THE CONCHENTA CONUNDRUM

The Conchenta Conundrum

Paul Anthony

The Right of Paul Anthony to be identified as the author of this work has been asserted by him in accordance with sections 77 and 78 of the Copyright, Designs and Patents Act of 1988.

All the characters in this book are fictitious, and any resemblance to actual persons, living or dead, is purely coincidental.

~ ~ ~

First Published 2011
Copyright © Paul Anthony 2011
All Rights Reserved.
Cover Photography: Copyright © Margaret Anne Scougal 2011

First published in Great Britain in 2011 by
Paul Anthony Associates
www.wix.com/tscougal/paulanthony

By The Same Author

~

In Fiction…

~ ~ ~

The Fragile Peace

Bushfire

The Legacy of the Ninth

~ ~ ~

In Poetry…

~

Sunset

~ ~ ~

To Margaret – Thank you, for never doubting me.

To Paul, Barrie and Vikki – You only get one chance at life. Live it well, live it in peace, and live it with love for one another.

To my special friends – Thank you. You are special.

…… Paul Anthony

And 'Muchas Gracias' to 'Corralejo'
Where the waters of the Atlantic approach the harbour wall…

*

For Jess and Rita
Still reading somewhere…

*

Author's Note
~ ~ ~

For those who have followed the much applauded Boyd trilogy of *The Fragile Peace, Bushfire* and *The Legacy of the Ninth,* then many thanks for your support over the years. I hope you enjoyed reading about Boyd, his friends, and his adventures as much as I enjoyed writing about them.

I have worked on dozens of suspicious fatalities, sudden deaths and violent murder cases over the years. Sometimes I've been at the heart of the enquiry, and sometimes on the periphery of things; other times I've supervised such investigations. It's not surprising to be asked to explain why I have never written a 'murder mystery'. Well, now it's time to right that wrong. It's time to introduce a fresh set of characters for your enjoyment. It's time to stand on the cliff tops of a town called Crillsea and visit the locals at the Anchor Pub down by the harbour, and get to know a set of people you might imagine live like the rest of us: somewhere between normality and insanity, perhaps somewhere between innocence and guilt. Criminal investigation is occasionally simple, sometimes complicated, and always a challenge. You can deal with such problems as if they were pieces in a chess game because by being one step ahead, in the moves that you make, you have more chances of success. The problem with chess is you always know who your opponent is. In real life, this is not always the case. Created in Corralejo, on the island of Fuerteventura in the Canaries, and crafted in Cumbria, I have named my work *'The Conchenta Conundrum'*.

I hope you take pleasure in this tale of murder, mystery and deceit, of love and hate, of normality and insanity. And it would be quite wrong of me not to thank Pauline Livingstone and Mark and Julia Thompson for reading, advising, and editing the work. Thank you...

Paul Anthony

Conundrum....

A dilemma of some magnitude,
A riddle for consideration,
A problem encountered,
A mystery to unravel,
A puzzling question,
An enigma to solve,
A challenge,
A poser,

....Conundrum

*

Prologue

~ ~ ~

When she died on an island in the middle of an ocean, only her family cared. When she was taken from her people, only they noticed. When she had gone from the world she loved, it was too late to ask the question: Why?

Only her closest family knew she had died. Only her mother held her at the time of death. Only her mother knew the answer to why her daughter, Alicia Andorinha, died on a lonely island in the Atlantic.

But a tall white lady, with rings on her fingers and flowers in her hair, arrived on the island and asked, 'How? Why? And when did the pretty Alicia Andorinha die?

It was a dilemma of some magnitude originating on a tiny island a hundred nautical miles from the mainland.

The tall white lady, with rings on her fingers and flowers in her hair, wondered how many others had died, or might die in the next six months.

She called it the Conchenta Conundrum…

*

Chapter One
~ ~ ~

Dateline: Six Months Later,
Wednesday, Crillsea Cliffs:

Strolling in the garden one morning he had an idea. He remembered the traditions spoken of earlier, acknowledged their power, and developed and refined his evil notion. Then he took a walk in nearby woods and privately confirmed his intentions. He could not help but notice the wood was carpeted with a mass of foliage and wild flowers. There were so many, you see. Oh, so many. And so many different colours caught his eye. He returned to the house and thought it all out, planned it to perfection, and then picked lavender and white crocuses from the garden border because it seemed the easiest and most convenient thing to do. They were the dying blooms of spring and they were withered, wrinkled, and past their best, but he knew what powers lay dormant inside the plant.

Selecting a twelve years old bottle of his finest scotch, he broke the seal and poured himself a good two fingers before taking a substantial mouthful. The liquid hit the back of his throat in a rush but gently slid into his stomach. Carefully, he pulled leaves away from the corm and placed them in a wooden pestle. Taking a mortar he ground his dry crocus leaves until they were virtually dust. Then he added more crocus leaves and eagerly ground them into a fine powder. Another drink was taken and another two fingers were poured.

As spring died summer was born and an early bout of sunshine invaded the coastline. He invited her to his lair intending to finalise matters once and for all. He swept the patio and tidied the area for the episode he planned, and then prepared clean towels and chilled wine for their lunchtime swim.

He was frolicking in the pool when she arrived and he leapt from the water to welcome her and hold her close; deviant soul that he was.

'I'm glad you could make it,' he said enthusiastically.

'I wouldn't have missed it for the world,' she replied with a smile.

They swam together and bathed in the sunshine before relaxing on loungers he thoughtfully angled towards the sun. Caringly, he carefully massaged her neck and back and trickled his fingers down her spine and said, 'You like?'

She giggled in gleeful delight. It was as if they were such good friends, maybe even lovers.

Later, laughing and smiling, he donned his Japanese silk kimono and strutted along the patio to a barbecue and a chilled drinks cabinet.

'Time for drinks and a snack,' he announced happily.

'Fabulous,' she replied.

Striking a match, he lit the barbecue. He tossed a salad, reached inside the wooden drinks cabinet, and withdrew a bottle of rosé wine. He uncorked the bottle, poured a sample, and sprinkled his lethal mixture into her glass.

Offering the glass, he said, 'A premier drink for a premier lady.'

She accepted, laughed, and sparkled in delight as she drank in the ample softness of her wine.

Returning her laughter, he smiled and waited for her to die as he casually barbecued slices of chicken and prepared a salad. But she did not die. She did not even feel any discomfort, at first.

Eventually, as the sun rose in the sky and rays began to burn into her skin, she developed an unquenchable thirst due to an irritable tingling smarting in her gullet.

'Another drink please,' she asked in a concerned manner. 'I'm so thirsty with this heat. My throat is on fire.'

He obliged and she gratefully accepted another glass of chilled wine. But the time approached and he needed courage locked inside a bottle of scotch. Another two fingers were poured and drank in one and the half empty whisky bottle was unsteadily placed on the table.

The coldness of her rosé wine seemed to have no influence because she cried out anxiously for another drink that might kill the prickly itch in her throat. He chuckled deviously as he tried to hide the alcoholic state surely affecting his mind, remarked jovially on the fickleness of the English weather, and then poured her more wine.

'God, my throat is on fire now,' she said. And the worry in her voice became anxious and questioning. 'Is that just wine?' She queried.

Fear invaded her mind when she persisted, 'You didn't lace it with a dash or two of vodka, did you? Or was it cocaine? I hope not.'

He dismissed her remark instantly. 'Of course not, don't worry; I'm sure the sensation will soon pass.'

She drank quickly and clumsily hoping things would improve and her craving would subside. She asked again for a cold drink and said, 'I wonder if I might have swallowed an insect, perhaps a tiny wasp or a fly, because the burning sensation is still there, and it's getting worse.'

Laughing at her ridiculous suggestion, he said, 'Don't be silly.' Yet he took time to note her condition. It was, indeed, slowly deteriorating.

The heat of the poison burnt steadily into her, scorched her gullet, scalded her insides, and drove her to despair. When the mixture finally delivered a climax of pain she could bear it no longer.

'Oh no,' she uttered apprehensively, and then retched uncontrollably at the fiery sensation within her. Gradually, her heart gathered pace and beat faster. Her blood pressure was going through the roof and her lungs ultimately felt as if they would explode.

Draining her glass in desperation, she placed it on the table before her. It was then she saw a fine pinkish white residue covering the bowl of her glass.

She looked directly into his eyes and accused him, 'You, you bastard, you've...' Realising what he had done, she made a grasp for the empty glass as if by somehow snatching the evidence into her possession things would improve.

With a slight of his hand her glass fell to the patio and exploded into innumerable pieces.

She tried to scream but could not. Her throat was on fire when she slowly crawled to the pool and scooped water into her. She opened her mouth but could not scream, could not even raise her voice to cry for help. Her hands cupped the pool water and threw the liquid into her mouth. Almost immediately she could feel the benefit of the cold water. She began to gurgle, began to reboot her voice box, and began to utter a painful forced scream.

'Arghhh......'

The man realised something had gone terribly wrong with his murderous plan. He blamed her, of course. Her and those expensive reference books and well-thumbed paperbacks he'd scoured through. He was pretty sure he'd read them from cover to cover and knew the content inside out. The reality was he hadn't read and understood them properly, and a little knowledge was a dangerous thing.

The man waited patiently, like the printed word said. Repeatedly, he checked the time and watched her slowly wither away. She suffered retching and stomach pain but she did not die.

By then, she'd worked it all out and knew what he was doing. She accused him, 'You're trying to poison me; you're trying to kill me; you're trying to dispose of me forever with your poisoned wine... You bastard, you rotten lousy...'

She scooped more water from the pool and tried to escape, retched again, and tried to scream for help.

He checked the time and realised she was improving.

'Oh dear,' he said laughing. 'This isn't quite working the way I had planned but not to worry. Come with me, my dearest one.' Seizing her hair, he pulled her away from the water.

'Ouch! Oy!' she complained. She kicked out, struggling.

Dragging her like an old rag doll destined for a bonfire, he threw her onto her knees on the patio. She was exhausted. He watched her try to crawl from his presence. She gasped for breath and clutched her throat.

'You swine,' she gurgled fearfully.

Sniggering, he disappeared from her sight.

It was her chance to escape. She tried frantically to crawl away, to lift herself to her knees and slither to a place of safety.

Casually, but deliberately, he took a spade from the garden shed and returned to stand over her. He watched her trying to desperately slither away. He looked down upon her as she struggled to her knees for the last time.

'No... No, please, no,' she cried.

Smiling and laughing, he raised the spade above his head and violently beat her skull as hard as he could. He rained down two terrific blows to the back of her head and broke her skull into a dozen separate pieces. Blood showered his face, his clothes, and the patio surrounding the conspiratorial waters lapping gently against the side of the pool.

When it was over he rested for a moment. It wasn't a pretty sight and the affects of a twelve years old scotch did have an effect upon him but he hosed all the blood, bone and brain tissue from the patio area and placed her body inside a green plastic suit holder.

Dragging her to the garage, he bundled the corpse into the boot of his car then burnt his silk kimono and swimming shorts on the barbecue. Almost frantic in his desire to escape, he threw the spade back into the garden shed. Hastily, he gathered up her belongings: her handbag, sunhat, and bits and pieces, and threw them onto the barbecue. The man added more charcoal and stirred the contents of the tray until flames grew and enveloped all. Checking the area, he realised it was time to go and made for the garage.

Firing the car engine, he selected a gear, and drove off. Driving through a maze of leafy country lanes, he criss-crossed the green meadows and pastures of the surrounding area. Then the car began to climb and he eventually reached a place where only the sea visited the cliffs and few walked the lonely coastal path. The locals called this wild desolate place, 'No Man's Cliff'.

In summer, 'No Man's Cliff' boasted a spectacular panoramic view and was often visited by dog walkers, courting couples, and people looking for solitude. Yet it was such a wild and unforgiving place when the winter elements snarled at Crillsea's headland.

He pulled in and set the handbrake tight. Clumsily, he dragged the package from his car boot. Straining with the exertion of it all, he rested a moment, regretted the foolish fingers of courage he had found necessary to embrace, and with a mighty heave, threw her into the ocean.

Without remorse, he watched the green plastic suit holder gradually sink through the waves. Concerned things had not gone to plan and the scotch had been a stupid accessory in his plan, he looked out to sea and scolded himself for his ineptitude.

The tide smashed into the cliffs and withdrew. The tide roared and crashed into the cliffs again but left no traces of a lady who had been poisoned but did not die from ingesting an ordinary crocus diluted in a glass of chilled rosé wine.

With his back to the sea, he guided the car through the leafy lanes. It was as if someone had at last lifted a great weight from his shoulders when he slid his foot heavily onto the accelerator pedal and made good speed towards the house.

His mind soon wandered to a patio that needed checking. Had he washed the area thoroughly? Had the fire in the barbecue burnt out his kimono and swim shorts? Had he cleaned the spade with which he had pummelled her skull into a dozen little pieces? Had he... He did not see the big red two-litre tractor emerge from the meadow and lumber casually into the lane.

There was a rush of adrenaline and a squeal of tyres when he heaved onto the brakes and swung the steering wheel fiercely to his right. There was an almighty crunch of metal and a cloud of dust when the front of his car collided with the rear offside of a farmer's tractor and a rusting red mudguard crumpled to the ground.

Stunned! He was stunned for a moment but quickly jumped from the car and ran towards the farmer and his tractor.

With a hurried smile a hand was clasped and a head and face were checked for injury. No injury was found and reluctant smiles were forcibly exchanged. There was a quick inspection of a front bumper and a rear mudguard followed by a quick examination of debris and skid marks on the road; and there was recognition of how things might have been worse.

Then there were recriminations.

'It was your fault,' alleged the car driver. 'You didn't stop. You just drove straight out of the field onto the road.'

'No, lad,' retaliated the elderly farmer standing his ground. 'You were driving too fast. You are at fault, lad.'

'Too fast!' snapped the car driver. 'Don't be ridiculous, you are a typical tractor driver. No respect for anyone. You think you own the road, don't you?'

'You were at fault, lad,' argued the farmer. 'You been drinking?'

The farmer leaned closer to smell a whiff of alcohol on the car driver's breath. He stroked his chin then shook his head in disgust.

Suddenly, there seemed to be a cold nip in the air which burnt into the car driver's skin and kindled his mind.

'Drinking?' queried the driver innocently. 'Of course not; look, there's no need to bother the police. It's only a rusty old mudguard.'

'Rusty?' challenged the tractor driver, annoyed at such a suggestion. 'It'll still cost money. Rusty or not, it'll cost money to replace.'

Wisdom of a kind intruded and the car driver responded, 'Yes, yes, of course; perhaps this would help.' Digging deep into his wallet, he produced a wad of banknotes.

The farmer sniffed again, sensed an odour of alcohol, stroked his chin again, and hinted, 'Do you think that will be enough, lad? Mudguards for agricultural tractors aren't cheap, you know, and I'll need to go to the dealer at Tevington for this.'

'Well, of course. I understand; how silly of me.' His hand delved into his wallet again and more notes were delivered.

'That should do it, lad,' reacted the farmer with a smile.

'And we'll settle on that, shall we? No police, I mean.'

'Aye, we'll settle on that, lad,' replied the farmer. 'No need to be bothering the police when it's all sorted, lad.'

Cash changed hands and a big red two-litre agricultural tractor straightened in the lane. A car reversed and then slowly edged passed the tractor. There was a wave and a pip of a car horn and he was gone.

The farmer watched the car disappearing down the lane and examined his brand new banknotes. They were fresh, crinkly, new, and unfamiliar to a man with soil on his hands. He lifted his head again and allowed his eyes to zero into the disappearing vehicle.

Stepping up gingerly to his tractor cabin, he found a biro pen and his magazine stuffed into the side pocket. The car turned left at the end of the lane and moved out of sight as the farmer wrote the car registration number down on the front of the 'Farmer's Weekly'.`

'Funny money is it?' queried the farmer aloud. 'Well, I suppose I had a good day on the fields today.'

Tommy Watson, farmer of Crillsea Farm Estates, patted the side of his tractor, brushed away debris from the ground with his foot, and fired up the engine. Not a bad day's work, he thought, preparing to return to his farm. Not a bad day at all. Smiling, he crumpled the bank notes into his fist, pocketed them, and made for home.

*

Chapter Two

~ ~ ~

Dateline: Thursday,
Crillsea Meadows:

Tommy Watson endured a sleepless night tossing and turning in a gigantic four poster bed in his eighteenth century detached farmhouse set in a dozen acres of prime farmland. The sweat poured from his body, perhaps he had the 'flu, but despite a couple of paracetamol and a glass of ice-cold water, he couldn't get to sleep.

His wife, Betty, decided she couldn't put up with him anymore. She nudged her husband.

Tommy had no choice. He was suddenly up at the crack of dawn and into breakfast, a shower and a shave. By nine o'clock, he had checked their cattle and bossed his farmhands to the point of annoyance. Making an excuse to leave, to see a doctor, he reversed his battered rusting three litre Mercedes out of the barn and headed into Crillsea Meadows.

The chickens clucked wildly and a handful of Friesian cattle looked disinterested as a mud splattered rusting Mercedes negotiated the rutted entrance to the farm and lazily crawled onto the well worn tarmac.

Suddenly, Tommy sneezed and decided he was due a bad day.

In the nearby picturesque hamlet of Crillsea Meadows, a gathering of loose ivy tumbled down the whitewashed walls of the village police station and trailed away into a lawn begging for the close attention of a lawn mower.

A puff of smoke escaped the chimney pot when Elsie Tait threw more coal onto a fire and rattled the grate with a fierce iron poker.

Mark Tait laced his boots up, buttoned his tunic, and prepared for another day patrolling the country lanes lying on the outskirts of Crillsea, and beyond. And that was the problem for the village constable; 'beyond'. Mark was out of the link, out of the action, out of the hum drum daily excitement of city policing. It was also one of the arguments as to why the station was earmarked for closing soon. Indeed, it was just a matter of weeks, it was said, before Mark Tait and his wife, Elsie, were re-housed in Crillsea and he was drawn into the central police station command structure. Of course, Elsie directed him not to get so uptight about it all. She loved Crillsea Meadows; the rural aspects, a village life, a certain respected status in a small community, and the quiet undisturbed lifestyle of rural England. And she regularly reminded her husband, Mark, how police work tended to be long, boring, unpretentious, sometimes stimulating, but generally, pretty damn standard.

'Have you much on today?' asked Elsie.

'Nothing exciting, love,' replied Mark. 'Average, that's all.'

A Mercedes appeared in the roadway and stopped outside.

'Visitors?' called Elsie. 'Headquarters people, maybe?'

'Tommy Watson, Crillsea Farm Estates,' replied Mark. 'Poachers or a gun licence, I suspect.'

'Well, you did say you were expecting an average day, dear,' replied Elsie. 'I'll put the kettle on. Two for tea, is it?' She asked.

'Thanks,' said Mark as he moved to open the front door and welcome his first customer of the day. 'Everything is pretty damn standard here. When will I get something I can get my teeth into?'

'One day, Mark. Maybe not today though,' shouted Elsie from their kitchen. There was a rattle of cups and saucers and the sound of water running from a tap.

Mark opened the door, shook hands with Farmer Tommy Watson, and guided him to his office.

The two men spoke of the weather and the long winter ending with the birth of spring and the onset of summer. The farmer handed over his shotgun licence and renewal application. A cheque for forty pounds was produced accompanied by a certificate that was about to expire and a new set of photographs to finish off the paperwork. There was a shake of hands and agreement reached on when the village constable might visit and inspect the new security arrangements Farmer Watson had put in place to secure his various weapons.

'It's a serious matter, the handling of shotguns and firearms, Mister Watson. I'll be out to visit the farm to inspect the situation before the certificate is renewed. You understand that don't you?'

There was a nod of a head to the constable and a thank you to Mrs Tait when she delivered tea and biscuits and a slice of chocolate cake.

'Too early in the morning,' Tommy said, and he woofed the cake down so as not to upset the fine lady, and then he sneezed uncontrollably.

There was laughter followed by talk of new people in the villages and hamlets surrounding Crillsea Meadows. There was a nod and a wink when the latest births, deaths and marriages were discussed, and satisfaction was expressed at the newly built wall protecting school children in the nearby school.

Then Tommy sneezed again and Mark produced a roll of tissues.

Eventually, Tommy Watson produced a copy of the 'Farmer's Weekly' and a host of crisp banknotes no longer cold to his touch.

The story was told: his tale of a car colliding with a tractor and how the driver smelled of drink. There was talk of a damaged mudguard and a new agricultural supplier in Tevington on Sea, and there was the production of 'funny money' that was crisp and new to the touch.

Mark Tait lifted the bank notes, crinkled them to his ear, checked the paper and held it to the light so he might use his expertise in such things. He pronounced the money 'good'.

Tommy Watson smiled, pocketed his cash, and pointed at a car registration number on the cover of the 'Farmer's Weekly'.

Mark Tait's suspicions were aroused further when they discussed Tommy's bizarre encounter with a stranger who drove back down the lane from 'No Man's Cliff'.

Mark looked stern, did not produce his pocket book, did not produce a pre-typed form, but did produce a battered loose leaf notebook and a pencil, and then he expressed interest in the story he had heard.

'Was anyone injured, Mister Watson?'

'No.'

'Was there any damage to other property, you know, property not owned by yourself?'

'No, Mister Tait.'

'Did you exchange names and addresses and insurance details, or come to an arrangement at the scene?'

'Yes, we did. The man gave me money for another mudguard but I thought it was strange, thought it was weird, particularly as he paid me a lot of money. He had a funny accent. Not from round here, him; maybe up north or over west but just a wisp of an accent, I'd say. I thought you'd like to know.'

'Aye, that's right, so it is,' replied Constable Mark Tait. 'But this is a minor accident without injury or third party damage and we don't record such matters anymore.'

'So I wasted my time and yours, did I? I thought you would be interested in what went on in your patch?' challenged Tommy Watson with a sneeze that shook the house. 'Of course, the word is you're moving soon so you won't be all that interested, will you, Mister Tait?'

'I am always interested,' replied Constable Tait passing more tissues. 'I'll check out the ownership of the car to ensure it's not stolen but otherwise, there's nothing I need do. But I'm always pleased to talk about things on my patch, wherever my patch is. It's what I do.'

Mark Tait switched on his desk computer.

'Well, I'm sorry to have bothered you then,' replied Tommy Watson. 'I'll know next time.'

'We have a sleepy environment because people like you tell me what's going on,' delivered Constable Tait. 'I'll look into this when I need to, Mister Watson. I thank you for telling me about the matter. I know who my friends are and I will support them.'

Constable Mark Tait of Rural Command, Crillsea Meadows, pulled across the desk a copy of the 'Farmer's Weekly', slid it into a drawer and announced, 'I will read it later, Mister Watson, if I may?'

There was a nod of the head and talk of the coming whist drive in the village hall. There was talk of a youth club to be formed, and talk of flowers and shrubs in Mrs. Tait's garden. And then the meeting was over and Tommy Watson was gone and bound for his farm and his tractor.

Mark Tait turned his computer and checked his emails.

'Poachers, was it?' asked Elsie Tait.

'Just a non reportable road traffic accident, Elsie,' replied Mark. 'Nothing to get excited about but I have to keep my parishioners happy.'

Elsie chuckled and said, 'Tommy can talk for England. He's keen on the community. You know youth clubs, village halls and suchlike.'

'Oh yes, Tommy could sit all day and talk,' replied Mark.

It was the way of rural England. It was the way of the English.

*

Chapter Three
~ ~ ~

Dateline: Friday,
Crillsea and the Anchor.

Summer was truly on its way. The sun shone brightly and the sky was a cloudless azure blue. Someone had remarked what a lovely warm day it was but Max could feel a sea breeze nipping his skin and he was cold, miserable and abandoned. Max Fowler was a civilian in the Metropolitan Police Service. He held an honorary title of superintendent but he was alone in a street at the back of Crillsea library.

No-one had questioned the forty seven year old since he had arrived. They'd just left him to get on with his job. They were watching him now though. He was centre stage. It was his khaki uniform that held their attention and he could feel the weight of the Kevlar bearing down upon his broad shoulders. Max could feel everyone's eyes boring into his back as he walked slowly down the street.

Khaki wasn't his favourite colour, certainly not a colour for a nightclub suit or a wedding day, or even going to a football match to watch his beloved Liverpool. But as the ballistic materials used in the manufacture of the bomb disposal suit issued to him by SO15, the Met's Counter Terrorism Command, had been tested and evaluated to the very highest level of quality assurance standards, he decided to wear it well.

The suit, costing about £30,000 and weighing about 25 kilograms, or 55 pounds, consisted of a jacket with an attached collar, a helmet and visor, full length trousers, overshoes and protective gloves. His helmet was fitted with integral earphones, an encrypted radio system and a demisting device that prevented the visor from misting over to blur his vision. There was an air cooling blower circulating around his suit to keep him fresh and the whole outfit was made of Kevlar.

Watching him now, through binoculars, were members of the Forward Operational Police Control, known as Bronze Command. Today, Bronze Command consisted of Assistant Chief Constable Phillip Patterson and his colleagues and they had taken over part of the harbour-master's office for the immediate future. The building was equipped with utilities, telephones, computers and communication devices, and radio antennae glistening from a roof dominating the streets they were working.

Patterson was a ruddy-faced individual in his early fifties. Dressed smartly in full uniform he deliberately adopted a military style to his persona in the hope his peers and fellow man would consider him to be a leader: a commander-in-chief in waiting, perhaps. He twisted and stroked his greying moustache whilst standing next to Superintendent Bert Allithwaite and Detective Chief Inspector Keith Jackson.

Patterson had force-wide responsibility that day but it was Bert Allithwaite's divisional police area. Keith Jackson was there because Patterson had decreed it and Jackson was, after all, the recently appointed head of Crillsea CID. But Jackson, in his mid thirties, was also Patterson's prodigy and the primary driver of Patterson's new policy and procedure handbook that would put Patterson back in the frame for command of his own police force. The slim line weasel features of Jackson did not hinder his potential in any way. Keith Jackson was going places whether Bert Allithwaite and the others liked it or not. Assistant Chief Constable Phillip Patterson would see to that.

The trio looked through their binoculars, through the windows of the harbour-master's office, and into the streets close by. Completing Bronze Command, were Detective Inspector Davies King and Detective Sergeant Annie Rock. All five officers were supervising a demonstration; a prime-ministerial motorcade, and, at that precise moment, the examination of a suspected improvised explosive device.

Fingers turned the binocular focus wheel and their faces pressed tight against the soft of the eyepiece, refining and honing the image of Max Fowler and the target he approached.

Annie Rock operated their radio system and maintained links to both Silver and Gold Command; such was the hierarchical arrangement of the day's policing operations. Silver Command was headed by a deputy chief constable responsible for tactical overview of the operation whilst Gold was headed by a chief constable who would take any final strategic decisions needed.

Detective Sergeant Annie Rock was tall and slim with light brown hair flowing to her shoulder line, but no further. She held a first class honours degree in economics and public administration and she didn't suffer fools gladly. She was in her early thirties, youthful looking, sometimes obsessive, mostly professional and a big fan of denim and colourful scarves.

Annie smoothed her denim jeans, adjusted her headphones, tapped the black and white keyboards of her computer, and updated the status of their operation.

Assistant Chief Constable Patterson leaned across Annie, took control of the radio, and said, 'This is Bronze calling Silver. We are evaluating the threat level at this location and recommend increased personal protection for Charlie One, over.'

'Roger, Bronze,' from Silver Command.

Patterson smiled at his acknowledgement and returned to the window and his binoculars. Raising the apparatus to his eyes, he said to Superintendent Allithwaite, 'Nothing's going to go wrong today, superintendent. Not on my watch. Better safe than sorry, I say.' His fingers gently caressed the focus wheel.

Davies shook his head in annoyance, even a touch of contempt.

A message from Gold Command flashed onto Annie's computer screen. She flicked a switch and radioed, 'Gold Command asks if you can see any explosives, Superintendent Fowler?'

Out on the sunburnt tarmac street, a quarter of a mile away, Max Fowler received the question in his earpiece but merely shook his head.

'He's shaking his head, Annie,' said Detective Chief Inspector Keith Jackson focusing his sights.

'What's taking him so long?' asked Patterson.

'The target is at the far end of the street, sir,' suggested Allithwaite, softly. 'Perhaps we should give him a little time to reach it.'

'Mmm! Very well,' replied the assistant chief constable peering through his binoculars towards the khaki figure.

Max felt assurance in an armour plated breast plate, groin plate and spinal protective unit that seemed to be half a second behind his body as he made towards the target in a street at the back of Crillsea library.

A drop of sweat formed on his brow and was guided gently away by the cooling system circulating inside his suit. Max neared the target and slowed his step. Carefully, alert, watchful, he took his time and used all the senses in his body to work out the target. It was a game really, thought Max, just a game. But he knew he had to know the game inside out to win it and it was his target, no-one else's. Max Fowler often lived right at the edge of vigilance.

Firstly, he used his ears to listen then he used his eyes to see. Then he used his nose to smell. Eventually, he began to walk to the left of the target. He stopped in his tracks and took a long hard look. He walked to the right of the target, stopped, and took another long hard look. He exhaled and carefully took stock of it all.

It had to be done, he thought. But why does it have to be me and why today of all days?

Max felt the armour plates drag when he decided to get up close and personal with the target. He knelt down and began to crawl on his hands and knees towards the target.

It was just a game. It was just a stupid game we have to play from time to time, he thought; but why today of all days?

Finally, he removed an electronic probe from a pocket and, slowly and warily, pointed his probe towards the target. He sucked in taking a deep breath.

There was a sudden unexpected screech of static in his ears and then a voice queried, 'Gold Command repeats its question, sir. Can you confirm the presence of explosives?'

'Stand by, control,' growled an agitated Max.

Annie Rock sat back in the control room and voiced aloud, 'He needs time and space, sir.'

'Quite,' consented Patterson. 'But I need to advise Silver and Gold as soon as possible.' He smiled smugly and added, 'Who am I to keep the powers that be waiting? And they wait for my word, don't they?'

'Personally, I think we should evacuate the immediate area, sir,' suggested Superintendent Allithwaite. 'Just in case it's not a hoax.'

Patterson lowered his glasses and stared at Allithwaite. 'Not on my watch, Superintendent Allithwaite. In any event, we've time yet.'

'Ask him if he can see any wires, Annie,' suggested Chief Inspector Jackson. 'He's close enough for that surely.'

Annie tapped her black and whites as she radioed, 'Are there any wires visible, superintendent?'

'I say again, stand by, control,' replied Max. A slight hint of annoyance was audible in his reply.

Detective Inspector Davies King, forty two years old and time served, wore scuffed down at heel shoes with worn out laces. Leather patches clung anxiously to the elbow area of his sleeve and highlighted the jacket he had favoured for nearly ten years. His trousers were in need of a sharp ironed crease and he sported a dog-eared shirt collar winging above a clean but crumpled shirt front.

Frustrated, Davies lowered his binoculars and said, 'No disrespect intended, gentlemen, but why don't you all leave him to get on with it? It's what he's paid to do, to be a professional, and, in his case, also an expert. He needs time. Be patient and give him time.'

'We need to know the answers now so that we might warn the motorcade. They might abort, advance or hold,' snapped Assistant Chief Constable Patterson. 'It's a decision I need to make, no-one else.'

'No coded warning has been received,' advised Davies King. 'We've found a suspicious device, that's all. It's a device that might be a bomb or it might be a hoax. It might even be a leftover parcel from a mail delivery. A bigger worry might be if we'd found a suicide bomber wearing his bomb jacket beneath a coverall on those streets near the library.'

'So what you do you advise?' asked Patterson tetchily.

'Tell them to slow down,' replied King.

'That's a bit indecisive, isn't it?' argued Jackson.

'I've a tenner in my pocket says it's a hoax,' offered Davies King. 'Anyway, lighten up, Keith.'

'It's Chief Inspector now, Mister King. Detective Chief Inspector Jackson, not Keith,' directed the assistant chief constable. 'Remember?'

Jackson felt slightly embarrassed but side-stepped the comment, nodded and said, 'I'll cover your tenner, Davies. I reckon it's not a hoax.'

Assistant Chief Constable Patterson smoothed his moustache, flicked a switch on the radio system, and radioed, 'Gold this is Bronze. Recommend the motorcade to hold at the outer marker and stand by for further instructions.'

They focused their binoculars and turned their attention to the street, a suspect device, and a bomb disposal officer bestowed the rank 'superintendent'.

Davies King leaned across Annie, winked cheekily, flicked a switch and radioed, 'One nil to the Reds, Max.' There was a pause before he radioed again. 'Anyway, Max, I'll catch up with you later but it's one nil and I thought you'd like to know.'

Out on the sun-kissed tarmac the information invaded Max's ears. He dropped his electronic probe and rolled to one side as high pitched static penetrated his brain.

'Max....' from Davies King.

There was no reply on the radio net, only static.

'Happy birthday, Max!'

Opening his eyes, Max felt sweat trickling down the back of his neck. He shook his head and reached for his probe on the tarmac before him just as the tide turned and a slight breeze transformed the weather.

'Davies...,' radioed Max. And then Max grasped the limp probe with his hand and realised the end of his probe had broken on impact with the tarmac. 'Davies I'm going to kill you just as soon as I have a moment to spare.'

There was a rattle of static in his ears, then only silence when Max lay on a street behind Crillsea library with a broken probe in his hand and the target beckoning before him.

In Crillsea, the motorcade came to a standstill. Police motor cyclists stopped the traffic, a double-decker bus carrying demonstrators incurred a puncture and discharged its angry passengers into the streets to vent their wrath, and Peggy MacDonald joined a long queue of vehicles held at the traffic lights. She knew she was going to be a late arrival at the house on the cliffs that day, just knew this traffic would make her too late; and, as she was approaching her sixtieth year, she did not look forward to pushing her plump frame along the cliff paths to her employer's house.

Sunshine invaded her battered old mini as she sat patiently growing hotter and hotter in the confines of a traffic jam. Peggy wound the window down, welcomed a slight breeze, listened to the car horns blaring, watched the vehicles build up around her, and decided to cancel her visit to Crillsea Cliffs. Spying a telephone box at the corner of the street, she edged into a parking place at the kerbside and went to make a call. Peggy MacDonald wouldn't be visiting the house on the cliffs today.

At the rear of Crillsea library sunlight was kissing tarmac and burning into Kevlar. A Yorkshire terrier cocked it's leg up outside a local baker's, paused for relief for a minute or two, and then sauntered on towards a man wearing a khaki uniform with a funny helmet and visor.

'On target,' mouthed Max into his radio. 'Electronic probe confirms no wireless activity emanating from target.'

'Roger!' replied Annie Rock.

'Or it did just before the football results,' whispered Max.

'Roger!' from Annie.

'Target is four by four with cardboard packaging. The target emits no smell. No unusual features. No wires visible.'

'Roger!' from Annie.

Max closed his eyes for a moment, took a close and considered look, and said, 'Target is grade A.'

'Roger!' from Annie.

In the control room Patterson and Allithwaite exchanged worried glances and Jackson asked, 'What does that mean? Is it a bomb?'

'Might be,' offered Davies, sensing the tempo. 'If it is then the man who would be a hero might only be another petal on Poppy Day, sir.'

The radio burst again with, 'Probe away, moving to cutters and primary physical contact.' Lying on the tarmac, Max pushed his probe behind him, clenched and unclenched his fingers, and took a deep breath before asking, 'Where the hell did this bloody dog come from? And who on earth is Roger?'

There was no reply from Annie, just silence and muffled static from a radio net.

A dog barked: a Yorkshire terrier. It barked again to the annoyance of Max who snarled at the dog. The canine hero held its ground and growled menacingly before moving on down the street to explore the back of a butcher's and anywhere else offering easy pickings.

Lifting himself to his feet, Max watched the dog scampering away down the street. Then he studied the target he'd been sent to neutralize.

The target consisted of cardboard boxes stacked on top of each other. It was held together with a piece of twine encircling the structure in a haphazard manner.

Max shook his head because he knew deep inside there was something wrong. CCTV footage from his robot had shown wires and composition in the peculiar target. But it didn't seem right to him. He knew there was a framework of metal and wires hidden deep inside those cardboard boxes. He just knew it, felt it, could almost smell it.

Such a feeling was born out of experience and he could feel it now. Max had seen so many devices over the years. In the Falklands, Northern Ireland, Bosnia, Sierra Leone, Iraq, Kuwait, the Yemen. All over really when he'd been in the Army. Bomb God, they'd called him. He was a man who lived and breathed incendiary devices to the point of bordering on religious belief. But Max retired early because he was sick of travelling the world and so was his wife. On returning to England, he volunteered for the Met bomb disposal job he'd read about in a magazine. He was a civilian. He would never be a policeman. The title of superintendent given to him was honorary and related to his status in the service and his pay cheque at the end of the month. He knew next to nothing about police work.

'Roger!' shouted Max into his radio.

'Roger!' replied Annie in control, worried perhaps as she trained her hair from her forehead with the flash of a hand. 'That's my line superintendent. What's the matter?'

'Check this out', said Max.

In Bronze Command there was a movement closer to the windows and a refocusing of binoculars.

Max turned and started to walk towards the end of the street; the comfort of his van, the warmth of control, a bossy female voice on a radio, safety, and a man he'd promised to murder when he found the time.

Then Max Fowler suddenly spun on his heel and ran full-bloodied at the cardboard boxes. Max launched a terrific kick at the target.

There was a tremendous thud when his armour plated boot struck the boxes full on. The boxes took to the air and landed about five feet away. Then a growing sea breeze recognised the flimsy of cardboard and lifted it ten feet into the sky before abandoning it to its own devices.

A box landed on tarmac, rolled over and over, and eventually detached itself from a layer of twine to reveal a collection of music stands clanking repeatedly on the tarmac.

Clank! Clunk! Clank! And then someone's precious powder coated nickel metal music stand died on a street when Max followed through and drove the heel of his armour plated boot into the framework.

.

'Grade A piece of shit,' said Max. And then he watched another cardboard box roll down the road towards the harbour wall when a breeze began to gather with the turn of the tide.

'Music to my ears,' quipped Max, and then he chuckled.

At the far end of the street a Yorkshire terrier began to bark threateningly at a black Jaguar cruising towards Crillsea library.

In Bronze Command, Assistant Chief Constable Patterson looked disapprovingly at Davies King, flicked a switch on the radio system, and snarled into the radio net, 'Gold Command, this is Bronze. The device is a hoax. Recommend the motorcade to advance.'

Davies King smiled politely at Keith Jackson, held out his hand, and waited for a ten pound note.

Peggy MacDonald was on her way home shuffling through the heavy traffic with windows down and blistering sunshine bearing through the windscreen. She ignored the prime-ministerial motorcade; it was of no interest to her. But out in the nearby streets, the motorcade was up and running and heading towards Crillsea library and an unpleasant welcome from a demonstration slowly building in numbers out on the streets.

'Troops out! Troops out!'

Shoulder to shoulder, noisy and boisterous, they were chanting and baying for blood.

'Troops out! Troops out!'

Jostling and manoeuvring for position, they strode forward.

'Troops out! Troops out!'

And further along there was another group, and then another. They were all there with their opinions and problems, and all expecting immediate solutions from the Prime Minister.

There were hundreds of them there to see him; to glimpse him, to photograph him, to snatch a word or express an opinion. They were all there to see the Prime Minister. They were linking arms and marching forward alongside the harbour wall. Hundreds of them advancing upon a double line of unyielding blue uniforms huddled together to confront the protesters.

Police tightened down their helmets, interlocked their shields, and prepared to deny them passage along the road to Crillsea library.

'What do we want?' squealed a quick fix man into a megaphone.

'No more bankers' bail outs!' from a group of middle-aged, middle class hippies for the day. 'No more bankers' bail outs!'

A news crew panned and zoomed.

'When do we want it?' implored the quick fix man.

'Now…Now…Now.'

A camera flashed. A photographer took a step backwards, aimed and his camera flashed again.

Further along the road, another chant could be heard. 'Long live the BNP! Long live the BNP! No more immigration! No more immigration. Na-na-na! Na-na-na!' Like a gang of football fans raving from the kop, a gang of protesters intent on having their day.

A video camera came into play and a microphone was thrust forward to capture noise and mayhem, and acquire the trembling voice of a news reporter filing his thirty seconds of fame on nationwide television.

Of course, the protagonists weren't orchestrated, or didn't seem to be. There was no mysterious dark figure in a hooded blue anorak with a mobile phone glued to his ear controlling crowd movements. No it was spontaneous, perhaps a smidgen of planning born out of frustration and a few pints of bravery in the pub. But the Prime Minister was coming and it was time to give voice to pent-up feelings, time to let it rip and let him know what they thought.

The hundreds stretched back into the town of Crillsea and became a thousand. Thousands stretched back and grew thicker and denser with placards and scarves and flags, and much more raucous and noisy with chants of complaint born out of unemployment, dissatisfaction and irritation.

And Peggy MacDonald's car overheated in the centre of town and she wondered if she'd get home through the crowds and traffic, never mind the house on the cliffs and her part-time job.

Yet for others it was a happy time. A thousand or more red, white and blue union flags, fluttering in the breeze, complimented deafening cheers from the smiling masses that had come to welcome the Prime Minister.

A police helicopter circled purposefully in clear skies above Crillsea as the tide ebbed from the harbour wall, the sun beat down on the streets below, and Bronze Command focused on a gathering demonstration.

Crillsea had not seen anything like it. Well, nestled on the coast so far from the capital, you wouldn't expect Crillsea to be familiar with the responsibilities of hosting a large scale national demonstration. But today, Crillsea was on the map. Well and truly, and virtually the entire population of a hundred thousand or more people knew about it, as well as its similar sized neighbour along the coast: Tevington on Sea.

It was all about Crillsea library and a statue of marble standing outside its entrance: a statue of marble covered in purple velvet: the velvet the Prime Minister would remove soon, once his motorcade had carved its way through the horrendous traffic.

There was a distant sound of a siren wailing from the outskirts of the crowd. The locals knew it would be soon; it had been in all their newspapers and magazines for more than a week. The wailing sirens were growing louder and police were looking a little more agitated.

The crowd didn't care. Those that weren't smiling and laughing and waving flags were still hoisting placards high and exalting their cause. They were linking arms, moving down the esplanade chanting their beliefs and police horses, blinkered and padded for protection, balked and whinnied as their riders tried to reign them into position, tried to hold them at an imaginary 'out of bounds' marker.

A bunch of young anarchists, clad in black but wearing white scarves, rushed the police line and shoulder charged into a line of rigid plastic shields. The line of shields billowed inwards, quivered slightly, and then rendered the youths away and to the ground. Scarves and bags littered the street when police withdrew momentarily before eventually pushing protesting anarchists away.

A young brunette wearing a Saint John's ambulance uniform ran into the roadway and dragged a scrawny youth away from the melee, away from a line of slowly advancing police and whinnying horses. She noticed blood seeping from his nose and reached into her first aid bag.

It was as if there had been a signal of some kind for at that precise moment the crowd bellowed a roar of approval when a little old lady wearing pink trainers, a well worn black two piece suit and a pink floral hat, struck a policeman viciously over the head with her rolled up yellow brolly.

A single errant shield, ill tempered, undisciplined, badly trained, and unworthy of its credentials, billowed out from the regimented line of reinforced plastic in a fierce moment of sudden retaliation. Down she went amid a surplus of swearing. The little old lady might have been younger than she looked but she crumbled to the ground close to an anarchist wearing a black hooded top and a Saint John's ambulance woman rummaging in a first aid kit.

A pink floral hat was lifted by the breeze, hovered fleetingly above a line of police shields, and then blew unceremoniously into a line of police horses. The hat attached itself to the corner of a protective eye blinker and a police horse jiggled her head in annoyance and frustration.

Unable to detach the hat from her blinker the horse shook, whinnied, baulked, and kicked out nervously as its rider struggled with the reins to retain control and hold the line.

A little old ladies yellow umbrella rolled forlornly down the street pretending some kind of wind assisted pursuit.

A camera flashed, a video camera panned and zoomed, and a microphone sought to capture a roaring crowd. A smiling news reporter turned to face the lenses and secure his moment of fame. It was the picture of the day; the one that said it all: the weak attacking the strong.

A voice above others suddenly shouted, 'Save our local post office! Bail out the local postie. Bail out the local postie.' Part of the crowd burst into laughter at the comedy of it all.

A news camera flashed again and the police helicopter bore menacingly down towards the crowd; its rotor blades clearly visible from street level and the sound of it engines throbbing in the ears of all below.

There was a push and a jostle, a kick and a punch, and another body fell to the ground as a microphone rolled into the street with a news reporter chasing after it as if it was his pay cheque. His thirty seconds of fame was lost in the farce that was street theatre.

Suddenly, a police car with blue and yellow Battenberg squares on the sides and blue lights on its roof was in the street nearing the library.

Its driver brought his patrol car to a standstill with the entrance to the library behind him and a crowd ahead of him. It grew noisier when police motor cycle outriders roared into the street with their lights flashing and sirens blaring and resounding from Crillsea's harbour wall.

The crowd responded, grew impatient, knew the Prime Minister was coming and surged forward.

Police lines held firm and felt the weight of frustrated protesters against them and slowly and surely gave way, quite deliberately, quite controlled, as the weight of numbers pushed them slowly back towards Crillsea library, a stationary patrol car, and police outriders.

Police horses baulked and whinnied and turned to lead the pushing crowd towards the entrance to the library. Slowly horses, police, and protesters, neared Crillsea library. They were jostling, shouting, struggling, and inching yard by yard towards the entrance and a purple cloth cloaking a marble statue.

A black four by four, with mysterious blacked out windows, swung into the street closely followed by two black Jaguars and another black four by four.

The statue stood tall, shrouded in purple velvet, waiting.

The newly appointed Chief Executive of the County Council, Mister George Samuels, stuck his chin out, his chest out, and his right hand out, then quickly recoiled his hand when he realised it wasn't the Prime Minister and he was far too eager to make his mark. It was all going on in his mind and it was his first time in the line-up. He was the new boy and he was nervous. Glimpsing sideways he caught the eye of the chuckling Mayoress, Abigail Ashton.

Abbey, he thought, and saw a sly seductive smile escape her lips and engage him. His nerves disappeared momentarily as he held her eye and then allowed his eyes to appreciate the curves of her body.

Abruptly, Mayoress Abigail 'Abbey' Ashton turned away and prodded her husband, Maurice, the Mayor, gently in the ribs as a line of black saloon cars entered the street. The Mayoress gripped the Mayor's hand tightly and then glimpsed over her shoulder at her would-be suitor.

'We have an arrival,' spoken into a detective's concealed radio. 'Charlie Two at Crillsea library.'

The Jaguar doors opened and the tiny blonde Secretary of State for Culture Media and Sport stepped from a rear seat waving to the crowd.

There was a round of applause from well-wishers on a pavement and a Union flag waved at the tiny blonde lady dressed in a powder blue two-piece suit. There were 'boos' from the mass of protesters struggling and jostling with a line of police.

The blonde Minister, all five feet tall of her, stepped towards the pavement, a crowd, and the entrance to the library; smiling, she smoothed the skirt of her two-piece and waved again to the waiting crowd.

Crillsea's grey-looking Mayor was tall and slim but drab in appearance and drab in temperament. No-one quite knew how he, Councillor Maurice Ashton, had ended up married to the stunning Mayoress, Abigail, who was once a former lingerie model, but he had. Readjusting his chain of office, he steadied his spectacles, and readied himself for a limp handshake.

The Mayoress wished she'd had time to practice one more curtsey or bow as she tidied her hair for the third time in as many minutes. And then Abbey wondered if she should curtsey for a Minister or was that just for royalty, or should she bow at all? She couldn't remember the protocol when it mattered and it mattered now. But oh, she was gorgeous with her long golden hair and dazzling looks, and didn't she know it. Stealing another glance at the handsome and elegant Chief Executive of the County Council, George Samuels, she looked away again when his head began to turn.

Cyril Leadbetter, a short, fat, young, Chief Librarian, fingered his tie, smoothed his hair, and scratched the end of his nose.

Simultaneously, as if on cue, the line of council chiefs all fidgeted in their own private ways and tried to look more sombre than the person they were standing beside.

Suddenly, they were all joined by a trio of dark suits and crackling ear pieces and the Chief Executive of the County Council felt himself jostling for position with the Mayor and Mayoress on the pavement as dark suits marshalled the entourage towards the front door of Crillsea library.

There they all stood; Abigail Ashton, her husband, Maurice; Cyril, the librarian, and the handsome and suave George Samuels. They all shared two things in common: nerves and standing where they had been told to stand.

The reinforcements arrived at the behest of Patterson and sanctioned by Gold. The team of police protection officers dressed in dark suits and sobriety encircled the area preceding the blonde Secretary of State as Cyril Leadbetter fingered his tie and scratched the edge of his nose again.

In anticipation, Cyril stepped forward to be recognised by the principals of government but, despite his weight, felt himself edged to one side as George Samuels gently shoulder-charged him into temporary obscurity and gave a look to the Mayor suggesting he needed to adjust the Chain of Office.

A second black Jaguar took centre stage and cruised to a standstill outside the front of Crillsea library.

'Charlie One at the library,' on the police net.

The Jaguar hunkered down closed and dark. A second ticked away and became two. Anticipation was rife.

There was almost a cheer when the Prime Minister's Personal Protection officer uncomfortably eased himself out of the front passenger seat of the car. But mistaken identity persuaded the crowd to falter and delay their applause when the Prime Minister's Personal Protection Officer stepped onto the tarmac at the front of the library. Gradually, he surveyed the street as another team of police bodyguards leapt from the entourage and formed a protective circle around the short blonde Minister of State. The Prime Minister's Personal Protection Officer stood six feet seven inches tall and two and a half feet broad across his shoulders and chest: a mountain of a man. He gradually moved to the rear nearside door of the Jaguar and placed his left hand near the door handle. But he used his eyes to scrutinise the street and those who were lined up to greet two principals of government. He guided his eyes to comprehend the body language of those nearing the library entrance under the slow deliberate control of a double line of police carrying riot shields and supported by a line of police horses whinnying and baying at no-one particularly. He listened to chanting, read insulting placards, and saw some flags waving a welcome. It was just another day at the office. The street was his office and the Prime Minister's personal protection was his job. His eyes dissected people, gradually and unkindly. It did not matter to him whether they wore black hooded tops and white scarves, Saint John's ambulance uniforms, floral hats, chains of office, or smart suits and designer dresses. It did not matter to him that they might be police officers riding horses or carrying riot shields. They were all potential enemies and he had no friends when he was at the office. He wasn't paid to be friendly, just mildly diplomatic when needed.

Grasping the door handle, the Prime Minister's Personal Protection Officer sought to engage the eyes of his seated Prime Minister. A moment passed before he instructed, 'Come,' and he opened the Jaguar door.

Growing to six feet six inches tall, the portly Prime Minister alighted from the vehicle as the crowd enveloped the area, pushed over flimsy barriers, and began cheering and clapping. Some were chanting their chants and mouthing their opinion; others were waving their Union flag and smiling; others were fidgeting on the pavement waiting anxiously to be introduced to the Prime Minister. Standing on the tarmac the Premier held his chubby stomach in and waved. Smiling, he looked for a television camera. He saw satellite dishes, communication cables, a television crew, and placards raised high. He heard voices grow to a crescendo and then saw a statue covered in velvet and wondered how well the sculptor had captured his image in marble. Soon, I will see myself in marble, he thought, and then waved again to the seething crowd.

Seagulls straggled along the harbour wall of Crillsea when the portly Prime Minister waved once more to the mass and moved towards the grand opening of a new three-storey library and the first of many handshakes.

Surging forward, the crowd tried to encircle the Prime Minister and a tiny blonde as a line of uniformed police tried to repel the swelling crowd.

A youth clad in black and wearing a knee length long black coat suddenly emerged from the multitude. He ran towards the Prime Minister and lifted his placard high.

Fanatically, he shouted at the Prime Minister, 'Shame on you! Shame on you!' Throwing his placard to the ground, he opened his coat to reveal a samurai sword dangling from a belt on his jeans.

There was a gasp from the crowd and the Prime Minister's Personal Protection Officer placed his left hand on the Prime Minister's shoulder preparing to push him forward out of harm's way.

Unsheathing his sword, the assailant felt its weight in his hands and saw the fine edge of its cutting blade sparkling in the sunlight.

The Protection Officer brusquely steered the Prime Minister forward whilst drawing his pistol with his right hand. In a split second the Protection Officer aimed his pistol at the youth and picked his spot: a double tap to his chest, he instinctively thought. And he was still directing the Prime Minister away from the attack, away from the assailant.

Raising his sword high with both hands the assailant charged towards the Prime Minister and screamed. 'Comply or die.'

Lowering his gun to target level the Protection Officer curled his fingers around the trigger and gently squeezed in the slack.

A figure wearing a worn out suit appeared running from the crowd, reached out a hand, and grasped the hood of the assailant's top. The youth lost his momentum and tumbled backwards kicking out into thin air.

Regaining his feet, the youth turned to face an intruder who was wearing a suit that had seen better days. The intruder was barring his way to the Prime Minister, foiling the attack. Angrily, the youth screamed, 'Die,' and hurled his sword at the Prime Minister who was behind the intruder.

Smartly, the unwelcome intruder ducked beneath the sword and deflected it with his elbow high into the air.

The crowd gasped as a samurai sword spiralled through the air towards the Prime Minister.

In a split second the Protection Officer relaxed his trigger finger and quickly pushed his charge towards the library entrance. The mouth of the Prime Minister fell open in shock and his chubby stomach flopped gently up and down above his trouser belt as he rushed towards the library entrance with the Protection Officer pushing him intently and shouting to everyone to get out of the way. Then a sword spiralled into a statue and decapitated the Prime Minister's marble head.

A terrific *crunch* could be heard when marble met tarmac and exploded into countless pieces on the ground.

Cheers and jeers accompanied a tubby Prime Minister when his Personal Protection Officer propelled him swiftly into the library whilst the remnants of a marble head of a statue wrapped in a slither of velvet rolled to a standstill near a Yorkshire terrier with a wagging tail and an annoying bark.

A body-crunching blow took the youth to the ground and the intruding figure announced, 'Hello, Sunshine. My name is Davies King. You're nicked.'

Detective Inspector Davies King, forty two years old, dishevelled, and a stone overweight thrust a warrant card into the youth's face as half a dozen dark sombre suits united pinning the miscreant to the tarmac.

On the pavement, the Mayoress fainted with excitement into the degenerate arms of George Samuels. The Mayor clutched his chain of office, looked skywards, and swore under his breath. The short fat Chief

Librarian, Cyril, stepped over Abbey, the Mayoress, nudged her husband, Maurice, in his ribs and rushed into his library in pursuit of the Prime Minister and the entourage of police who were hustling their charge along.

The film cameras rolled and the media had a field day snapping each and every movement for their editors to dissect.

Cheering! The sound of cheering greeted Davies King when he emerged from the scrum of police holding a youth clad in black who had tried to kill the Prime Minister with a samurai sword.

Cheering! The sound of cheering for Davies King followed by a round of applause as he led the youth towards a van and a stretch inside.

Cheering! The sound of cheering from photographers snapping and filming every second and then thumbs up from reporters hurriedly speaking into their mobile 'phones.

When the applause had ceased, when the crowd had moved away and normality began to return to the streets of Crillsea, two uniformed senior police officers stood on the terrace of Crillsea's new library and looked down into the street and across to the harbour and beyond.

Assistant Chief Constable Patterson turned to his colleague, smiled smugly, and said, 'Congratulations, Superintendent Allithwaite. I call that a rather splendid example of the management of resources with specific regards to security and public order. Don't you agree?'

Allithwaite replied abruptly. 'The Prime Minister's man doesn't think so, sir. He's hopping mad we didn't put proper metal barriers up and prevent the crowds from encroaching onto the Prime Minister. He tells me that if it hadn't been for our man King then we'd have been burying the yob who was armed with the samurai sword. He nearly shot the thug. Anyway, basically, he's not happy with security and....'

'Security?' interrupted Patterson, a hint of derision in his voice. 'Every high profile visit from a Prime Minister is likely to bring with it hoax bomb calls, protesters, placards, rotten eggs, and an opportunity for every Tom, Dick and Harry in the area to come out onto the street and vent their feelings, man.'

'Quite, sir, but...'

Patterson interjected again. 'Democracy upheld; library opened. The Prime Minister and the Minister are safe. Job done! What more does he want?'

'To meet Davies King,' summarised Allithwaite.

Patterson shook his head and walked away but then spun on his heel and snapped, 'Who?'

'Davies King, Detective Inspector,' replied Allithwaite as he smoothed back his greying hair and took a step forward, 'The chap in Bronze Command: Our man who disarmed the swordsman, sir.'

Patterson shook his head in disbelief and insisted, 'Yes, I know who he is. He was yesterday's man until today.' Patterson thought for a second and then said, 'He deflected the sword, superintendent. He didn't disarm anyone.'

Bert Allithwaite tried an agreeable smile and argued, 'Mmm… But it's not how everyone will see it I'm afraid, sir.'

'No!' contended Patterson. 'I know this Davies King from old. Trouble is his middle name. No, we've got our man in position here and it's not that bloody King man. If the Personal Protection Officer wants to speak to King put Jackson in the frame.'

'Keith Jackson, sir? Detective Chief Inspector Jackson?'

'Yes, who else?' responded Patterson with a knowing smile. 'He's the man who got the job heading up criminal investigation in this division, isn't he?'

'Yes, I appointed him myself, sir,' replied Allithwaite, limply.

'No, you didn't,' countered Patterson tetchily. 'I told you to specifically consider Jackson and you wisely took my advice and suggested he be promoted into the new position. I, however, arranged for his promotion through the various….' There was a subtle pause whilst Patterson found the appropriate words and eventually continued. 'Yes, that's it; through the various confidential procedures we have in place for these personnel issues. Remember?'

'Jackson it is then, sir,' smiled Allithwaite with a look of surrendered acquiescence on his face. 'The problem is the Prime Minister wants to speak to the man. King that is.'

'That's not going to happen,' ordered Patterson. 'The Prime Minister will be in a car headed for the capital in ten minutes time and King will be tied up at the x-ray department getting his arm looked at. Let Jackson deal with the media and milk it for the overall excellence of an operation we put in place.'

Patterson's anger seemed to reach another level when he snapped, 'Don't personalise it using that has-been King. We don't need heroes who are flabby and fifty.'

'He's nearer to forty, I think, sir. King, that is. He used to be a rather good amateur boxer, I'm told, and he's very much engaged in helping to run the local sports club for the youth of the area.'

'What? Never mind what age he is. I really don't give a damn. I want Jackson on the front page and on everyone's television screen tonight taking credit for today. Jackson is the future. King is the past. Now get on with it.'

'Will do, sir,'

The assistant chief constable stopped in his tracks, turned to his colleague and said, 'Superintendent Allithwaite, they don't teach you everything at training colleges and universities. You must remember to promote around you the people you want to take with you on your career. We've picked Jackson to do a job for us. He's got what I want and he's got a very positive attitude. He understands senior management requirements. He always complies and I like my people to comply.'

'I understand the various concepts of power, assistant chief constable,' smoothed Allithwaite.

'Good.' The assistant chief constable looked out to sea and ordered, 'This Davies King must go.... Understood?'

There was a silent agreement made with a nod of the head and a shared smile when three seagulls flapped their wings and headed from the harbour wall to the nearby cliffs of Crillsea.

The walk from Davies King's flat to the Anchor at the harbour was about five minutes, maybe ten. Davies and Max strolled along in dying sunshine reflecting on days gone by: days when they had first met.

Davies had been seconded in London for three years with the Specialist Crime Directorate working with the Central Robbery Squad - better known as the Flying Squad - when Max left the army and joined the Metropolitan Police. The two met when a team of gangsters took exception to one Detective Sergeant Davies King snooping into their affairs and promptly rigged his car up with an explosive device in order to get him off their backs. The device was discovered and Max was called in and defused a bomb under Davies's car. The pair instantly became firm friends and soon realised they shared the same passion in a game they both enjoyed, and a football team they both supported. Eventually, Davies transferred back to Crillsea as a Detective Inspector but they'd stayed in touch.

There was laughter from the duo as they walked down Harbour Place towards the area of Crillsea known as Harbour Wall. They approached Crillsea's brand new library and a headless statue covered with a grey tarpaulin sheet and surrounded by temporary scaffolding.

'So it finished one nil?' asked Max.

'Yes. Close game, I understand. We should catch the highlights in the pub tonight. Apparently our goalie tips the ball over the bar in the last seconds of the game otherwise it could have been a draw.'

'That reminds me,' enquired Max. 'How's your arm?'

'Badly bruised, that's all,' replied Davies, checking his left arm above the elbow. He was coming at me like a bloody lunatic, Max. I ducked and put my hands up to save my face. The sword handle hit my elbow. I didn't know where it was going.'

'You do now,' laughed Max nodding towards the covered statue.

'Yeah, crazy that, Max,' said Davies. 'I'm told there was something wrong with the composition of the statue. The sword struck a fracture in the marble apparently. They realised last week but didn't have time to fix it so decided to let it stand until after the visit. It didn't really change things though.'

A few steps later Max stopped in his tracks and asked, 'You mean you wouldn't have taken the blade full on to save the Prime Minister?'

Davies continued walking and replied, 'Give over, Max. Do I look like a complete idiot?'

'Well… Sometimes…' responded Max, thoughtfully. And then he followed on retrieving lost ground in seconds.

'Anyway,' challenged Davies. 'What possessed you to kick a suspect bomb into eternity?'

'Some clown reading the football results upset me.'

'Oh…' and Davies shut up for a moment or two before he countered, 'You didn't defuse a bomb and I saved myself then?'

'That's about right!' Max nodded and they strolled on. 'By the way, Davies, we call these things a device; not a bomb.'

'I know. You defused one under my car in Finchley years ago. If you hadn't I wouldn't be here, Max.'

'I remember it well,' chuckled Max.

A motor cycle roared past at high speed unnoticed by the pair.

'It was probably one of the worst devices I've ever encountered,' continued Max. 'An under car improvised magnetic explosive device fitted with a timing mechanism powered by a flat battery.'

'Bomb with a dud timer!' summarised Davies.

'Call it what you will,' said Max.

'Bet you don't get many like that?' enquired Davies.

'We don't that's why I keep it intact for the lecture tours. It's a perfect specimen to show people,' replied Max.

'Glad I could be of assistance,' mused Davies.

'No problem,' replied Max.

'How long you stopping?' asked Davies.

'A week or so, if that's okay with you. My kits in the van and I'm booked in at the Anchor for the duration.'

'Where's the big suit?' asked Davies.

'In your nick; it's Kevlar, you know,' replied Max.

'And it's five times stronger than… Yeah, I know.'

'I've always thought it ought to be six, Davies.'

'So you've repeatedly said over the years, Max. Never mind. You can stop at mine if you want,' suggested Davies.

'I know but you're working and I don't want to be a nuisance in your flat. Thanks all the same but I thought I'd do a bit of walking; take a break, crack a few bottles, move a few pieces. I've plenty of time owed and the office is covered. I've actually consigned my van keys to your office drawer.'

'Why my office drawer, Max?'

'You never use it. They're as safe as houses in there.'

'Great!' replied Davies 'Is Big Al still in charge of the office, or rather the squad?'

'Thank God, yes. The legend lives,' answered Max. 'Big Al is still the hardest man in the Met. He's just gone all technical and sophisticated.'

'You mean he's gone computerised?' suggested Davies King.

'And some, but he's just the same below the skin once you get past all the gismos and high tech gadget stuff they do nowadays,' replied Max. 'By the way, Davies, talking about gadgets, I bought you a present for old time's sake; it's a new clock.' Max rummaged in his clothing and produced a gift box. 'It's inscribed!' He passed it to Davies and said, 'Ordinarily, there would have been two names on it but, well, I wasn't quite sure what to put and …'

'There's no need, Max. Really! I've convinced myself she's in a better place,' replied Davies sadly. 'Angela rests now but one day I will have my revenge. Until then, I take each day as it comes.'

Broken memories of a shared past threatened their stroll but Max eventually said, 'I can't believe you stayed in Crillsea near the harbour. Her death must come back to haunt you surely?'

'I thought about moving away after Angela drowned, Max, but part of me thinks she would want me to stay here and work with those young people in Crillsea Sports Club. Then there's my job in the police, of course. I could never leave the police. It's my bread and butter and pays the bills. No, I worked out a long time ago that I'm surely not the only one who has lost his wife in such tragic circumstances. It's not fair; it's not right, but I have to get on with life.'

'Davies, how do you manage to pass those yachts in the harbour every day? Do you ever stop and ask yourself, was it that one?'

'Yes, Max, I do,' said Davies. 'There's never a day goes by when I don't think about her, and you're right; I often see an oceangoing yacht in Crillsea harbour and wonder if that's the one we collided with. Why didn't they stop? Where is it now? Why did Angela have to go that way?'

'I'm sorry, Davies,' said Max. 'I didn't mean to....'

'Forget it,' interrupted Davies. 'It happened two years ago and I need to let go.'

They walked on in silence before Davies eventually asked, 'Are you still rubbish at playing, Max?'

In a deliberately lighter mood, Max joked, 'Actually, it's you that's rubbish at the game, Davies, not me; but to be fair, I haven't played for a while.'

'In that case you'd better prepare to be slaughtered,' declared Davies, fondly examining his gift.

Night was rushing in and the sound of a cruel inbound tide was crashing harshly against Crillsea's harbour wall. The beam from the lighthouse flashed across the bay occasionally and gathered reluctant shadows against the harbour wall. Fishing boats, speed boats, and motor cruisers, strained at their anchors and nudged each other as the tide rolled in and a smidgen of escaping oil threatened Crillsea's sea life.

Davies King and Max Fowler rounded a corner and entered the Anchor pub. It was a fairly large pub with a function room, two bars, and a restaurant section. Trading in a tourist area, the pub was also equipped with half a dozen guest rooms and a bed and breakfast tariff. The Anchor served locals and holidaymakers alike. A low hum of noise greeted them as they made their way towards the bar.

'A chessboard, Bill,' shouted Davies. 'In fact... Davies turned to Max who nodded. 'Yes, make it two Magno and one chessboard.'

Bill Baxter, the slightly tubby licensee, replied, 'On the house. We don't get many heroes in here and two in the same night is worth a free drink.' Bill raised his voice to the crowd of locals near the bar. 'What do you think ladies and gents? On the house or are the heroes in the chair?' Reaching beneath the bar, the ruddy-faced and weather-beaten Bill searched for a dog-eared chessboard and associated chess pieces.

'I've got a chess clock, Bill. It's brand new,' said Davies winking at Max, 'Just the board please.'

'And the brandy,' added Max.

A group assembled near a darts board started chanting, 'Heroes... Heroes... Heroes...'

One of the committee members of Crillsea Sports Club beamed a huge smile, flicked her ginger pony tail across her shoulders, and shouted, 'Six pints here, Davies and make it snappy.'

'Watch it, Gloria. I'm not easy you know,' replied Davies.

'Course you are, Davies. You just play hard to get all the time. Hey, hero,' joked Gloria, 'It's a sponsored darts game for the sports club. The kids need new tennis rackets. Can I put you down for a tenner?'

'Of course, you can,' shouted Davies. 'Who's sponsoring it?'

'You are, Davies,' laughed Gloria. 'I'll put you both down for a tenner; that's twenty quid then, okay?'

Davies smiled, nodded his agreement, looked across the bar and said, 'Shut her up, Bill. Six pints of whatever she wants and don't forget the chess pieces as well please.'

'Who's your friend?' asked Gloria, flirting.

'This is Max, a pal of mine.'

'Mmm.... Tasty,' replied Gloria with a suggestive wink.

'Married,' countered Max.

'Damn,' shrugged Gloria.

'Lots of friends you have, Mister King,' and an elderly but rugged Archie squeezed between them towards his seat near a bay window.

Archie doffed his cap, ran his arthritic fingers through a mop of white hair, and declared, 'Even government friends. It's on the telly and in the evening papers. Heroes you are, both of you.' Archie placed a pinch of snuff near the base of his thumb. 'I remember you, Mister Bomb Man. You chased Yorkie away, so you did.'

'Yorkie?' cracked Max.

'My dog,' snapped Archie. He sniffed, replaced a lid on his snuff box, and prepared to sneeze.

'A Yorkshire terrier, scruffy little thing?' suggested Max.

Archie sneezed and said, 'Watched you with the bomb, so I did; good job you didn't kick my dog, Yorkie, Mister Bomb Man. Yorkie is not happy.'

'Max! My name's Max Fowler. Not Mad Max. It wasn't a bomb and I'm sorry if I upset Yorkie. That's such an imaginative name for a Yorkshire terrier, Archie, if you don't mind me saying.'

'Yorkie isn't happy, Max, the Bomb Man. He wouldn't let Mister King and you buy me a drink if he'd been kicked like you kicked the bomb. I mean not with you and Mister King getting knighted soon, I shouldn't wonder.'

'I doubt it, Archie,' interrupted Davies. 'Max, this is Archie. He knows everything about everybody and…'

Archie broke in, 'It's in the Crillsea Chronicle, Mister King.' Tapping his nose with the end of his finger, he removed a newspaper from inside his jacket to reveal a front page photograph of Davies King.

"Well if it's in the Chronicle then it will definitely happen won't it, Archie?' Davies laughed and quietly asked Max, 'Married? Thought you were divorced?'

'I am,' whispered Max. 'Once is enough. Don't tempt providence with that Gloria woman. Anyway, what wife wants to wait at home for a man that might not come back that night?'

'Well, put that way I suppose it's a nuisance being a hero every hour of the day, Max,' chuckled Davies, snaffling a handful of salted peanuts from a bowl on the bar.

Archie exploded with a sneeze.

'And you?' asked Max. 'I mean anyone since….'

'No,' snapped Davies. He threw a peanut into the air and caught it in his mouth. 'Sorry, Max. No, no-one else.'

Archie engaged them again. 'I told you so, Mister King. Knighthoods and things! Look you're on the telly.' Archie pointed to a screen on a distant wall and then offered them both a pinch of snuff, which they declined.

The image of Davies King leaving casualty department nursing his sore arm dominated a large plasma television screen usually reserved for sports coverage. Noise in the bar denied any audible sound from the screen but the caption *A King saves a Prime Minister* occupied the bottom of the screen. Television coverage followed Davies walking to his car, shaking his head and waving away a cameraman and reporter. Then an image of a man smartly dressed in a pin stripe suit filled the screen. The caption *Detective Chief Inspector Keith Jackson, Senior Investigating Officer*, was displayed on the screen for a moment. He read briefly from a prepared script on a piece of A4 paper and then the screen shot cut back to Davies King driving away from hospital with a smile and a wave to the camera. There was another image of Davies King warily turning into a compound at Crillsea police station followed by a shot of the Prime Minister outside 10 Downing Street paying homage to his saviour with a quotation filling the bottom caption of the screen with *If a man has to be saved, then let it be by a King*. And then there was some still colour photographs of Davies King confronting a youth carrying a samurai sword.

Davies nudged Max and said, 'Trial by television, Max. Any minute now some retired detective is going to be dragged willingly onto the screen and asked to analyse every movement ever made.'

'Watch it then. You can retire soon, can't you?' chuckled Max.

Suddenly the image was gone with the click of a remote and a football stadium took centre stage. People in the bar began to root for their team as twenty two men lined up to do battle in the name of sport.

'Politics,' mused Davies. He sighed and reflected, 'Sad thing is, Archie, I didn't even vote for the Prime Minister.' His hand scooped peanuts from a bowl on the bar.

'Oh dear, Mister King! Mistake! Mine's a mild when you're ready.'

Davies turned to Max and quipped, 'We only came in for a game of chess and a couple of quiet brandies and we end up supplementing every loafer in Harbour Wall who can't stand their own round.'

'You've a bruised arm remember?' suggested Max. 'It might hurt putting your hand in your pocket.'

'It always does,' agreed Davies.

On the other side of the bar, in the lounge and restaurant area, some form of celebration was taking place and Davies caught a brief glimpse of ladies in fine dresses and gentlemen in smart lounge suits.

Davies nudged Max when a tall good looking blonde appeared at the bar in the restaurant and lounge. 'You sure, Max?' asked Davies. 'I mean about not giving marriage another go?' He turned to the bar rummaging in a trouser pocket for his wallet. 'What's on, Bill?'

'Works do of some kind, Mister King. Someone leaving Crillsea, I think,' replied Bill.

'Best do a mild for Archie whilst you're at it, Bill.'

The pints were being pulled and Davies was searching his pockets for a wallet that was on a bedside table a mile up the road in his flat.

'Max,' prompted Davies.

'No! Don't tell me.'

'Be a hero, Max. I've forgotten my wallet.'

'Why am I not surprised? Here, Bill.' Max pulled a wad of twenty and fifty pound notes from a pocket and paid for the drinks.

'Oh my God, Max. You won the lottery?' asked Davies, and then quietly said, 'You'd best put that away before someone gets tempted.'

'Chill out,' smoothed Max.

'Where'd you get that kind of money, Max? Robbed a bank?'

'Holiday break, remember?' smiled Max.

A youth wearing a black leather motor cycle jacket and jeans stepped between them and placed himself next to Davies. The youth had attitude when he looked at the back of Davies's head and challenged, 'So you're him.'

Davies was carefully handing pints over from the bar to a bright and breezy Gloria.

'Hey, you,' threatened the youth. 'You… Big hero! He was my mate. He was my best mate. It's time you were put in your place.'

Gathering his leather jacket around him, the youth jutted his head forward preparing to confront Davies. 'You, are you listening or what?'

Davies heard a huge groan from some fans watching a football glance across a crossbar on the television screen, and then handed two more pints over to a waiting Gloria, saying, 'I'll be in the gym in the morning. I'll leave the money in the office for you, okay?'

'Thanks, Davies,' replied Gloria. 'But don't forget to tidy the weights away when you're finished with them.'

Davies agreed but, still oblivious to the youth's challenge, he accidentally nudged a bowl of peanuts from the bar and watched them scatter on the floor. 'Bill...' offered Davies apologetically.

Shaking his head again, Bill asked, 'Why didn't I see you coming tonight, Mister King?'

'Sorry!' offered Davies. 'Nuts everywhere, Bill.'

'You can say that again,' muttered Bill Baxter.

Max leaned forward and whispered into the youth's ear, 'Excuse me, son. I think you've got the wrong man.'

'What? Who the...?' Then he winced when he felt Max's foot pressing down onto his toes.

Max hinted again. 'You've got the wrong man, son, and my foot carries more weight on it every day than you could ever imagine.'

'Get your foot off mine,' squealed the youth. 'Or you'll be next.'

'Oh dear! That's my problem. I'm always putting my foot in it.' Max leaned further forward transferring more weight onto his foot.

'Oh no. No...!' The youth met agony for the first time in his life and did not relish the engagement.

Davies passed his last pints over to Gloria as Bill attacked salted peanuts with a pan and brush.

Max suggested, 'Were you just going?' He moved eyeball to eyeball with the youth and transferred his full body weight onto one foot. It was as if a hammer was driving into a cockroach.

Ashen-faced and weakening in resolve, the youth nodded and then seemed pleased when Max stepped back and released him.

Davies turned to Max and asked personably, 'Friend of yours?'

The youth looked at Davies and then frowned at Max.

'No,' replied Max. 'I don't think so.'

Davies, still oblivious to the youth, carried a chessboard and two glasses of Magno to a nearby table and asked, 'Black or white?'

'Black will do. I've never been a white knight,' smiled Max looking deeply into the youth's eyes. 'And I don't think I ever will be.'

'I like things in black and white myself, Max,' offered Davies.

The youth was gone from the bar, gone from Max's penetrating grey eyes, and gone from a game of chess that was about to start with the swift movement of the white king's pawn.

Davies sampled the first taste of the night by toasting, 'Magnificent Magno! Happy birthday, Max! By the way, thanks for the time.' With an abrupt *thud* Davies activated his chess clock and announced, 'Game on!'

As the front door of the pub banged tight behind a disgruntled youth there was a cry of 'GOAL' from those eyeing a television screen rather than a bulls-eye or chessboard.

Within minutes the chessboard was littered with fallen pawns, knights and a rook as Davies surged into an attack. But then Max laid out a trap and began to slow the pace of the game down to his choosing.

Davies sunk his Magno and suggested, 'Another?'

'Why not,' replied Max and slid his glass towards Davies.

Carrying two empty glasses Davies made his way to the bar.

'Hey, Davies,' prompted Bill. 'You being a clever type and having had a private word with the Prime Minister will know about this.'

'What's that, Bill?' asked Davies.

'This letter from the Chamber of Commerce.' Bill pushed a document across the bar towards Davies.

Davies took a cursory look at the paper and said, 'You need a businessman.' Thrusting his hand into a bowl on the bar, Davies dug out some peanuts and popped them into his mouth.

'Well, have a proper read of it anyway. It's an invitation to a seminar about beating the credit crunch,' said Bill, moving the peanuts out of reach.

'Great!'

'The fee for the seminar is fifty pound. Tell me, what sense is there in spending money to learn about saving money?' asked Bill.

Davies looked around and lowered his voice, 'Sounds like everyone's making money out of this recession except the workers. Are you in trouble? You know… financial trouble?'

'Well, busy today but you know what it's like.' Bill started dusting the top of the pumps. He avoided eye contact for a moment but then offered, 'I'm hoping things will pick up in the summer. Busy one day, quiet the next.'

'I always thought business was okay, Bill?'

'Deceptive! Mister King. It's been busy this week because the Prime Minister is down to open the library so we've had press and television people, visitors, holidaymakers, and the like.'

'That's good.'

'Next week it'll be back to reps selling outboard motors and yacht paint to the rich and fancy in the harbour and I'll be hoping we get a good draw in the football to get the punters in on Saturday. Yeah! I wouldn't say no to some extra money. It's not easy, Mister King.'

'Maybe you just need a break. You know, a long weekend away.'

'I just got back from the Lakes.'

'Climbing?'

'Yeah! Pillar and Gable.... Rock climbing.... I got to the top and decided I'd rather be a climber than a licensee. Mind you, it won't be long before the place is full of wind turbines to climb if they're not careful.'

'How long you been at the climbing then?'

'More years than I've been a licensee, I can tell you. It's what I'd rather do with my life.'

'Better make it two more Magno then, Bill, and one for yourself.'

'I don't drink when I'm behind the bar, Mister King.'

'And one for yourself,' insisted Davies, 'When you're not behind the bar, Bill.'

'I'll take a drink later then.'

'Put it on the slate though. I forgot my wallet, didn't I?'

Bill shrugged in mild disgust, shook his head, poured two Magno Spanish brandies and reached for a notebook and a pencil.

Davies gathered his glasses and was gone from the bar.

'Evening, Mister King. What's your pleasure tonight then?' A dapper looking gentleman in his early forties and wearing a striped blazer followed Davies back to a table.

'Thought you'd be here, Harry,' said Davies. 'Business good?'

Davies sat and handed a glass to Max.

'You know me, Mister King. Just making a living like the rest of us, scraping a crust from where I can. A little bit here; a little bit there. You know how it is.' Harry's eyes took in Max and he enquired, 'Who's your friend?'

'A friend,' replied Davies, denying information.

'A friend?' Harry persisted. 'A friend, you say?'

'Okay, Harry! This is Max. Max, this is Harry Reynolds. Purveyor of all things cheap and questionable.'

'No, no, no, Mister King. You got me all wrong. I'm just an honest businessman, so I am.'

Harry offered a hand to Max but the greeting wasn't taken up.

'Who hasn't been caught yet? What you selling?' asked Davies.

Feeling the leather patches of Davies King's jacket, Harry Reynolds offered, 'You need a new jacket, Mister King. Even the elbow patches will need replacing soon.'

'Watch it, Harry,' replied Davies. 'Hands off the threads!'

'Threads?' queried Harry. 'No matter, I've a nice line in jewellery doing the rounds at the moment, Mister King. Only the best costume jewellery mind you. No trash. I might have a few good quality well-priced radios and a couple of vacuum cleaners next week, Mister King. Good prices for good friends. Bankrupt stock and seconds! You know me, Mister King?'

'Oh, yes I know you, Harry. Not tonight, okay!'

'Big game on?' asked a relentless Harry.

'All our games are big, Harry,' replied Davies.

'Well, any time you want a good deal let me know, Mister King.'

'I surely will, Harry. I surely will.'

Harry Reynolds sniffed politely, adjusted his blazer, bent low, and whispered into Davies's ear. 'They tell me Jackie Striker is back in town.'

'Who tells you?' asked Davies concentrating on the chessboard.

'Voices, Mister King. I hear them everywhere. Voices!'

'I'd get your ears tested if you ever want to hear those dodgy radios, Harry. Or clean them out with your toxic vacuum cleaners.'

'You're so kind, Mister King,' squirmed Harry.

'Is he busy?' responded Davies quietly. 'Jacky Striker?'

'I wouldn't know, Mister King. I don't mix with such people.'

Davies raised his glass and offered, 'Mind how you go, Harry.'

'Next week, Mister King! Nice radio maybe?'

'Maybe!' suggested Davies, pushing a knight into a defensive position. 'Maybe!'

Harry Reynolds winked at Davies and moved on.

'Do you know everyone here?' asked Max.

'No,' replied Davies. 'Problem is they all know me.'

'Often the way,' replied Max with the considered movement of a pawn in the attacking mode.

There was a shout of 'Goal' from a crowd by the television screen as the black and white chess pieces fought their battle on a worn out chessboard.

A delicate scent wafted across their game and warned Max he was being watched. He looked up to see the same tall good looking blonde Davies had pointed out in the restaurant lounge earlier. She smiled when their eyes met and he became aware she was not alone. She was truly beautiful, thought Max.

'Your move, Max,' prompted Davies.

'Sorry, so it is.' Max reached out to move a piece when a hand fell onto his and gently lifted it away from their chessboard.

A man's voice announced, 'Allow me. If you do this you can win now.' His finger hovered above the black queen and then pointed to a vacant square in the centre of their board. 'Sorry, but chess fascinates me.'

'And you are?' asked Max.

'They call me Rob. This is Carla.'

Carla, tall and beautiful, smiled a smile broad enough to fill the harbour, ignored Davies, and looked directly into Max's eyes.

'But you both have me at a disadvantage,' continued Rob, tall, smart and elegant in his pin stripe suit. 'They tell us you are both famous and I wondered if I might have seen you in a film or something like that.'

'Your wife, I presume?' Max asked.

'My secretary actually,' replied Rob.

Davies was annoyed. 'We're not famous; we're trying to have a quiet drink and play chess. No disrespect intended but get your hands off my chessboard.'

'Everyone seems to know you,' suggested Rob. 'Apparently you were on television tonight but who are you if you don't mind me asking?'

'Me?' replied Davies. 'Oh, I'm just a pawn on a chessboard.'

'You are the bomb man,' smoothed Carla. Her eyes penetrated Max.

'Of course, the army bomb disposal men down for the day,' confirmed Rob. 'The Prime Minister and a cardboard box! Well, that's our mystery solved. Come, Carla. It's been wonderful to meet you army chaps,' said Rob. He turned to Davies and offered, 'My apologies but I think the game is mine.' And then Rob moved the black queen and said, 'Checkmate, I think.'

Davies studied his chessboard as Carla smiled and Rob guided her outside to a waiting taxi.

Max allowed his eyes to follow the curves of the blonde and inhale the last remnants of her fading perfume.

'Sure you're never going to get another wife then, Max?' asked Davies as he watched Rob guide the gorgeous blonde out of sight.

'I could be tempted, Davies. Yes, I could be tempted,' sighed Max.

'Last one?' suggested Davies, checking the time.

'Why not?' replied Max who was setting the pieces up once more.

And so they played on as Gloria concentrated on her arrows; Bill smiled and checked a growing wad of notes in the well of the till; Archie asked for another mild to go on Davies's slate, and Harry Reynolds plied his trade quietly hidden in the darkest corner of a neighbouring bar.

Without warning an empty pint glass flew through the air and crashed into a wall close to Max and Davies. Then a chair was thrown against the side of the bar and disintegrated into matchstick. There was a mighty *roar* from a man's voice followed by the sickening sound of bone smashing into flesh.

'Oh dear,' said Davies.

There was a rush of falling bodies colliding with each other. Tables and chairs toppled over as customers tried to escape a giant of a man who had decided televised football scores were not to his liking.

'Shall we?' suggested Max.

'Nah,' replied Davies. 'Leave it to Bill. I think it's that Jimmy Riley kicking off again. I've heard he's a bit of a handful when he's had drink.'

There was another roar from the crowd of drinkers and then Gloria crashed into Davies King. Another pint glass hit a wall behind the bar. There was a surge of bodies trying to escape the wrath of an angry man. Archie was knocked to the ground and in the mayhem that followed Max and Davies found themselves under their table with thirty two black and white chess pieces rolling along the floor and a chessboard in danger of being trampled on.

Seeing the chessboard endangered, Max reached out.

Seeing the chessboard endangered, Davies reached out.

Both men grabbed the chessboard and pulled at the same time. There was a rip of cardboard and cloth and Davies scrambled to his feet holding one side of a damaged chessboard.

Moments later, Max produced the other half laughing, 'That's torn it.'

'That's it,' said Davies. 'That's bloody it. Football is one thing. Chess is quite another. Bill!' he shouted.

'Three nines! I know,' replied Bill, reaching for the phone.

Advancing against an oncoming tide of people, Davies marched straight up to Jimmy Riley: a lumberjack of a man, six foot up to his armpits, and then some, who sported a fierce heavy beard and a temper to match.

'Ambulance, police or both?' shouted Bill.

Immediately, Jimmy Riley struck out at Davies who dodged the full weight of the punch but took a glancing blow on the side of his face slightly below the eye.

Davies King took a step back and then to the side. He ducked and weaved and curled his fists. He took up a boxer's stance and released a searching jab just to test the distance between him and his opponent.

'Ambulance then,' decided Bill, watching. He dialled.

Davies stepped right into the man and barked, 'Oy! That's my chess board.' And then for the first time he took in his adversary properly. His eyes worked slowly up from chest to armpits but struggled to find a face hidden behind a big hairy beard.

'Oh, my God!' conceded Davies.

Jimmy Riley reached out a hand to grab Davies by the throat but Davies King closed his eyes and launched himself upwards with a fierce head butt that connected with Riley's chin.

Jimmy Riley swore and Davies King followed through with a thundering right striking deep into his enemy's lower stomach. Riley crumpled like a pack of cards and Davies stepped round him, grabbed his neck, and pushed him headlong into the bar in a move he did not learn in the boxing ring. There was a dull *thud* when bar and Jimmy collided and his lights went out.

'Hello, Toxic. My name's Davies King and you're nicked.'

Davies King's announcement was greeted by sporadic applause and a beaming licensee.

'On the house, Mister King,' smiled Bill as he placed a pint of best bitter on the bar in front of Davies.

Davies took a mouthful, then another mouthful, and downed half a pint before replying, 'Excellent timing, Bill. Excellent!' Then he stuck his fist into a nearby ice bucket and winced in pain. 'My problem is that I'm not as young as I used to be and I could do with more time in the gym.'

'Your jacket, Mister King,' said Bill. 'The patch on your elbow is torn. Needs fixed, so it does.'

Running his fingers along the sleeve, Davies felt the tear where the leather patch and cloth had parted company. 'It'll fix,' he pronounced.

Jimmy Riley stirred, shook his head, looked up, and tried to struggle to his feet to come back at Davies King.

Davies delivered another brisk jab to Jimmy Riley's glass chin and said, 'And that, my man, was a copper's short caution.'

This time Jimmy Riley's lights stayed out as the front door burst open and four police officers rushed into the bar.

Davies sank his beer in one continuous swallow.

'What the hell has been going on here?' shouted a uniformed sergeant surveying the scene and standing above Jimmy Riley.

'Hi, Tom,' offered Davies who caught a reflection of his black eye in the mirror. 'He's nicked. Chuck him in the van, will you! He broke my chessboard.'

'Oh dear,' offered Max. 'The end of a perfect day.'

Davies slammed his empty pint glass on the bar, considered his aching fist and bruised knuckles, and then walked past the sergeant and towards Max, and thirty two rolling black and whites lying on the floor.

In a street outside a youth in motor cycle gear pulled out a mobile phone from inside his jacket, worried about his badly bruised toes, and fiercely hit the digits as the night clouds moved in and the tide edged along the coast.

Within the hour the Anchor was closed and Crillsea settled down for the night.

But elsewhere, and later that night, there was a sudden sound of breaking glass when a pebble fractured an old street lamp and extinguished its light. The silence of the evening was broken only by a distant hum of traffic, a few night birds, and the twanging sound of his catapult wriggling its way into the thigh pocket of his combats. He stood still, watching and waiting. Minutes passed in the shadow of an alley as his eyes gradually became accustomed to the sure and certain black of night.

Darkness enveloped the narrow passageway but his knowing hands reached out to find a rusting drainpipe. The pipe metal remained firm. A deep breath was taken and a huge step found a corner of brickwork where mortar had perished and bequeathed a toe grip.

With a heave his toe launched his limb upwards and his arms clung to the drain pipe. He stretched out with his other foot and eventually located a bracket of an external air conditioning unit. Tentatively, he transferred his weight onto a slender bracket and grasped a window ledge above him.

A siren sounded somewhere in the near distance but the climber dismissed it from his mind and sought the comfort of another crevice in the brickwork. Gradually, he turned and pushed his back into the wall whilst his feet pushed against the opposing wall of the alley. It was as if he was inside a thin and gloomy open-aired chimney and he slowly, but expertly, shuffled up the walls of the alley, climbing defiantly, grunting occasionally, but with the slow determination of one destined to win. Sweat trickled down his neck and flowed onto his throat. He could hear his heart and lungs pounding in unison as he climbed to the top.

There was a shared silence on Crillsea's roof tops. Only the sound of his breathing and a distant rumble of an incoming tide crashing against the harbour wall comforted him.

Glimpsing the horizon he picked out the faint lights of a distant oil tanker bound for the world's oceans. Then there was a brief flash from a lighthouse on nearby Crillsea Rock as an arc of light swept the bay as if it were a sentry searching for an escaped prisoner.

Catapult, darkened torch, gloves, jemmy, magnet and wire! Kneeling down he switched on his torch and followed the passage of thin beam across the rooftops.

*

Chapter Four

~ ~ ~

Dateline: Saturday,
Crillsea Cliffs.

A log fire warmed a spacious lounge, took the chill from a colder than usual morning, and provided comfort to the long-haired brunette who was alone in the house. She prodded burning logs with a poker and inspired more flames into the grate before returning to the comfort of her white leather sofa.

Memories were flooding back to her as she toyed playfully with her diamonds and sapphires, a collection of gold and silver rings, and a particularly unique and personal wedding ring made of eighteen carat gold but semi-paved with diamonds. The ring was skilfully crafted, dazzling and resplendent, and inscribed with her name on the inside.

Such beautiful jewellery, she thought.

With a poignant tear in her eye, she held nostalgia closely to her chest and smoothed the precious stones with her slender fingers. So many memories, she thought as she meticulously arranged her collection of precious stones into her jewellery box.

After a moment of thinking and wondering, she laid the jewellery box onto the marble table and sat back into a deep velvet cushion. Then she chuckled and appreciated how she had received the jewellery box as a present from the Spanish girl and her family: the family on the island.

Yes, she thought, in view of what happened it probably was appropriate to adorn a cheap jewellery box with jewellery valued at twenty five thousand pounds or more. She thought back to the time of the island, the very first visit, and the receiving of such a well intentioned gift. Then she closed the lid on her box, ran her fingers across the unique embroidered motif, and smiled wistfully.

There was a far-away screech of a rusting hinge and she knew it was the garden gate at the end of the path. She shook her head in annoyance and took a mouthful of coffee before placing her mug on a table next to the jewellery box. Casually, she pressed the remote and watched her television screen die into a thick blackness.

There was a gentle crunch of leather on gravel and she knew he was coming. He was expected and she was waiting for him and the argument that would surely follow. But she would stand her ground because she knew she was right. She knew what needed to be said.

Throwing the remote to one side of the sofa, she smiled smugly, and ruffled her hair with a casual brush of her fingers.

There was another crunch on the gravel, louder this time, followed by hungry seagulls squawking loudly above Crillsea cliffs. She stood up and slowly moved towards the hall to greet him and deny him.

There was a sound of heavy breathing at the door and she knew the steepness of the path from the cliffs had taken its toll upon him. Then quickly, full of anticipation and desire to have her way, she glided elegantly to the door. Pausing for a moment by the mirror, she checked herself, grinned at her reflection and turned to greet the visitor.

She reached out for the handle but, simultaneously, the handle turned slowly, a gloved hand appeared curled around the edge of the door, and then he was in and upon her.

'What are you doing with my keys? Where did you get them?'

'You left them in the office,' he replied.

'You had no right to keep them. You could have 'phoned me to tell me you had them. I didn't think you would let yourself in. You swine!'

'I phoned. You knew I was coming to see you. But oh, am I sorry if I've ruffled your feathers.'

'Well,' she calmed herself. 'You're here now. What do you want?'

'I came to see if you would change your mind.'

'Change my mind?' she challenged. 'Why on earth should I change my mind? I've no reason to change my mind. I know I'm right; you know I'm right, and very soon everyone else will.'

'You haven't thought this through, have you?' he suggested.

'My mind is made up. I've made my decision.'

'It's the wrong decision. I could be ruined. We could be finished. Things are bad enough as they are without you being God Almighty.'

He began to stalk her like a predator tracking his prey.

'I said you could come and see me about this but I expected an adult conversation not a shouting match with a bully,' she contested.

'There you are again with your God Almighty attitude.'

'God Almighty! God Almighty! Leave.' She moved away from him. 'I want you to leave please. I was happy to discuss this matter with you but I'm not going to be bullied. My mind's made up and my papers are waiting to be sent. There's nothing you can do.'

'Your papers are waiting to be sent,' he queried. 'Where are your papers?' he demanded.

'Safe! Away from your prying eyes and greedy hands! One little finger that's all it takes. One little finger and the world will know and there's absolutely nothing you can do to stop me.'

'Where's your laptop?' he demanded angrily.

Realising her mistake, she gasped. 'You can't be serious?'

'Oh, I'm serious. Now I'll ask you for the last time to sit down and discuss this with me.'

'I do have copies,' she argued.

'How much do you want?' he reasoned. 'How much will it take for you to change your mind?'

'Bribery and corruption! It's all in the open now, isn't it, and no surprise really. Just what one might have expected from the likes of you.'

He laughed in her face and said, 'Actually, that's the difference between us. I live in the real world and deal with these types of problems every day of my life. You, on the other hand, live in a land you really do believe is utopia. All flowers! Sugar and spice and all things nice! Now stop and think for minute. You've made your point and you've made it well. How much do you want? Name your price and we'll sort it.'

'There's no price and nothing you could ever do to make me change my mind. What you do now is up to you,' she snapped. 'Get out.'

Suddenly, she felt his powerful body pushing her backwards, pushing her against the framed mirror on the wall, against a telephone trolley and a double-glazed door into the lounge.

There was a crash and the mirror fell from its wall and smashed to the ground. Slivers of glass spilled across ceramic tiles that laid out a welcome for an unwanted guest. There was a grating of wood and a telephone trolley was upturned in the rush of the moment.

She tried to move away but strangely did not want to resist him, could not resist him, could not deny her will to beat him. She wanted to stand against him. She did not expect his hands to be so hasty and demanding in their desire. She retreated from his advances, retreated from his heavy breathing and perfumed fragrance, and slithered along the wall into the lounge.

Stumbling over a coffee table, she fell backwards onto the mink carpet lying in front of the blazing fire. The jewellery box fell from the table and spilled its contents onto the fur. Diamond earrings; a pearl necklace, a sapphire brooch, a wedding ring semi-paved with diamonds, private memories, odds and ends and dazzling trinkets of an insatiable expense account littered the carpet. Then a pink and white porcelain coffee pot slid against a silver sugar bowl, fell from the table, crashed to smithereens, and emptied onto the carpet.

He grinned and stretched out his gloved hands to grasp her.

'No,' she cried. 'Not this way,' she begged. 'This is not what I…'

Forcing himself upon her, the jewellery and coffee pot were trampled when he grabbed a cushion and tried to smother her.

Kicking out limply, she tried to scream, tried to scratch his face, his eyes, his very being. She tried to bite him as he overpowered her but he was too strong for her and pushed her down. And then she felt his leather gloves encircle her pretty long neck, felt them tighten and press against her throat. She began to resist again for all she was worth, began to punch and kick out furiously at her assailant. She struggled and fought for her existence. Gradually, she managed to move backwards and wriggle away an inch or two, maybe three.

Before long, he overcame her completely. The veins in his neck stood out as he brutally shook the life out of her by throttling her to death in the lounge in front of a blazing fire in a house on Crillsea's cliff tops.

When he had squeezed and shaken the life from her body and felt her fall limp against him, he allowed her corpse to slide to the ground and lay upon a mink rug next to an overturned sugar bowl and a coffee pot.

Holding the jewellery box, he inspected the gems. He held her jewels to the light and ran a careful eye over the glittering trinkets. Then he pocketed his hoard, sniggered and threw the jewellery box haphazardly onto the carpet. He made his way towards the front door. In the hall he took one last look back at her lifeless body, checked his appearance in a random shard of glass lying at his feet in the hallway, and carefully closed the door behind him.

There was the turn of a key followed by a slow shuffled movement of leather on gravel as a hungry seagull squawked above him and a far-away wave crashed against the foot of the cliffs. A rusting hinge creaked and he was gone from the house on Crillsea Cliffs.

There was a drizzle in the air when Detective Inspector Davies King parked up in Crillsea police station car park and got out of his vehicle. He locked his rather bruised and battered Ford and instantly became aware of voices from above. Gazing up, he saw people waving from his office. There was a low hum of cheering and jeering escaping an open window.

Davies hid a bouquet of flowers behind his back when he entered the station. Nodding to the sergeant, he smiled and said, 'Morning, Joe.'

Joe nodded a brief response as Davies hurried past.

Taking the stairs to an open plan CID floor, Davies King passed a poster on a wall advertising the Mayor's Ball at Tevington on Sea. As he approached his workplace he heard again a low hum of sarcastic cheers.

'Alright you lot, I'm no hero and you're not bloody saints. I presume you are all cheering because my team won yesterday. Am I right?'

There was a shuffled silence and a shake of the head.

'Shall we get back to work?' suggested Davies.

Walking towards his private domain, Davies shouted, 'Claudia…'

He swung into his office and threw his mobile phone into a tray. Davies took a seat at his desk and looked directly into the face of an enormous chocolate medal that had been carefully placed on a blotter in the centre of his desk to assume prominence amongst his clutter. Tied to the medal was a piece of red ribbon upon which was written the words *King of the Chocolate Soldiers.*

Davies glanced through the window and watched fellow detectives gradually making towards their seats as telephones rang and a mail man dropped his bundles on their desks.

One or two were giggling and chose to sneak a look at Davies's reaction to his chocolate medal.

Davies obliged them by snatching the delicacy from his desk and holding it up for them to see. With a smile that went from ear to ear, he devoured the chocolate in two mouthfuls.

'Claudia!' He shouted again.

Claudia Jones, widow of this parish, pushing towards a well-deserved old age pension, but strikingly elegant in a long black pencil skirt and a grey woollen cardigan walked into his office.

'No need to shout, Inspector King,' she scolded. 'No need at all.' Claudia immediately tended to a rubber plant that was barely surviving in a pot in one corner of his office. 'All the years I've known you, all the years I've been your personal assistant, you've never shouted for me. Not once. It's not to my liking, Inspector King, and I won't be having any shouting, hero or not. Is that understood, Inspector King?'

'Sorry, Claudia! I just don't like it when you're not here to sort things for me first thing in the morning.'

'Not to worry, inspector. I'm here now.'

Claudia removed his mobile phone from the tray and placed it on his desk beside a landline telephone. 'The battery for your phone is dead, as usual. Would you like me to put it on charge, inspector?' she asked.

'Yes please, Claudia. I think it must have a fault,' said Davies.

'Mmm…' she mused and put the phone to one side for a moment. All the years she had known him, she thought, he was never one for understanding even the most simple of devices. Bit of a bumbling blunderer sometimes, wasn't he, thought Claudia Jones. He really drives me mad, she thought, to the point of distraction, actually. But then Claudia was compelled by the wisdom of her years to be both judge and jury over those whose actions she witnessed daily. Yet she was somewhat isolated by the solitude of her widowhood despite enjoying the respect bestowed upon her by those who cherished her bluntness.

Flicking a switch, Claudia caused a kettle to burst into life.

'Jacket!' she instructed.

'What? Oh, yes. Would you?' suggested Davies removing his jacket and fingering the torn elbow patch. 'Must have got torn somewhere.'

'Needle, thread, five minutes! That's all it takes,' she scolded.

'You are a star,' he quipped. 'What would I do without you?'

'You'd find somebody else to torment,' she replied. Then she started to organise his documents. She moved a bunch of files and instructed him, 'These are letters you requested, typed and ready for your signature. These ones are copies to initial and file, and you need to read these ones, inspector. Okay?'

'These are for you,' offered Davies extending her a bunch of lilies. 'Happy birthday for last week, Claudia.'

'How kind, Inspector King, how very kind but actually…'

'What, wrong colour?' asked Davies, dismayed.

'No, not at all. Actually, lilies are generally a funeral flower but it's the thought that counts,' replied Claudia.

'Oh, well, I asked for something big and colourful for a big and colourful lady and that's what the florist gave me,' replied Davies, pleased he had made his secretary smile.

'Big?' she alleged.

'I meant the flowers,' countered Davies. 'I mean you're not big. The flowers are; if you see what I mean.'

'Which florist?' she enquired with a sharp turn of her head.

'*Flowers for special occasions*, down by the park,' he replied.

'Ha, well. They saw you coming,' she suggested.

'Oh, yes. I know they did. I paid cash,' replied Davies.

Claudia looked quizzically into his eyes, shook her head and said, 'Well, thanks anyways. A week late is better than never, I suppose.'

Davies pushed a button on his computer. 'This bloody thing…'

'Inspector!' She scolded him. 'I will not have you swearing!'

'Sorry, but this thing is not working again.'

'I'll switch it on for you,' suggested Claudia.

'Get the IT department to sort it out,' retorted Davies angrily.

'Did you switch it off when you left?' she demanded.

'Of course I did.'

'The IT department would tell you to leave it on all the time.' She rebuked him. 'It saves time and preserves the processor longer.'

'Well, you learn something every day,' sighed Davies.

The kettle came to a boil and she rattled two cups before announcing, 'Your coffee.' She served him, sipped her own, and settled into repairing his elbow patch. She asked, 'Did you have a good night with Max? I hope you didn't get him any flowers.'

'No, I got him a bottle of brandy and he gave me a chess clock.'

'Chess again!' she challenged.

'He's my mate.' Davies paused and said, 'Not a stalemate.'

Claudia returned a blank stare.

'Stalemate,' he announced. 'Chess! Get it?'

'Stupid board game,' she replied.

Davies changed the subject. 'How's our butterfly man?'

Claudia handed him the finished jacket, tidied the kettle away, and tetchily replied, 'I do wish you'd stop talking about Mister Jackson like that. He's not a garden insect. He is a gentleman. He has a lovely manner…'

Davies interrupted, 'He has an O level in domestic science and an A level in art. Jackson has no qualifications at all other than his standard police entrance exams. I've got a degree in sociology with the Open University and a master's degree in criminology from Edinburgh and…'

Claudia stared at him disapprovingly.

'You're right,' continued Davies. 'I'm bloody annoyed at not getting that job. Why did Bert Allithwaite pick Keith Jackson and not me?'

'Because Mister Jackson has connections in the right places, inspector; he does as he is told and doesn't upset the apple cart. He's socially responsible, dresses in smart suits, and has a well cultured voice,' professed Claudia. 'Everyone in the office knows you're the best detective in this division but you wear some of your jackets until they are threadbare, have absolutely no fashion sense, and never go to the officer's mess. What did you expect?'

'Respect!' snapped Davies.

'Take a look in the mirror,' advised Claudia. 'Why didn't you get a personal invite to the Mayor's Ball, for example? Well, I'll tell you why because no-one else in this place will. You need a haircut. Your tie's askew and you need a new shirt. I'll pop out and get you one later on this morning. But the bottom line is that you need to get your act in order.'

The telephone rang.

'Why don't you say what's on your mind, Claudia? Don't be shy.'

The telephone rang again.

'Shall I answer that or will you?' asked Claudia.

'I'll get it but your beloved Chief Inspector Jackson is a butterfly man. He's only here for a couple of years to gain experience and then move on to the rich and fertile grounds of ethnicity and diversity, developmental training, community relations, or professional standards; something like that, probably in another force somewhere. But more likely some irrelevant department that has absolutely nothing to do with everyday policing as I know it.'

Davies eventually answered his phone, killed the ringing sensation and held the mouth piece closely to his chest. He continued ranting, 'Butterflies never stay long enough to leave their mark on anything. They avoid direct contact with the public; anything to avoid strife with law breakers and criminals, anything but to avoid real life. No, they engage only in a succession of meetings, associations and institutions where life is governed by committee…'

Davies smashed his phone onto its cradle without speaking into the mouth piece and continued his tirade. 'Not like the reality of a society influenced by street life at street level and criminality but lost in the austere surrounds of the higher and idle classes who have no interest in the lower classes other than their continued subjugation…'

'Take three paracetamol,' snapped Claudia, cutting in sharply.

'What?' barked Davies.

'Take three paracetamol and get a strap for your arm. I saw you on the television. Your arm needs looking after.' She paused for only a moment. 'And look at your hand. It's badly bruised. Was that the sword too?'

The phone rang again but this time Claudia answered it, listened and replied, 'He's briefing the department at the moment, sir, but I'll tell him as soon as he gets back.'

Claudia quietly replaced the phone and said, 'Here! Drink your coffee and stop twittering on about Chief Inspector Jackson. What would your detectives think if they heard you going on about him?'

'But they won't,' softened Davies. 'You're my sounding board. What is said in this office stays in this office.' He rifled his drawers for a tablet and then challenged, 'Doesn't it?'

Claudia smirked and said, 'In that case, lilies are for funerals and I'd like pink roses next time, and on time. Not a week late.'

Davies winced in acknowledgement and said, 'Still, I got a tenner off him yesterday.' He considered his coffee and asked, 'What we got?'

'Chief Inspector Jackson would like to see you in his office at eleven o'clock to discuss his new policy on generics,' advised Claudia.

'Generics?'

'Yes, I gave you the policy papers on it last week,' she chided him as she rummage amongst his paperwork. 'Look, they're still in your in tray. You should read these things, inspector.'

'I read everything I sign, Claudia, and for your information I took Keith's papers with me to the gym and read it whilst cycling on the machine. By the way, you can file it under P for policy, if you don't mind.'

'How on earth did you do that, inspector?' she asked.

'By propping it up against the controls, of course,' replied Davies.

'I'll file it under G for generic. In any case, what's it about?'

'File it under P for policy then I'll know where to find it, Claudia.'

Arguing, Claudia decreed, 'I do all the filing and I'll put it under G for generic because the next time you want it you'll ask me where it is, inspector. Now tell me what it's all about? I work here too you know.'

Davies shook his head woefully and replied, 'Keith's guiding principle is about deploying staff with basic knowledge throughout the entire organisation. It replaces specialists. The effect is a significant

67

reduction in payroll expenditure, recruitment, training, petty expenses, and pension costs. It leads to a flat model of hierarchical bureaucracy requiring much less qualified specialist staff. Most services like the police and the NHS, for example, are pyramid shaped bureaucracies with a boss at the top and various layers of managers and specialism cascading downwards to the bottom. If you drew the structure of the organisation it would look like a triangle or a pyramid. Keith's policy is like an inverted T. It still has one boss but there are less managers and specialists.'

'That must be better then?' suggested Claudia.

'No, it's worse,' argued Davies. 'In the pyramid there's room to specialise, to climb a ladder, to improve your lot in life. This new plan is not good for moral and makes people think they are just being messed about. I call it the 'as cheap as chips' policy because it doesn't support workers. It's about saving money not delivering professional services.'

'It must be good if it saves money, inspector?' suggested Claudia.

'Well, that's the problem, Claudia. Theory and practice don't always make good bed fellows. Practically, Keith's policy might require my staff, indeed, possibly me as well, to drop all our crime enquiries and go and deal with a domestic dispute on a housing estate.'

'Why's that?'

'Because we'd have less staff but still the same amount of work,'

'I wish I hadn't asked, inspector,' said Claudia.

'What else is there?' asked Davies, abandoning a visit to an important paper and a paracetamol tablet he couldn't find in a drawer.

'Burglary, at a jeweller's, the second at a jeweller's this week.'

'The second?' queried Davies King. 'Same team?'

'Now how would I know that, inspector? All I know is that it's a big one. Constable Webster has gone to it. He wants you to join him at the scene. There's also a couple of assaults reported, theft from cars, about twenty still inside for public order and criminal damage from the protest march yesterday. Sergeant Rock is overseeing things in the cell block with Constable Barnes.'

'Oh yes, our young Detective Constable Webster. A man marked by inexperience and constrained by the inability to decide what or to whom loyalty should be bestowed. His perception of duty, loyalty and reliance might just extend to the boundaries of trust but certainly not beyond it.'

'You picked him!'

'There was no-one else in the pile to choose from at the time, Claudia, I was desperate. There are too many jobs on the slate, not enough detectives!'

'Not like you to make such a decision.'

'I made a mistake. Look, can we move on, Claudia?'

'Well, a good surgeon doesn't blame his blade when things go wrong.'

'You don't need to use our ranks. We've all got proper names, you know. In fact, we're real people,' said Davies.

'Thank you, inspector,' smiled Claudia. 'But none of you have ranks in my eyes, just titles showing everyone's standing in the office.'

'Titles and labels don't prove anything. It's the difference a person makes that count.' Davies sighed, 'Oh, never mind. Did you say jewellers?'

'I did,' replied Claudia. 'Young Mister Webster has gone, like I said. Keen that one, inspector. One to watch, I tell you.'

'Okay it's on my board. I'll take a look later,' said Davies. 'Tell me about the jewellers, Claudia. Slowly, properly! I like things in black and white.'

'Oh, there's a surprise.' She produced a bottle of tablets, threw them onto his desk and ordered, 'The Tablets are white; the coffee is black. Get them inside you. And, by the way, inspector, how did you get your black eye?'

There was a solid wooden door marked Superintendent tucked onto one corner of Crillsea police station. Inside a telephone rang and it was answered almost immediately.

'Superintendent Allithwaite...' Listening intently, he replied. 'It's like this, assistant chief constable, I briefed the media people but their editor obviously thought he was a better piece to show than our man. I can't make them televise what we want them too I.....'

He was interrupted but eventually argued, 'I understand, sir, but Davies King carries the respect of the men with him everywhere. He's, generally speaking, quite popular, and actually he's very good at his job. If he supports our new policy then there will be no problems but he's old school and won't even have read the papers yet. But I do think we should give him time and...'

Chastened, he listened for a moment and then said, 'Well, I....'

Interrupted again, he held his breath before suggesting, 'But perhaps we should....' There was another pause. 'Yes, his friend Max Fowler is the bomb disposal officer. Why?'

Superintendent Allithwaite reached for a pencil and suddenly became motivated saying, 'A complaint of assault in the Anchor, you say?'

Scribbling, he said, 'Mind you, sir. This bomb disposal chap is a superintendent in the Metropolitan Police Service.'

After listening, he offered. 'On holiday! He's off duty then? Mmm... How do you want this one played?'

There was a brief silence in Bert Allithwaite's office as he settled into his chair and listened to the questions that were instructions: the instructions that had to be followed because an assistant chief constable had deemed it so.

'Max Fowler and Davies King were together. Was King drunk?'

'Was he gambling? Is King a homosexual?'

'What else happened in the pub? Who did he speak to?'

'Get King! I mean, he's not quite with us, is he?'

'Get Keith Jackson to investigate and report in confidence!'

There was a quiet expectancy in the air when Superintendent Allithwaite replaced the phone and considered his next move.

Allithwaite considered Assistant Chief Constable Phillip Patterson: passed over for advancement in the northern metropolitan areas of Merseyside and Manchester; not short-listed in the former Yorkshire boroughs or the Black Country, no joy with the Scottish forces, no luck with the Shire counties, not in contention for an assistant commissioner's job in London, passed over and striving to be reborn on the strength of new policies and procedures that could change the face of policing and would have a major impact on public services. Such matters needed to be considered carefully and at length, thought Bert Allithwaite. Phillip Patterson was striving to be on the map again. It was Patterson's last chance to reach the very top of the police profession and it was in Bert Allithwaite's power to support that policy in his division or deny it. Bert Allithwaite could play the game for Patterson or not play it at all. Phillip Patterson needed Bert Allithwaite, he just hadn't realised it.

But what of the young pretender, thought Allithwaite? Detective Chief Inspector Keith Jackson: the new boss in his division; Patterson's weasel pawn who had been injected with a dose of deep desire that addicted him to succeed by the shortest route possible, a man of rank and substance that had taken such advantages by befriending and beguiling the most naive around him. It was Keith Jackson who would attend every promotion party, transfer bash, raffle draw, retirement celebration, or any social gathering to which he was invited or could coerce an invitation. It was said he would attend the opening of an envelope if it was advantageous to him. A social man was Keith Jackson. Yet he was seldom asked to a private shindig, a private bash, or a private do.

And then there was Davies King, thought Allithwaite. Davies King was ignited only by a need to find answers to questions. Davies was fuelled by his contempt of what he perceived to be a withering, ignorant system and was primarily inspired by an inner self discipline that lesser mortals would strive hard to understand. But Superintendent Bert Allithwaite understood Davies King. He knew him very well indeed. Warts and all!

How many bunkers must I negotiate before I reach my goal, thought Bert Allithwaite? Three, by the look of it, he thought. Three problem people all to be dealt before it's time to go. He drummed his fingers on his desk as he wondered which way he should jump.

A clock was ticking on a dull pastel wall and Bert was watching it.

Bert tidied and reset a framed photograph of his wife and daughter on his desk. Then he edged his family portrait slightly towards a framed image of himself, stood proud, with his *Class of 2001* taken at the Police Staff College at Bramshill in Hampshire. Yet pride of place was given to an empty gold frame waiting patiently for a colour photograph of an inbound golf club president.

Soon, thought Bert Allithwaite. Soon I shall be President of Crillsea Golf Club and then I shall retire from this overburdened desk of antiquity, inconvenience and problems.

Allithwaite checked the clock again. He watched the hands of the clock move slowly towards the end of another hour, towards the end of another day. Coasting! Sure but slow, the hands of the clock coasted towards the end of his working day and Bert Allithwaite would coast with them unruffled by the passage of time, not wanting to rock any boats as he glided safely towards the Presidency of Crillsea Golf Club and an overdue retirement.

He strode casually to the window of his office and looked out over Crillsea. Allithwaite took in its castle, church spires, roof tops and undulating skyline. After a moment or two, he returned to his desk and lifted the phone. He dialled a number. When the phone was answered Superintendent Bert Allithwaite instructed, 'Keith, have you a minute? My office!'

The youngest edition to Crillsea CID was Detective Constable Terry Webster: a bachelor in his early to mid twenties, tall, dark, and handsome, fresh faced and fresh out of a regional detective training college. Dressed smartly in a thin pin stripe suit and highly polished shoes, he was first at the scene. He'd studied the building, found a point of entry, taken details from the owner along with an estimate of property stolen, and then filled in his time by making notes. He was wondering what he should do next when he saw the down at heel Davies King arrive.

'What you got, Webby?' asked Davies. 'Black and white, short and sweet, please.'

'This is Wight's Jewellers, Main Street, Crillsea; twenty five thousand pounds worth of jewellery stolen, boss. Roof entry via a forced skylight; egress by the front door. Good stuff only. No costume jewellery. No money. No attempt at the safe. In and out and gone, and it's the second jewellers in a week. The other one is up the street. More or less the same method of entry and another twenty five grand's worth of gear.'

'CCTV?' enquired Davies.

'It's an internal system with a standalone power unit. It shows a body totally blacked out for five seconds before it's knocked out,' confirmed Webster. 'The burglar alarm seems substandard and it was bypassed using a set of wires earthed to the roof. I'll ask the crime prevention officer to suggest an upgrade.'

'Point of entry in the roof then?' suggested Davies.

'Come with me, boss.' Webster escorted Davies to a lane at the side and pointed up and across the roof tops saying, 'I think he climbed up here somehow and then scrambled across those roofs and down through a skylight.'

'Which he forced! Yeah, I agree. Well done, Webby. You been up on top?' asked Davies.

'Just a look from inside the shop. I've not done the roof top tour. Not yet, boss. I'm waiting for a scientific support officer.'

'Good lad. Got a list of stolen property yet?' asked Davies, surveying the roof tops.

'Being done now but it's only a couple of dozen rings.'

'A grand a time, Webby?' suggested Davies.

'Yes. Two dozen good quality wedding rings! Total cost twenty five grand-ish, give or take a hundred here or there.'

'That's an old fashioned lamp that's been knocked out in the lane. Ask around. Was it on last night? Who uses the lane?'

'Wouldn't have thought anyone, boss.'

'You're probably right, Webby, but think courting couples, kids with bikes, tramps and homeless people who doss down for the night.'

'Bit out of the box?' suggested Terry Webster.

'So are roof climbers. They don't think inside the box either. They're usually good toxics who study these places until it's like second nature to them. They don't smash the front door down and nick a couple of watches from the display. They study what they're doing and only take what they know they can place. Our man will know the roof tops like the back of his hand and he'll have taken a look at this lane in broad daylight. Who saw him? Street CCTV and anyone who uses the lane, okay?'

'But it's only twenty five thousand?'

'So far,' said Davies, studying brickwork. 'Anyone coming to mind?'

'Not yet, boss. But I haven't had time to knock on any doors.'

'Reginald Arnold Cuttleworth: climber, jewel thief, recently released from prison within the last six months,' suggested Davies. 'Where is he and what's he doing? Last I heard he was looking at post offices and security vans. Could be he's looking for a step up.'

'Forensics?' suggested Webster. 'Glass, brickwork...'

'The works, Webby. Get them to vacuum that roof if you have to. These types of breaks never come on their own. Two so far, you say?'

Webster nodded.

Davies declared, 'Someone's had a nice look at this one, knocked the lights out and made a nice little earner, as they say.'

'Plenty of glass broken inside,' advised Webster.

'Tell you what, Webby. Ever heard of a Jackie Striker?' asked Davies. They began to walk back to the front of the jewellers.

'Before my time, I think, boss.'

'Jackie's a good burglar and he's got form for robberies. He's a nasty piece who can be quite violent. I put him away for a climbing job a few years ago. I think he's out now. Check with Intelligence but pull the files on any locals with a conviction for a climbing job. By the way, Reg lives at Tevington on Sea. Check with the Tevvies. And, whilst I think about it, find out if we've any climbing clubs in the area. You know, rock climbing clubs.'

Davies's phone rang and he answered it immediately with, 'Davies King.' He listened and replied, 'That's okay, Claudia. There'll be at least a dozen or more people in the Anchor last night. I've nothing to fear. Let Chief Inspector Jackson have a look at my diary for yesterday, if he must. Problem is, of course, I was off duty and playing chess with Max when it happened.'

Davies looked up at the rooftops as he listened to the voice on his mobile. He continued, 'There's no entry in my diary for the Anchor pub. Why should there be? I was off duty. No problem for me. It's his problem.'

Davies King stowed his mobile 'phone and thought for a moment.

'Problems?' asked Webster.

'Not at all,' replied Davies. 'Come on. Let's knock on a few doors.'

*

Chapter Five

~ ~ ~

Dateline: Sunday,
Crillsea Cliffs.

Morning broke. The tide turned. The seagulls were in fine voice to welcome a host of executive style coaches bringing the latest troop of mystery tour 'one day a week' holiday makers into Crillsea. Slowly but surely, Crillsea woke to the splendours of the day.

Knocking on sixty years of age, plump, perhaps a little overweight, Peggy MacDonald struggled up the path to reach a detached house standing prominently on the cliff tops.

An annoying grating noise greeted Peggy when she unfastened a rusting garden gate. Making a mental note to oil the offending hinge she strolled down a garden path between the townships of Crillsea and Tevington on Sea. Humming a tune, smiling, she was happy with her lot in life as she looked out across the cliffs. The only annoyance to her day so far was a grating hinge and an enormous shopping bag, which was full of cereals, bread, jam, butter, eggs, margarine, bacon, a few vegetables, wine, marmite, and nuts bought from the shops of Crillsea. She planned to prepare a light lunch once she'd settled into the kitchen and got her breath back. At least she had made it today. There were no traffic jams to contend with, no prime-ministerial cavalcades to cause the rescheduling of her day.

She fumbled for a key, laid her shopping bag down, and removed the key from her dress pocket. Opening the front door, she shouted, 'Hello, it's Peggy. Yoo-hoo!'

The response was silence. It was as if she wasn't expected but it was Sunday and she was always expected on a Sunday.

Peggy saw a broken mirror and upturned trolley. 'Oh, my goodness me! Whatever's going on?' she said aloud.

She pushed a door into the lounge open and saw a body lying on a mink rug. Peggy screamed and dropped her shopping bag.

A wine bottle cracked and a deep red wine spoilt the ceramic tiles and formed a pool around the base of a marmite jar and half a dozen broken eggs.

Peggy's scream reached a crescendo and a couple of seagulls winged from the roof of the house to escape the scene of the crime.

Detective Chief Inspector Keith Jackson was in attendance, in full uniform, and as smart as a tailor's dummy with his buttons shining and scrambled braid on his peaked cap sparkling in the morning sun. He stood beside a gate leading to a garden path talking to Detective Sergeant Annie Rock and Detective Constable Ted Barnes when Davies King and Terry Webster arrived at a house on the cliffs.

'Glad you two could make it,' scowled Jackson. 'It looks like we've got a murder. I'm far too busy with a special project to take this on board. The body's cold and I'm giving it to you to sort out.'

'Are you indeed, sir? How kind,' replied Davies with a huge smile and a soft hint of sarcasm.

'Yes, Sergeant Rock can look after your office while you work with Webster. I want you to keep an eye on him but I want Webster to handle everything. It'll beef up his experience on domestic murders and set him down well for the future. Tidy the loose ends up, Davies.'

'A domestic murder?' queried Davies King.

'Yes, it's an easy one by the looks of it,' explained Jackson. 'It shouldn't take a lot of clearing up. There's no sign of a break in. The husband hasn't been seen for quite a few days. The family car is missing and there's nothing stolen as far as we can tell.'

'Oh, it's that simple?' asked Davies.

Sergeant Annie Rock stood tall and slim wearing blue denim jeans and a blouson. She could feel a certain tension growing between the pair. Stepping forward, she volunteered, 'May I?

Davies nodded and acquiesced, 'Please do, Annie.'

'The victim was found by her house-keeper: a Peggy MacDonald, who arrived as usual at the house, unlocked the front door and found the body. She identifies the victim as Elena Jayne Martinez nee Morgan,' said Sergeant Rock. 'The husband is one Manuel Martinez and he hasn't been seen for a couple of days. He works in London, in the city, and he's gone missing by the looks of it. We're still filling in the pieces but it looks like death by strangulation.'

'Good, at least you made a start, Annie,' said Davies, taking comfort from an early identification. 'Where are you setting up the incident room?'

'There'll be no incident room,' advised Jackson, smartly.

'Why ever not?' queried Davies.

'No need to waste public money. I won't be setting a murder squad up either. I'll spell it out for you. There's no sign of a break-in so the victim obviously let the murderer in. The victim knew the murderer. It wasn't a stranger-murder. This is a nice and easy one for you, Inspector King. All you need to do is formally identify the murder victim and put some meat on what we already know. Who is she? Where's the husband? Who's the next of kin? Is she insured? Who gains from the insurance? The basics! I'm sure you remember the basics. Don't you, inspector?'

Terry Webster nodded vigorously at Chief Inspector Jackson's remarks but Davies King enquired, 'You seem pretty certain it's open and shut, chief inspector. Presumably Annie here will fill me in on the finer details?'

'Whilst we are on about the finer details, Inspector. You might as well know that you are no longer a member of the Criminal Investigation Department. My new policy includes the rebranding of the department. You are now a member of the Strategic Crime Intelligence Directorate.'

'The Strategic Crime Intelligence Directorate! What on earth is that all about?' asked Davies.

'It's a new title to celebrate a new way of doing things, inspector. For example, it won't be long before civilian investigators are assigned to minor domestic murders.'

'Oh, yes. I've heard. That'll be a few civilians who work nine to five with every weekend off. I've heard they're recruiting retired detectives in some places, aren't they? All well and good but when the retired ones have gone who teaches the new kids on the block?' asked Davies.

'We don't need detectives on this kind of job. It's straightforward, Inspector King, or is that too hard to take in?'

'Straightforward?' queried Davies. 'I'm so pleased.'

'At least you've got one thing in common with the deceased, Davies,' pronounced Chief Inspector Jackson.

'What's that then?' enquired Davies.

'She's got a black eye too.' There was a look of triumph in Jackson's face. 'Oh yes! She has an earlier black eye than you. Domestic violence, I expect. It's pretty obvious, Davies. The husband did it.'

'Why did her husband murder her?' asked Davies.

'That's for you to find out,' challenged Jackson, 'Or rather Webster under your guidance and my supervision. There's a lover[i]

77

somewhere, isn't there? There's always an affair in these domestic murders, isn't there?'

'The lover could be the killer then?' proposed Davies.

'Wow!' exclaimed Jackson. 'You've just made an easy job hard. Now you've got two suspects when you only needed one.'

'Actually, I haven't got a suspect yet,' revealed Davies.

'It's just a lesson for you, Davies,' suggested Jackson turning to connect with all present. 'Things are changing here. So-called stranger murders might need an incident room and a murder squad of some kind but these run of the mill domestics don't. They only need a desk and a couple of filing trays, if you see what I mean. We don't need to spend a fortune in manpower, overtime and forensic tests. Understood?'

'Run of the mill murders?' asked Davies. 'What's a run of the mill murder, may I ask?'

Ignoring the question, Jackson continued, 'I intend to make my mark on this division and then move on to higher things.'

'A butterfly!' declared Davies, deliberately looking towards nearby floral borders.

'Pardon?' quizzed Jackson.

'I can see a butterfly amongst those flowers, chief inspector,' offered Davies. 'Butterflies! They appear in spring during sunny periods, seldom settle, flit from flower to flower taking the best out of the heart of a flower, and then disappear to God knows where. Jack of all trades and master of none, they are.'

Sensing tension, Terry Webster suddenly took a deep interest in a far away ship on the horizon whilst the balding old hand, Ted Barnes, stood his ground and concentrated his eyes on the gravel path as he tightened his anorak.

'Forget your chess and your butterflies, Inspector King. Concentrate on this murder and get young Webster on the map,' instructed Jackson as he moved into overdrive. 'From now on we are generic, Inspector. I'm in uniform today and I'm illustrating to everyone I can do any job despite the fact that I am handling a special investigation.'

'Special investigation?' queried Davies.

'A confidential enquiry, inspector,' replied Jackson. 'The point is I might be a detective one moment but traffic officer the next. My uniform is my qualification. There are no expert theories or higher educational standards required. Basic knowledge is our key to success and there will be no room for clever and fancy so-called experts. Understood?'

Terry Webster nodded vigorously again.

'Utopia you mean when everybody has knowledge of everything,' challenged Davies. 'That's the only time you don't need expert staff.'

'Come and see me about it if you don't understand it,' ordered Jackson. 'I'm not arguing with you. I'm telling you. We'll do it my way from now on. No messing about, no major incident room, no dedicated door to door staff, no murder squad, no wasted public money. No experts pontificating on the whys and wherefores. Just a pruned to perfection organisation with a straight down the line policy; do as it says in the manual. Find her husband, find her lover. It'll be one of them. You don't need an army of detectives. Just do it.'

Finality filled the atmosphere but then Davies's mobile rang.

'Hello?' said Davies, turning away slightly. 'Not now, Max.... What....? What have you been questioned about?'

'Problems?' demanded Detective Chief Inspector Jackson.

'Not at all, just a contact of mine! Nothing important,' replied Davies. He spoke into his mobile again, 'Not now, Max. I'll ring you later.'

'By the way, Davies,' countered Jackson, 'Butterflies are famous for pollination. They visit each and every flower, sniff out the best, and take it with them on life's journey.'

Davies stowed his phone. Worry beads formed on his forehead. He wondered whether he was anxious for Max or for berating Jackson.

'Wrap it up, inspector,' advised Jackson 'This new policy is going to work and I'm going to make sure it works. Wrap it up by the end of the week.' Jackson walked away but then turned and ordered, 'Let me have daily briefings. Keep on top of it, inspector. Wrap it up and move on.'

'Daily briefings?' queried Davies.

'Daily briefings on a daily basis, Davies,' smiled Jackson.

Detective Chief Inspector Keith Jackson was gone from Crillsea cliffs, gone from a gravel garden path, and gone from the scene of the murder of Elena Jayne Martinez nee Morgan.

Davies King watched him go and stood with his mobile wondering, worrying, pondering his future.

Ted Barnes quietly asked, 'Anyone got a butterfly net? There's a dead woman inside and the only thing our divisional head of criminal investigation is interested in is using amateurs to make savings and his next promotion, or did I mean posting?'

Annie Rock offered, 'Strategic Crime Intelligence Directorate, Barney! Not CID. Now that's put the skids on everything, hasn't it?

Davies chuckled and said, 'The SCIDs, Annie? How long before the uniforms pick up on that one? But you've seen it all before, Ted. What did you expect from a new broom?'

'Respect, Davies! I got twenty nine and a half years service in three different forces. Here, the Met and the RUC. I've worked more murders than most and...' Ted Barnes drifted off into forlorn disappointment.

'I know why, Ted. We all do,' offered Davies, placing his hand on Ted's shoulder. 'You've forgotten more about murder investigations than most people know about speeding tickets.'

'As far as murder enquiries are concerned, Davies, we've a lot in common,' said Barney. 'We've done it all, seen it all, bought the tee shirt and opted out.'

'That's as maybe,' replied Davies. 'Yeah, I think we did opt out somewhere along the line.' Davies chuckled and then said, 'You have to opt out to be able to do this job, but I think you've been around long enough to design and patent the tee shirt.'

Ted Barnes said, 'I don't know anything about speeding tickets, traffic laws, parking or the brakes on pedal cycle regulations, Davies. But this is my forty-eighth murder scene and I'll tell you now things are never as they seem. Never take the basics for granted. Never! He couldn't even be bothered to step inside and take a proper look.'

There was a look of concern on Terry Webster's face and then Ted Barnes took a step away and signalled Davies King to join him.

In muttered tones Barney advised Davies. 'You do realise Keith Jackson has just set you up, my old friend? If the job is detected then young Webster will get the credit whatever happens but if it remains undetected or any mistakes are made in the investigation then you'll carry the can. It's called politics and it's a game Jackson plays well. It's not your game, Davies.'

'Hadn't looked at it that way, Barney, but thanks,' replied King.

'Mind yourself on this one, Davies,' suggested Barney 'Our new chief inspector lives in a different world to us and he knows sweet sod all about murder enquiries.' Ted Barnes took a deep breath and then turned to the group and volunteered, 'They say the first forty eight hours are the most important. Are we waiting for the tide to change?'

'Thanks for the reminder,' replied Davies. Then he turned and asked, 'Annie, who's been inside? What's on the board?'

'A Peggy MacDonald, house-keeper, cleaner, shopper, and this and that lady, found the body,' replied Sergeant Rock, keenly. 'She visits three or four times a week as and when required. She turned up as usual this morning, unlocked the door and, more or less, walked into the body. I was first on the scene along with Barney. We just left the cell block and came straight here. It's hell down there, by the way.'

'It always is, Annie. It'll keep. Go on,' instructed Davies.

'Doctor Scott confirmed death to me and I called out Professor Jones and the circus. Uniforms have cordoned the scene off and Professor Jones is inside at the moment examining the body in detail. It's a clean scene otherwise. No-one's trampled it. A scientific support team and a search team have just arrived but I'll cancel them in view of the chief inspector's remarks about saving money.'

'No, you won't. Leave the arrangement as it is,' ordered Davies.

'Well, in that case,' considered Sergeant Rock, 'I was about to take a statement from the lady who found the body, if she's settled down and isn't in too much shock, and of course, Mister Jackson wants…'

'Thanks for keeping the scene clean, Annie' interrupted Davies. 'I heard our chief inspector. He wants Webby to be well involved in this one. I don't have a problem with that. If you can do the initial statements, Annie, I'll take Webby and make a start. I'll be a while.'

'I know,' replied Sergeant Rock. 'By the way, I'm not going near your desk or your paperwork.' She smiled an impish smile.

'I've got a secret weapon, Annie,' offered Davies.

'What's that?' she asked.

'She's called Claudia.' Davies drew a smile from the sergeant's face as he turned and said, 'Come on, Webby. Welcome to your first murder scene. Just try to ignore the body for a while. We'll come to that in due course. The best thing we can do for this lady is to find her killer. Nothing else! Now get your thinking cap on because I like to sort things into black and white. What do we do next? What does the manual say? Fingerprints and photographs, forensics, DNA, video, move the body and investigate? What are you going to do?'

'I'd rather watch you chaps if you don't mind?' volunteered Webster.

'Okay,' replied Davies. 'Now put your hands in your pockets and follow me…. Barney?'

'Right behind you, Davies,' from Ted Barnes.

Dressing in white coveralls, they entered the murder house.

'Everyone does things differently, Webby,' explained Davies. 'I like to take a good look at a murder scene without touching anything and without doing anything and I don't let every Tom, Dick and Harry trample all over it destroying evidence. When I've an idea of what has happened then I call in the scientific support team and discuss with them what scenarios are in play. They're the experts. They will examine the scene of the crime in great detail and from the perspective of securing evidence by scientific means. Let them take control of the scene once you're happy you know what the set up is. For now, I'm trying to get into the mind of the players by looking at lifestyle patterns of the victim whilst trying to establish the actions of the murderer.'

'I understand,' replied Webb.'

Davies noted and remarked upon a grating hinge when they approached the house; and a gravel path needing microscopic fingertip, and grass and floral beds of daffodils, crocuses and snowdrops that might yield footprints or evidence of someone's former presence. Warily, he entered slowly, almost reverently, as if the house were a cathedral or mosque demanding total respect from its congregation.

Standing in the hallway, with his hands in his pockets, Davies studied a front door, a broken mirror, an upturned telephone trolley and an entrance into a lounge.

Davies met Professor Jones: a consultant forensic pathologist who examined the body in an attempt to determine a cause of death.

Professor Jones was eminent in his field. Approaching his mid fifties he still sported long flowing golden locks curling over the collar of his jacket and complimenting his bushy sideburns. Some said he resembled General George Custer of the legendary American Seventh Cavalry but Custer was a frontier soldier who was probably strong and fit. Professor Jones was tubby and fiddly who liked detail and minutia. He was not a leader of men but he did study the minutia of the human body.

Davies listened to details of a post mortem intended, discussed a provisional cause and time of death, and agreed that Professor Jones would do all his tests and examinations before determining undisputed fact. Davies learnt the body had laid for at least a day, maybe more.

Ted Barnes made notes whilst Webby watched and listened and knew that one day it would be his turn; one day he would ask such questions, one day he would be in charge. One day he would take notes and one day he would have to remember all that needed to be done at the scene of a murder. He shuddered at the thought of forgetting the precise detail of what they required.

Professor Jones asked Davies how he had incurred a black eye but Davies merely answered, 'in the execution of my duty,' and left it at that. Davies joked with Professor Jones and suggested that his General Custer locks might get a haircut soon. Jones laughed aloud and his belly flopped up and down. Then he reminded Davies that he too needed a haircut. But Professor Jones also explained the victim had an old injury: a black eye. It was faint now but he had seen enough in his time to know a black eye when he saw one. Perhaps it was indicative of domestic violence, Professor Jones suggested, and then he gave a detailed description of how Elena Jayne Martinez had been strangled to death in the living room of her classy house.

Davies did not worry on precision of scientific fact at this time and accepted the initial findings from the prominent Professor Jones. Davies stood with his hands in his pockets, thinking, scanning, looking, and thinking again. Slowly and patiently, he visited each and every room in the house, always stopping in a doorway, always looking, scanning, planning, thinking, never touching. In his mind the scene was a chess board and he was setting out his pieces and working out his game plan.

When they returned to the lounge Davies asked what they could all see. He agreed they could see a porcelain coffee pot broken and lying on the carpet, and grains of sugar loose on the carpet where the attack might have taken place. But Davies pointed to the body of a victim and explained that beyond the physical presence of her body there had once been a real person: Elena, a beautiful tall brunette who wore rings on her fingers, perhaps flowers in her hair. Davies King explained he had taken in expensive aftershave and exquisite perfume in a bathroom, gigantic plasma televisions and surround sound music systems, and expensive porcelain in the lounges. He'd marvelled at a collection of crystal glassware, of Meissen porcelain dinnerware, of classical figurines, and a strangely unique collection of various wooden and marble mortar and pestle. He spoke of silk bed sheets, dimmed lighting and furs in bedrooms, stunning mink carpets decorating floors, and exceptional paintings of boats and ships hanging from walls. Davies wondered if the family owned a boat because of such paintings and Barney made a note. Davies spoke of a wall safe hidden behind a framed picture and wondered what its combination might be. And Barney made a note.

They saw an outside swimming pool, Jacuzzi and sauna, surrounded by elegant Italian ceramics reminding Barney of a five star hotel with leisure facilities. There was a drinks cabinet, a barbecue, a garden shed, a garage and an outhouse or two to be conscious of and to be sure of. They studied a framed photograph of what might be her husband and her sister. Maybe it was her close friend, they did not know.

Davies saw such a lot of normality for a rich and wealthy family but then closed his eyes and concentrated on what he could not see. He told his colleagues he could not see a computer, or a mobile phone, or a private telephone directory. He could not see a radio, or photographs of parents and children. He could not see memorable friendly bric-a-brac collected over the years from a holiday here or there. He could not see the casual lived-in normality of newspapers and magazines strewn across a sofa or stuffed into a wooden magazine rack. There was no evidence of a dog, a cat or a family pet. He could not feel an atmosphere of warmth, of family, of love. It was a strangely cold house to him.

Looking into her face, the face of Elena, Davies shivered with the coldness of death at his feet. Shaking himself awake, Davies wondered what such people considered to be normal. The house reminded him of a show house specially prepared for sale on a prestigious estate.

'Barney... What do you see?' asked Davies.

Barney waved his notebook and answered, 'I don't see any unclaimed lottery tickets lying about. I don't think they needed to play the lottery, Davies. Rich, I would say but I see a wall safe we'll need to get into. Shall I get onto the manufacturer?'

'Agreed and check with them if they've ever put a floor safe in. There's nothing visibly moved or disturbed. There's a wealth of things that haven't been touched but then if the toxic knew where the safes were and what the combinations were... Anything else, Barney?'

'I see an electric razor and a toothbrush in the bathroom. If they belong to her husband then he's on the run without them...'

'Or he's got spares,' mused Webster.

'Good, you're catching on, Webby,' smiled Davies. 'How many men do you know who are organised enough to have a spare toothbrush and a spare razor, Webby?'

'Not many, sir.'

'Right on! Just now, it's the front door that's bugging me. The front door?' pondered Davies.

Webster looked again at the front door, stared through it, round it, and then shook his head.

'Barney?' quizzed Davies.

'Five lever Mortice lock, standard construction, not forced and I'm not on the board with you,' chuckled Barney as he stroked his balding head with the sweep of an arm across his skull.

'Just something not right,' said Davies. 'I can't put my finger on it.' He paused, considering things, and then said, 'One thing's for sure, I'll go with manual strangulation, no doubt.'

'Agreed,' said Barney. 'Which probably means the murderer is a man because I can't ever remember a woman strangling a man or another woman. It's a question of strength, you see, Webby.'

'I understand,' replied Webster.

'Strange way to kill,' suggested Davies, now studying the body closely. 'Strangulation, I mean. I can pull a trigger from three hundred yards or three feet and drill a bullet into you and kill you. I can plunge a knife into your chest or slash a blade across your throat and then run away in the sure and certain knowledge that you might easily bleed to death. I can leave a bomb beneath your car and rig it so that when you drive off the car explodes and you're blown to kingdom come. I can poison you by giving you weed killer in your hot chocolate every night and watch you drift away, eventually, but strangulation… now that's different.'

'But you're still dead,' suggested Webster.

'True, but only strangulation needs me to get up close and personal with you. To strangle you I have to be face to face with you. I have to look in your eyes and put my hands around your throat and squeeze. I have to squeeze your throat so hard and so long that the blood stops going to your brain and you lose consciousness. I have to squeeze you and shake you until you die. It's going to take me a minute, thereabouts, maybe longer. It depends on how hard you struggle and believe me you'll struggle because you'll know you are dying a horrible death. But when I strangle you, God I really mean to kill you. It's a very personal murder, full of really deep hate, I think.'

'Can I ask something?' pleaded Webster.

'What's on your mind?' asked Davies

'How many murder cases has Chief Inspector Jackson dealt with?' asked Webster.

'I really don't know, Webby,' replied Davies. 'Not many, I reckon... Barney?'

'None,' replied Barney. 'None that I know of, that is.'

'Why?' queried Davies.

Terry Webster bent down near the body and said, 'Listening to you guys, I'm reading Elena was murdered in this room. The chief inspector is surmising there's nothing stolen without ever entering the house. He's thinking that because he's been told nothing's been disturbed anywhere, other than the hallway and the lounge where the attack took place.'

'What you driving it, Webby?' asked Davies.

'I wondered what she was doing with an empty jewel box.' Webster pointed at the empty jewel box lying on the carpet and said, 'Women like this never have empty jewel boxes. Where's the jewellery? Were the contents stolen to order? Did the jewellery box have a big blue diamond in it?'

Davies and Barney exchanged glances before Davies asked, 'You're suggesting robbery is the motive, Webby?'

'Could be,' nodded Webster.

Ted Barnes smiled, 'You'll make a detective one day, maybe?'

Bending down, Davies studied the jewellery box and the motif, intricate in its design. 'A flower of some kind, I think,' suggested Davies.

'Not a rose or anything British by the look of the design,' said Barney. 'Swiss? One of those mountain flowers? Who knows?'

'Here we are playing florists when we are supposed to be trying to catch a murderer,' winced Davies. 'But there's just something not right though,' said Davies. 'I can't identify the flower but I think I finally sorted the door out.'

'What's wrong with the door?' asked Barney.

'Something Annie said. Basic really, obvious, so bloody obvious,' offered Davies. 'I'm such an idiot. Peggy said she unlocked the door to get in. That means the murderer locked the door when he left. The murderer has a key, doesn't he?'

'Of course… And he might still have it,' suggested Barney. 'I'll make a note in the murder book. Are we keeping a murder book on this one, Davies?'

'Oh, yes. Chief Inspector Jackson told us it was a run of the mill domestic murder but he made no mention of the murder book. We'll keep a book because that's the way I do things, Barney. Make a note so that we can come back to it at a later date.'

Barney nodded approvingly.

Davies added, 'Our chief inspector suggested the victim must have let the murderer in because there's no sign of a forced break in and therefore the victim knew who the murderer was.'

'But if the door was locked when Peggy arrived it means the murderer took the keys with him and locked the door behind him,' said Barney.

Webster continued. 'But if robbery is a motive then where are we?' he asked. 'I mean the husband would have a key so he's probably locked the door behind him when he's left. Or are we looking for a burglar who has been disturbed and killed this woman in order to escape? But then he decides to lock the door behind him and take a key which is no good to him! I don't know.'

'I don't know either,' stated Davies. 'I do know pawns only move forward, never backwards. And today, we're pawns. I don't think this is going to be as easy as some might think. I'm worried that strangulation is a pretty personal way to kill. If it were a burglar who was disturbed then you'd expect the murder weapon to be a knife, a poker, a blunt instrument of some kind that has been picked up and used without any prior planning. No, this one needs some thought and we need to try and think like the killer did. But we'll do a forensic examination. We'll take some samples of the coffee pot, for example. We'll have DNA procedures in and around the body and the point of death and I think we'll have the jewellery box examined for fingerprints and DNA. That's down to the crime scene investigators: the scientific support team. They'll decide what to do for the best once we've briefed them.'

'Will they do the whole house and gardens?' asked Webster.

'Quite likely,' replied Davies. 'They'll find DNA all over the place but the problem is people think DNA is a panacea in criminal investigation; the reality is DNA matches from the national database help solve as few as one crime in every thirteen hundred. We have about five million crimes a year, that's not all that many detected purely by DNA.' Davies studied the jewellery box again and continued, 'But then you have to consider that to get a DNA match you have to hold the existing DNA profile. If you haven't got the profile already, you're stuffed. You have to hope someone gets locked up for something else and his DNA matches an old crime held on the books. The fingerprint data base started the same way if you think about it.

'Well, congratulations, chaps,' chuckled Barney. 'We are at last discussing the merits of our leader's generic policy and procedures paper. Indeed, we're talking to some extent about the science of dactyloscopy, or the science of fingerprints to the uninitiated, together with the finer practical points of gathering DNA samples for analysis and comparison. DNA, that's Deoxyribonucleic acid, to be precise, Webby. Now, let's get the scientific support team and the search team working.'

Davies nodded in agreement, walked across the lounge, took another look at the front door lock, and said, 'That reminds me door to door enquiries, Barney. Can you put together a house to house enquiry sheet?'

'Of course, the usual questions, I take it?' said Barney.

'Yes, please,' replied Davies. 'Who lives here? Where do you work? What do you do? Where were you over the last seven days? What do you know? What did you see? Do you know the victim? Have you seen anything unusual in the area lately? Or, indeed, have you seen anyone unusual in the area? Who walks the dog? Who drives a car? Who knows who and why? Can I leave it with you, Barney? We could go on forever but I think the main thing, in the short term, is to concentrate on people who visit the cliff tops. This isn't a housing estate job in the middle of town.'

'I know the score, Davies. I'll knock something together for starters. We can always go back for a second knock when we know more. Two problems...'

'Like what, Barney?' asked Davies.

'Number one, how far do you want us to do house to house, Davies? There are probably only forty or fifty dwellings in Crillsea Cliffs. I'd do them all plus anything inside a three mile radius of the scene for starters. Agreed?'

'Absolutely, Barney, but the second problem is...?' asked Davies.

'Who is going to do the house to house enquiries when the chief inspector won't sanction a murder squad or an incident room?'

'Good point, I hadn't thought of that,' replied Davies.

'I'll use the search team once they've finished and I'll use some of the detectives back in the office to do some of Barney's house to house sheets, inspector,' replied Annie Rock. 'He didn't say anything about a minor enquiry room, did he?'

Terry Webster said, 'No, the chief inspector mentioned an incident room, that's all. What's a minor enquiry room?'

Davies King beamed, 'No idea, Webby. Thanks, Annie. I knew I could count on you. Action that list, Barney! Let's get the job rolling. It's going to be a long day.'

The tide was on the turn and the Anchor was quiet with only Archie and a couple of locals playing pool by the bay window overlooking the harbour. Davies King had thrown some weights up and down in the gym for an hour as he was finished for the day. He was sat on a bar stool cradling a brandy and mulling over chess pieces on a chess board when Max joined him.

'What the hells' going on?' asked Davies, irritable. 'Where've you been?'

'Archie and Gloria have been interviewed and so has Bill,' replied Max. 'I bumped into your wide boy on the cliffs. Harry Reynolds, was that his name? I'd just been for a walk up on the cliff paths and….'

'You were walking on the cliffs?' interrupted Davies, surprised. 'What were you doing on the cliffs with Harry Reynolds?'

'Well, I just bumped into him, that's all?' said Max.

'We'll get back to that later; what were you interviewed about?'

'An assault here the other night, you know, the lad in the motor bike jacket,' replied Max.

'Motor bike jacket!' barked Davies. 'That bearded giant, Jimmy Riley, was no biker. What are you on about?'

'He means the kid who was having a go at you,' soothed Bill, leaning over the bar. 'Don't worry, Mister King. 'It's all for the best. I told them you had nothing to do with it.'

'I had nothing to do with it?' stated Davies. 'Bill, I haven't a clue what you are talking about.'

89

'I told them, Bill,' interrupted Archie, muscling in with his pool cue and a half empty glass. 'I told them everything I saw, Mister King.' Archie doffed his cap and shouldered his pool cue. 'Prime witness, I am; prime witness, according to Detective Jackson.'

'Jackson!' quizzed Davies. 'Detective Chief Inspector Jackson?'

'He's the new governor now is Mister Jackson,' offered Archie, emptying his glass. 'He's been doing all the interviews, him and some men in suits. You aren't the governor anymore, Mister King. He told me so.'

'I never was the governor, Archie,' countered Davies. 'Look will somebody please tell me what's going on?'

Max took Davies by the arm and explained, 'When you were getting our drinks a thug in a leather jacket tried to have a go at you. I sorted it. You were miles away, as usual.'

'Oh! What did you do?' asked Davies.

'I stood on his foot,' acknowledged Max.

Davies chuckled but then laughed aloud and said, 'You stood on his foot and you get interviewed for assault?'

'Bit more to it than that,' elected Max. 'Bill…'

Bill obliged. 'They took the CCTV tapes and everything. He wanted to know everything you were doing. You, Mister King! Not just Max here. He wanted to know how much you had to drink. He wanted to know who you were talking to. He even wanted to know if you were drunk when you arrested Jimmy the giant who was cutting up rough. You know, he wanted to know if you'd had one too many.'

Davies and Max exchanged glances and listened more intently.

'Mind you,' offered Bill. 'He saw the funny side. You should have heard him laugh when he watched you on CCTV downing that pint I gave you after you'd arrested Jimmy Riley. Well pleased, he was.'

'He laughed?' queried Davies. 'Why would he laugh?'

'It wasn't so much of a laugh; more of a snigger really, Mister King.'

Archie interrupted and offered the contents of a snuff box. 'I told him you were a regular in here, Mister King. I told him you did business with the spiv, Harry Reynolds, and the like.' Archie tapped his noise twice, looked round, and whispered, 'I told Detective Jackson you know all the hooks and crooks in Crillsea and Tevvie, Mister King. I told him you often do business with the likes of Harry Reynolds. You know, buying and selling stuff. I never miss a thing, Mister King. I hear things. I see things, so I do. But I'm the soul of discretion, I am. And that's what detectives do, isn't it. Get to know the hooks and the crooks. I told him, so I did. You can trust me to tell the truth, Mister King. Pinch of snuff, Mister King?'

Archie sneezed.

Davies looked almost scornfully at Archie, then Bill, and finally Max before saying, 'If they're investigating an assault by you, Max: an off duty superintendent; why is the butterfly man asking questions about me? Is this the confidential enquiry he was talking about?'

Max shook his head but Archie pushed forward and interrupted, 'Search me, Mister King. I'm just the prime witness, is what I am. Maybe they don't like you. Your bosses, I mean. Maybe they want rid of you, Mister King. Upset someone, did you?'

Archie drained his glass in one swoop.

'But…' staggered Davies, somewhat puzzled. 'I get landed with a murder to preside over and Chief Inspector Jackson spends his time doing confidential enquiries, as he calls them, it doesn't make sense.'

Archie banged his glass on the bar and demanded, 'It'll be a pint of mild, Mister King, if you please. On the slate is it, Mister King?'

*

Chapter Six

~ ~ ~

Dateline: Monday,
Crillsea, Soho, and Chinatown, London.

Troubled, Davies King spent the night tossing and turning and trying to get to sleep. Eventually, morning arrived and he did not allow a bad night's sleep from focusing his mind on the quest ahead. He clambered from bed and quickly showered before spending an hour at the gym in the Sports Club. Then he called in at the office and collected Annie. A fairly short drive took them to their destination. It was his first appointment of the day and he lost no time with the lady before him. 'Are you okay now, Mrs MacDonald?' asked Davies.

''Much better thank you,' she replied. 'I was upset yesterday.'

'It must have been a very nasty shock for you,' said Davies.

'It was but I'm fine now,' replied Peggy MacDonald.

'Then I'll get straight to the point, Mrs MacDonald. How did Elena Martinez get that black eye?'

'I don't know, Mr King,' replied the house-keeper.

'Did you ever see her husband Manuel assault her?'

'No. Your lady sergeant asked me the same question yesterday.' Peggy nodded to Annie Rock as if she might confirm her statement.

'I appreciate that but I just wanted to get to know you, ask a few questions, tidy a few things up, Mrs MacDonald; if that's alright with you?

'Well, if I can help, Mister Davies. I don't mind trying to help.'

'Did you see anyone ever assault Elena?' asked Davies King.

'No. It's just like I said yesterday. Why are you asking the same questions, inspector?' Peggy looked again to Annie Rock for help.

'Did she ever complain or mention to you that she was a victim of domestic violence?'

'No, Mister King. Not much use to you, am I?'

'Actually, you are a very big help to me Mrs MacDonald.' He leaned forward and with a smile asked, 'May I call you Peggy?'

She nodded acquiescence with a slight smile.

Annie looked on approvingly and sat beside her on the sofa.

Davies King sat opposite in an old and battered armchair that was shrouded with a threadbare blanket and asked, 'You have a lovely home here, Peggy. Do you have any family?'

'Just a younger brother, Mister King, but I don't see much of him now that he's married and everything.'

'Oh, I see,' replied Davies. 'Have you lived here long?'

'All my life, Mister King. Of course, it's not in the posh row up on the cliffs or down by the harbour where the young money and new developers live. But I like it here and I like my garden.'

'Good for you, Peggy,' replied Davies King.

The chill was gone from him; the importance of questions and answers not lost. Davies smiled a soft empty face that pleaded with her for help and understanding. He softened in his gestures; his tone, his look.

'Shall I pour, Peggy? The pot, when full, is heavy.' Davies King weighed the teapot and continued, 'And I'd be happy to oblige.'

'Yes, why don't you pour, Mister King?'

'Do you like it weak, Peggy? Or shall I leave it a while? Let it stew a while longer?' He twisted a wondrous smile and asked, 'Did Elena take afternoon tea or was she a coffee person, Peggy? I don't know.'

'Coffee, Mister King? They both drank coffee from that fancy coffee machine they had. Cappuccino or something like that. Italian or Spanish I think… Cappuccino… Not sure. Well, when they weren't drinking champagne, of course.'

'Champagne?' His eyes flickered with slight interest. 'Expensive!'

'Oh yes, Mister King. Bollinger it was; always on my list. I always placed a weekly order for a crate or two of 'Bollies' at Crillsea wine merchants whenever they were up from London.'

'Regular then?'

'Yes! Crillsea Cliffs is their second home, or rather, was their second home now what with all this and such like.'

'Tell me about the London house, Peggy.'

'Not much to tell, Mister King. I never went to it. I was never invited. Not that close, Mister King, you understand.'

'Do you know the address of the London house, Peggy?'

'Oh, yes. Canary Wharf it is. It's in my address book. I used to forward on the mail when I needed to.'

'The address would be good, Peggy. Very helpful! And, if you don't mind, we've brought some photographs from Elena's house for you to look at. Perhaps you can tell us who is who… Annie…'

'Oh, I don't know if I could, Mister King. But I'll try, so I will.'

Sergeant Rock removed a number of framed photographs from her shoulder bag and spread them out on the table.

'Would you like a biscuit, Mister King? A chocolate one! Homemade they are,' suggested Peggy as she began to scrutinise the images.

'Oh, I couldn't.' Davies King sounded disappointed but then he smiled and said, 'Well, why not, indeed. And I know Annie here likes them when she's not on a diet.'

There was a ripple of laughter as the three reached for biscuits.

'Oh, your sergeant lady doesn't need to diet, Mister King,' volunteered Peggy.

'No she doesn't, Peggy. Now then,' explained Davies. 'I just need you to think back over the last few months or so, Peggy, and ask yourself if anything funny, strange, or out of the ordinary has happened in the area. That's all, Peggy.'

Peggy rummaged in her handbag and produced a leather diary saying, 'Well, here's the diary. I don't suppose you would be interested in the swimming, would you, Mister King.'

'Swimming?' quizzed Davies. 'What swimming, Peggy?'

'They were swimming naked, so they were,' said Peggy. 'Naked as the day they were born!'

'Who?' queried Annie Rock.

'Yes, who was swimming naked?' asked Davies.

'Those two,' replied Peggy MacDonald pointing to figures in a framed photograph.

Davies King nodded as Annie reached forward, directed her fingers over the images and asked, 'This one?'

'Yes, that's Manuel. He's Elena's husband.

'And he was swimming with...?' asked Davies.

Annie offered the photograph again.

'Elena,' stated Peggy conclusively.

'Which one is Elena?' asked Annie Rock.'

'Why this one of course,' replied Peggy MacDonald pointing to an image on the photograph. 'The lady I keep house for.'

'That's the lady wearing a very large ring on the finger of her right hand, Peggy. Is that the one?' asked Davies.

Peggy took another look at the photograph but didn't reply.

Davies looked longingly at the photographs and asked, 'I need you to be sure. I need you to have faith in your eyesight and look again at the photograph of the man and his two female companions. I need you to be absolutely sure of what you see and what you tell me, okay?'

'Of course, Mister King,' replied Peggy. Then she rooted in her handbag for a pair of spectacles. When Peggy MacDonald had scoured the depths of her handbag, she produced a battered spectacle case and eventually perched her reading glasses onto the end of her nose. She scrunched her eyes as she sought the images once more before nodding and saying to Davies, 'Yes, Mister King. I see what you mean.'

Davies smiled and said, 'It's important you see, Peggy.'

They drank tea and Peggy fed them home-made chocolate biscuits and told them of the champagne life style of Elena and Manuel Martinez, and a naked swimming session. Then Peggy MacDonald patiently told them of who she thought the killer might be.

They took their seats in Davies King's office and settled into their sandwiches. Davies rattled some mugs and poured the coffee.

'Catch up time,' announced Davies, handing out drinks. 'And I need some caffeine. Okay, what you got from the safes, Barney?'

'Manufacturers were fine,' replied Barney, gathering crumbs on his plate. 'It took most of the day to get into the wall safe. It was empty.'

'Empty? Well I never,' replied Davies.

'But the search team found a stack of documents and paperwork in a floor safe in one of the bedrooms,' smiled Terry Webster.

'Anything interesting then?' quizzed Annie Rock.

Detective Constable Barnes swept a hand across his bald patch and enthused, 'Oh, yes. According to a passport; bits and pieces of paperwork, and various documents, the husband is one Manuel Martinez, a Spaniard from Barcelona. He's a corporate lawyer in London. He has plenty of rich customers and associates, by the look of it. We're talking pin stripe suits, fancy cars, stock brokers and bankers.'

'Money!' suggested Annie with a flick of her shoulder length hair.

'Lots of it,' replied Webster. 'I'd say new money, by the looks of it. Money earned this generation, not inherited from the previous!'

'Keys?' demanded Davies, nodding.

'In the floor safe,' answered Barney. 'We found keys tagged with a fob showing an address in Bartholomew Wharf, wherever that is.'

'South London! Canary Wharf area,' interrupted Davies. 'I know it from my squad days down there and Peggy MacDonald confirms that address. Go on, Barney. Anything else?'

'Keys for I don't know what.' Barney produced a set of keys on a ring and said, 'Take your pick and make a guess.'

'Were they found in the floor safe?' asked Davies.

'Yes,' nodded Barney. 'But there's no trace of car keys which suggests he's off in the car somewhere. The hubby, that is.'

'Vehicle documents?' challenged Davies.

'They're in the document bundle. Top of the range Porsche and a Mercedes for the lady,' revealed Barney. 'But there's no trace of either vehicle in the area, so something is amiss. Actually, I'm guessing these keys might be spares but who knows?'

'Apart from that,' offered the pin striped young Webster, 'There's some basic bank accounts, utility bills, receipts for jewellery: about one hundred thousand pounds worth, by the way, and a stack of business cards, and odds and sods of a rich lifestyle. The worry is there's a shotgun certificate in Manuel's name amongst the documents we found but no trace of a gun in the house.'

'That's disturbing and something we'll have to bear in mind, but let's not jump to any conclusions, just yet,' decided Davies.

'But there's another rub, Davies,' said a puzzled Barney. 'The search team found remnants of burnt clothing in a barbecue and a bloodstained shovel in a garden shed.'

'Human blood?' asked Annie Rock.

'Not known yet,' replied Barney. 'The forensic scientists will take a look at it. I'm going to guess animal blood because they live in the country. The blood might be from a rabbit or a pest of some kind but the results are awaited. Same with the clothes, the lab will let us know what they find in due course.'

'Strange,' queried Davies King. 'We have a strangulation victim who has a bloodstained shovel in a garden shed. It might be something, might be nothing. Burnt clothes and bloodstained garden tools! What's going on there then? Any trace of a dead hedgehog?'

'I'll keep you posted, Davies,' chuckled Barney. 'Of course, we don't know what happened. Maybe the victim used the spade to resist her attacker and whopped him one with it? I don't know but I think we should check with the local hospital and the local surgeries. We need to find out if anyone has called in with cuts and bruises.'

'That'll keep us busy,' noted Webby.

'It'll keep you busy,' said Barney. 'You've just won the job.'

'Yeah, give it a whirl, Webby,' said Davies. 'Meanwhile, keep the house closed and a guard on it for a day or two.'

'Chief Inspector Jackson won't like using a uniform for that,' suggested Terry Webster. 'Bad use of resources he would say.'

Davies seemed a little exasperated. 'That's my problem, not yours. What have you done about the jewellers?' asked Davies.

'Nothing, boss, I've not had time,' explained Webster. 'The only thing I've done is get a list of stolen property.'

'Good! Is there a link between the jewellers and the murder? We don't know but get that stolen property circulated pronto,' ordered Davies. 'Ask Sergeant Rock here for help, if you need to.'

'I'll get on it right away, sir,' replied Webster who acknowledged Annie Rock's nodded agreement.

'Good! Sergeant Rock has a knack of making things happen in this team. If you get stuck or bogged down, you've a top sergeant who knows this job backwards. Don't be afraid to speak up. Now then, I'll need to make time too and put some feelers out amongst my informants in due course,' advised Davies who then enquired, 'Whilst we're on the subject, Webby, how many climbing clubs have you located in the area?'

'I've not had time yet,' replied a worried Terry Webster.

'Then make time, Webby. I want all the stones turned over and I expect my team to be the best beachcombers in the nick, understand?'

'Yes, sir.' replied Webby.

'Davies, how did you get on with the cleaner, Peggy?' asked Barney changing the subject.

'Lovely lady,' replied Davies. 'A bit slow but obviously well suited to her role in the house. She filled Annie and myself in on a lot of background but then couldn't tell me everything.'

'Why not?' asked Terry Webster.

'Well,' chuckled Davies. 'Peggy told me the couple were happily married, so, if they were happily married how come one of them was murdered? And how come Elena has an old injury, that black eye? You see, Peggy told me she'd caught them once swimming together naked in their swimming pool. When I pushed her on the matter, Peggy eventually

97

admitted her eyesight wasn't that good and she only presumed it was Manuel and Elena.'

'What's her eyesight got to do with it?' asked Barney.

'Remember the photograph in the lounge? There was a man and a woman in it. We thought husband and sister, maybe best friend, agreed?'

The pair nodded.

'Peggy told me the woman in the photograph is called Sophie. So I'm just wondering where this Sophie fits in,' said Davies.

'I'm lost,' surrendered Webster. 'Is this Sophie a suspect?'

'It's an option, that's all,' suggested Davies. 'Manuel might have been swimming with Sophie, not his wife, Elena. So, for me, the motive might be jealousy but it could also be money or something else. At the moment, I suggest we take a look at the eternal triangle thing!'

'And Sophie could be part of the triangle?' suggested Barney.

'Yes,' advised Davies. 'It's a possibility but we need to locate her and Manuel before we can bottom it. It just might tidy things ups for us if we can trace Manuel and Sophie at the same time and in the same place.'

'Here's hoping,' said Annie Rock.

Davies continued, 'Peggy shops, cleans, and odd jobs. She's in and out and can give us background but not a true picture. We'll need to find out much more about the victim, Elena. According to Peggy, she's a laboratory assistant in a school but she doesn't really know where she works so we'll need to bottom that out as we build up a picture of Elena. Knowing her blood group, cause of death, height, hair colour and what she had for her last meal is fine but it doesn't take us very far and it certainly doesn't take us to the murderer.'

'I'll do the schools,' volunteered Webster. 'Phone calls!'

'Thanks. Problem we have is that Elena lives in a house on a cliff top midway between Tevington on Sea and Crillsea. There's no immediate neighbours and very little known about her. I hate these bloody mystery people. I like things in black and white and easy to work out.' Davies knocked back his coffee and continued, 'Meanwhile, talk to me. What else should we be doing? What have we missed? Come on, you must have something to say.'

'Forensic report is going to take time,' replied Annie Rock.

Terry Webster said, 'The post mortem confirms cause of death is manual strangulation.' He dealt out appropriate copy reports to his colleagues whilst saying, 'The search team paper focuses on what we've just discussed, documents and the like; telephone records are attached here, and....'

'You've been a busy young man,' interrupted Annie Rock.

'One thing I can see, boss,' offered Webster, 'The 'phone records refer to payments for broadband on a dedicated line but as you know...'

'We didn't find a computer in the house, did we?' stated Barney.

'But Manuel Martinez is paying for broadband piped into the house and there's a receipt for a laptop computer, a web cam and download instructions for Skype, in the papers we've recovered.' Webster flicked through his paperwork, 'General paperwork bundle A, exhibits 48 through to 51 refers.'

'What's Skype,' asked Davies, awkwardly.

'Voice over internet protocol,' announced Claudia, breezing into the office with a large bunch of pink roses and a selection of shirts wrapped in see-through packaging. 'That, Inspector, before you ask, is free calls, video calls, and instant messaging to anywhere in the world through the internet. You need broadband to set that up properly now.'

'Oh! Thanks, Claudia. I wondered where you were,' said Davies.

'Out, inspector, I've been out. The roses are a late birthday present from Chief Inspector Jackson and these are the shirts I promised to get for you. I've made you an appointment for a haircut, inspector, and, by the way, you're all in trouble.'

'Why? What have we done now?' demanded Davies, angrily.

'According to our chief inspector his generic policy came into force today. Constable Barnes should be on two to ten in uniform on an area car. Sergeant Rock is custody sergeant in the cell block and ought to be there now.'

'Oh dear,' said Davies King.

Claudia continued, 'But apparently Sergeant Rock has blotted her copybook already. She put herself on day shift and was with you this morning when you interviewed the woman who found the body of the murder victim. You, Inspector King, and our young Mister Webster here are seconded to 'Murder', or so it says on the duty sheet. Only two detectives on the murder not four! By the way, they're looking for officers to take the last of the demonstrators arrested the other day to court. Where will they find them from, I wonder? The good news is that I'm still your personal assistant until this murder investigation is sorted and then I don't know what. Maybe it's time for me to look for another job.'

99

With a swirl from her long grey cardigan Claudia switched the kettle on. 'I'm fed up of it all already. Total chaos in the police station and you're all sitting having a coffee break, or are you having a meeting about the murder? Nothing to do with me; I only work here.'

Annie stood and announced, 'I'll be downstairs in the cell block then. Keep me in the loop if you please.'

Davies nodded agreement when Annie made her departure.

Claudia tidied her roses into a temporary vase arrangement and closed the door tightly behind her as she left.

'Claudia.... Claudia.....' shouted Davies almost apologetically.

But Claudia Jones was gone from the office and charging down the corridor at high speed to her next port of call.

'Nice shirts,' pronounced Davies examining his purchases. 'Snazzy! Different colours too, now then, where were we?' asked Davies.

'On an area car by the sound of it,' suggested Barney. 'The generic policy really has arrived thanks to the butterfly man.'

'Not yet,' scowled Davies picking his telephone up. He dialled a number and said, 'Chief Inspector Jackson…' He waited and then said, 'Hello, sir. It's Davies King. You wanted a daily briefing on the murder so here it is. We've had a breakthrough and we need to move fast.'

Webster and Barnes exchanged inquisitive glances.

Davies continued. 'We've got a lead on the husband and a female accomplice who may well be the reason behind the murder: the other woman, as they say. Anyway, I've left a uniform guard on the murder house in case either returns but we think he's in London, possibly with the other woman.' He paused, listened and said, 'Canary Wharf area. My problem is I'd like Detective Constable Webster to follow this one through, just as you instructed.'

There was more listening before Davies said, 'Of course it's possible to save money, sir. We don't have to go to London. Look, I can phone the Met and ask for a visit to the address and an arrest to be made for murder but I'd rather go myself with Webster and Barnes as back up.'

Davies winked at Barney and continued, 'I do need Barnes as an exhibits officer with me if there's an arrest to be made and I certainly don't want to tie up Webster on his first murder case with exhibits to sort out. So the thing is, sir, the press will no doubt get to hear of it and it will be on the front page of the Crillsea Chronicle, at the very least, probably some of the nationals too. So my question is who do you want to take the credit for the arrest, the Met or us?'

Barney closed his eyes and shook his head.

Terry Webster stared at the phone trying to follow the conversation in his mind.

Davies King listened for a moment and said, 'No worries, Chief Inspector Jackson.' He slammed the 'phone down, grinned and ordered, 'Bartholomew Wharf! Let's go.'

Detective Chief Superintendent Alan Jessop: Big Al, to his friends, stepped out of the Flying Squad Jaguar and onto the tarmac. Splashing into a puddle, he was not amused but chose to ignore the rain soiling his trouser leg and the dozen or so Londoners rushing up and down the street with their umbrellas flapping in the wind. Dressed immaculately, tall, with a mop of black brushed-back hair and a prominent square chin, he considered the falling rain with heartfelt scorn, smoothed his dark Armani two piece suit, and looked up to read a neon light flashing intermittently from the club entrance.

Jessop turned up his collar and smiled gratuitously when he hurried towards Lucy's Party Place in Soho, just off Greek Street. He approached its entrance with his sergeant behind him.

A large man, broad across his shoulders and wearing a long black coat, stepped forward and held his hand up preventing entrance. 'Members only, squire,' announced the doorman.

'That's good because I've got a membership card for the whole world,' replied Detective Chief Superintendent Jessop. 'What did you say my name was? Squire? No, actually my name is Alan Jessop. Everyone remembers it usually. Don't you know me? J E S S O P Jessop…Sergeant….'

Sergeant Jim Adams produced his warrant card and announced, 'Metropolitan police! We have a search warrant and…'

The doorman immediately held up both hands, laughed, and replied decisively, 'I really don't give a damn who you are and what you've got. I've heard that one before from coppers like you: coppers looking for free drink usually. No, this is a private members club and the owner is very particular about who is allowed in. Why don't you go somewhere else because there's no free drink for you and your police friends today! You aren't coming in, squire. Oh, and by the way, we…' He waved three more burly doormen to his side, 'We don't want you and if you do go inside, well....' There was a threatening pause. 'We'll enjoy escorting you out. Understand, squire?'

'Oh dear,' replied Jessop. 'What don't you understand about the words police and search warrant?'

The doorman clicked his fingers and three more doormen appeared, making seven in all.

'Wrong decision, squire,' smiled Jessop, grasping the doorman's fingers. There was a twist of a wrist and the doorman was suddenly on his knees screaming in pain. 'I'll break them if I have to,' said Jessop, engaging the eyes of the advancing doormen. 'Sergeant...'

Sergeant Adams produced a handheld radio from inside his clothing and instructed, 'Strike.... Strike.... Strike...'

Within seconds four marked police vans and four Flying Squad cars were outside the front door and two signed patrol cars had sealed off either end of the street. A police helicopter appeared hovering overhead and three police dogs and their handlers bounded from a dog van.

Plain clothes and uniform police swarmed into the club trampling half a dozen doormen in the process.

Jessop overpowered the doorman, pushed him to the ground, and said, 'Later, son. I didn't come for you.' Then he twisted his fingers again and listened to a sickening cry from his adversary. 'And the name's Jessop, not Squire.'

Stepping over the debris Jessop was inside Lucy's Party Place and down a darkly lit passageway, passed a cash desk, passed a toilet block, passed the first of many scantily dressed girls, and through a maze of running, panicking customers who had no chance of escaping the timely midday police raid.

Jessop's foot suddenly made wicked contact with an office door and its wood splintered as he crashed through and into a well lit room that was dimmed only by cigar smoke and a haze of what might have been the essence of cannabis resin.

'Benny!' announced Big Al, coolly. 'Benny Abbott! It's been years, Benny. Actually, it's going to be years, Benny.'

Benjamin William Abbot, strip club owner, gambling club owner, tax evader, and professional criminal, shifted his seventeen stones of human blubber from one cheek to another, inhaled on a huge Cuban cigar, motioned to his assistants to relax and said, 'Superintendent Jessop!

How nice of you to call. Do you have an appointment? Why didn't you let me know you were coming?'

'What and spoil the party? No chance! We've a search warrant and it's your turn,' smiled Jessop.

'My turn? I think someone's made a mistake, superintendent.'

Abbott clicked his fingers and pointed at empty champagne glasses, expecting them to be filled immediately by his closest henchmen.

Jessop covered the glasses with his hand, smiled, and said, 'No mistakes, Benny, and I'll let you into a little secret; I'm not relying on a search warrant. You're nicked so ring your brief because you're stitched up good and proper. Listen to me. My men are all over Chinatown taking down your cover operations: you know restaurants and slot machine joints. Listen to me. I don't make mistakes, Benny.'

Abbott started to look a little concerned at the confident manner in which Jessop was coolly dominating his office and offered, 'Maybe it's my mistake. Am I behind with the rent? Perhaps the widows and orphans need topping up, superintendent?'

'Actually, Benny, it's chief superintendent nowadays.'

'Sorry, chief superintendent. Now how much would it take to cover your expenses, rent and suchlike?'

'Nah, you've watched too many seventies films and too many police dramas, Benny. You see, it's like this…'

'I'm listening.' Smiling, Abbott reached for his wallet and placed it on his desk. Opening it, he revealed a huge wad of fifty pound notes and a cheque book which he flicked open to a clean page. Abbott then produced a pen.

'Listen well, Benny,' suggested Jessop. 'We've been on your back for eighteen months. I'm so far up your backside I'm tickling your throat. Benjamin William Abbott I'm arresting you for conspiracy to commit armed robbery, robbery with violence, extortion, conspiring to import drugs, drug dealing, human trafficking, arms smuggling, and money laundering… Oh yeah, and attempted bribery. Sergeant Adams, read him his rights and cuff him.'

'You just made a huge mistake, Jessop,' snarled Abbott. 'You bastard! A big mistake!'

'I don't make mistakes, Benny, you know that. You have one chance and one chance only.'

'What's that?' asked Benny Abbott.

'Sing to me, Benny. Sing to me like a canary and do a deal.'

'I don't do deals with the filth, Jessop, you bastard.'

Al Jessop lowered himself into eyeball contact and said, 'Benny, I got television people and cameras outside so that when my nice kind sergeant takes you out in his shiny handcuffs and puts you into to a dirty old police van, the whole of London will see you on the box tonight.'

''What the hell for?' pleaded Abbott.

'Just smile for the cameras, Benny. I want all your friends to see you on television in nice new handcuffs then they'll know that no-one is immune from the Flying Squad. We're coming for your shitty little friends, one by one. I'm taking you down and there's not a thing you can do to stop me. Your only chance is to make it easy for yourself and spill the beans on your competitors, you know, the east side, save me some time and I'll put a good word in for you to the judge. Who knows, it might mean your old lady will wait for you if you get a short sentence.'

'Drop dead, Jessop.'

'Take him away, Jim,' ordered Jessop.

Benny Abbott offered no resistance when Jim Adams applied the handcuffs and led him away whilst more officers burst into the office.

Jessop answered his mobile phone, 'Jessop!' he snapped. Then he listened, and joyfully replied, 'Davies King! Bloody hell, Davies King! To what do I owe this pleasure, my old son?'

Pointing to a computer and a safe in the office, Jessop signalled his officers to secure the items, listened and continued, 'Of course, it's Big Al! Who did you think it was? Are you still boxing or is it chess, which? Where are you, Davies?' he demanded. 'You're famous now, my son. If you're in town I'll buy you a drink or two. I expect you've heard that a cat can look at a king.'

Jessop watched as his colleagues unplugged a computer and began rifling desk drawers. He spoke into his phone. 'Davies, what do you want from London's finest?'

As an aside Alan Jessop spoke to a nearby officer and ordered, 'There's a doorman at the entrance with dodgy fingers. Do me a favour and nick him for police obstruction, conspiracy to pervert the course of justice and littering the streets of London.'

There was a rushed nod of agreement and Jessop returned to his call. He listened intently and allowed another grin to form on his lips.

Striding into a dance floor area, Jessop couldn't help but chuckle at a lone pole dancer desperately gyrating on a circular stage. He signalled to two uniforms to have her removed and then watched his colleagues begin searching a line of customers.

Grinning broadly, almost laughing, Jessop said, 'Of course, I can help you, Davies, my old son. This is London, Davies. It's my London. But what's in it for the Met?'

Britain's three tallest buildings dominate London's skyline and are anchored at Canary Wharf on the Isle of Dogs in the London Borough of Tower Hamlets in London Docklands. The ubiquitous buildings of Canada Square stand proud beside Canary Wharf Tower and gather around them the banking giants of HSBC, Citigroup, Credit Suisse and other goliaths of a global banking industry that located there from 1990 onwards. Now, flying above this key financial sector, a British Airways A318 airbus lifted steeply from London City Airport and ascended into the clouds bound for Barcelona with a full cabin of business passengers and a splattering of holidaymakers. Beneath the shadow of Canary Wharf Tower, beneath the ascending airbus, it was business as usual for Al Jessop and Davies King.

King's Crillsea men and Jessop's Flying Squad watched the first floor apartment at Bartholomew Wharf for any signs of life hoping someone might turn up at the residence; but the exclusive apartment overlooking West India Docks appeared to be empty. Checks on a Porsche and a Mercedes parked at the end of the street, close to Prestons Road, revealed they were registered to Manuel Martinez and Elena Martinez respectively, but the vehicles were empty. The seconds grew to minutes and then into hours. Oily grey waters of the West India Docks mixed with the adjacent Blackwall Basin and divided the reaches of the Thames. From Poplar to Millwall, the people of the Isle of Dogs went about their business unaware of the hunt for a suspect in a murder case.

When they were sure there was no-one in the premises, Davies took a key from his pocket, walked down the path, and unlocked the front door of the exclusive apartment in Bartholomew Wharf.

'Nice work, Barney. You said the key would fit,' chuckled Davies.

They were inside very quickly searching and rushing from room to room shouting, 'Clear…. Clear…. Clear….' Penetrating the apartment, they confirmed its emptiness.

'Sorry, Al,' offered Davies. 'The cupboard is bare!'

'You said you had keys. `Let's try them,' suggested Jessop.

'The floor safe in Crillsea was in one of the bedrooms. What's the betting here?' asked Davies.

'I'll take the bedroom any day,' replied Barney. 'These people like their belongings near them even when they are asleep.'

'Do you see what I see, Davies?' asked Barney.

'I see photographs of family and friends. Empty milk bottles on the front step, magazines and mail on the floor in the hallway....'

'And a sink full of dishes still to wash,' finished off Barney. No sign of a cleaner though. Why's that?'

'Yes! Home is what I see, Barney. Not a second home on the cliffs of Crillsea but a main base in the heart of London and close to work, by the look of it. Agreed?'

'That's the way I read this house, Davies,' suggested Barney. 'But I still don't see a desktop computer or a laptop. And there's no trace of the missing shotgun either.'

'Mmm...' reflected Davies. 'It makes you think someone has got their laptop with them.'

'Yes, I agree,' replied Barney. 'An important laptop, I suspect. There's nothing in the cars. It's interesting, isn't it? We know they have broadband but there's no trace of a computer either here or in Crillsea.'

'Oh yes,' agreed Davies. 'It's very interesting! I'm looking forward to finding this phantom laptop; although it's always possible that they just don't have a computer anymore.'

Al Jessop said, 'I don't like guns of any kind. I think you should upgrade your wanted notice on this man. He could be armed and dangerous, exercise extreme caution!'

'Agreed,' responded Davies. 'We don't want someone getting their head blown off through lack of knowledge of the man we're after. I'll see to it.'

Barney and Webster then entered a bedroom, shifted a rug, felt the floor with their hands and rolled back the carpet to reveal a floor safe.

'I'm impressed,' said Jessop.

'Me too,' replied Davies. 'And it's good that you took time out to help, Al. We really appreciate it.'

'No problem, my friend,' replied Jessop, and then, thoughtfully, almost painfully, he said, 'I was sorry to hear about your wife, Davies, so very sorry.'

Nodding, Davies replied, 'Yes, well, thanks. Yes, thank you.'

'Tell me, Davies,' asked Al Jessop, compassionately. 'I understand you and Angela were on your yacht when there was a collision with a big forty foot oceangoing yacht that didn't stop. Is that right?'

'Yes,' said Davies. 'It was getting late and it was getting dark. We were lit up but the other yacht wasn't. I didn't see it coming but it barged along the side of ours and dumped us into the sea, I never saw Angela again until she was washed up on shore some days later. It hasn't been easy, Al. Not easy at all.'

'Did they ever locate the other yacht, Davies?' asked Al Jessop.

'No, extensive enquiries, but never traced and never identified,' said Davies. 'A ghost ship.'

'Boss?' interrupted Terry Webster.

Davies acknowledged Webster and handed him a bunch of keys. He watched Webster select an odd looking shaped one and insert it into the floor safe. The safe opened and Webster reached in, hauled out a tin box, and selected another key from the bunch.

Jessop went outside for a moment and spoke to one of his men. When he returned he said, 'The boys have been talking to the neighbours.'

'Anything interesting?' asked Davies.

'Yes,' replied Jessop. 'They've heard loud outbursts of fury between man and wife! Regular, and sometimes quite violent apparently; I think the term is domestic violence, Davies.'

'More pointers to suggest the husband really is the murderer,' suggested Davies. 'I thought it was going to be someone else but it looks like I'm wrong and he's right.'

'Who's right?' asked Jessop.

Webster opened the tin box and pulled out its contents.

'My boss! A certain Detective Chief Inspector Jackson,' replied Davies. 'I'm sorry but it looks like this just might be a straight forward domestic after all and I know your squad doesn't usually touch such things. I'd hoped there might have been something else but I was wrong.'

Webster and Barnes began to spread the documents on a table.

'Armed robberies are our main course, Davies. Major organised crime! Nothing's changed since your days,' stated Jessop. 'But you're ex

Squad and you used that to get some quality help from the Met. No problem because if I'm ever in Crillsea I'll know who to call. I'm retiring soon and I just might be down your way for a holiday. I'm going to treat my wife to some sunshine and peace and quiet instead of late night calls and twenty four seven work.'

'Sounds good,' replied Davies. 'Give me a bell when you throw in the towel and I'll come and join the festivities.'

'I'm fed up with the job. When I joined you got life for murder and that meant thirty years. Now it's twelve years on average. It's what they used to give armed robbers when I joined. Sorry, I've no confidence in the system anymore. They expect us to police the scum of the earth with cheap community support officers and specials. God bless them all. There are some good ones. But it's still cheap policing by amateurs.'

'Tell me about it,' said Davies.

'Only a few years ago there were about six hundred murders a year. Now we're knocking on the nine hundred mark.'

Jessop was sifting the paperwork. Davies was looking inside an empty tin box. Barnes was on the telephone. Webster was looking inside the floor safe.

'Where did we go wrong?' asked Davies.

'We didn't go wrong, Davies,' laughed Jessop. 'The government went wrong. It lost its focus on the things that matter: police, crime, health, doctors, nurses, fire-fighters, prisons, education, even the military. It systematically replaced professionalism with a cheaper brand and put the wrong people in charge at the very top. Do you want me to go on?'

'Public services?' queried Davies. 'Generics?'

'On the cheap,' replied Jessop, scanning the contents of a folder. 'Professional services delivered at amateur prices. But this isn't getting your murder solved. Look at this, Davies. You were telling me the victim was a lab assistant at a school somewhere on your patch.'

'That's right, so we're led to believe. We're not too sure where she works actually. We're still learning about our victim. She's a bit of a mystery in some ways.'

'Well, this is obviously their London base and she's a scientist at a research establishment. Not a lab assistant. Here, have a look at this.' Alan Jessop handed over a folder entitled *Conchenta*.

Davies allowed his fingers to smooth over a drawing of a flower that adorned the centre of the Conchenta folder. 'We're back to Swiss flowers, Barney,' shouted Davies. 'A flower just like the one on the jewellery box is on the front of this folder.'

Flicking though the file, Davies saw a hand-drawn map of an island named *Conchenta*, ownership papers for an ocean going yacht named *Conchenta*, some share certificates in the name of Elena Jayne Martinez relating to a scientific research establishment called The Farringday Trust at Tevington on Sea, share certificates in Barclays, Abbey, Jennings Brewery, and receipts for a crate of Bollinger champagne from Fortnum and Mason. Then he read an old P45 tax statement from the Farringday Trust to their former employee, Elena Jayne Martinez.

Ted Barnes walked into the room, chased his eyes over the title of the file and the drawing of a flower, stowed his mobile phone, and said, 'That was Annie Rock, Davies. The harbourmaster at Crillsea has a record of a berth issued to Manuel Martinez. He has a vessel called Conchenta. Have we hit pay dirt? The husband's on a boat, isn't he? That's why we can't find him.'

'There's more,' offered Terry Webster, producing a stack of bank accounts, note books and address books from the bottom of the safe. 'Much more, boss. We need a proper search team and an exhibits officer.'

'Later, Webby. What we got?' asked Davies.

'Bank accounts, share certificates, an address book, and a…'

'An address book kept in a floor safe?' quizzed Davies. 'And something called the Farringday Trust. I wonder what that is.'

Davies King glanced at the business cards and then seized the red leather bound address box and slowly turned its pages.

'My God!' cried Davies. 'Look at this! Jack Creighton! Do you remember Jack Creighton, Al? You'd be a DI back then not top brass.'

'Jack, You mean James Alistair Creighton, one time professional boxer of this parish and beloved gangster of the east end?' asked Jessop.

'His name is in this book, Al,' stated Davies. 'I mean there can't be two Jack Creighton, can there?'

'Well, as I recall he floored you in that fight you had with him at Bermondsey,' laughed Jessop. 'A real sweet uppercut, so it was!'

'I got up again,' retaliated Davies, aggressively.

'Then he knocked you down again,' laughed Jessop. 'A hard man is Jack Creighton. We've had our claws into him since I was a DS and you were at training school leaning how to direct traffic.'

109

Davies King rubbed his chin and recalled, 'He's younger than me. He was on the way up and I was…'

'Past it and on the way down!' cracked Jessop with a cruel laugh.

Davies King flicked through the pages of the book, and then offered it to Jessop saying, 'Back pages, what do you make of that?'

Jessop read the pages and said aloud, 'Lydia Bryant, drug dealer; Katrina Helen Kitchener: she's a bent property developer, and Jack Creighton. Now that's what I call tasty, Davies. Very tasty!'

Big Al Jessop continued reading and said, 'This little book more or less lists our version of the London crime scene on one page.'

'Who's tasty, Lydia or Katrina?' asked Webster.

'Lydia,' said Jessop. 'Katrina is not heterosexual.'

'You mean she's a lesbian?' asked Davies.

'She is an extremely attractive woman,' replied Jessop. 'And yes, she is a lesbian! Remember her, Davies? She never fancied you but she did like a good blonde if I remember.'

Davies chuckled, thought for a second, and then shook his head. 'Al, sorry, Chief Superintendent Jessop, I keep forgetting. No, I don't remember her. You were a lowly sergeant when…'

'Rank is immaterial, Davies,' interrupted Jessop. 'It's what you do that counts. And we go back a few years.'

Jessop turned a few pages at the back of the book and was visibly moved when he read a line and said, 'Oh, my God. Would you believe it? Would you Adam and bloody Eve it. Benny Abbott's name and telephone number is in here.'

'Benny Abbott?' quizzed Davies.

'Yeah, big time criminal in the west end: club owner, racketeer, drug pusher, you name it he's at it. Well, he was at it until I nicked him earlier today and closed him down.'

'Is he talking?' asked Davies King.

'No, but then we've got enough on him to put him away for a long time,' replied Jessop. 'I don't need him to sing but it would help if he did because it would cut the time of some of our bigger investigations down and we might get a good result against some of his mates.'

'Such people don't usually do deals, Al,' said Davies.

'Sometime they do and Benny has a wife and kids, even grandchildren. You just never know with people like that. Put someone under pressure and promise them the inside of a cell for a decade or more and you never know.'

'I suppose they reach a time in their lives when they'd rather be free than locked up,' said Davies.

'At a certain age, yes,' replied Jessop. 'And every now and again someone talks and makes the job easier, more focused, more intelligence led, as they say. It just bothers me that after eighteen months I find out about this connection from a book in a house connected to Crillsea. I thought we knew everything we needed to know about Benny Abbott.'

'There's always something,' said Davies, but Davies King was miles away, thinking and wondering.

'What's eating you?' asked Jessop

'Nothing, well, I know you reckon I'm past it but, Lydia, I'm wondering why you haven't had a go at taking her down,' asked Davies.

'I know,' interrupted Jessop again, suddenly grasping the issue with both hands. 'Lydia has been on the board for years. She works out of a really posh restaurant in the Shaftesbury Avenue area but she has minders that cover all her moves, rarely uses the phone, and is well switched on to the technical issues we can range against her. And she has a legal team that protects her against the slightest intrusion of her privacy. She's not at all stupid and isn't a very easy duck to shoot off the rack. We've tried surveillance, only to find she never moves about a lot, and we've even tried 'undercovers' without success. She's a cocaine dealer: a big fish. Katrina is into some very shady property deals and uses dodgy money to do it and Jack is a minder for anyone who needs protection. He's just a gangster really.'

'With a good uppercut,' remembered Davies.

'He still doesn't pull any punches, Davies,' stated Jessop.

'Have you ever met, Lydia Bryant, Al?' asked Davies.

'A long time ago, not recently, why?' replied Jessop.

'I just wondered if the intelligence you have on her is up to date. I mean her personality profile. You know, what newspapers she reads, her hobbies, whether or not she's excitable, is she...'

'Are you doubting the intelligence, Davies?' interrupted Jessop.

'No, just asking if it's as good as you seem to think,' said Davies

Chief Superintendent Jessop paused for a moment, reflecting.

'Why not pull them all in, spin the drum, and see what turns up?' suggested Terry Webster, listening intently to the conversation.

Jessop smiled thoughtfully and responded, 'We could pull them all in, interview them forever and a day, and, do you know what that would accomplish?'

'They'd pull the shutters down,' said Barney.

'Absolutely,' replied Jessop. 'They'd crawl all over us with their expensive solicitors, writs of *habeas corpus*, and total silence. It's a total waste of time unless you've got cast iron stand up in court evidence and there's no such thing. It's just a game, you see, but we aren't always rolling the dice.'

'But you must have something?' asked Barney. 'You just said you had Benny Abbott taped up good and proper.'

'We've a ton of intelligence against them but it's all a question of putting the final piece into the jigsaw at the right time,' replied Jessop. 'Criminal investigation at the serious crime level is a precise science. It's like a set of dominoes all lined up to all fall down one after the other. If you don't get it right at the first knock then there's always remnants of the organisation left to dirty the waters, move the evidence, destroy the evidence, or get rid of key witnesses. Do any of you really understand what we are up against here?'

'Mmm,' considered Davies. 'A visit or two, here and there, might be appropriate in the circumstances; a quiet word perhaps?'

'Oh, dear,' chuckled Jessop. 'You're not thinking of a rematch with Jack Creighton are you, Davies?'

'No, but Lydia Bryant might be worth a word.'

'A word about what?' demanded Jessop.

'This and that!' Davies replied.

'Forget it,' advised Jessop. 'She has a bodyguard with her all the time.' He reached inside his jacket, flipped open his mobile, and fingered some digits. 'When it's time for the gloves to come off, Davies, I'll be in the lead. Okay?'

Davies King rubbed the end of his chin and said, 'Maybe it's time to play the game in an unorthodox fashion, I don't know. Doesn't matter really, Mister Jessop; it's your patch, not mine.'

'You remember that, Davies. It might be your murder but it's my patch,' said Jessop. 'I know you of old. No funny business, okay?

''Okay,' agreed Davies. 'You're the boss.'

When Jessop's phone was answered he ordered, 'Jim, how's it going? Good, look, get hold of the River Police division at Wapping nick.

I want to know if there's a record of a vessel called Conchenta using the dockland waters, West India docks, Blackwall Basin, anywhere. Use your contacts and get into any registers, membership lists, harbour master records, anything. If Conchenta floats on water I want to know where, why and when. Put a team on it. Okay?'

Jessop walked round in a meaningless circle as he listened intently to his phone. When the listening stopped, he said, 'Good, and send a small search team down to Bartholomew Wharf. Then run…'

Davies handed him a sheet from a bank account and Jessop read the details of the account holder saying, 'Thanks, Davies… Jim, run Manuel Martinez through our system, and start an initial financial investigation into him. You know, do the basic stuff to start with. Press some buttons. No date of birth but…'

'Spanish,' stated Davies.

'Born in Spain,' continued Jessop. 'Put the name thorough Interpol and Europol, Jim. Spin the drum and see what comes out the other end.'

Jessop snapped his phone shut and watched Davies reading papers from the safe.

Handing a flimsy piece of paper over, Davies asked, 'What does this mean, Al?'

Jessop read the writing written in a scrawled hand and said aloud, 'VXW3091 failed on thirty six months. What on earth is that about?'

'Sounds like a catalogue number,' suggested Webster. 'You know a catalogue number for an oil painting, an antique, something like that.'

'Could be a car registration for that matter,' suggested Ted.

'Why did this VXW3091 car registration number or whatever it is fail then?' demanded Davies.

'Search me, boss,' answered Webster.

'Is it a court file reference number?' asked Barnes. 'According to these papers I'm reading Manuel Martinez is a senior partner in a corporate law firm,'

'Which one?' asked Jessop.

'Chipperdale, Wallace and Palmerton…. Belgravia?'

'Fortnum and Mason are in Piccadilly, that figures,' said Jessop. 'Belgravia is just down the road from Piccadilly. The Belgravia pigeons are so posh they only nick caviar and champagne. Take another look. Is VXW3091 the number of a Fortnum and Mason invoice?'

113

There was a rustle of paper followed by, 'No, sir!'

'Well there's one thing we've found out,' suggested Davies.

'What's that?' asked Jessop.

'If Manuel Martinez really has strangled his wife in a fit of domestic violence then he's opened up a right can of worms, hasn't he?'

'Double life?' suggested Jessop.

'Could be!' responded Davies King. 'Spanish corporate lawyer from Belgravia has criminal friends in the east end of London and ends up murdering his wife in a fit of domestic violence. Indeed, we reckon he has important criminal connections in the west too, by the look of it. Friends! Not just contacts? What do you think, Barney?' asked Davies.

'Nothing ever surprises me, Davies,' replied Ted. 'You'd better take this call from Annie. Your mate has done a bunk from the Anchor.'

'What?' asked Davies, surprised.

'And he's been circulated by our butterfly man as wanted on suspicion…' added Ted Barnes.

'Butterfly man?' quizzed Jessop.

'Max? Suspicion of what?' snapped Davies.

'Suspicion of grievous bodily harm,' stated Barney, handing the phone over. 'And it doesn't look good for the man from the Met.'

'Max?' asked Jessop. 'Max Fowler?'

Davies grabbed the phone and spoke to Sergeant Annie Rock. When he had finished he turned to Jessop and said, 'Yeah, Max Fowler. You remember, Max?'

'Oh, I know Max Fowler,' replied Jessop. 'He's one of ours. Saved your life once if I recall, and a few others.'

'That's him,' said Davies. 'But it looks like we've got a problem.'

'No,' replied Jessop, decisively. 'You've got a problem, Davies. 'Tell me, what has Max done?' His eyes penetrated Davies King's skull and bore into him as if his life depended on it.

'Nothing really! Thing is,' replied Davies. 'I think they're using him to get at me. He stood on someone's toes and they seem to be putting a case together to prosecute him for assault, that's all.'

'Assault! Get my man out of there. He's saved too many lives to be used in this way,' ordered Jessop. Turning, almost angrily, Jessop said, 'He's a top Bomb God and too damn important to be used as a pawn in a game, Davies. Understand?'

'Understood,' replied Davies.

'Max Fowler is a Met man, a superintendent of police, and he's one of mine. Now sort it!' demanded Jessop with a hint of threatening finality in his manner.

'It'll sort,' offered Davies. 'It's on my board and it's my move. I'm not telling you how to handle your squad down here so please don't tell me how to handle my problems at Crillsea. It's my patch. I'll clean it.'

'Be sure you do, Davies. It would be a shame to fall out over such a thing, wouldn't it?' suggested Jessop.

'Perhaps!' considered Davies. 'Now then! First things first! Witness statements from the neighbours and then we'll process these exhibits. Once we're cleared up here, I've business in Crillsea.'

Chief Superintendent Jessop looked carefully and deeply into the eyes of Davies and finally said, 'It's what I like about you, Inspector King.'

'What's that, sir?' asked Davies.

'Your ability to bring everything down to an irrelevant stupid board game, but this time, Davies, this time a stalemate won't do.'

In Crillsea, that night, a man in black dragged himself onto the roof and lay for a moment looking at the sky above. Panting, he could hear himself breathing heavily from his exertions. 'I'm getting too old for all this,' he said quietly to the heavens. 'Far too old!'

Gradually, he pulled himself together, rolled over and switched on his torch. A thin beam of light trickled towards a skylight window and more easy pickings. He checked for an alarm system but could find none.

He listened for the sound of running feet, of police sirens, of anything unusual that might give him cause for concern. He remained calm and cool as he slowly brought his breathing under control.

The man wondered if his favoured point of entry was protected by a radio beam of some kind, he did not know but he sought the mirror and a spray in the thigh pocket of his black over-trousers and decided he had all the tools he needed to force an entry.

Tightening his gloves, the man in black crawled towards the skylight, sought his jemmy, and gently forced his way into the jewellers below.

Out at sea, headed south, a sailor plotted his escape route.

His was a steady hand on the tiller, strong and resolute. His hand moved gently and guided the vessel through the dark waters of the ocean.

The cliffs were a long way to the rear. Only the deep black of night kept him company as the bow of the yacht cut through the waves and ploughed on relentlessly.

*

Chapter Seven

~ ~ ~

Dateline: Tuesday.
Crillsea and Tevington on Sea.

A telephone rang on Detective Chief Inspector Keith Jackson's desk in Crillsea and he answered it sharply, 'Jackson.' Within minutes he was on his way to Tevington on Sea, just along the coast, having pulled Sergeant Annie Rock out of the custody suite at Crillsea. He took her with him. He hated driving and threw Annie the ignition keys saying, 'Jewellers shop in Tevington; forty thousand pounds worth through the night, roof entry again. Quick as you can.'

'Why us?' asked Annie.

Jackson explained, 'The Tevington DI is off sick with a bloody squash injury; King isn't back from London yet, and I've too much work on to be investigating burglaries.'

'Okay, it'll sort,' replied Annie firing the engine and slamming the car door closed.

'Well, it's a jeweller's again, the third, so I need to show face and be able to fend any questions emanating from the local Chamber of Commerce or any individual police authority members,' said Jackson. 'And then there's the Crillsea Chronicle to deal with. It won't be long before they're on my back asking more questions.'

'You mean you want me to investigate the burglary?' asked Annie.

'Of course, you haven't got those nice new shiny stripes on your uniform for nothing. Is that a problem for you, Sergeant Rock?'

'Not at all, chief inspector,' replied Annie Rock.

'Anyway, the stripes suit you,' replied Jackson.

Annie scowled.

'And it's exciting, isn't it? One moment you're in the cell block dealing with prisoner reception, and the next investigating crime. That's the way to do it, I say.'

Booting the car into traffic, she accelerated hard as Jackson checked his mobile 'phone.

Smiling politely, Annie retaliated, 'You might call it exciting, sir, even part of your new policy, but I don't know whether I'm coming or going. One minute I'm on telephone enquiries for Inspector King and the murder, the next I'm in the cell block processing prisoners. At the same time I'm supposed to be running a CID office. Now I'm an operational detective again wearing a new uniform rushing off to a burglary.'

'I told you my ideas would work,' countered Jackson. 'This policy is saving us a lot of money and we're getting the best out of our resources. But you need to be reminded the department is no longer called CID.'

'Actually, sir,' ventured Annie, 'I don't think your policy is working very well at all.'

Chief Inspector Jackson said, 'Sergeant Rock, if you want a meaningful career in my Strategic Criminal Intelligence Directorate then you must be much more flexible in your attitude to working practices.'

Annie scowled, adjusted the interior mirror, flicked her hair across her shoulders, and sped towards Tevington on Sea.

Jackson sensed tension between them when Annie broke the silence saying, 'If everyone in the division is involved in your policy, then why can't the 'Tevvies' look after the job. If your plan is being adhered to and working correctly, then a uniform bobby with six months experience ought to be able to look after a forty thousand pound jeweller's break-in and do all the immediate enquiries before handing it over to....' She paused for a while thinking and then said, 'Who do you hand it over to under your fancy generic policy?'

Jackson contained his growing resentment and merely said, 'Just drive, Sergeant. My guidelines allow for expert input when appropriate.'

Annie Rock tried to contain her growing resentment, pressed hard the accelerator, and drove along the dual carriageway running parallel to the coast. 'Detective Constable Webster is dealing with a couple of similar roof top burglaries at jewellers in Crillsea,' she stated. 'We're already looking for a 'climber'. There's probably a connection, isn't there? A connection to a series of high value crimes committed by the same person or persons could be lost if a degree of quality control wasn't implemented at an early stage. Don't you agree, chief inspector?'

'I know!' Jackson finally snapped. 'Generics is working, can't you see? You are proving how versatile you really are, how versatile we all are.'

'So I'm not being messed about then?' demanded Annie with a look of slight bemusement.

'No!' barked Jackson. 'It's just that the others aren't doing what they're supposed to do.'

'Oh!' exclaimed Annie, surprised. 'That explains everything then! I thought they were on murder enquiries in London. Are they supposed to be here, there, or somewhere else?'

Jackson slammed the dashboard with his fist and barked angrily, 'Where are they when you want them? London, bloody London!'

Annie drove on in silence.

Jackson's mobile rang and he answered sharply, 'Jackson!'

Annie pulled out and overtook a line of traffic as she listened to Davies King updating Keith Jackson.

Jackson eventually spoke into his mobile and ordered, 'King, circulate Manuel Martinez to all British Forces as wanted for the murder of his wife, Elena. Make sure the circulation shows that he is believed in possession of a double-barrelled shotgun, armed and dangerous, treat with extreme caution. Inform Interpol and Europol the Spaniard is on the run and is wanted in the UK. Do the necessary paperwork and do some draft extradition papers, just in case he's traced abroad. Have the documents on my desk as soon as possible. I'll brief Superintendent Allithwaite on the Interpol, Europol, and extradition interface as soon as possible.'

'What's an interface?' asked Davies, deliberately being awkward.

'Business speak, inspector,' explained Jackson, tirelessly. 'Scale down this murder enquiry until our Manuel Martinez is found. We're busy in Crillsea. Tevington's inspector is off sick from a squash injury and I need you and your team back here as soon as possible.'

Davies King was in the back of a car returning to Crillsea but that didn't stop him asking Chief Inspector Jackson, 'Why has Superintendent Max Fowler been circulated for GBH?'

Jackson responded, 'We had a complaint of an assault made against a serving officer. I acted upon it.'

Annie and Keith Jackson were off the dual carriageway and on the main drag into Tevington on Sea. Annie blasted her car horn at a pedestrian ambling across the road.

'Which serving officer would that be?' pleaded Davies King.

'The nature of my enquiry is confidential, inspector.'

'Ah, those confidential enquiries again, chief inspector; am I being investigated?' enquired Davies.

'Whatever gave you that idea?' countered Jackson.

'My black eye and you asking questions in the Anchor,' suggested an inquisitive Davies. Then Davies leaned forward in his car and said, 'Give it some welly, Webby; time and tide and all that!'

Terry Webster guided their car into the fast lane and squeezed the accelerator pedal to the floor as the telephone conversation continued.

'I understand you got a black eye in the line of duty although it was in a pub fight, Inspector King,' explained Jackson. 'Luckily for you, you arrested the man who gave you the black eye otherwise…'

'My friends at the Anchor told me you were asking questions and examining CCTV,' interrupted Davies. 'Why don't you give me it in black and white? I'd much rather know what's ahead than behind.'

Annie Rock couldn't help but listen to the conversation as she pulled up outside a jeweller's shop in Tevington on Sea.

'I'll level with you,' stated Jackson. 'A file has gone up to Headquarters via Superintendent Allithwaite to Assistant Chief Constable Patterson. He'll decide whether police regulations have been breached.'

'Why did you do the enquiry and not the professional standards department, complaints and discipline?' asked Davies King.

'It's my prerogative, inspector, and an example of how I foresee my new policy working. I expect all officers, of officer rank, under my command to be able to investigate their fellow officers in such ways.'

'Wow!' exclaimed Davies. 'That'll be good for moral. Is that in the team building section of your policy, sir?'

'Tetchy, aren't you, Inspector King, and on dangerous ground if you continue this line of conversation,' warned Jackson.

'You've already circulated Max Fowler,' snapped Davies. 'They're even looking for him at his old haunts in London. If he's circulated then you've already made the decision to prosecute him when you catch up with him, haven't you? It's a *fait accompli*.'

'That may prove to be the case, inspector,' suggested Jackson, stowing his seat belt and preparing to get out of his car.

Davies challenged. 'And you're going to find I'd been drinking.'

'Correct,' replied Jackson.

'That I assaulted a man in the course of an arrest,' explained Davies. 'That I sustained a black eye in the execution of my duty, and a whole lot more. By the way, the yanks do things in the line of duty. I'm British; I do things in the execution of my duty. You're going to find I mix with criminals. I do when I need to. I'm a detective. A bloody good one too! Now get off my back and let me get on with my job.'

Detectives Webster and Barnes closed their eyes fleetingly as their car passed beneath a motorway bridge and they shuddered at the festering ongoing squabble they were witnessing daily.

Detective Chief Inspector Jackson closed his mobile without another word to Davies King, got out of his vehicle and smiled graciously at Annie Rock, 'All we need to do now is catch us a jewel thief, Sergeant Rock. Let's go. We don't need the others for this one.'

They were touching eighty five miles an hour on the motorway heading for Crillsea when Davies stopped thinking about his run in with the butterfly man and hit the buttons on his mobile again.

'Claudia, it's me….Fine thanks…. Any word from Max?'

Davies King was looking out of a window watching sheep pass by and motorway marker posts run into oblivion when he casually asked, 'Claudia, could you do me a favour? Have you got a pen?'

There was a slight pause before Davies continued, 'I need some really top class quality clothes and a couple of things done. You know; shirts, suit, new shoes, a silk tie even. I tell you what; make a list would you… Yes, yes, I know. Haircut!'

Davies listened and then confided, 'Socks? Oh, yes, black.'

There was another pause followed by, 'No, I'm not going to Cinderella's Ball. Whatever gave you that idea?'

The car descended into silence as the speedometer crept slowly towards ninety miles an hour.

Oversized Wellington boots wallowed in the soft sand and then rubbed ferociously against his shin as the rubber of his boots found the shingle. A seagull, or two, played in the sky, perhaps hovered momentarily, and then dived in pursuit of prey. Or were they just cavorting for onlookers? Jake Muncaster didn't know and he didn't care. He was late for work and he pushed on, collar up, against the breeze and across the fairly isolated beach.

Moments later, he saw a green bundle well above the water's edge where an earlier tide had deposited the flotsam and jetsam of the British coastal waters, and where the holidaymaker and day tourist didn't seek to stretch out their towels in this particularly unkempt area. As coxswain of

Crillsea's lifeboat, he walked the area regularly and he was used to finding all manner of things washed up on the beach.

Jake approached the bundle, couldn't quite make out what it was, and decided to investigate further.

Curiosity got the better of him. Jake pulled back the sheeting and was horrified to see the dead, cold body of a human being.

A sudden gust of wind and spray slashed across his face as he ran, squelching and wallowing in his Wellingtons, towards the lifeboat station and a telephone.

Signed police cars lined up on the green and flowery esplanade above Tevington on Sea's beach. Their occupants questioned trades people and spectators asking whether or not anything suspicious had been seen or heard on the beach recently. An ambulance moved off, not required for the collection of flotsam and jetsam found on a beach. Then an undertaker's car slid to a quiet halt near Tevington's lifeboat station and waited to be called forward.

Detective Chief Inspector Keith Jackson was first detective at the scene, diverting his attention from the jewellery job to 'a body on the beach.' He bent over a body and spoke to Professor Jones.

Sergeant Annie Rock was taking a statement from Jake Muncaster when Davies King, Terry Webster and Ted Barnes trudged across the shingle towards the scene of the body on the beach.

When they hit shingle, Davies suddenly lost his footing and floundered unceremoniously into Jackson before crumpling to the ground, arms outstretched, near the green plastic bundle.

'Typical!' announced Chief Inspector Jackson. 'You certainly know how to make an entrance, Inspector King.'

'Yeah! It's been a long day. Sorry.'

'It's going to be a bit longer yet, Davies,' suggested Jackson, sarcastically. And then with a look into Davies King's eyes, he said, 'You'd best not fall in it anymore.'

'I take your point,' replied Davies, thoughtfully. 'What we got?'

'Another one for young Webster,' pronounced Jackson, beaming a huge smile to the detective in question. 'You've one under your belt this week, Webster. How about making it a double?'

'Mine's a single brandy,' laughed Davies, rubbing his knee and accepting a helping hand from Ted Barnes.

'Humour is for the station canteen, Davies,' revealed Jackson. 'And drink has caused you enough problems lately. Black eye, now bruised knee, I shouldn't wonder. Can you concentrate on the job?'

'What we got, sir,' asked Ted Barnes.

'A body on a beach: female, thirty or so, I would say. Clothed in casual loose trousers and a top and her underclothes look to be a swimming costume. Her head is badly smashed up; no wedding ring, but a real corker of a ring on her right hand, otherwise no identification. What more do you want?'

'Knowledge is power,' cracked Davies King. 'Professor?'

'Mister Jackson is right, Davies. I'll need to remove the poor woman's body and do a proper examination to determine the cause of death,' stated Professor Jones. 'But as you all seem to be getting rather good at murder cases perhaps you ought to tell me what you think. My first question would be has she been murdered?'

'Webster?' asked Jackson. 'What do you think?'

'She could have fallen off the cliffs or fell from a boat,' offered Webster. 'Did she fall or was she pushed? Isn't that what they say?'

'Think man,' suggested Ted Barnes. 'Read the scene. Did she wrap herself in a plastic bag before she jumped?'

Webster looked away, slightly embarrassed, but then added with a reluctant chuckle, 'There's no family photographs here; no giveaway clues to wonder about; just a dead body on a cold and windy beach.' He blew air into his cupped hands and added, 'Bloody cold when that sea breeze bites into you. Anyway, why aren't the Tevvies dealing with this one?'

'Because it's yours,' smiled Jackson. 'All yours, and the local DI is off sick and you've got it so don't complain.'

'And this is your starter for ten,' revealed Davies, unzipping the plastic sheeting. 'When I fell down my hand hit the zip. Of course, you can clearly see it's a suit cover in which a body has been wrapped. But this, I believe, is a handkerchief.' Carefully, he removed what appeared to be a square piece of white cotton.

'Bravo, Inspector King,' ridiculed Jackson. 'Bravo! Is there a white rabbit in there too?'

'Thank you, chief inspector,' replied Davies. 'Humour for a theatre stage as well as a works canteen. Maybe we should set up a Punch and Judy whilst we're at it. Professor Jones, allow me…'

Professor Jones signalled with a gentle movement of his hand and stated, 'Be my guest, Inspector King. I'm all ears but I'm getting a little tired of you two sniping at each other.' His golden locks played on his collar and crept down his back as he bowed, smiled, and stepped back saying, 'It needs to stop. It's not professional from either of you.'

Davies confessed, 'You're right. My apologies, Professor, anyway, as you can see, the body is wrapped in a green plastic suit cover: a man's suit cover. And I'm sure you were going to ask the question, Chief Inspector Jackson, did a man put this body into a suit cover? Well, I think so because a body is quite heavy to lift. I'm sure you were also going to reveal to young Webster here that this body has been deposited at the top of the beach, well above the present water mark.'

Jackson was silent as Davies looked to the rolling waves and ordered, 'Barney, find out when the last high tide was. Last night's low tide didn't reach this part of the beach. The body's been here a day or two.'

Ted nodded in agreement, produced his battered notebook, and began scribbling furiously. He wrote 'number 49' at the top of the page.

Davies resumed. 'There are five stages of decomposition. This body has recently entered the second stage: it's the so-called bloat stage of decomposition. The first decomposition stage commences immediately after the heart stops. You see, the heart stops pumping so all the blood drains to the lower part of the body. That's why the lower part of the body is discoloured. It's called *livor mortis*. Very soon after death *rigor mortis* sets in when muscular tissues become rigid and incapable of contraction. Finally the body loses heat to the surrounding environment and the overall cooling of the body is called *algor mortis*. Sadly, when the heart stops, changes occur inside the body and the cell structure breaks down and releases enzymes that initiate the breakdown of surrounding cells and tissues. This is known as autolysis.'

Davies paused for a moment and studied the deceased's face before continuing, 'Sometimes you get blistering of the skin but on this occasion blistering has not quite set in. That should help Professor Jones when he tries to determine time of death. The skull is an obvious place to concentrate upon here because it's in a really bad way. The skin of the upper jaw and mandible stretch into what looks like a smile but I'm guessing she wasn't overly happy at the time of death. It's the way death has contorted her body. Her hair and skin are still securely attached to her head but her body has become a little bloated. This bloating is caused by gases that bacteria in the intestines give off as they feed on dead tissues. She's been lying here for a couple of days, I would say, but how long in the sea…. Now that's another matter.'

'What else do you need to know, Davies?' enquired the Professor.

'What she had for her last meal and her time of death?'

'Anything else?' asked Professor Jones.

Davies considered the remark for a moment but then replied, 'If she had been dumped on the beach above the high water mark then we would be looking at heavily embedded footprints in the sand, drag marks, and a dried out plastic bundle. No, it hasn't happened that way.'

Professor Jones nodded in agreement.

Davies continued. 'She could have been thrown into the sea from a boat or pushed off the cliffs close by or further along the coast. We'll have a search team do a search in the area for us and scientific support can see what they can find. If there's anything to find, those guys will find it. But I reckon she was battered to death with a blunt instrument. If that's the case can you tell me what kind of murder weapon we're looking for?'

'I believe so, Davies,' replied Professor Jones. 'But she could have sustained head injuries from being thrown from the cliffs whilst alive and still inside the suit cover. But I doubt it. I'll need some rock samples because if her head hit the rocks I'd expect to find traces of rock and sand in her hair, and on the outside of the suit cover, and possibly in her skull.'

Barney nodded and made a note.

'You see,' remarked the Professor, 'I have to consider whether or not those head injuries were caused by the skull smashing against the cliffs or colliding with the rocks below. Anyway, there are so many imponderables when you think about it. No, if pushed, and at this early stage, I would think you're right by the look of her skull, what's left of it.'

Professor Jones carefully re-examined the skull and said, 'Poor woman, I'll need to be certain with a microscope and a proper examination but I think the indentations into the line of the skull are all fairly flat. That would make the murder weapon have a flat surface the size of....oh, perhaps a hand or two; hard to tell at this stage.'

'A spade?' suggested Barney to Professor Jones.

'Yes, something like that, similar shape, I would say.'

'We found a blood stained spade at the last murder scene up on Crillsea Cliffs,' said Barney.

'Yes, but that was a strangulation,' intervened Jackson.

'A very personal murder this one though,' offered Webster. 'I mean battering someone to death is horrible.

'Indeed,' agreed Professor Jones. 'Potentially that in itself is a good lead for you all. Very personal murder means cold hatred!'

'With incompetence and ill conceived planning,' revealed Davies.

'Why's that?' asked Chief Inspector Jackson.

'Because death might have been caused by pure cold hatred but disposal of the body hasn't been thought through very well.'

'Interesting,' implied Jackson. 'But not necessarily incompetent.'

'No, but what kind of inept person bundles a body into a suit cover and then leaves a handkerchief behind? Look…' Davies displayed the handkerchief and watched it blowing gently in the breeze.

Ted Barnes looked up from his scribbling and said, 'Gents suit cover! Is there a bow tie in there? A gentleman might ordinarily keep a bow tie and his tuxedo in a suit cover.'

'Well, it's not my tuxedo, chaps,' revealed Jackson with a slight chuckle. 'I need to collect mine from the dry cleaners today though. Big night coming up soon! The Mayor's Ball, you know; lots of VIPs and toffs to rub shoulders with, shakers and movers to shake and move with, lots of gushing and brushing to do. Not my scene, of course.'

'Oh, I was invited to that myself once,' said Ted Barnes but I…'

'Is anyone looking at this?' asked Terry Webster.

Jackson turned his head. Ted lowered his pencil. Together they studied a handkerchief blowing in a sea breeze.

'Yes, Ted,' announced Davies. 'The hankie bears the monogram MM in one of the corners. Find MM and we're half way there.'

'Manuel Martinez!' declared Terry Webster.

Detective Chief Inspector Jackson grinned broadly and said, 'Good work men, Good work.'

'Of course, it could still be a two a penny basic domestic murder,' suggested Davies without a hint of challenge or disdain in his voice. 'You see, we don't know who she is, do we? Someone's wife or girlfriend perhaps? And I wonder if the handkerchief was left behind by accident or was it left behind deliberately for us to find?'

'It wouldn't be the first time a murderer has left us a false trail to follow, Inspector King,' said Ted Barnes. 'It's entirely possible someone is trying to put us off the scent.'

'In your experience of suspicious deaths,' suggested Terry Webster, 'What do you think has happened, Chief Inspector Jackson?'

'We'll keep an open mind, shall we, gentlemen,' suggested Jackson. 'Right now we're clueless because she hasn't got a husband, hasn't got a friend we know of, and I can't think of a good reason or a good motive, at this time, to suggest why she's been bludgeoned to death.'

Terry Webster tried to look consoled at Jackson's remarks but his face betrayed him.

Sergeant Annie Rock joined them clutching a statement and brushing sand from her uniform tunic. 'Success?' she asked.

There was a look of disdain from Davies King.

'Two in a week, wow! A serial killer is it?' asked Annie.

'Not quite, Annie,' replied Davies. 'She's been battered to death with a blunt instrument.'

'I know, inspector, it's my scene and my crime. I was first here with the chief inspector and he's allocated it to me. I've taken a few statements including one from a Mister Jake Muncaster who found the body. I've never carried a murder enquiry before.'

'It's not your crime anymore, sergeant,' interrupted Jackson. 'Sorry, Sergeant Rock, but young Webster needs trained up if he is to make the grade. He's carrying the crime on his desk. It will be in his portfolio in due course.'

'And I don't carry the crime, chief inspector? I don't have a meaningful portfolio, is that what you mean?' replied Annie Rock. 'I don't get trained up to carry my first murder case under the guidance of Davies King and Ted Barnes here. They've handled more murders and suspicious deaths than Terry Webster has had breakfasts.' Annie looked aside and said to Webster, 'No offence meant, Webby,'

'None taken,' replied Terry Webster.

Annie said, 'Is this your policy working again, chief inspector, or is it because I'm a female and you'd prefer me to be a beer swilling man with balls for brains? Or would you prefer me to have a lipstick, and a perfume spray instead of a CS spray, handcuffs and a steel baton?'

Jackson ignored Annie's attack. 'I think we should wait for the Professor's report and double our efforts to find this Martinez man.'

Davies King bent down beside the body of the woman and allowed his fingers to part her hair. Carefully, he exposed the remnants of deathly beauty struggling to find a place in the bloated features of her full face. He studied her appearance; he studied her features.

Looking up at Keith Jackson and Ted, Davies shared his revelation when he quietly announced, 'You suggested we were clueless, chief inspector? I don't think so. Take a look here. Isn't she familiar?'

Keith Jackson peered over and declared, 'Probably similar to a mug shot you've seen at the nick, I would say.'

Annie Rock took a closer look at the woman's face and said, 'If anyone respects my opinion the injuries don't really help but a facial reconstruction might assist us. God bless her but I couldn't recognise her as she is now, but that said, inspector, do you mean the ring?'

'Yes, I do, Annie,' replied Davies.

'Then I agree with you, inspector,' replied Annie. 'The so-called corker of a ring on one of the fingers of her right hand looks very similar to what someone in a photograph frame I'm thinking of was wearing.'

'That's exactly what crossed my mind, Annie,' said Davies. 'Is this Sophie and was she battered to death at Crillsea Cliffs with the blood stained spade we found in a garden shed? I wonder, no, surely not.'

'I'd try dental records,' said Annie. 'And I find it interesting that she's wearing a swimsuit underneath her top clothing. It's consistent with her going for a swim and then throwing on a set of loose fitting clothes after the swim. And, of course, the house at Crillsea Cliffs has a swimming pool.'

'Professor, Annie is right. Can you do a dental examination with a view to comparative analysis?' requested Davies King

'There's one more way to find out,' proposed Barney interrupting. 'We need to compare the indentations on her skull with the curvature of the spade and the blood on the spade with the victim's blood. Is that okay with you, Professor Jones?'

'Of course, it is. My office will take care of the dental records and we will be able to help more when I have completed my examination in the laboratory,' advised Professor Jones. 'But you are absolutely correct, Ted, I will give it my closest attention but I'll need your help collating all your local dental records to start with.'

'I'll sort that for you,' volunteered Barney. 'There can't be that many dentists in Tevvie and Crillsea.' Barney made a note.

'What about DNA? If Manuel Martinez's DNA is on the spade we've cracked it,' suggested Chief Inspector Jackson.

'Mmm... Interesting,' said Davies. 'Manuel Martinez lives there. I'd expect to find his DNA everywhere.'

The look on Jackson's face did not accompany a reply.

'I'm sure we'll ask the scientists to take any DNA,' smiled Davies.

'Just a minute,' interrupted Chief Inspector Jackson regaining composure. 'It's not just the murderer who is useless in getting rid of the body, is it? What about you guys?'

'What do you mean by that?' asked Davies.

Chief Inspector Jackson rounded on Davies King and demanded, 'Are you seriously telling me your questionable investigative skills have reached a level where you think you know who the murder victim is, where she was murdered, and what the murder weapon is?'

'Something like that,' said Davies King.

'Yet your bungling ability extends to the point that you didn't examine the last murder scene properly and you didn't secure the murder weapon for what we now know is 'the body on the beach' murder?'

'Oh, we have the spade, Chief Inspector Jackson,' said Barney.

'It was strangulation not a battering,' added Davies.

'We were expecting to find animal blood on the spade but now I'm not so sure,' said Annie Rock. 'After all, I'm just a woman; what do I know about criminal investigation?'

'Incompetent blundering stupidity!' growled Jackson. 'You haven't a clue have you? I give you all a straightforward domestic murder to sort out and you mess it up by not examining the scene properly. As a result, you've now got a second murder to investigate. As I understand it part of the evidence for the second murder might have been found at the scene of the first and...'

'We have no time of death for either murder at the present moment,' advised Davies King.

'Be that as it may, Inspector King, but I have absolutely no confidence in you and your team and no belief that you will carry out your enquiries properly. It's preposterous. I can't believe we have to reopen the first scene to investigate the second murder.'

'Oh, we examined the scene properly, chief inspector, that's how we know who the victim is,' responded Davies. 'Or, to be precise, we have a damn good idea on who the victim might be and there is a distinct probability that the murders might be connected. I'm thinking the same man may have committed both murders.'

'Who found the spade and where?' barked Jackson.

Davies King sighed deeply but then responded, 'The search team found the spade when I arranged them to attend and cover the scene. They were brilliant and turned over every square inch but, as I recall, you didn't want them to attend under this fancy policy of yours.'

'You got lucky, inspector, don't push that luck because you're close to being removed from this investigation and being suspended.'

'We're just behind the game instead of ahead of it. Maybe it's time to sacrifice the Queen and turn the tide,' reacted Davies.'

Close by, there was a roll of an angry sea as it crashed onto the beach and wave after wave of brine collided with the sand.

'Coffee, inspector?' asked Claudia.

'No thanks, Claudia, I'm too busy,' replied Davies King.

'You need to eat and drink, Inspector. You have a reputation for working long hours and I don't want you falling asleep on the job.'

'I'm fine, Claudia, thank you. I was scheduled to referee a five a side match at the kids sport club but I had to cancel, that's all.'

'Another body, I understand,' stated Claudia. 'On the beach this time, how sad, is the woman local or don't we know yet?'

'Not sure, Claudia,' replied Davies. 'We've a good lead but no confirmation as yet. Look, did you get me those clothes I asked for?'

'But of course, in the bag by the side of your desk.'

'You are a treasure, Claudia. I don't know what I'd do without you,' stated Davies checking his purchases. 'How much do I owe you?'

Claudia produced an invoice; Davies sighed and transferred the money to her outstretched hand.

'Any news on Max Fowler?' asked Davies.

'Not a word, but I understand they are looking for him.'

'Mmm.... I'd like to find him first,' said Davies reaching under his desk for a dumbbell which he began casually hoisting into the air with his right hand.

'Well you won't find him here. You have a haircut booked in half an hour,' Claudia said. 'Special occasion, is it?'

'Not really, I'm going to war, I mean work,' laughed Davies, curling his dumbbell repeatedly.

'Oh dear, I hope you're not going to war with young Mister Webster, inspector,' advised Claudia. 'He's in Sergeant Rock's office where he's set up the murder enquiry computer.'

'The murder enquiry computer?' queried Davies. 'More fancy technology. I thought they'd have binned that under Keith Jackson.'

'Come, come, inspector, it's his new policy you are having another go at and if you are honest you will admit you've heard of the computer before and you've used it,' chided Claudia. 'Constable Webster is loading it with all the relevant information. It's like an Encyclopaedia Britannica of information on the two murders.'

'Great, Claudia, I know how it works but we have one confirmed murder and one suspicious death until Professor Jones determines the cause of death for the body on the beach.'

Claudia asked, 'So you think it was natural causes then?'

'No, but I'm waiting for Professor Jones's telephone call and that will end all the speculation,' advised Davies, still curling his dumbbell.

'Well, be that as it may, but you should give Terry Webster credit where it's due. Sergeant Rock is pleased with the way he's taken to it.'

'Good, I'll look in on my way to the library?'

'The library, what are you going to the library for?'

'The Encyclopaedia Britannica,' replied Davies. 'And a few other books I could mention.'

'Oh, I'm so pleased you are trying to find some relaxation, inspector. It will do you good to read once in a while,' said Claudia. 'Don't you think you should put that big weight down before you hurt yourself?'

Davies King chuckled, put the dumbbell down, placed his bag under his arm, and said, 'I'm off. I'll catch you tomorrow, Claudia. Finish up here as soon as you can and have an early night.'

'How kind, inspector, how very kind,' replied Claudia suspiciously. 'Are you looking for a particular book?'

'I've a lot to do, Claudia, and a lot to find out about. I've no murder squad to speak of so some of the basics I need to know may be hidden in Crillsea's new library.'

'Oh, I see,' replied Claudia.

'Yeah,' said Davies. 'The peace and quiet helps me think.'

'Well, good luck, inspector,' acknowledged Claudia. 'I hope you find what you're looking for.'

Two minutes later, Davies King was studying the murder enquiry computer with Annie Rock and Terry Webster.

'So, as I understand it, you've loaded the computer with all the information about the two murders and then imported into the computer all the local information about crime, incidents, local criminals, criminal intelligence, the works. Am I right, Webby?'

'That's it, inspector,' replied Webby with a sideways smile to Annie Rock. 'With Sergeant Rock's help, of course, and, have you noticed, this isn't the Holmes computer it's a new one called Detect.'

'Detect?' queried Davies.

'Brand new and under trial from the Home Office. It's part of Mister Jackson's new guidelines; more technology and less manpower.'

'Kind of him to share his secret, Webby, but tell me does it record lost and found property?' queried Davies.

Annie nodded, 'Everything that comes into the Force area is on the computer, every incident you can think of. Detect reads the Force database, duplicates the records and integrates them with our enquiry.'

Thinking deeply for a moment, Davies asked, 'Good, but how about speeding tickets, parking tickets, oh, I don't know, stop checks, person searches, vehicle searches, fishing permits?'

Terry Webster beamed and replied, 'And the rest, inspector; if it's reportable and recordable it's on the system, even traffic accidents.'

'Well done but what are you going to do with all that information?' asked Davies thoughtfully.

'We're looking for common denominators for both murder scenes and trying to find connections between people and vehicles moving between the beaches and the cliffs,' replied Webby. 'Particularly amongst the criminal community; you know travelling burglars, robbers, door to door conmen, anything out of order. But we've a lot still to input into the computer and, to be honest; we're also hoping something will suddenly jump out at us that we might ordinarily miss.'

Sergeant Rock said, 'And we've loaded some of the completed house to house enquiry sheets that Barney sorted.'

'Well, that's what I like to hear,' said Davies. 'Acceptance of the fact that a little bit of luck might play an important part in this enquiry.'

'We always need luck, inspector,' said Annie. 'Some of the door to door enquiries throw back descriptions of people walking on the cliff tops, some names for people walking their dogs, parked cars, all kinds of insignificant information.'

'Intelligence isn't it?' commented Davies. 'Pieces of straw that make up the haystack; all we have to do is find the needle.'

A slight smile crossed Webster's face when he said, 'The Detect computer is showing some early suspects based on what we know so far.'

'Suspects?' queried Davies. 'Who?'

'Manuel Martinez, Harry Reynolds and Max Fowler,' replied Terry Webster. 'Harry and Max have been sighted by one or two people in the area meeting on the cliff tops but there's no apparent reason for such a meeting.'

'Maybe it was a chance meeting?' suggested Davies.

'Maybe we'll get to ask the questions in due course,' said Annie.

'Yes, all in good time,' replied Davies. 'Anyone else in the frame?'

'Computers are funny things,' replied Annie. 'It's throwing up an unidentified person responsible for the jewellery breaks; it's obviously tying the jewellery thefts together and suggesting whoever committed the jewel thefts might have committed the murders.'

'Mmm...' muttered Davies. 'It's just like us then, no idea really.'

Davies walked towards the door but then turned and asked, 'I thought Chief Inspector Jackson had made it clear there was to be no incident room and no murder squad.'

'That's correct,' replied Annie.

'Who did all this work and when?' asked Davies.

'We need to get on,' replied Webby. 'There's a lot still to do. Didn't you have an appointment, inspector?'

Davies looked across at Annie but she remained non-committal.

'Nodding slowly, Davies said, 'I see. Very well.'

'By the way, Inspector King,' disclosed Webby. 'I've determined there is one climbing club in the area: Crillsea Climbing Club. It specialises in cliff climbing but often runs courses and weekends in the Peak District and Lake District doing climbing activities.'

'Good,' acknowledged Davies. 'I suggest you get hold of a membership list and see who's a member.'

'I've already done that, sir,' replied Webby. 'I'll let you know the full results but I can tell you now I've uncovered one interesting trace.'

'Oh, who's that then?' queried Davies.

133

Terry Webster replied, 'Bill Baxter, the licensee at the Anchor, sir. He's a member of Crillsea Climbing Club and he has a caution recorded against him for theft. Apparently, some years ago, on a pub outing, he shinned up a flagpole and stole someone's flag.'

'Interesting, Webby, very interesting,' acknowledged Davies. 'There's a man who is not afraid of heights then.'

Annie Rock nodded a supportive smile towards Webby when Davies King closed the office door behind him.

A computer screen flickered gently whilst one volume of the Encyclopaedia Britannica sat on a corner of the desk. A small pile of other nonfiction books, some of which were open at various pages, occupied the mind of Detective Inspector Davies King

Only the hand of a clock moved silently forward, only a solitary leg of a chair scraped annoyingly on the marble floor of Crillsea library, only the turn of another page held King's attention.

It was one of his ways: a methodology to discover the origins of Crillsea Cliffs; and of the industries and institutions making up the area he policed and felt responsible for. Davies King was a dedicated man in his own way. He was a man set apart from the others, often a solitary man who relished his own individuality, but he was a man determined to soak up knowledge so that he might win, so that he might conquer his enemies.

'Mister King..... Mister King,'

Davies was half way down a page when he became aware of a short fat man standing beside him. The chief librarian shook his shoulder.

'Mister King, it's time for me to close up. It's gone ten o'clock, Mister King. I'm sorry but it's time to close.'

'What, oh I'm so very sorry,' replied King. 'I do apologise. I'll put these books back and I'll be off for the night. Ten o'clock, you say.'

'No, Mister King, why don't you keep them for now.'

'Oh I couldn't, they're reference books.'

'I know but you obviously need them. I've been watching you. You've been here all evening. Look, just between the two of us, you take them and return them when you're ready.'

'Don't I know you?' asked Davies.

'The Prime Minister's visit, I'm Cyril Leadbetter.'

'Of course, Mister Leadbetter!' acknowledged Davies shaking hands. 'Please forgive my ageing memory. I remember now, sir. Look, that's very kind of you but that's not right. Other people might want these books and if I've got them at home...'

Cyril interrupted and said, 'Other people can wait a little while, Mister King. I can tell you need the books for something special you are doing. I've been watching you. Is it the murders, perhaps? I don't know. I probably shouldn't ask but murder does fascinate me.'

'Why's that?' asked an inquisitive Davies.

'All day, I'm surrounded by books. I'd love to do a murder just to see if I could get away with it,' laughed Cyril Leadbetter.

'What?' asked Davies. 'What did you say?'

'Oh I'm joking, inspector. Still, this is none of my business. But do take them with you. Bring them back when you're ready. Okay?'

'Well, that's very kind, of you, I'll just take this one then, if I may.'

Cyril examined the book and said, 'Oh yes, from the science section; a heavy choice for bedtime reading, if you don't mind me saying.'

'Yes, indeed, Mister Leadbetter,' replied Davies. 'One often comes across a heavy and strange choice of words.'

Clutching his book under his arm, Davies King stood and walked from the library reflecting upon a strange remark uttered by one Cyril Leadbetter.

*

Chapter Eight

~ ~ ~

Dateline: Wednesday Night,
London's West End.

The express hurtled beneath the bridge and darkness invaded the first class carriage for a few seconds. Suddenly, England's green and pleasant lands flashed past the windows again as the train sped towards London and an unscheduled appointment Davies had made for himself.

'Tickets please, sir!'

He rummaged inside a pocket and then handed over his ticket for inspection, Davies asked, 'How long?'

'Not long to Waterloo, sir. There's time for a nap, or a fresh coffee, if you've the mind for one.'

There was a clip of a train ticket and the conductor moved on.

Davies rubbed his eyes, closed the library book, and swallowed the last of a cold coffee.

His mobile rang. 'Davies,' he answered.

'Ah, glad I caught you, Davies. It's Professor Jones. I have cause and time of death for you.'

'Fabulous,' replied Davies. 'Thanks for ringing, Professor.'

'Elena Martinez probably died between nine o'clock and two o'clock last Saturday,' reported Professor Jones. 'I can confirm manual strangulation, as we thought, but you'd better sit down because I have some quite odd information for you.'

'Go on,' insisted Davies looking casually out of the window.

'The body on the beach and your blundering murderer have just taken another interesting turn.'

'I'm all ears,' replied Davies King. 'Do tell!'

Conscious of others in the carriage, Davies slid out of his seat and went to stand in the area where the carriages connected. He could hear the continuous rattle of the train wheels on the rails beneath him but with his privacy assured, he held the mobile close to his ear.

Professor Jones said, 'Time of death for the body on the beach is last Wednesday lunchtime, give or take twelve hours either way. I will do more tests to try and refine the time even further. It's very difficult to establish a precise time due to the seawater but I can confirm the bloodstained spade is the murder weapon. Indentations on the skull match the spade and I have a blood match so there is no doubt.'

'Are you sure, Professor?' asked Davies. 'I mean am I right in thinking we have two murders in the same place? The body on the beach first, battered to death on Crillsea Cliffs with a spade, then another victim strangled to death in the same place a couple of days later.'

'Precisely, Davies, but the twist is that stomach, bladder and kidney tests on the body on the beach reveal traces of a light meal: chicken, bread, wine, and a common or garden crocus.'

'What's so funny about that?' asked Davies.

'Why the crocus, of course, Davies,' declared Professor Jones. 'Unless she has a history of cultivating wild flowers for scientific research and digesting them then I would say someone has laced your victim's wine with crocus.'

'What would that achieve, Professor?' demanded Davies, somewhat confused.

'Ordinarily, absolutely nothing, Davies, other than the likelihood of a violent stomach ache and a thirst to die for, if you'll pardon the expression. The thing is I think your murderer used the wrong crocus.'

'What? What are you talking about, Professor? You've lost me.'

'There are crocus all over the United Kingdom, Davies,' explained Professor Jones. 'One crocus isn't significant but I think someone ground a big bunch of crocus together and sprinkled it into her drink to try and poison her.'

'But she didn't die from poisoning,' stated Davies King.

'No, but your murderer tried to poison her. It didn't work so he beat her to death with a spade.'

'And then stuffed her into a suit bag and threw her from the cliffs in a flash of panic when things didn't go to plan,' surmised Davies. 'What makes you think the murderer tried to poison her, Professor?

'Only the rare Meadow Saffron, sometimes known as the Naked Lady or the Naked Virgin, is poisonous. It's not a real crocus. It looks exactly like a crocus but it's one of the lily family,' explained the Professor. 'The toxic Meadow Saffron is capable of lethally poisoning an individual. The victim would suffer a burning throat, intense thirst, and vomiting. Difficulty in swallowing, stomach pain, muscle weakness, delirium, and cardiovascular failure, follow. The victim suffers a slow and painful death and I think that is what your murderer planned to do. I suggest your murderer did some research and decided crocus could poison. They were wrong. Crocus mixed, grinded and put into a drink would turn the victim upside down and inside out with pain and discomfort. And there would be traces of crocus in the stomach, just as I found. If your murderer had used Meadow Saffron, and I suggest that's what he thought he was using, I would have found traces of the alkaloid colchicine. I didn't find colchicine, I found only common crocus. I suggest your murderer made a mistake. They thought all crocuses poisoned and they were wrong. Your murderer reverted to battering the victim to death in a fit of panic when the crocus didn't work.'

'Wow, your some detective, Professor. Now tell me, did he plant the monogrammed handkerchief to lead us onto a false trail or does the MM monogram indicate the murderer is Manuel Martinez?'

'I don't know, Davies. You're the detective. I can only help with time and cause of death,' replied Professor Jones.

'And you have. I am very grateful to you,' said Davies, looking out of the window. 'And you're right about one thing, Professor.'

'What's that?'

'I've never seen a Naked Lady in these parts,' chuckled Davies.

There was laughter and Professor Jones said, 'I've taken dental impressions but I'm waiting for Barney to turn up with dental records. It could take a day or two but I'll come back to you once that's been done.'

'Thanks, Professor.' Davies ended the call politely and immediately dialled Annie Rock as he dodged the ticket collector going about his business.

'Annie…'

Sergeant Rock responded and Davies King conveyed Professor Jones's information on cause and time of death.

'That's interesting,' replied Annie. 'So we're looking for a suspect who grows crocus for research purposes and sews hankies for a hobby.'

'Something like that. Feed that into Detect and it will blow a fuse. Look, I want you to do something for me,' said Davies.

'Such as?'

'I want you to send an email to every officer in the force. I want to know if any of them dealt with any incident between Wednesday and Saturday in the Crillsea Cliffs area.'

'But all those incidents are already in the computer.'

'Yeah, I know but I've been thinking about what you said.'

'And?' queried Annie.

'I recall you told me only recordable and reportable incidents are on the computer. I want to know what's not on the computer.'

'Okay,' replied Annie. 'You're the boss but I think it might be a waste of time.'

'Well, such things often are but can you also raise an enquiry. I want to know if there are any research centres in the area.'

'Research centres? It was a joke, inspector,' stated Annie.

'Yeah, I know, but that's the point. You never know until you've asked,' said Davies. 'Give it a whirl.'

The train continued gently rolling from side to side.

Annie said, 'Will do but while you are on, inspector. We have some results from the scientific support examination at Crillsea Cliffs.'

'Excellent,' replied Davies. 'Anything interesting?'

'There are some surprises. Some expected, some suggested, some unidentified, and some identified; and some that are going to open up a whole new can of worms.'

'Who, Annie?' asked Davies. 'Can you be specific?'

'I think you ought to know that the bill from the forensic science department for all this work is going to blow Chief Inspector Jackson's cheap as chips policy right out of the window,' stated Annie. 'I don't think he was expecting a major trawl to check any DNA found on the murder site against the national database. I kind of think he was expecting you to put a couple of names up for comparison, not the whole bloody nation.'

'Mmm... I forgot to discuss the financial implications of a murder enquiry with him, Annie. Tell me, how much do you think we should spend on catching criminals; a tenner, twenty quid, a thousand? How much is it worth to the public to catch a criminal?'

'Please, inspector, don't drag me into office politics. I've been put in my place already, thank you very much. Look, Harry Reynolds figures as a prime suspect on the Detect computer and he's mentioned in this report. His DNA and fingerprints were found at the scene. He's top suspect. I'll read the reports out to you, shall I?'

Davies King replied, 'Yes, please, Annie. Take your time whilst I make a note or two.' Davies fumbled for his notebook and pencil, listened intently, and eventually said, 'Thank you, Annie. That helps us, I think.'

'Inspector,' asked Annie. 'Where are you?'

'I'm just about to go for a walk, Annie. Thanks, I'll see you tomorrow.' Ending the call, Davies closed his eyes and sank back against the window thinking.

Fifteen minutes later, he was walking out of Waterloo station and into the noisy vibrant capital. Passing the National Theatre, he headed across Waterloo Bridge towards Somerset House and Covent Garden.

Harry Reynolds, he pondered at length as he crossed the road dodging taxis and cars in the process. So the scene of crime officers had used their scientific knowhow and identified his old adversary, Harry Reynolds. Actually, thought Davies, Harry is more of an informant to me than a criminal. Agreed, he's got criminal convictions but he's more use to me outside than inside. Life and criminal investigation was all played out on a giant chess board, wasn't it? No, let's be scientific, thought Davies. In line with the latest developments in crime scene investigation, evidence now existed that Harry Reynolds, local criminal, had left his fingerprints on a table lamp in the second bedroom and his DNA on a chest of drawers in the main bedroom.

There was a blare of a car horn and Davies jumped from the tarmac onto a pavement.

What had Harry Reynolds been doing in the bedroom, speculated Davies? Yet there was also evidence that Peggy MacDonald had left numerous sets of fingerprints throughout the house, as one might expect of a housekeeper who had given her fingerprints voluntarily. But there were a list of suspects which included Jack Creighton, Lydia Bryant and Katrina Helen Kitchener, and others. So much for putting the name of a particular suspect against a crime scene swab, he thought. His request to initiate a national trawl of the DNA database was based on a hunch, and the result had probably provided as much confusion as it did evidence, and a host of names he would never even have considered in normal circumstances. As far as he could tell, Harry Reynolds was a prime suspect since his DNA profile was lodged on the national database and matched the crime scene examination. But Manuel Martinez, Chief Inspector Jackson's primary suspect, had no criminal convictions, had never been arrested in the UK, as far as could be established, and held no such profile on the national database. So, was it right to presume that unidentified DNA found at the scene was that of the suspect Manuel Martinez?

Scientists had revealed Elena's DNA, taken from her body, clearly indicated where such finds had been located and in every place you would expect the resident of the house to be. It just narked Davies that some politicians and self appointed community leaders criticised DNA gathering techniques and strategies whilst failing to recognise the importance of community safety in its widest, and sometimes its narrowest, context. He supported the Commissioner of the Metropolitan Police, who, in March 2008, attended a European Serious Organised Crime Conference in Liverpool, and called for a Europe wide DNA database to be established. Given the notion that the UK was a haven for east European migrants and numerous middle-eastern refugees seeking to escape oppressive regimes, these comments were not lost on the chess playing Davies. He liked to be ahead of the game, not behind it; and the DNA national database was good, but behind the game as far as Davies was concerned. In any event, Davies could not establish from the DNA system whether or not Manuel Martinez's DNA had ever been taken.

Davies startled passersby when he laughed aloud and thought, all I have to do now is work out why all this DNA and fingerprint evidence has been found in the house. Well, Peggy MacDonald? She worked there, but Harry Reynolds and the others? What were they doing there?

Crossing another stretch of tarmac, Davies cut through some side streets and headed into a maze of concrete buildings.

But what occupied Davies's anxious mind? It was that niggling part of the report Annie read out to him on the telephone: DNA analysis reveals a genetic family relationship between Harry Reynolds and Peggy MacDonald! Well, surprise, surprise, thought Davies. So what was Peggy to Harry? Presumably they were brother and sister; he seemed to recall Peggy telling him once she had a younger brother that she seldom saw.

Walking in the density of London, Davies thought deeply about the task ahead of him, and the evidence behind him.

The capital's sinister anonymous streets offered no welcome to the visitor. The best of the day was gone; now there was only the dust of a squalid night. But when Davies walked through the capital he quietly contemplated the value of parked second hand Fords, a couple of old Vauxhalls and one or two rusted wrecks bearing dodgy tax discs that might tell a story. It was as if he were in the overflow of a used car showroom that had been relocated to a never-ending pavement. Yet as he moved through the streets, he gradually realised he was approaching the opulence awaiting him. Progressively, Lexus, Mercedes, Aston Martin,

BMW and Porsche, replaced the cheaper brands and were seen parked next to high end four by fours and an occasional Bentley.

He knew he was getting close when the parked cars seemed to become more and more expensive and colourful, then blooms suddenly appeared in flower boxes employed by a row of exclusive apartments.

'No denims, no jeans, no trainers,' advised a huge but polite doorman at the entrance to *Bella Madras*. On the other side of the street at *Piccallis* someone was saying, 'No casual wear, over eighteens only.'

Ignoring them all, he tracked the scent of money and fast cars until he located *Banano* buried in the streets lying between Shaftesbury Avenue and Covent Garden in the west end of London. Named after the Spanish for banana, Banano offered meals, tapas, snacks, and drinks to tourists and residents alike. But Davies King and London's street wise hustlers also knew that 'banano' is slang for either marijuana or tobacco cigarettes laced with the bitter taste of cocaine. A dark expensive Italian suit, a silk shirt, silk tie and luxurious black leather shoes carried him into the heart of affluence. There were few who would have recognised Davies King that night. And his hair sat fine, cut and smoothed to perfection.

Carrying an overcoat and arranging his loosely draped silk scarf, Davies climbed slight three steps into a luxuriously presented restaurant. Skipping the last step and displaying an amiable grin, he acknowledged a man in a black tuxedo with a nod of his head.

The door was swiftly and obligingly opened for him with the words, 'Welcome to Bananos, signor. Have a pleasant evening.'

Exuding confidence, Davies ambled to the bar and placed his overcoat on a bar stool. He took his time, deliberate and precise in his carefully tuned movements. He knew he was being studied, being watched, being considered by the rich and affluent that were present. It was part of the game he played.

Slowly, he presented his back to the bar and a stylishly dressed barman who was anxious to serve. Davies carefully scanned row upon row of diners, scrutinising faces, checking body language, playing his game, reading the room in the manner he had taught himself. Satisfied with the company, he turned his attention to the barman and with a smile asked, 'Silly question but I presume you have a Spanish brandy?'

'Of course, sir, we have quite a few actually. Did you have a particular brandy in mind?'

'Magno, if you please, young man, a large one.'

The barman attended to a balloon of brandy whilst Davies used reflections in a mirror behind the bar to work out a pecking order of suits, tuxedos, gowns and dresses. The eatery was decked with Spanish décor throughout but its clientele was quite obviously rich and varied. There were no cockney accents to be heard, just a mixture of higher middle class and lower upper class self made nouveau rich that were moving onward and upwards by being seen in the best places in town.

Eventually, his eye caught a woman of distinction sitting alone in a far corner. Her table was roped off, visibly private, and protected by a solitary henchman dressed in a white tuxedo and black bow tie. The man in the white tuxedo, whom Davies assessed as being a bodyguard, stood quietly with his hands crossed in front of him.

The woman was dressed in a low cut white gown. Her hair was dark and trailed away to rest on her ample bosom. She wore dark spectacles and smoked a cigarette whilst reading an evening newspaper.

'On business, sir?' asked the barman, placing a Magno on the bar.

'Always,' replied Davies. 'Perhaps you can help me!'

'Well, I'll certainly try,' offered the barman with a huge grin.

Davies lifted the balloon to his nose and gently swilled the golden liquid wafting the essence of Spain to his nostrils. Then he said, 'Lydia!'

The smile waned slightly from the barman's face when he reluctantly offered, 'Pardon?'

'Lydia Bryant!' replied Davies. 'She's not expecting me.'

The barman looked at him blankly.

Davies nodded his head towards the woman in white sat alone behind the roped area guarded by a man in a white tuxedo. 'But I have business with her. Be so good as to deliver her my card, won't you?'

Davies flicked a business card from a silver case, offered the card with a twenty pound note and said, 'And have one yourself.'

The barman struggled to attract the bodyguard's attention and then responded to Davies with, 'Appointments only, I'm afraid, guv.'

Davies King looked again at reflections in a mirror and saw the bodyguard bent over talking into the ear of the woman wearing white.

'I've been many things in my life but I've never been a guv,' said Davies, laughing politely. 'I've come to do business with Lydia Bryant and do business I will. Who is the man in the white tuxedo, pray tell?'

'Mister Blackstock is Lydia's personal assistant, sir. You'll need to speak with him before you get anywhere near the first lady.'

'Ahh,' chuckled Davies. 'You mean Lydia's bodyguard.'

Davies looked into the mirror, directly into the eyes of Lydia Bryant sat behind a roped area speaking to Blackstock in his white tuxedo. He held her eyes and raised his business card so it could be clearly seen.

She casually removed her spectacles and studied him. He looked very smart, she thought, a man of wealth and substance dressed in such finery. She nodded, and Blackstock approached, gathered his card, and returned to the lady.

Swilling brandy again, standing tall, supreme, and with an air of total confidence, perhaps even a hint of sublime arrogance, Davies inhaled brandy fumes and placed his glass on the bar without letting the liquid spoil his lips. Looking in the mirror he saw her beckon him to her table.

'Look after these, won't you?' ordered Davies, leaving his coat on a stool. Casually, he approached Lydia and stood in front of her table.

She read his business card aloud, 'Manuel Martinez, corporate lawyer. Belgravia address! Now then, Mister Martinez, why on earth would I need a corporate lawyer?'

'Because the Flying Squad is coming to take you down; you and your empire of snow and bananos, and you need a fixer, someone like me, to get you out of it.'

She laughed aloud and then selected an apple from a fruit bowl and began to peel it with a knife.

'And because I can help you and because you know and I know that I'm not Manuel Martinez.'

Lydia was lost for words for a moment but said, 'Police are you?'

'I forgot my brandy,' said Davies. He turned to the man in the white tuxedo and instructed, 'Be a good chap, won't you, Blackstock? The brandy on the bar?'

Lydia thought for a second and then nodded. Blackstock went to retrieve a glass of brandy.

Davies smiled at her and suggested, 'No, I'm not police and I'm certainly not stupid.'

Blackstock returned and placed a drink on the table, Davies thanked the man with a smile and waited for him to retire before he gazed across the table and said to Lydia, 'I'm David Gladstone and I'm a businessman. I'm looking for Manuel Martinez. Unfortunately for him he owes me a lot of money; one million pounds to be precise. You do business with Manuel. He does business with me. Believe me, we have mutual business interests. I believe you can help me, Lydia.'

'What makes you think I'm Lydia Bryant?'

'What makes you think I'm David Gladstone?'

Lydia raised a finger. Blackstone was by her side in a flash waiting for his orders. 'Get Jack,' she instructed softly.

Davies watched Blackstock move away and flick open his mobile.

Somewhere in the restaurant a group slightly the worse for drink began singing 'Barcelona' and a uniquely rotund lady on a neighbouring table clicked her fingers to attract a waiter. She huffed and puffed and muttered at such baseness. 'They need to be reminded of what kind of establishment this is,' she was heard to say in a rather haughty voice.

'The thing is, Lydia, I have absolutely no interest in you,' continued Davies. Reaching inside his jacket pocket, he removed a photograph, placed it on the table and said, 'Other than the fact that you can help me find this man.'

Lydia studied Davies before looking at the photograph.

Allowing his fingers to trickle across the images, Davies said, 'This is Manuel Martinez.' He moved his fingers, 'And this is Elena, and of course, this is the bitch that started it all. She's dead now, of course.'

'Sophie! Dead?' exclaimed Lydia, suddenly taken by surprise.

'Oh, Lydia, how fast your brain works. Have you been on the snow or do you just sell it to your customers?'

The sound of 'Viva Espana' replaced 'Barcelona' and grew in the background. Davies qualified his statement with, 'Not these customers, Lydia. They're high on music…. Aren't they?'

'Sophie is dead? When? How?' she asked.

'Washed up on a beach yesterday I'm afraid. Did you know her?'

'Everyone knew Sassy.'

'Sassy? But that surely wasn't her real name?'

'Sophie,' replied Lydia. 'Sophie de Lorenzo, she was well known here. She adored the west end. How did she die?'

'Well,' replied Davies. 'Someone murdered her.'

'What, how?' quizzed Lydia, concerned.

'They dumped her body on a beach,' said Davies. 'That's all I know. No disrespect intended, Lydia, but I need to catch up with Manuel before he…' Pausing, Davies removed a leather case from a pocket, withdrew a ridiculously large cigar, and rolled it between his fingers.

'Before he what?' Lydia asked.

'Before he spends the million I loaned him and we all end up in court one at the Old Bailey.'

'You are one hell of a cool guy coming in here with a load of bullshit like that, David whatever your name is,' she challenged. Lydia displaced the apple and said, 'Now I suggest…'

'No,' snapped Davies, leaning forward. 'I suggest you listen to me. Manuel moves snow for you. He uses his business contacts and his financial friends to move money around but he relies on your elaborate network of dealers and hustlers to create and sustain demand.'

'I think you'd better leave,' replied Lydia, suddenly drawing deeply on her cigarette. 'You don't know what you're talking about and I resent your implication that I'm some sort of drug dealer. I am a business woman with half a dozen restaurants to run and…'

Davies interrupted, 'Manuel Martinez was using your friend Sophie to help him. I helped finance his last buy from you and now he owes me a million pounds. The Flying Squad is coming for you and you're going down. But if you can help me trace Manuel I can give you a lifeline and a way out.'

'A lifeline! Why would I need a lifeline?' she asked.

Lydia stood up, stubbed out her cigarette and smoothed her dress preparing to leave. 'I made a mistake inviting you over,' she snapped.

'Sit down and listen to me,' demanded Davies.

Lydia looked towards Blackstock but he merely shook his head.

'Oh, you needn't worry about Jack Creighton,' revealed Davies. 'Jack's in the melting pot too. They might even have taken him out already. You never know do you, Lydia?'

'Jack?' Surprised, almost dumbstruck, she sat down and asked, 'What do you want? How do you know such things?'

'A short time ago Benny Abbott was taken out of the game. It was on television. Did you see him?'

Lydia nodded.

'It's even in the Standard tonight. Yes?'

She glanced at the front page of the Standard and nodded.

'The Squad was on Benny for a couple of years before they moved on him. He's history now. His name will be in the paper for weeks, on television maybe, and there will be a trial and he'll be famous until the sentence is passed.'

'So?' she was bemused. 'What's this got to do with Sophie?'

'Hear me out. The Flying Squad will dismantle his business, his family, his finances, and his empire. He'll have nothing unless…'

'Unless what?' she asked interested.

Davies slowly unravelled the wrapping from his cigar and said, 'Unless he talks to them about you, Manuel, Katrina, Jack Creighton: people like that. It's the only bargaining chip he's got left and if I know you're all sitting at the same table eating out of the trough then be assured the Flying Squad does too.'

'Katrina? Jack?' Lydia quizzed.

'Benny will kick and fight but there's no exit for him. He'll take you down and your cocaine network in return for a lesser sentence, somewhere for his wife to live, something for when he gets out, anything to ease the pain of prison. It's not easy going from caviar to porridge.'

'Where do you come into all this?' asked Lydia.

Davies reached across and helped himself to her cigarette lighter. He casually but confidently lit his cigar and said, 'I'm your early warning system. I have friends in France, Italy, America, places like that… even Russia….. They are interested in developing their interests in this country. The Euro and the dollar are so much stronger now since the banking crisis. No, Lydia. I have the contacts to smooth and facilitate the business associates that you need to sell up, take the profit before the sky falls down on you, and walk away. I'm a fixer.'

Lydia studied him.

Davies said, 'Yes, I fix things quietly and without fuss so that people like you can disappear into the woodwork whilst my friends take over your business empire and you sit back in the sunshine and enjoy your ill-gotten gains. I don't create problems; I sort them and fix things.'

'You fix things?' she asked, unconvinced.

'It's hard work but someone has to do it,' smiled Davies.

'Presumably you have credentials?' asked Lydia.

'Where would you like to live? Spain or Brazil?' replied Davies.

Lydia laughed for a second but then changed the subject and said, 'You seem to think Sassy was my friend but I can't tell you much about Sophie,' offered Lydia. 'Go and see Katrina. She had an affair with her.'

'An affair?' asked Davies.

'Didn't you know? When Sophie broke up with Katrina she hooked up with Manuel but it wasn't Manuel she was interested in, was it?' suggested Lydia. 'It was cocaine and money, to some extent, but her main interest was in Elena. She was addicted to Elena, not cocaine. Manuel went mad. He couldn't shift Sophie from Elena, that's why he bought Elena the yacht.'

'Conchenta?' stated Davies.

'Yes, Conchenta, Manuel bought the yacht as a gift for Elena and in an attempt to turn her head from Sophie.'

'Strange name... Conchenta, I mean,' suggested Davies.

'Manuel named it after an island Elena visited regularly, that's all.'

'Interesting but this isn't helping me find Manuel,' said Davies.

The back door of the restaurant burst open and Jack Creighton burst into Bananos and moved swiftly to Lydia's table. Heads turned momentarily at the bar. A doorman wearing a black tuxedo at the front door stepped inside and looked towards the noise. There was a chink of glass, music, the slurred words of 'Viva Espana', and a female customer complaining before everything subsided into normality again.

Approaching the early side of middle age, Jack still enjoyed the physique of a retired middle-weight boxer. His square chin and muscular shoulders seemed to be contained within his well-cut cream-coloured suit, but he sported a cauliflower ear and a nose that looked as if it had been broken more than once. Stepping towards Davies King, Jack's body gained extra strength and bulk when he looked into his adversary's eyes and asked, 'Problems. Lydia?'

Comfortable now, more relaxed, Lydia looked somewhat confident when she said, 'Jack... This is...'

'David Gladstone, Mister Creighton. I'm so very pleased to meet you. I am a business acquaintance of Manuel Martinez,' revealed Davies with a broad grin. 'Who, as we were discussing, owes me a lot of money and I'm extremely grateful to Lydia here for helping me.'

'Don't I know you?' demanded Jack Creighton.

'I doubt it, Mister Creighton. Not unless you've been involved in the fight game, of course,' replied Davies. 'I've many friends in the ring.'

'You a boxer?' suggested Jack, his speech trying to keep up with the speed of his brain.

'Oh no, Jack. I'm a fixer but I'm also a punter! A ringside hustler, that's all I ever was. Now think on this. Benny Abbott is going to grass everyone up,' announced Davies. 'Tell me where I can find Manuel Martinez and leave the rest to me.'

'I know you from somewhere, don't I?' Jack was ordering his mind back, thinking, going through the thought processes of a hundred fights. 'You a copper?' demanded Jack.

'Do I look like a copper?' laughed Davies. He flicked the finely tailored cloth of his suit and tipped cigar ash into an ashtray.

'What's a copper look like these days?' asked Jack thoughtfully. Decidedly, he revealed, 'A man asking questions is not a welcome man.'

'Mistake,' laughed Davies. 'Big mistake, little fella.'

Jack might have had a middle-aged physique to be proud of yet one look at him told you he wasn't the sharpest tool in the box. Jack snarled at Lydia and barked, 'What have you told him, you stupid bitch?'

Puzzled, confused, Lydia backed away.

Jack Creighton closed with Davies and said, 'I think you'd better leave. You're an odd ball if I ever saw one. Weird, you are to come in here with all your fancy ideas and funny questions.'

'Weird?' queried Davies.

'Yeah, weird!' said Jack suddenly seizing Davies by the throat and closing his fingers around Davies King's windpipe. Jack squeezed hard.

Unable to take a breath, gurgling for air, Davies pushed his thumb deep into Jack's eye. Jack screamed and broke his hold allowing Davies time to hunker down low and deliver a jab into Jack's testicles.

There was a terrifying scream from Jack who retaliated with a failed humdinger hitting thin air.

Cruelly, Davies delivered another short but powerful jab into Jack's groin. Seconds later, Davies was attacked by Blackstock, the doorman, and a barman. Over they went rolling into chairs and a table. A balloon of Magnos fell to the ground and splintered across a plush carpet. Golden liquid stained the carpet and a fruit bowl ousted its contents of apples, oranges, and a fruit knife onto the floor.

Davies King reached out and grabbed the knife. Simultaneously, he felt pain shoot through his fist.

'Viva Espana' was replaced by screaming customers and the sound of broken glass as the fracas gathered pace.

Taking two blows to his head and face, Davies pushed away two tuxedos and grabbed Jack by the hair. He dragged him towards the entrance of Bananos knocking over more chairs and tables and bumping into flower vases and other furniture. Screaming people ran away, crockery tumbled over, knives and forks and spoons hit the carpet. And a barman held the neck of a bottle of wine and smashed it against the bar.

Screams and terror violated the atmosphere when Davies pulled the blade of the knife across Jack's throat and threatened, 'Back off! I'll cut him.'

The barman threatened with a broken bottle.

'Don't! Don't!' pleaded Lydia.

Jack squealed, kicked out, and remonstrated with his free hand. 'Keep away,' he managed.

'Manuel Martinez! Where is he?' shouted Davies, moving the blade of the knife closer to Jack Creighton's throat. 'He owes me money. Now tell me.'

Lydia Bryant was close to screaming but garbled, 'At sea in Conchenta; he's in his yacht, you idiot. Let Jack go.'

Davies seized Jack's neck and twisted it saying, 'Whereabouts?

'Don't tell him,' squealed Jack.

'Whereabouts?' demanded Davies, threatening the knife.

'The Azores,' screamed Lydia. 'Now leave him for God's sake.'

Gradually, Davies pulled Jack to the front door holding the knife to his throat as more staff threatened to liberate Jack Creighton.

Fresh air invaded Davies's nostrils, and then there was a bump, a bang, and a clatter as Jack's body met a swinging wooden door, cold cement, and Davies King's helpful knee.

'Sorry,' mocked Davies. 'It's just me making a blunder of things as usual. You should have tried an uppercut.'

A glint in Jack's eye might have been recognition of a fellow boxer from years ago. But he had no name to shout in agony, and no memory that went back that far.

Looking up, Davies feared a barman with a broken bottle and another with a carving knife carrying a blade measuring twelve inches. Hearing the knife swish through the air, Davies rolled, still clinging to Jack, and felt the blade slash across his shoulder. He cried out in pain but dragged Jack Creighton to the front door. Blades and broken glass threatened and challenged Davies King. Screams of panic penetrated the air. Chaos overflowed inspiring Davies to escape.

Davies bumped a squealing, screaming Jack Creighton down three steps onto a dirty, dusty, gutter and then onto oil stained tarmac.

Bump! Bang! Clatter! Car horns blared; tyres squealed, the sound of brakes on dry tarmac! And all the time Jack tried to wriggle away.

Pulling and dragging Jack into the roadway outside Bananos, Davies held the fruit knife to his throat. It was his flimsy ticket to freedom: his getaway. He was on the street feeling the grime beneath his feet and suddenly aware of traffic in the highway. There was a blare of a car horn and Davies turned his head to see a grey Vauxhall nudging towards him.

'Get in!'

The voice was familiar but Davies held Jack Creighton tight and pressed the knife constantly against his skin. Veins in Jack's throat bulged when the blade of the knife threatened to rupture his carotid artery.

'Get in, Davies. For God's sake!'

'Barney?' quizzed Davies.

Opening the nearside door, Ted Barnes leaned across the passenger side and shouted at the top of his voice, 'Get in!'

Davies lifted Jack to his feet and then threw him savagely towards the restaurant as a crowd quickly gathered to watch the debacle.

Diving into the passenger seat, Davies sensed a broken bottle and a knife hurtling through the air into the interior of the car. The bottle smashed against the dashboard; the knife glanced harmlessly from the inside of the door.

Barney heaved onto the accelerator and drove off as Davies fell to the floor with a smidgen of blood slowly oozing from his shoulder.

There was a crash when the front of the Vauxhall collided with a parked car. Barney reversed, gunned the engine, and drove off into the night leaving a badly bruised and beaten middle-weight boxer in a torn cream suit bent double, screaming in agony, and clutching his testicles.

'He's getting away,' shouted Blackstock.

Galvanised by Blackstock, but still in agony, Jack Creighton reached inside his jacket and pulled a revolver from his shoulder holster.

Pointing his weapon unsteadily at the Vauxhall, Jack pulled the trigger. A bullet whistled through the air and smacked into the rear bumper of the car.

People ran screaming from the street. They were terrified.

Three more bullets followed in quick succession, all spraying the rear of Barney's Vauxhall saloon car.

Lydia Bryant, dazed and bewildered, watched the bullet-peppered Vauxhall slew across a street junction and out of sight as she asked, 'Who the hell was that, Jack?'

On all fours now, pained and wrecked with his revolver lowered before him, Jack Creighton sniffed the last exhaust fumes emitting from the disappearing Vauxhall and vowed, 'That's a dead man. That's who. A dead man when I catch up with him.'

'Did anyone get the car number?' shouted Blackstock.

Hours later, Davies closed the door of his flat in Crillsea behind him. He opened the fridge and stuck his swollen hand into a bowl of ice. The ice surrounded his right fist and he prayed it might heal the swelling.

Eventually, he slowly withdrew his hand and wondered if he had finally fallen victim to Boxer's Knuckle. He tried desperately and carefully to straighten the fingers of his right hand but pain struck deep into his fist and electrified his forearm. The sweat poured from his head. Selecting the nearest can of orange he pulled it from the cold and pressed it against his head, his face and his eyes. Flipping the top, Davies chased cool juice down his throat and crumpled the can into oblivion with his good fist.

Bruised and with his fine and expensive clothes torn, Davies undressed quickly, slung everything into a black plastic bag, and headed for the shower. He relished the hot water trickling down his body and tingling damaged parts as the cubicle steamed up and his back rested against a marble wall. Remnants of a black hair dye dribbled down his chin, smeared his throat, and then filtered through the hairs of his chest on the way to a plug hole. On route he noticed his fist was still swollen, perhaps broken. A trace of blood flowed down his body from his shoulder and soiled the shower tray. Davies cried out in pain and anger as the reality of his minor flesh wound struck him.

Plundering a bathroom cabinet, Davies located a pad and secured it to his shoulder with Elastoplasts. Finding his mobile 'phone, Davies rang Al Jessop in London and waited for a response.

'Big Al...? It's all gone wrong, Al. I'm wrecked.'

Davies listened and said, 'Yeah, fun and games in the west end but I bet no-one makes a complaint about a fight in the restaurant.'

Screwing his eyes up for a moment, Davies listened and replied, 'Unconfirmed reports of gunshots but no witnesses that want to talk to the police! Well, well, well! Everyone frightened of retaliation, I presume?'

There was a period when Davies King merely listened before saying, 'Look, I'll never solve these murders bumbling about in Crillsea with an idiot for a boss. I've opened up the door for you; can't you see that? I'm returning Max Fowler in one piece now please, do as I ask. All you need to do is pull the rug from under everyone's feet and play them all off against each other. You said you have a ton of intelligence on these guys, well now is the time to use it and strike while the iron is hot.'

Davies listened, shook his head and said, 'No, do it my way for a change. Lydia is petrified. She's confused, frightened, and not averse to looking for a way out. The intelligence you have on her criminal operation may well be correct but your understanding of her personality is out of date. She's vulnerable to change and she's interested in getting out free, I can tell you. I think Benny Abbott will spill the beans. Katrina will link financially to Manuel and a Sophie de Lorenzo, one of my victims, will too because she's had an affair with Sophie and you can bet your life something will show. Jack is brain dead but he's armed and dangerous and needs to be taken out early doors! The thing is can you provide the killer punch and make it happen?'

Davies King twitched and said into the 'phone, 'I know it's a gamble but the stakes are high and I like winning.'

There was another pause and Davies checked his bandage before replying, 'Max Fowler? Don't you worry about Max Fowler, Chief Superintendent Jessop. I have a plan to help him walk away a free man.'

The 'phone call ended and Davies stowed his mobile.

Checking his swollen fist, he looked into the bathroom mirror and said to himself, 'The trouble is, I don't know what the plan is yet.'

Fifteen minutes and another can of juice passed before Davies King staggered into his bedroom and collapsed on top of the sheets. It was approaching dawn when he finally drifted into a deep sleep in his flat close to Crillsea harbour.

*

Chapter Nine
~ ~ ~

Dateline: Thursday,
The Anchor and Crillsea.

Hauling himself from bed, Davies realised he had slept most of the morning. He felt a twinge in his fist as a bolt of pain shot from his knuckles to the muscle in his forearm. His phone hadn't sounded and no-one, as far as he was aware, had knocked on the door of the flat, or called for him. He'd slept deeply and long. He hadn't been missed, and he knew he owed Barney a big favour.

Fully awake now, he checked the flat for notes left by Max. Interrogating the phone for messages, he decided there were none. Without further delay, he made his way to the Anchor. It was just a short walk to the quiet venue.

'Morning, Bill,' said Davies. 'Any sign of Max today?'

'None at all, Mister Davies, more importantly, what have you been up to? You look terrible.'

'Yeah, would you believe me if I said I fell down the stairs, Bill?'

'No!'

'In that case I'd like a black coffee, please.'

Bill turned to an expresso machine and filled a mug.

'I suppose your mate Max is with Harry Reynolds?' said Bill.

'What? Why do you say that?' asked Davies.

'Oh, weren't they together on the cliffs or something?' ventured Bill. 'They met here, didn't they? Maybe Harry plays chess I don't know.'

'Harry Reynolds playing chess,' laughed Davies. 'I doubt it.' Then more seriously, he asked, 'What were they doing on the cliffs?'

'Well, Harry lives on Crillsea Cliffs with his wife,' offered Bill.

'Never,' said a surprised Davies. 'I thought he lived in town.'

'He did until last year. Harry used to live with his older sister but then he got married and moved to the cliffs,' said Bill.

'Married?' said Davies. 'I'm losing my touch. No-one told me.'

'You've met his sister, of course haven't you, Mister King?' said Bill. 'Peggy, Peggy MacDonald. It's a sad business, and, to be honest, not a good way to meet someone. Through a murder enquiry, I mean.'

'Are you telling me Peggy MacDonald is Harry's sister, Bill?'

'It's common knowledge, Mister King. I thought you'd know.'

'Well, I never,' said Davies taking a sip from his coffee.

'I thought you knew everything about everyone, Mister King,' said Bill, chuckling as he tidied the bar top.

'I wish,' replied Davies.

Turning towards the bay window, Davies spied a couple sat at a table. The man's hand was resting across hers. A loving couple, thought Davies casually. He turned away but then caught their reflection in a mirror behind the bar and turned to look again.

'Yes, indeed, Bill. You learn something every day,' said Davies.

He couldn't believe his eyes for a moment but then he thought back to the two vehicles in the car park outside: the grey Ford Mondeo and the blue Vauxhall Corsa he'd passed on his way into the Anchor. And there before him were the happy couple. It was a meeting, wasn't it? They'd travelled separately in separate cars.

Davies studied the couple as he enjoyed his drink.

He saw the gentle probing touch of his finger on hers, then his hand closing over hers and taking hold of her hand. Davies heard her soft laughter and saw her smile. He saw the deep look of affection in his eyes. Love or was it lust? There was no chauffeur; no mayoral car, no chain of office, no hangers-on, no secretaries, no-one carrying the mace of office or links to the local authority. Just the two of them, it seemed: the Chief Executive of the County Council and the Mayoress of Crillsea. And there he was in the Anchor pub witnessing their moment of indiscretion. What were they called again, he wondered, turning his mind back to the Prime Minister's visit? George… George Samuels that was it, and Abigail Ashton. That's them, he thought and they are besotted with each other.

Pity, thought Davies King, if the chief executive had been a local criminal coveting the woman of a man serving time in her majesty's prison then how well he could have used that moment of indiscretion to cajole, to apply leverage, to encourage, to blackmail, one against the other.

Davies considered himself to be a detective. He wasn't a saint or a vicar, a social worker or a community worker bringing smiles and encouragement to the masses. He was a solver of crimes by any means available to him and if that meant the use of canny blackmail then so be it.

Raising the mug to his lips, Davies tipped the coffee into his mouth and watched George and Abigail enjoy their moment of pleasure.

Davies drank it all down as he planned how Max might be freed. He wasn't bent or corrupt; he was a watcher of people and an analyst of their strength and weaknesses; either to be used when it served his cause.

Davies King was in his office by early afternoon.

'Coffee, black,' Claudia instructed. 'What have you been up to?'

'I fell on a bar of soap in the shower, that's all,' offered Davies.

'Too much to drink, was it?' she asked. 'It's a good job Chief Inspector Jackson isn't here. You've been fighting again, haven't you?'

'It's a long story, Claudia; all about tactics and taking the lead.'

'Fighting over a stupid chess game again, was it?' she suggested.

'Not quite. I played that stupid chess game, as you call it, and offered a knight to try and fool a pawn. I was doing very well. I had all the board laid out and all the pieces in place. Everything was going my way then this other knight suddenly appeared and I had to retreat.'

'Drink this.' Claudia thrust a mug of coffee in front of him and ordered, 'Two paracetamol and some ice for your black eye. I'll swear it's worse than last week.'

'Claudia,' said Davies, conspiratorially. 'I'm one step closer to finding out what happened. Let me tell you…'

'I think you should be asking where everyone is, inspector,' stated Claudia. She shuffled papers into an order pleasing her proficiency and thrust them in front of Davies with a pen. 'Sign,' she demanded.

'Where is everyone, Claudia?'

'They're all busy except Chief Inspector Jackson. He's putting more papers together for his case apparently. There have been some developments recently. That's all I know.'

'What kind of developments?' asked Davies.

'It's all a bit hush-hush.'

'Oh dear, that's something we can do without,' replied Davies.

Claudia Jones became uneasy and turned away from Davies. 'Inspector, it's time I told you something,' she said.

'Please do, what's bothering you, Claudia?'

'I've applied for another job,' replied Claudia.

'What? You've done what?' asked an incredulous Davies.

Claudia passed over the Chronicle and said, 'Page twelve; there's an advert for a personal secretary at the Farringday Trust. The pay is better although I'd have to drive there every day. It's out in the country.'

'Why?' asked Davies. 'I don't believe it's about money.'

'The money has nothing to do with it, inspector. I'm just sick and tired of being taken for granted by everyone and I'm fed up of not knowing who's doing what where. There is so much talking behind people's backs in this place that there is no comradeship to speak of. No-one seems to be interested in doing a good job anymore. It's a disaster.'

'The new generic policy, you mean.'

'Partly, well, the way things are going I will be everyone's assistant soon, not just yours. Apparently there's talk of pruning civilian support staff down and sharing resources. I'm getting out before things get worse.'

'I don't blame you, Claudia, but I'm damned if I'm going to let you go that easy. Now tell me about the Farringday Trust.'

'Not until you tell me what you wanted those new clothes for.'

'A fancy meal out at a Freemason's lodge,' stated Davies.

'You expect me to believe that?'

'Claudia, it' a bit hush-hush as Chief Inspector Jackson would say,' replied Davies.

'God give me strength. I'm surrounded by idiots,' she snapped.

'It's not quite like that, Claudia,' soothed Davies. 'I think you know me better than that.'

'Mmm,' considered a suspicious Claudia. 'Have you been up to something, inspector? Something you'd rather not talk about perhaps?'

'This coffee smells really good, Claudia,' said Davies with a hint of vagueness. Then he took a drink and set his mug down on the table. 'It's nearly as good as my Freemason's banquet.'

Claudia knew the man, had known him for years, knew he was a bumbling, bungling near genius of a man who lived somewhere between the first stage of normality and the last stage of insanity. She also knew when he'd overstepped the mark, gone out on a limb, gone the extra mile.

Intrigued perhaps, she asked, 'Were you careful, Inspector King?'

Davies King questioned her hazel eyes.

'I mean careful not to slurp the soup?' she asked.

'I was careful, Claudia.'

Tending his thriving rubber plant she revealed, 'A little care in what you do can get results. Look how this plant has turned out.'

'Fabulous,' agreed Davies. He completed his reading and activated his pen on paper scrunching the nib as pain invaded his forearm.

'By the way, Constable Webster is awfully busy,' said Claudia. 'He's got another roof job at a jewellers last night: the third, as well as the body on the beach.'

'Good, I'll drop in and see him soon. Is he still on the Detect computer with Annie?'

'I believe so, inspector. Have you heard about our CID car?' asked Claudia.

'What are you on about?' asked Davies.

'Apparently one of our cars was stolen last night. It's been found on the outskirts of Crillsea with bullet holes in the back bumper. Chief Inspector Jackson is looking into it with Detective Constable Barnes.'

'Barney?' queried Davies. 'Why Barney?'

'Because he was first in this morning and went straight to the job,' replied Claudia. 'Apparently Chief Inspector Jackson isn't happy because there are no records of who last drove the car and where it was all last week. It's obvious really, when the car was used exclusively by CID then everyone knew which team had the car. Under this new procedure every Tom, Dick and Harry in the police station has had access to it for a whole manner of reasons. No-one actually knows who last drove it and where it was last parked. Even the log book in the car is missing.'

'So that's the latest developments for Chief Inspector Jackson to look into, is it?' suggested Davies. 'I expect local yobbos with an air rifle are responsible, Claudia. Joy riders, I suspect.'

'That's what Constable Barnes thinks,' answered Claudia. 'Now isn't that remarkable: you and he thinking the same thing.'

'Not really,' Claudia. 'We've known each other a long time. You were going to tell me about the Farringday Trust before we got waylaid.'

'So I was, inspector. It's a pharmaceutical research institute situated inland from Tevington on Sea.'

'I know,' replied Davies. 'I've been reading about it lately.'

'Oh, have you indeed.'

The telephone rang. It was Al Jessop who said, 'Davies, I thought you would like to know; Benny Abbott was remanded into custody for further questioning. I've got him for three more days and then he's back in court.'

'Well done, sir,' replied Davies who turned away from Claudia and said into the hand piece, 'And?'

Jessop replied, 'I've been considering your madcap idea. Benny isn't singing. In fact, he's saying absolutely nothing. I can't push things here when he isn't singing. I can put him inside for a long time but not the others.'

Davies said, 'You need to play chess, Al, if you don't mind me saying so. When you nicked Benny Abbott his arrest was on television and in the newspapers. He was dragged handcuffed unceremoniously into the streets and stuffed in the back of a van. Most of London's top criminals know about his arrest and the closure of his clubs and various toxic businesses. They know there's always a chance a man in his predicament will turn Queen's evidence and do a deal with you. If you do nothing and don't follow up on his arrest then that will confirm in their minds he has kept silent. They don't know anything about his current mouth shut attitude and they won't as long as you have him under lock and key. Are you with me on this?'

'What you driving at, Davies?' demanded Al Jessop.

'Why not move him from West End Central to Paddington Green, sir? It's the most secure police station in the United Kingdom with underground cells and a reputation for housing our top terrorists whenever they are arrested.'

'He's not a terrorist, Davies. We're not talking national security.'

'I didn't say put him in an underground cell and treat him like a terrorist prisoner, Al. No, move the pieces around on the chess board. Can you get the police station transfer on the telly? The toxics will wonder why he's been moved to a top security nick. Once he's remanded in prison, as opposed to a police cell block, he'll get word out that all is well. Our strength is in using this time to act and convey the message to his criminal mates that he has talked and dropped everyone in it.'

'Is that what you call chess, Davies?' quizzed Al Jessop.

'Yes, and it's your move,' replied Davies.

'Most people at my rank sit on their arse in the office and get fat,' replied Jessop. 'I should have stopped in my big fancy office and pushed paper around and not got involved with bloody stupid board games and middle-aged ex-boxers with lifestyle problems who think they are God's gift to the Criminal Investigation Department of police forces and specialist squads they don't even belong to. You come up with some crazy-minded off-the-wall ideas at times.'

'Finished?'

'No, I've not started yet,' barked Jessop.'

'Did I ever let you down?'

'Max Fowler?' growled Jessop.

Davies lied, 'On his way back to the capital soon, I expect.'

There was a brief silence before Jessop acknowledged the statement with, 'I'll need to think about this, Davies.'

'As I say, sir, it's your move.' Davies ended the call abruptly by slamming the 'phone down onto its cradle.

Turning to Claudia, Davies asked, 'Max, any word?'

'Max Fowler was arrested on the cliff paths between Crillsea and Tevington on Sea by uniform staff earlier today,' replied Claudia.

'For what?' asked Davies.

'Assault in the Anchor, by all accounts, but Chief Inspector Jackson has also instructed that Max Fowler is detained overnight pending enquiries into his involvement in the murder of Elena Martinez. Inspector, did you know this new murder computer indicates Max might well be responsible along with someone called Harry Reynolds?'

'May the Lord save us from this imbecile,' argued Davies.

'How can you say such a thing, inspector, Chief Inspector Jackson surely has the best intentions?'

'The man's an idiot, Claudia. Computers are an aide to investigation. They do not replace the senior investigating officer.'

'But the computer is the latest technology available, inspector. Are you going to live in the past all your life?' asked Claudia. 'Are you going to stand in the way of progress every day? It's well known you're not particularly computer literate. Is that why you are not in favour of Chief Inspector Jackson and his intentions, or is it because Max Fowler is a friend of yours?'

There was no reply from Davies King. He was lost in thought somewhere between normality and insanity, reality and fantasy, and Crillsea and Canary Wharf. His mind was on the board, plotting.

'Okay, Inspector King,' announced Claudia. 'If you can sign and date all these papers I'll file them for you and you can get on with tonight's assignment,' she decided.

Reading, then scribbling a signature carefully and slowly, Davies did not look up but asked, 'I'm not going to fall out with you over Chief Inspector Jackson and his computer, Claudia. I value your friendship too much. Understood?'

'I understand. Things are so very confusing at the moment,' she replied. 'I don't quite follow what's going on in this police station.'

'What assignment are you referring to, Claudia?'

'I shouldn't say it. I mean it's nothing to do with me, inspector. Not having upset you once already today.'

'What's on your mind, Claudia?' Davies reached into his desk drawer and ferreted about rummaging with his hands. 'Black and white, get it off your chest and on the board! What's the problem? You've just had a pop at me now I'm entitled to ask.'

'I'm not happy the chief inspector has gone on these hush-hush enquiries and left you a surveillance file to put together on the jewellery shops. He just wants you out of the way completely, and he's more interested in the Mayor's Ball than any murder enquiry. He's dropped everything on your plate if you must know, Inspector King.'

Withdrawing a package from his desk, Davies popped it into his pocket. Then he rummaged for a clip board, pencils, and a police manual.

Claudia continued, 'I think they call it delegation. Isn't that what leadership is about, delegating?'

'No, that's management. Leadership is entirely different, Claudia. So, the chief inspector has left me a surveillance operation to put together on jewellery shops, and no staff to speak of; well I never.'

'Perhaps, Sergeant Rock could help, inspector,' suggested Claudia.

'Don't concern yourself with the surveillance. It will be done.'

Davies smiled, squeezed Claudia's arm, and left his office carrying a police manual and a clipboard. He made his way to Annie Rock's office.

Turning a corner, Davies saw two young uniformed officers standing beside a poster advertising the Mayor's Ball. As Davies neared one of the officers said, 'That's him, say nothing.'

'Everything alright, lads,' asked Davies,

'Yes, sir; no problem, sir,' came the answer.

Davies King watched as the pair scuttled away nervously before exchanging sly smiles.

Strange, thought Davies. He knocked, and entered Annie's office.

'Annie, Webby, how's it going?' asked Davies.

'Wonderful, inspector,' replied Webby. 'We are almost up to date with all this information and all the house to house enquiry sheets have been completed and put onto Detect. And before you ask I've circulated all the property stolen from Crillsea Cliffs and the jewellery shops and...'

161

'Great,' interrupted Davies. 'And what does Detect show now?'

'A seventy-five percent likelihood the two murders were committed by the same person,' replied Annie. 'Manuel Martinez scores seventy five, Harry Reynolds seventy, and Max Fowler sixty per cent likelihood. Chief Inspector Jackson is absolutely delighted with all the work we've put in.'

'Oh my God,' replied Davies. 'A mathematically intelligent computer from Chief Inspector Jackson's mates in the Home Office; can it tell me if Stevie Gerrard will score a hat trick on Saturday?'

Annie Rock laughed and said, 'I'm sure it can give you an estimate of potential if we put in all the relevant information, inspector.'

'Well, try this for potential, Annie. I want you to create a file on Sophie de Lorenzo. I believe she is the body on the beach: the victim. Also known as Sassy, Spanish, I believe, no date of birth, but she's the other lady in the photograph from Crillsea Cliffs. Put her name through the system; find out what you can; detect, if you please.' Davies tapped the Detect computer playfully and added, 'We'll try and help this little man out, shall we?'

'It's a girl,' replied Annie.

'Yes, Sophie is a girl's name. I know that.'

'No, the computer; Detect is a girl,' replied Annie. 'It's a female computer. It must be female it never goes out.'

'What you doing the rest of the week?' asked Davies.

'Washing my hair,' replied Annie.

'Poker,' said Webby.

'You were,' replied Davies. 'I'm sorry but I want you to cancel arrangements and watch this space. You're with me tomorrow, Annie.'

Davies reached into his jacket pocket and withdrew a library book. Handing it to Annie, he said, 'Read this before tomorrow morning, Annie. You'll find all you need to know in Chapter three.'

Taking the book, Annie read the title with interest.

Turning to Terry Webster, Davies instructed, 'Webby, I want you in the harbour at Crillsea. I want a description of the yacht, Conchenta, and then I have a stack of telephone enquiries for you. Somewhere along the line, we have a night surveillance operation to do. Now then, any replies to my email about non recordable incidents, Annie.'

'None whatsoever, inspector, but that's no surprise.'

'Keep on top of the job. I need you two to be on top of the evidence chain and on top of the intelligence and enquiry chain.'

'We're there,' replied Sergeant Rock.

Davies King was buzzing as he closed Annie's door and headed smartly for Superintendent Allithwaite's office.

Knocking on the door, Davies heard, 'Come,' and entered.

Superintendent Bert Allithwaite sat behind his expansive desk neatly arranged with his telephone, his in tray, his out tray, and a trio of photograph frames. There was a photograph of his wife and daughter, an image of himself with his *Class of 2001* taken at the Police Staff College at Bramshill in Hampshire, and an empty gold frame waiting for a photograph of the next President of the Crillsea Golf Club.

Bert Allithwaite immediately opened up with both barrels. 'Ah, Inspector King, I've been trying to contact you. God you look terrible. What have you been doing? Never mind, sit down. We need to talk. I'm told your daily reports are no longer daily; you might have a drink problem and the pressure is getting to you, and, frankly, you're no longer up to the job. Chief Inspector Jackson also tells me you made a cock up of the first murder scene reported. Apparently you missed vital evidence and compromised the investigation of a very serious offence, possibly a double murder. A bloodstained spade missed, he tells me. Not good enough, Inspector King, not good enough at all and perhaps a clear reason why you didn't get the job you thought you deserved. Indeed, Mister Jackson has submitted a confidential file to headquarters, as you know, and to be perfectly blunt, he's called for your suspension pending criminal charges of assault and various contraventions of the Police Discipline Regulations. He has asked me to suspend you forthwith. I'm inclined to agree with him, inspector.'

'And a good afternoon to you too, sir,' replied Davies, 'How nice to see an old friend who's memory is slipping. How's the golf handicap?'

'For God's sake, Davies, have you no understanding of what's at stake here? It's your career, man.'

'I know our two murders may not have been committed by the same person. The Detect computer is wrong. It needs to be sent back to its maker, and at least one of our murders, if not both, is connected to serious organised crime in the United Kingdom. What Chief Inspector Jackson initially perceived to be a minor domestic murder, if there is such a thing, turns out to be a significant murder in the scheme of things. The victims and suspects in these two murder enquiries link to the west end and east end of London, organised crime, money laundering, drugs importation and God knows what. And you want me to quietly walk away with my tail between my legs and conveniently pretend I made a mistake because we didn't see the significance of a bloodstained spade. With respect, superintendent, your chief inspector hasn't got a clue and his cheap as chips policy needs to be....'

'Okay, okay, I get your point, Davies. For God's sake sit down and let's discuss this properly.'

'With respect, sir, you pulled the trigger. I merely held up a shield and dodged the bullets. I came to ask you to authorise a Superintendent's Authority for the Royal Navy to search at sea and to fill you in with the enquiry as it is at this moment in time.'

'Are you involved in this stolen CID car, Davies?'

'Not directly, sir. It's a SCID car now: Strategic Criminal...'

'Enough!' exploded Superintendent Allithwaite

'How long before you retire, sir?' asked Davies.

'I'm not going anywhere until this mess is sorted out, Davies. Jackson is the new kid on the block with all the powers that be behind him. You're the grumpy old guy jealous. He got the job and you didn't, so don't patronise me with jovialities about my golf handicap.'

'Point taken, sir, but I'm not jealous. I'm a King and I should be wearing a crown. Indeed, good luck to Keith Jackson, sir. He got the job and that's fine but I just wish he'd do it properly.'

'Now listen to me, Davies. I see it this way,' continued Allithwaite. 'Jackson is squaring up to put Manuel Martinez, Harry Reynolds and Max Fowler in the frame for the murders on the strength of a Home Office computer being trialled in this station. In thirty years police experience, I can't ever remember a computer detecting a double murder without the so-called senior investigating officer stepping out of the office to speak to witnesses and trace suspects. Now then, Davies, you've got five minutes to convince me why you shouldn't be suspended.'

'I didn't steal any CID car. I went to London to make undercover enquiries in order to trace Manuel Martinez,' revealed Davies. 'I discovered he's on his way to the Azores in Conchenta: a yacht owned by himself, and recently berthed here in Crillsea Harbour. I'm not sure he committed both murders but we need to trace him and shake him upside down to see what falls out. He links strongly to organised crime in central

London and we are on the verge of making a massive strike against some major crime gangs in the capital.'

Bert Allithwaite sat quietly for a moment and considered the tale. 'Undercover, you say, on whose authority?'

There was no reply.

'Organised crime, major London crime gangs, on whose analysis?'

'Detective Chief Superintendent Al Jessop, Head of the Metropolitan Police Flying Squad and the officer I have been dealing with in respect of our London enquiries.'

Pausing for a second, considering the matter, Bert Allithwaite then said, 'In any case the Azores are African, aren't they? If my memory serves me well, we have no extradition treaty with Africa.'

'The Azores are off the African coast but they are owned by Portugal, sir,' replied Davies. 'The Extradition Act, 2003, covers arrest and legal procedures. It's a category one country, sir.'

Davies passed over a manual opened at an appropriate page.

Bert Allithwaite glimpsed at the manual and said, 'Yes, I know what a category one country is, Davies, thank you. Is that why you want a search at sea authority?'

'Yes! The Royal Navy have what they call a Fleet Ready Escort. It's a warship maintained at a high state of readiness around the UK on short notice standby for deployment anywhere in the world. HMS Albion, for example, in April, 2010, rescued over five hundred personnel from Santander in Spain when those volcanic ash clouds grounded European air flights. Historically, they've deployed for counter narcotics operations off the coast of Spain and elsewhere and they seem to be the correct tool, sir. If you'd turn to page 139 in the manual, you'll see what I mean.'

'Your wife, Davies,' said Bert Allithwaite. 'She was thrown overboard when a yacht collided with yours and she drowned. We never traced the offending yacht despite all the enquiries we undertook. Are you obsessed with this Conchenta yacht for all the wrong reasons?'

'There's never a day goes by when I don't think....' Davies paused for a moment but then said, 'I need the authority for a search at sea, sir. I think we'll find Manuel Martinez on board.'

'Bert Allithwaite cradled the manual before quickly turning to the relevant page. He read briefly and said, 'It's a long time since I've signed one of these but let's give it a go. I'll give you authority and I'll make arrangements with the Ministry of Defence and draw up the paperwork.'

'Thank you, sir,' replied Davies.

'But you still have a big problem, Davies.'

'And that is?'

'Chief Inspector Jackson! He'll be at the Mayor's Ball and you can bet your life he'll be sidling up to the assistant chief constable and querying why you haven't sorted these murders out and why you haven't been suspended. He's a dangerous man, Davies, and his game is politics.'

'You sound just like a friend of mine, sir,' said Davies.

Davies King reached the door before Bert Allithwaite asked, 'Davies, how did the CID car get bullet holes in its bumper?'

Turning briefly, Davies replied, 'Yobbos, I suspect, sir; young toxics with an air rifle and a couple of bottles of cider inside them.'

Davies King was gone from Superintendent Allithwaite's office before a reply was heard.

Bert Allithwaite shook his head. He didn't believe King for a moment but he knew him well enough to know he was probably onto something important. He drummed his fingers on the table, reached for a pen and a page from a manual, and then set them on his desktop. He paused to reflect. Quietly, he studied his photographs and thought to himself, it's only a game of golf. Do I really want to be president of a golf club when I can make or break so many people? To sign or not to sign, that is the question? If I sign and they locate Conchenta, Davies has a fighting chance. If Davies is correct then Jackson and Patterson will be finished. If I don't sign, King is finished and Jackson and the wolves from headquarters will tear him limb from limb and drool over the carcass.

'What the hell,' said Bert Allithwaite aloud, 'There's plenty of years left to be a golf president.' He pushed over an empty gold photograph frame, took up his pen, and signed on the dotted line saying, 'It's my division, isn't it?'

Outside in the corridor, Davies walked to the cell block and stood at the entrance. He knew he would see Max in a few minutes.

Davies paused, contemplated the door in front of him, and thought for a moment. Slowly, he turned and walked out of the police station and headed home to change a dressing and confirm his shoulder had stopped bleeding.

Yards away, Max stood in a grey dank cell studying the dark tiled walls in the half light shining from the ceiling. He shrugged his shoulders and listened to the moans and groans of neighbouring cell mates. Lifting his hands to his head, Max wondered if anyone knew; if anyone cared, and how the hell he was ever going to get out of his predicament.

That night in Crillsea Meadows police station, Police Constable Mark Tait buttoned his tunic, booted up his computer, and prepared for the start of a new tour of duty. Two emails caught his attention. The first indicated that the station would close in three weeks time and he would be redeployed to Crillsea Town Centre on uniform patrol. There were details of when the removal van would call for his furniture and belongings, and where he and his wife would live in Crillsea. The second email was from Annie Rock of CID.

Opening his desk drawer, Mark Tait rummaged inside as he read Annie's email. He withdrew the 'Farmer's Weekly' magazine and recounted in his mind a conversation with Tommy Watson. Hitting his keyboard, Mark Tait began to formulate a reply. It might be of use, he thought; probably not, but he would send it anyway.

The telephone rang and Mark answered it.

'Crillsea Meadows, PC Tait... A missing person...A young child...' Reaching for a pad and a pencil PC Tait continued, 'Name, age, description.... Yes, I'll be there right away. Mark Tait tore the message from a pad and stuffed it inside his tunic pocket. 'Missing child,' he shouted to his wife. 'I'm off.'

'Take care,' he heard her reply.

'Love you!'

'Love you too!'

There was a slam of a door and a crunch of a leather shoe on a gravel driveway when Mark Tait hurriedly left the police station with an unsent email sitting in a computer waiting for a finger to press a button.

*

Chapter Ten
~ ~ ~

Dateline: Friday
Central London, The Farringday Trust, Tevington on Sea, and Canary Wharf.

It was rush hour in the capital.

There was a blue light flashing and a siren wailing when the big double doors of West End Central police station in Saville Row opened and a white liveried police van emerged onto the street with its headlights on full beam.

Police outriders filtered into place escorting the vehicle as it threaded its way through central London's traffic on its way to Paddington Green police station. Uniform officers stepped into the roadway and stopped traffic as the motor cycles sped ahead of the vehicle and ensured its uninterrupted passage. The streets were a mass of sirens and flashing lights supported, here and there, by strategically placed armed uniform officers carrying a range of firearms to protect their charge.

Escorted by six prominent motor cyclists as it travelled on its high visibility journey to Paddington Green, the police van became a focus of attention for many interested parties and passersby.

The van travelled along Regent Street, across Oxford Circus, down Portland Place passing Broadcasting House, and turned left into Marleybone Road. Here, it skirted Regent's Park. Within a few minutes the van roared past Madame Tussauds Wax Museum and reached Edgeware Road where it turned into the United Kingdom's most secure police station.

The two miles from West End Central to Paddington Green, through the busy streets of London, took only five minutes but the carefully planned prisoner transfer was seen by countless thousands of people, and a gaggle of cameramen and television reporters who turned out for the rush hour news story dominating London's television screens and newspaper stands for the rest of the day.

The Press had received a 'tip off' apparently, from an official source that was unofficially official, it was said. It's 'just to fill a ten second news slot' it was said, and 'just to keep the police-press relationship meaningful', it was said. The unspoken establishment of life was in full flow. What was the story? The police had moved Benny Abbott to the most secure cells in the country.

Why? What was so important about Benny Abbott? He wasn't a terrorist, was he? Was he a Supergrass? Had he turned Queen's Evidence? He'd been remanded in police custody according to the newspaper, but why had the police moved him to Paddington Green? Was it because he was seen as a really important prisoner? Had he tried to escape from police custody? Was it because the police didn't want anyone getting anywhere near Benny Abbott?

The word was on the street, and the word was Benny Abbott was doing a deal.

Back in Crillsea, Annie Rock and Davies King were on their way to Tevington on Sea. Davies was driving and the leather patches continued to dominate the old jacket he insisted on wearing.

Annie was asking questions. 'I take it the book you gave me to read is an important part of this enquiry, inspector?'

'Did you find it interesting, Annie?'

'Well,' replied Annie, 'I recall putting the details of the share certificates and documents you found at the house in Bartholomew Wharf onto the Detect computer. The Farringday Trust was amongst them; there was an old P45 in Elena's name, but I never gave it much thought until you gave me that book to read and told me about Sophie de Lorenzo.'

'I want a clear mind on this subject, Annie. You're a good judge of character when you're not biting Chief Inspector Jackson's hand off and I'd value your opinion on today's outcome. You're my sergeant; I've let you down lately because I've wandered off into my own little world. I'm sorry.'

'Thank you, inspector,' replied Annie. 'I don't think I did myself any good falling out with Chief Inspector Jackson but tell me, did you know Sophie de Lorenzo used to work at the Farringday Trust?'

'No, I didn't know,' replied a surprised Davies.

'You asked me to put her name through the system. I did. She has a national insurance record linking her to the Farringday Trust. She worked there for a few months some time ago then the record ends, presumably because she was no longer in full time paid employment with them, or anyone else for that matter. And Professor Jones rang; her dental records match his findings. We've successfully identified the victim as Sophie de Lorenzo.'

'Interesting,' mused Davies. 'Two women murdered and they both once worked at the Farringday Trust. It has always bothered me why Elena kept an old P45 from her former employer in a floor safe, strange?'

'Oh, some people just don't get round to sorting out paperwork, inspector. I still owe the milkman for last month,' advised Annie. 'If you were Keith Jackson I'd be telling you that a proper murder squad and an incident room would have sorted out who worked where and when within twenty four hours of the deceased being identified, and a whole lot more.'

'Yeah, well, it didn't work out that way, Annie,' replied Davies. 'You wouldn't expect resources to deal with a minor domestic murder would you?'

Annie chuckled and replied, 'Not under this new policy, no.'

Davies changed gear and overtook a slow moving wagon.

'The library book records the history and complexity of the pharmaceutical industry but obviously doesn't supply much local information,' said Davies. 'Certainly, not what we want to know as far as the Farringday Trust is concerned.'

They were through Tevington on Sea, off the dual carriageway, and onto a main road leading inland through England's green and pleasant countryside.

'I was astounded when I read those pages, inspector. It's hard to get your head around the size of the industry. There are over two hundred pharmaceutical companies throughout the world fighting for a share in a global market in prescribed tablets worth more than seven hundred billion dollars a year. I just cannot imagine that kind of money.'

'What's that in beer and brandy vouchers?' asked Davies.

'Close to four hundred and fifty billion British pounds, I believe. I looked it up on Google,' chuckled Annie.

'Oh dear,' laughed Davies. 'You're a secret computer geek, aren't you? 'You're probably on Twitter, Facebook and every other social networking site imaginable.'

Annie laughed.

'Talking about Google, Annie, what do you make of our Detect computer?'

Annie considered, winced, but then answered, 'It's good. I'm impressed with it. I love the ability to scan in about a dozen sheets of documents, statements, and such like, at a time, and the system reads and analyses everything. There's no need for a team of input clerks to sit typing data into the machine every day. If you query a word; well, take blue for example, Detect will look up blue as a colour or colours; you know dark blue, light blue, or azure blue, and it's also a mood. Hey I'm feeling blue today. Understand? Never mind, Detect is quicker and holds more information than the last one we had.'

'And the mathematical function?' queried Davies.

'Well, there's the big problem; Detect gives you a read out based on a statistical analysis of probabilities that a suspect committed the murder and then expresses them in percentage terms.'

'Mmm...,' said Davies. 'Is there a likelihood someone could just say Google it and then totally believe in the results without any objective investigation?'

'Yes,' agreed Annie. 'It's a great computer with a dubious outcome if the user doesn't stand back and ask the question, 'What's not on the computer'. It's like you reading a murder scene then you eventually stop what you're doing and ask everyone what's missing; you know, like that lap top in the Crillsea Cliffs house the family are paying for but isn't present, for example.'

'And you'll be reporting your findings to the Home Office via Chief Inspector Jackson will you?' asked Davies.

'Of course, that's what he wants, and Chief Inspector Jackson is right about one thing, inspector.'

'What's that?' asked Davies.

'Good technology is time saving, labour saving, and a great attribute to the police service provided it works well.'

Davies said, 'Hey, maybe there is something to this generic policy after all, but tell me, Annie, what's the current possibility the murderer works at the Farringday Trust?'

Chuckling, Annie answered, 'About five percent, unless he's a jewel thief in which case it's seven.'

They were approaching a cross roads when Annie advised, 'Left here, inspector. It's another five miles according to the signpost.'

Onto a minor road with Tevington and Crillsea disappearing fast behind them, they headed into the countryside. The road narrowed further and a series of bends and a hunch back bridge followed.

'Good, we'll be there soon. Apart from enquiring about our two victims, I'm interested in finding out who owns the Trust and how long they've been in business,' said Davies as he slowed to accommodate the changing road. 'Most of today's major pharmaceutical companies were founded in either the late nineteenth or early twentieth century. The discoveries of insulin and penicillin in the Twenties and Thirties created a market for mass-manufacture and distribution. Switzerland, Germany and Italy seem to have driven the industry in those days with the UK, America, Belgium and the Netherlands following on behind.'

'Yes, I saw that,' stated Annie. 'It quite fascinated me but I wondered if you were looking at the law on the testing and approving of drugs and the need to label them correctly. Have you come across something I've missed?'

'Not that I'm aware of, Annie.'

The road straightened out into a long level lane where a stream ran parallel to the road and a high palisade fence could be seen in the far distance.

'Okay, it's just that I do understand the difference between prescription and non-prescription drugs and I studied all the papers on that crocus poisoning scenario Professor Jones put together. It's interesting reading about scientific research, don't you think? You don't suppose, no, surely not?'

'Do you think one of these research scientists is going to tell us they've been experimenting with crocus, Annie?' chuckled Davies.

'Well, it all seems to start with something like that. Research took off big style in the Fifties when DNA and a microscopic understanding of human biology led to more sophisticated manufacturing techniques.'

'You have been busy, haven't you?' stated Davies.

'And you haven't, inspector?'

'We'll need to find out what kind of drugs this Farringday Trust develops, Annie. And who owns the Trust? All kinds of drugs were developed during the Fifties and Sixties: the Pill, Cortisone, blood-pressure drugs and heart medications, and then tranquilisers ushered in the age of psychiatric medication. Did you know Valium is the most prescribed drug in history?'

'Yeah , I'm taking ten a day to calm me down and get some sleep with all the problems we have at work,' replied Annie.

'I'm taking brandy myself,' laughed Davies.

'Don't forget thalidomide, inspector; that was a disaster: a tranquilizer taken by pregnant women which caused severe birth defects. Do you think the Farringday Trust had anything to do with that?'

'I doubt it, Annie, but I don't know.'

'Well, the thalidomide problems led to the World Medical Association issuing its Declaration of Helsinki in 1964. They set standards for clinical research and demanded that people give their informed consent before enrolling in any experiments. Pharmaceutical companies had to prove beneficial change in clinical trials before they could market drugs.'

'It's a never-ending industry; drugs for cancer, AIDS, heart disease, everything,' said Davies. 'So, in my mind I'm wondering what scientific research might have to do with crocus, drugs, pills, a yacht, and an island in the Azores. There's a link somewhere and we need to find it.'

'I think we're here, inspector.'

'Oh yes, I think you're right,' said Davies turning left and following a signpost to the Farringday Trust. 'Oh my God, it's a prison.'

They had arrived but they weren't at the entrance, not yet. And it was obvious to them both the Farringday Trust was more than just a building in England's green interior.

Davies slowed and drove parallel to a high palisade fence bordering a compound where the Farringday Trust was situated. The exterior fence protected an interior fence sporting razor wire that looked cruelly down upon the observer. Every hundred yards or so there was a plain grey mast that towered upwards and carried close circuit television cameras focused on No Man's land lying between the two fences. But what really caught their eye was the third interior palisade fence which created yet another area of No Man's Land. It was as if the compound were protecting nuclear materials or top secret military equipment such was the security precautions in place.

Annie pointed and said, 'Armed guards?'

Following her outstretched arm, Davies replied, 'No, but they might as well be by the look of this.'

Stopping at the security barrier, Davies smiled when a uniform officer approached the vehicle and politely asked whether they had an appointment.

'We're police officers here to see Mister Rupert Farringday, by appointment,' replied Davies producing his warrant card.

The guard checked his clip board, nodded and said, 'Inspector King and Sergeant Rock, yes; you're expected. You'll need a visitors pass. Please step into the control post and sign in, sir. You can park your vehicle inside the control zone where CCTV will monitor your vehicle as a precautionary measure. A security officer will escort you to the main building. Please observe the signs, sir. Smoking, mobile 'phones and cameras are not permitted inside the main building.'

Complying with their request, Davies and Annie soon found themselves walking down a tarmac drive towards a broad based building. The building was surrounded by gardens but an immaculate lawn, decked out with a croquet court, dominated the front of the premises. The double doors at the entrance were guarded by two smartly dressed burly uniforms but as they entered the building they soon became aware of a tall moustachioed gentleman descending a marble staircase.

Rupert Farringday exuded elegance and confidence in equal portions. Dressed in a grey lounge suit, white shirt and matching tie, he extended his hand and said, 'Inspector King, I presume. Allow me to introduce myself. I am Rupert Farringday. My secretary dealt with your appointment in my absence but it is so nice to meet you, inspector. Please do come and join me.' Turning to Annie, Rupert smiled and said, 'And Sergeant Rock, welcome to the Farringday Trust.'

There were handshakes before Rupert swivelled his arm and instantly dismissed the uniform escort with, 'That will be all, thank you.'

Pointing up the staircase, Rupert suggested, 'My office is on the first floor. Will you join me for tea, coffee perhaps? I hope you don't mind me saying so, inspector, but you look terrible. Have you had a fall?'

'Nothing to worry about, Mister Farringday; just a minor altercation with a wall, that's all,' acknowledged Davies.

Annie threw a disbelieving sideways glance.

'Well, as long as you're alright, inspector,' replied Rupert Farringday. 'It's all very exciting having the police call; we haven't had a visit since the crime prevention officer popped in last year, or was it the year before? I expect you want us to look at some materials of some kind but I have to tell you both that we are a research establishment; we are not licensed to carry out forensic examinations for the police. Mind you, I expect we would be cheaper, don't you think?'

Rupert led the way up the marble staircase, twisted the end of his moustache, chuckled to himself, and then said, 'I understand you are from

Crillsea, we usually get the odd visit from Tevington police if there's any poaching or suchlike in the surrounding area, and, of course, we always make some form of donation to the children's Christmas party, but Crillsea police! Well, what brings you all the way from Crillsea, may I ask?'

'You mean you don't know?' asked Annie.

'Know? Know what?' asked Rupert Farringday.

'The two ladies who worked here!' queried Annie.

Interjecting, Davies King said, 'I explained the reason for our visit to your secretary when I rang to speak to someone in charge, sir.'

'I'm sorry, inspector, but I presumed you were investigating a crime in the area of the Trust. I haven't a clue about two ladies. Now, can I help you or not. I've so much to do today,' replied Rupert Farringday.

'What's your position here, sir?' asked Davies.

'I'm Chief Executive Officer, inspector; I run the show for your information. At least that's what my shareholders tell me.'

'We're investigating two murders, sir. Do you know Elena Martinez and Sophie de Lorenzo?'

Rupert Farringday paused half way up the staircase, turned to face them both, curled the end of his moustache again, and said, 'But of course I do, inspector. Sophie was a personal assistant here and left us a couple of months ago but Elena is one of our top scientific research analysts. She's foremost in her field, actually. How can they help?'

Remaining silent, Davies King looked directly into Rupert Farringday's eyes, and allowed his message to sink in.

'No, oh no,' realised Rupert Farringday, paling slightly 'Tell me there's some been some kind of mistake; surely not, inspector, sergeant?'

'I'm afraid the inspector is right, sir,' replied Annie. 'We're sorry to be the bearer of such bad tidings but I can't believe you haven't heard about these murders. Details of these crimes have been in the local newspapers and on regional television. Surely, you must be aware.'

'Forgive me for a moment,' replied Rupert leaning against the banister, visibly shaken, obviously upset.

'I'm sorry, Mister Farringday,' intervened Davies. 'Sergeant Rock is right. Surely you are aware of the deaths of these two ladies?'

'No, no,' answered Rupert Farringday wearily. 'I'm shocked beyond belief. I've just returned from Switzerland, you see. It's actually my first day back at the Trust for over three weeks. I'm taken aback by all this.'

'I'm terribly sorry, sir,' said Davies, 'We seem to have unintentionally delivered bad news. Would it be better if we continued this in your office?'

'Yes, yes indeed; come with me please,' replied Rupert.

Struggling to keep his composure for a moment, Rupert Farringday took a deep breath, fingered his moustache at length, steadied himself, and then led his guests to the first floor and into a salubrious office decorated with a palatial desk, coffee machine, computer monitors, bookcases, a drinks cabinet, armchairs, and a television set.

Immediately engaging with the television, Davies watched a clip of a police van being escorted through London by a number of police motor cyclists and armed officers. The clip ended when the police convoy turned into Paddington Green police station.

Switching his television off with a remote control, Rupert Farringday approached the drinks cabinet. Opening its glass doors, he turned and said, 'I need a drink; whisky, brandy, anyone?'

'No, thank you,' replied Annie swiftly. She stole a sudden sideways glance at Davies King and replied, 'Coffee would be good though.'

'Of course,' replied Rupert Farringday. Turning to a coffee dispenser, he poured two cups, mounted them on saucers, and handed them over.

'Okay, let's start again,' announced Rupert. 'How can we help?'

'Who owns the Trust, sir?' asked Davies.

'It's a family concern, Inspector King. The Farringday family own the Trust and we've been in business over thirty years. We're quite well established in the field of pharmaceutical business.'

Rupert Farringday poured himself a drink in a fine crystal tumbler.

'And why is it called a Trust, sir?' asked Davies.

'Yes, I understand why you are asking that question, inspector. Actually, we are not a charitable trust or anything like that. No, the Farringday Trust is our trading name and we use it to promote the company logo to our business partners,' explained Rupert Farringday knocking back a large whisky.

'The company logo?' queried Annie.

Farringday turned to Annie, smiled and said, 'If you can't trust a Farringday, who can you trust?'

'I don't trust anyone myself, Mister Farringday,' stated Davies.

Rupert Farringday stared at Davies King and tried to penetrate his innermost mind.

Noting his opponent's distrustful eyes, Davies asked, 'So, if the Farringday Trust is your trading name, what's your business name, sir?'

'Farringday Pharmaceuticals plc.'

'You explained you are Chief Executive Officer, Mister Farringday. Which other family members are involved in the business?' asked Davies.

Taking another small mouthful of whisky, Rupert discreetly depressed a switch on the underside of his desk and then replied, 'I am the oldest of three brothers. My younger brother, Richard, is Operations Director and my youngest brother, Robert, is our Finance Director.'

'Thank you,' replied Davies, 'Annie?'

Davies King ambled to the bookcase and eyed some titles.

'Elena, Mister Farringday, what was her role in the business?' asked Annie Rock.

'She was one of our top scientists, sergeant,' replied Rupert Farringday. 'She worked exclusively on drug research and she was very good, highly qualified, and a scientist of the utmost integrity.'

'What kind of work did she do, sir?' asked Annie.

'Highly confidential, sergeant,' replied Rupert curling his moustache.

'Such as?' pressed Annie.

'I'd rather not say. There's too much at stake,' replied a cautious Rupert.

'In general terms, Mister Farringday, that's all I'm asking at this stage?' said Annie Rock.

'Mmm...' considered Rupert patiently. 'Very well, in general terms, the Trust trialled and tested a vaccine on monkeys in Africa and...'

The door opened suddenly and in walked a clean shaven gentleman bearing a close resemblance to Rupert. He too wore a smart casual suit with a crisp shirt and a silk tie.

'I came as soon as I could, Rupert. Are you having problems?'

'Not at all, Richard; I want you to meet Inspector King and Sergeant Rock from Crillsea police.' Rupert Farringday turned to his guests and introduced his brother saying, 'This is my brother, Richard, our Operations Director. He's much better placed than me to discuss these things with you. Richard, they are investigating the murders of Elena Martinez and Sophie de Lorenzo.'

'Oh dear, Elena and Sophie, how terrible, can I help at all?' asked Richard Farringday.

'I take it you have heard about the two murders, sir,' suggested Davies. 'On the television or in the newspapers, I presume.'

'No, this is my first day back at the Trust in three weeks. I've been abroad, inspector,' replied Richard Farringday.

'Abroad? Were you with your brother Rupert?'

'Not at all, Rupert was in Switzerland following up on some possible staff acquisitions - research people we are interested in employing - I was in Barcelona attending a seminar on the latest industry developments. Why do you ask, inspector? You surely don't think we had anything to do with this?'

Davies King turned and looked out of the window, thinking, whilst he took in the croquet lawn below.

'How well did you know the two ladies, Richard?' asked Annie. 'You don't seem overly concerned they are no longer with us whereas your brother, Rupert, was quite shocked.'

Richard stole a sideway glance at Rupert who snapped, 'Oh for God's sake, Richard, tell them. They'll find out anyway.'

'I didn't get on with Sophie,' stated Richard emphatically. 'I sacked her.'

Richard made his way to the drinks cabinet, selected a glass tumbler, and poured himself a whisky before continuing, 'She was trouble and spent more time eyeing up other women than I could stand, plus she wasn't very good at her job. But as far as Elena is concerned, I hated her.'

Richard looked deep into his whisky before downing it in one gulp. Turning to face Davies King, Richard said, 'Elena wouldn't do a thing she was told and wouldn't keep to the budget Robert allocated her. She carried a torch for truth, honour and justice, and hadn't a clue about the cut and thrust of business in the modern world. She was a liability that couldn't be written into any set of business accounts I've ever come across. If you must know, I was looking for a way to dismiss her and would have done so without an ounce of remorse.'

Richard reached for a decanter in order to pour himself another drink but his brother, Rupert, gently covered his hand and shook his head.

'Well, thank you for being so honest with us, Mister Farringday,' said Davies. 'But can you explain to me what Elena was doing that threatened your budget and made her carry a flag for her own beliefs?'

'No, he can't,' said Rupert. 'It's commercially sensitive and we do not have to tell you such things.'

Annie Rock intervened and asked, 'You were telling us about research monkeys in Africa, sir. Would you care to finish telling us what monkeys in Africa have to do with the death of Elena Martinez?'

'Monkeys?' snapped Richard. 'Those bloody monkeys didn't murder Elena, if that's what you think.'

Sudden alarm dashed across Annie's face.

'Just as I was saying,' smiled Rupert Farringday moving in to reassure Sergeant Rock. 'Forgive my brother, sergeant, but he's upset and tired after so much hard work lately.'

Ignoring his brother, Richard declared angrily, 'Yes, we tested a product on monkeys in Africa under a strictly controlled budget that I, correction, we, had set. We were very generous in our allocation. But then what did she do? What did she do? I'll tell you what she did.' Richard became furious and began pacing the floor. 'She went to the Azores, found an island in the middle of a bloody ocean, and began testing the vaccine on the bloody natives without our permission; that's what she bloody did. The budget went through the roof, for God's sake. It cost us a fortune and there was no stopping her. Spend! Spend! Spend! That was her password.'

'Conchenta?' queried Davies King loudly.

Stunned! Richard and Rupert Farringday were visibly stunned to hear the word 'Conchenta' slip from the lips of Davies King.

'I said Conchenta,' repeated Davies forcibly. 'Was that the island in the Azores where the natives were tested?'

'I think it's time you left, inspector,' declared Rupert Farringday. 'You seem to know far too much about our operations in the Azores and...'

'So I am correct in my allegation regarding Conchenta,' demanded Davies swiftly interrupting Rupert and holding his ground.

There was a loud knock on the door followed by a bout of giggling and laughter. The door opened and a man and woman waddled into the centre of the room. They were obviously under the affects of alcohol, if not drunk. The curvaceous blonde female spoke first when she looked at both Davies and Annie. She giggled, and said, 'There's been a murder.'

Annie and Davies exchanged glances.

'Which one of you is Sherlock Gnomes and which one is Hercule Parrot?'

As soon as she spoke, Davies realised she really was drunk. Within seconds the man took hold of her and said, 'I'm terribly sorry, chaps, Carla has had too much to drink at a staff party. I do apologise.'

Carla tried to become more circumspect and sober saying, 'No, Rob, there really has been a murder. That woman has been killed while you were away, the one who keeps leaving her keys at work. Silly cow, she is, well, was,' Carla fell into a drunken giggle again and allowed her long blonde hair to tumble down her back.

Not at all amused, Rupert Farringday moved quickly to gather Carla into his arm and guide her to a seat. 'My youngest brother, Robert,' announced Rupert. 'There you have us all now, inspector. Satisfied?'

'I'll be satisfied when I get to the bottom of these murders, sir,' replied Davies. 'So, you are the Finance Director, am I correct, sir?'

'That's me,' replied Robert. 'They call me Rob and this is Carla my secretary.'

'Fiancée,' muttered a drunken Carla. 'I'm a financier's fancy fruity fiancée.' She frittered the sentence away and laughed.

'Yes, well, I think this is an appropriate time to close proceedings for the day, don't you agree, inspector?' implored Rupert.

'One moment, Mister Farringday,' replied Davies King. 'Haven't we met before, Robert?'

'I think not,' replied Robert. 'I would have remembered.'

'Oh well, my mistake,' said Davies. 'But a couple of final questions if you don't mind; for example, Robert, are you aware we are investigating the murders of Elena Martinez and Sophie de Lorenzo?'

'I was told by security you were here and quite a few of the secretaries and typing pool know about it. In my position I have to attend certain functions and we've just been to a leaving do for one of the secretaries. Carla is the worse for drink because she got involved with some of the ladies and, well never mind, it's just a couple of drinks too many. The thing is, inspector, the Trust is just a small village really, you know. You must forgive Carla for her silly outburst. There was nothing personal meant by it.'

'It's irrelevant, sir,' replied Davies. 'Did you get on with the two ladies, Sophie and Elena, that is?'

Rupert intervened and said, 'Enough, I think you should say no more than you need to, Robert.'

'Oh no, I always insist on a reply from the innocent,' demanded Davies. 'You've nothing to hide, have you, Robert?'

'She was a lovely woman,' replied a thoughtful Robert. 'I had a lot of time for her but she played hell with my budget constraints, totally ignored them, and did things her own way. It's terrible she's been murdered, inspector, but if I were you I would concentrate on her husband or a boyfriend. You won't find your murderer here, I'm afraid.'

'Why do you say that?' asked Annie.

'I've been away in America attending a seminar on the pharmaceutical industry. I think you'll find we were all abroad at the time of the murders,' replied Robert Farringday. 'I left here two weeks ago. When was the murder?'

'Obviously whilst you were in America, sir,' replied Davies.

'Thank you,' replied Robert.

'Whereabouts in America, sir; it's a country I've always been smitten with?' asked Davies King.

'Why, New York, of course,' replied Robert Farringday.

'Yes, indeed,' said Richard Farringday. 'That's all settled then.'

'All settled indeed,' confirmed Rupert. 'We are all obviously innocent of these terrible murders since none of us were in the UK during the relevant time period. Now will that be all, inspector?'

'I've a question,' said Annie.

Rupert Farringday was obviously growing a little frustrated but gave way and said, 'If you must, sergeant.'

'Well, it's simple really, Mister Farringday. We'd like to take DNA samples from the workforce, with your kind assistance, of course.'

'What! This is preposterous,' argued Rupert shaking his head. 'Inspector, your sergeant can't be serious surely?'

Davies King was a little lost in thought studying Carla but he turned and said, 'That perfume, I remember now.'

'I beg your pardon,' said Rupert.

'Oh, sorry, Mister Farringday, yes, my sergeant is absolutely correct. Have any of you been to the Elena Martinez house?'

'Absolutely not,' barked an irritated Rupert. 'Richard? Robert?'

There were no replies from the brothers so Davies imposed himself with, 'In that case we won't find your DNA at the murder scene, will we, gentlemen?'

'Come with me, Inspector King,' said Rupert inviting the two police officers out of the room. 'You two, stay here.'

Angrily, Rupert Farringday led the two police officers out of his office, barged his way down the marble staircase, and along a corridor. Reaching the end of the corridor there was a door from which a number of people were emerging. They all wore white coveralls.

Rupert Farringday announced, 'This is where Elena worked, occasionally Sophie. It's our laboratory. This is Farringday Pharmaceuticals.'

A white coverall glided passed them and stepped into a small recess in the wall. Davies watched the figure press a button on a display screen and then place his hand on the screen.

'Fingerprint recognition?' asked Davies.

'Indeed, yes,' replied Rupert. 'Fingerprint and palm, actually.'

'Can we see her workplace, sir?' asked Annie Rock.

'I'm afraid not, sergeant. It is forbidden to access the laboratory any further on the grounds of commercial confidentiality. We must preserve our industrial secrets, you see. You do understand that, don't you, inspector?'

'I can get a search warrant if I need to, Mister Farringday. I'm not here to play ping pong with you. I have a job of work to do. Look, I just want to have a look at their workspace, that's all,' explained Davies. 'Any letters, notes left, personal stuff that might help, that's all.'

Rupert Farringday placed his hand on the screen, watched his hand impression turn purple and the machine do its job, and then smiled warily when the door slid open. 'Come,' he said. 'Let's get this over with.

I'm trying to run a multi million pound business here and, quite frankly, I can do without this.'

Annie, Davies and Rupert walked into the laboratory where Rupert escorted them directly to a stainless steel work station situated in one corner of the laboratory. The worktop was exceptionally clean.

'Help yourself,' said Rupert. 'The cupboard's bare because the rules of our laboratory are nothing is brought into this building and nothing leaves this building that is of a personal nature.'

'Nothing at all?' queried Davies.

'No, nothing,' confirmed Rupert Farringday. 'That way, we don't allow any covert devices that might be tape recorders or cameras: apparatus likely to compromise our operations and lead to our competitors being au fait with our work, inspector.'

Davies nodded an acknowledgement whilst scanning the area.

Annie strolled, checking for anything out of place.

Spotting mortar and pestle and a variety of microscopes and scientific equipment stacked on one of the worktops, Annie alerted Davies with a tilt of her head in their direction.

'Notes are dictated into machines incorporated in the ceiling above the worktops,' revealed Rupert Farringday pulling a microphone cable down from the ceiling to head height. 'The notes are typed by our staff. We don't allow mobile 'phones or cameras because this site is protected and secure. Personal belongings are prohibited on site.'

'What's in there?' asked Davies pointing to a door at the far end of the laboratory where access to another room appeared to be apparent.

'That's the sharp end of the industry, inspector,' revealed Rupert. 'I can't take you in there because it's retina scan entry only and the complex does not have your retina scan on record. Apart from that it is potentially dangerous.'

'What's in there?' repeated Davies.

Rupert Farringday sighed deeply and said, 'Do you ever take no for an answer, Inspector King?'

'No, Mister Farringday, not when I'm investigating a murder.'

Pausing, Rupert Farringday considered his position for a moment and then reluctantly explained, 'Biotechnology, inspector: a field of applied biology using living organisms and bioprocesses in engineering, technology and medicine. In our case, medicine is the primary research factor. Here, or rather, in there, genetic engineering and cell and tissue

183

culture technology is the daily diet of some of our specialist staff: people like Elena. We use a wide range of procedures that can modify living organisms, cultivation of plants, and improvements to breeding programs employing artificial selection and hybridization. In other words, it's the application of scientific and technical advances in life sciences to develop commercial products, and this is where we do it, inspector. And, for your information, that part of the building is maintained at a constant temperature, inspector, it's the growing season.'

'You cultivate plants; how interesting! Do you cultivate crocus?'

'No,' replied Rupert Farringday. 'Most of the plants we have on site are from North America, South America, the Amazon basin, and, in some cases, the high plateaus of certain countries in central eastern Asia. We occasionally use reptiles, such as snakes, to extract their venom so that we can analyse toxicity and establish whether or not we can apply the snake venom extract to a medical application. That's fairly common practice, inspector, considering there are about three thousand known species of snake in the world. Why do you ask about crocus, Inspector?'

'I analyse toxicity in people, sir. I think someone tried to poison Sophie by administering a concoction of poisonous crocus to her.'

'Goodness me, inspector, that explains why you have been so direct in your questioning,' replied Rupert. 'Well, I'm sorry to disappoint you both but that's quite ridiculous. Scientists here have access to a wide range of ingredients all of which are under intense security. But if I were to commission any of them to poison someone it wouldn't be by the administration of crocus, inspector. No, not at all, that's quite ridiculous.'

'Oh well, I apologise, Mister Farringday,' chuckled Davies. 'I suppose that's the kind of stupid thing someone would do with a little bit of knowledge gained from reading books or suchlike. You know what they say about a little bit of knowledge in the wrong hands.'

'I accept your apology, Inspector King,' replied Rupert Farringday, smiling. 'It's about time you were brought to your senses.'

Annie said, 'There's mortar and pestle on some of the worktops. They are similar to mortar and pestle found in Elena's house. What use is a mortar and pestle to your scientists, Mister Farringday?'

'For grinding and mixing ingredients, Sergeant; but actually a lot of the work they carry out relates to studying the DNA of a particular organism, like a plant, for instance. This is usually accomplished by computer-aided microscopic analysis in advanced technical conditions.

Hence, our most secure unit is extremely commercially sensitive and access is restricted to a handful of individuals who have provided retina scans for comparison to our sophisticated security system. Our security policy is rigidly enforced and I have great difficulty in helping you any further due to the discreet, dare I say, Top Secret, nature of our business.'

'That makes sense now, Mister Farringday,' said Annie.

'Indeed, it does,' added Davies. 'Thank you for clearing up that mystery for us, Mister Farringday.

'It was my reason for bringing you both to the laboratory,' stated Rupert Farringday. 'I was getting very annoyed upstairs but I'm surprised you still haven't understood why I brought you here.'

'You'll have to explain, Mister Farringday,' suggested Davies. 'We're obviously missing something.'

'You suggested all staff in the Trust might give DNA samples. Presumably, this will allow you to compare them with samples you have found at the scene of the crime.'

'Correct!' stated Annie Rock.

'And my point is that people who work here, as I have quite clearly demonstrated to you, live and breathe, twenty four seven, fingerprints, retina scans and DNA analysis. Do you really think people from this type of background would leave such evidence behind at the scene of a murder, inspector? Of course, they wouldn't.'

'Not unless they panicked, Mister Farringday,' replied Davies. 'Not unless an individual panicked and made a silly mistake. But tell me, what was Elena Martinez working on? In general terms, sir, general terms only would suffice in view of your security policy?'

Rupert Farringday walked slightly away from them, considered thoughtfully, and then turned and replied, 'Elena was working on drug research in order to secure a patent. She wasn't working on generics. She had made a discovery and had applied for a patent. She just hadn't quite followed the full patent procedure through.'

'Why not?' asked Davies.

'Elena was in the process of tidying her application up. She'd submitted the patent application but I understand she was strengthening procedures before making a final amendment to the paperwork. She said she had to go to the island...'

'Conchenta?' suggested Davies.

'Yes, Conchenta, but the fact that you know about Conchenta bothers me, inspector. It troubles me a lot.'

'I know Manuel Martinez, Elena's husband, bought a yacht and named it Conchenta,' replied Davies. 'I believe Conchenta is an island in the Azores, Mister Farringday. Do you know the exact location of the island of Conchenta?'

'That's what troubles me, inspector,' replied Rupert Farringday. 'There is no such island as Conchenta.'

'The Conchenta Conundrum?' queried Davies King.

Smiling slightly, Rupert Farringday replied, 'There is a very small island in the Azores which Elena code-named Conchenta in order to protect her work. We live and breathe commercial security here, inspector, as you can see. You have obviously come across papers or a file or something that has led you to Conchenta.'

'Oh, just the yacht and a brief note pencilled in a book,' replied Davies 'That's all, Mister Farringday, nothing to get worried about.'

'Are you sure, inspector, sergeant?'

'Can we ask why you didn't push this patent through if it was so important?' asked Davies.

'I encouraged Elena to get the paperwork submitted before our competitors latched on as to why she was in the Azores, and then you tell me she has been murdered, inspector. I presume she has been murdered by some sex-crazed jealous lover,' said Rupert Farringday.

'Can you tell me exactly where the island is, sir, and exactly what Elena had discovered?'

'No, I will not, inspector,' replied Rupert Farringday vigorously.

'Why not?' demanded Sergeant Rock

'You have been told much today; much more than one might normally impart to non members of the Farringday Trust. But I want to make this clear to you. We have quite obviously indicated to you both that the three of us were out of the country when your victims were murdered. Furthermore, I have unmistakably explained to you the futility of taking DNA samples from people professionally and scientifically involved in DNA processes. I refuse to divulge the location of the island and I refuse to disclose what exactly Elena was working on. You see, these matters have a potential commercial value to us worth billions of pounds over the next decade or so. And you, sergeant, how much do you earn in a month?'

Annie exchanged looks with Davies but had no time to reply since Rupert Farringday followed through with, 'Don't answer, Sergeant, and you, inspector, what do you earn in a year? Don't tell me, I don't want to know about your overtime and your silly little allowances. What I do know is that you have made it clear to me that you do not trust people.'

'It comes with the job, Mister Farringday,' replied Davies.

'Such a pity for you both,' Rupert Farringday replied.

'What are you driving at?' demanded Davies.

Rupert Farringday replied, 'I have no intention of entrusting you with commercially sensitive top secret information worth more than the two of you could ever earn together in your entire futile irrelevant lives.'

Davies listened carefully, sighed, and slowly nodded his head.

'Now I'm asking you to leave for the very last time,' declared Rupert Farringday quite forcibly.'

Davies studied Rupert Farringday's eyes intently and responded, 'I think you've made your point quite expertly, Mister Farringday. Thank you for your time. We will be on our way. Come on, Sergeant Rock.'

Without further ado, Davies King was striding out of the room, down the corridor, and standing at the front step scanning the croquet lawn whilst waiting for Annie Rock to catch up.

With a crunch they were treading the tarmac towards the security control, their car, and a journey back to Crillsea.

As Davies King was slamming his car door shut at the Farringday Trust, Police Constable Mark Tait removed his boots and explained to his wife, Elsie, how he located a missing child sleeping in a barley field not far from home. He'd been up half the night and all he wanted was his sleep.

Mark yawned, yanked off his tie, and climbed the stairs to bed.

Downstairs, in Mark's office, Elsie shouted to her husband, 'Mark, do you want me to send this missing person report off. I see you've completed the incident log. Shall I send it for you?'

'Oh, yes please, Elsie. I just want my bed. I'm exhausted.'

'Okay, sleep well.'

Elsie Tait, wife of a village policeman, had picked up quite a bit of police procedure over the years.

Elsie held no fear of computers and police incident logs detailing the result of enquiries undertaken.

Carefully, and with interest, she read the missing child report detailing a successful outcome. No changes required, she thought as she pressed the send button and transmitted Mark's report to headquarters.

But still waiting patiently was an unsent email in the out box. Elsie read the email Mark had formulated for Annie Rock and quietly pressed the send button. Both emails would be on the headquarters server within the next fifteen minutes.

Elsie switched off the computer, tidied Mark's boots away, and closed the office door behind her. And so ended Elsie Tait's contribution to being a village policeman's wife: minor computer administration.

'I can't believe you wrapped up that visit so quickly, inspector,' argued Annie Rock. 'We were making headway there and I had a stack of questions still to answer.'

Davies was gunning the car back towards Crillsea at a fairly respectable speed when he replied, 'You're absolutely correct, Annie. Problem is we went there to ask a few background questions and ended up virtually interviewing the main man. We've too many unanswered questions and a score of things we must now do. And we seem to have rattled three brothers by the name of Farringday and I'm not at all sure any of them are telling the truth.'

'So what next?' asked Annie.

'I want you and Webby to do profiles on the three brothers. Start with the usual; employment history, things like that. But ring the Tevvies and see what paperwork they've got on the establishment. Didn't Rupert say they'd had a visit from the Crime Prevention Officer?'

Annie said, 'And they donated to the kids Christmas party.'

'Find out who they have been talking to in the police about crime prevention and such like, Annie. Somebody knows these people and I want to know what they know.'

'I'll make a start as soon as we get back,' replied Annie.

'And more jobs to do, I'm afraid. I want you in London first thing tomorrow morning. We've a list of questions and I want the answers. The next time we speak to Rupert and his cohorts we'll know the answers before we ask the questions.'

'Now you're talking, inspector.'

'Problem is, they only want to talk about what they want us to know. They don't want to answer the real underlying questions.'

'Well, can you answer me this?' asked Annie.

'I'll try,' replied Davies.

'How would Elena discover a drug on an island?'

'Ah well, discovering drugs is the process by which potential drugs and medicines are discovered or designed. Most drugs have been discovered either by isolating the active ingredient from traditional remedies or by pure chance,' explained Davies. 'For example, the plant Echinacea is found in north and Central America and it has proved quite effective in common colds, would you believe. They reckon Red Indians used it years ago long before scientists discovered its potential, Annie. The Indian squaws used to eat the leaves of the plant to get rid of a cold. Would you Adam and Eve it? But think of it this way, by handing down such recipes and old wives tales from one generation to another, a legend is born. It was only a question of time before the recipe fell into the hands of research scientists who visited the area. The rest is history.'

'Do you know something, I can understand that perfectly,' said Annie. 'And as I understand it government authorities have to be totally sure that a drug works before it can be used on real people.'

'That's right,' confirmed Davies. 'And that's the Trust's problem, I think. The patent hasn't been fully submitted. Why? We need to find out. It's important because historically there have been increasing accusations and findings that clinical trials conducted or funded by pharmaceutical companies are much more likely to report positive results than negative results. There's too much money at stake as Rupert Farringday made clear. Some researchers who have tried to reveal ethical issues with clinical trials or who tried to publish papers showing harmful effects of new drugs or cheaper alternatives have been threatened by drug companies with lawsuits. These things aren't as clear cut as they would have us believe. We're on to something, Annie, but how we get the answers to our questions is another thing.'

'What about the biotech laboratory?' asked Annie. 'Why can't we just get a search warrant?'

'Waste of time, I think. No, we need Elena's personal laptop computer; her husband, Manuel locked up; and a stack of answers to questions on our board.'

'Do you think Manuel murdered his wife?' asked Annie.

'Not sure,' replied a thoughtful Davies. 'There's too many balls up in the air at the moment. We need to do a bit more investigation; back to basics, Annie, I think.'

'What's a generic drug?' asked Annie. 'If I remember your library book correctly, it's the clustering of tablets into groups offering the same treatments. You know, the same drug is made by two or more different companies and does exactly the same thing. In fact, the drugs might even have different names but still do the same thing.'

'Yes, that's it,' replied Davies pulling out to overtake a slower moving vehicle. 'A generic drug must contain the same active ingredients as the original formulation. They are identical in dose, strength, route of administration, and safety. Funny isn't it, Annie?'

'I'm not with you, inspector,' queried Annie. 'What's so funny?'

'Chief Inspector Jackson's generic policy is about making the service cheaper, doing away with specialists, trying to get better value at cheaper prices. It's nearly the same with drugs,' laughed Davies.

'In what way?' asked Annie.

'Elena was working on a patent. If she'd successfully jumped through all the hoops and everything worked okay the Trust would have secured a patent licence agreement to manufacture a drug for, oh say twenty years. In that time, no other company could sell that drug. A drug, or what we call a medicine, which has a patent is a specialist; an expert, the only one of its kind.'

'Got you,' replied Annie.' But after the patent licence expires twenty years later, every other pharmaceutical company can then produce the drug at a cheaper and more affordable price because the patent has expired.'

'Generics!' laughed Davies King. 'General, basic, broad, common, nonspecific, standard, commonplace, that's what it means.'

'A patent: the longer exclusive rights licence lasts, the more money the pharmaceutical company is likely to make,' suggested Annie. 'That's what Rupert Farringday meant when he said he was running a multimillion pound business.'

'When generic products become available, market competition is bound to lead to lower prices for both the original brand and the generic forms,' explained Davies. 'Drug patents give twenty years of protection, but they are applied for before clinical trials begin, so the effective life of a drug patent tends to be between seven and twelve years. In that time the company who discovered a plant ingredient, for example, and then discovered a medicinal use for it, can make an absolute fortune.'

'The common denominator in the drug discovery and patent business is therefore money,' said Annie decidedly.

'Yes, big money!' confirmed Davies.

'So why didn't Elena Martinez apply for the exclusive rights a patent carries before clinical trials on that island in the Azores?' asked Annie Rock.

'That's what we need to find out, Annie.'

'Interesting, but we could just be running round like rabbits caught in the headlights, inspector. We've too many motives emerging here.'

'It's like chess, Annie. We need to take a few pawns out, that's all.'

Davies King found the open road, put his foot down, and headed for Crillsea.

Luke Lowther of Kendal would rather have been home in his council flat at Kirkbarrow, Kendal, with his young wife who was expecting their first child soon. But it wasn't to be. Today he was 'Starboard Watch' on board HMS Cumberland: a Royal Navy frigate. The ship was negotiating the English Channel on its way from Dogger Bank south towards the Channel Islands.

HMS Cumberland was the sixteenth ship of her name to be so called and was an ambassador for the glorious county of Cumbria lying in the north west of England and encapsulating the Lake District. The English Channel was about five hundred miles wide between the English mainland and the French beaches of Saint Malo, but only twenty one miles wide in the Dover Straits. Over five hundred vessels a day negotiated one of the busiest seaways in the world and the entire traffic system was policed by radar technology from a relatively small control room in the town of Dover.

Luke scanned the seas with his binoculars taking in the tankers and ferries carving through the waters as they weaved their careful way through the deadly passage. He saw a yacht out there. Focusing his binoculars he homed in on the thirty-five foot ocean-going yacht with her twin outboard engines dropped at the stern and her sails curled and at rest.

'Starboard Watch to Bridge, there's a yacht dead ahead, crossing our bow, range one thousand yards.'

'Roger, Starboard Watch,' echoed the reply. 'Confirm you are reporting a response to the search at sea message received this morning?'

Luke Lowther couldn't remember the name of the vessel they'd been instructed to look out for. Was it Concertina, Congenial, Cumcatch? He couldn't quite remember.

'Stand by,' he replied.

The yacht reduced speed, turned with the wind behind her, and her sails suddenly unfurled to display her true profile.

'Conchenta,' he whispered to himself quietly, and then loud and clear he bellowed into the radio, 'Confirmed the vessel dead ahead westbound at one thousand feet is named Conchenta. It's the one in the message, Bridge.'

'Roger, Starboard Watch, Bridge, come left ten degrees, slow ahead both; I'll notify Dover control.'

Following the yacht, Luke turned slightly as the frigate ploughed onwards towards an exercise with its French counterparts off the Channel Islands. He took in the outboard motors and the full sails now capturing the wind. There was a figure on deck. It looked like a man but from the distance and the mist hovering over the Channel, it was difficult to tell.

Luke watched as they journeyed south and Conchenta headed towards the mouth of the River Thames.

Minutes later, an operator sat in a control room in Dover located a small blip on a radar screen and reported, 'Target locked and held, designated Metro Alpha One. Route plotted, course plotted, speed one five knots. Metro Alpha One is on my screen and holding inbound east.'

Turning into the car park at Crillsea police station, Davies King wasn't surprised to find a lack of parking space for their vehicle. As usual, the area was cluttered with police vans, cars, motor bikes and visitors. Eventually, he found a slot, inched his way in, and pulled on the handbrake.

Slamming car doors behind them, Annie and Davies approached the rear door of Crillsea police station as Ted Barnes walked into the car park.

'Just the man,' announced Barney, withdrawing a book from inside his jacket. 'Here you are; one murder diary updated and ready for signature, Davies.' Barney handed the diary over.

Accepting the diary, Davies replied, 'Are you a mind reader, Barney?'

'Probably, but I'll tell you now, it's not totally up to date,' said Barney. 'I haven't fully written up the Bananos incident, Davies. You'll have to do that. I've declared an undercover operation in being to which I am not signed up to and have no knowledge of, okay?'

Davies King paused and returned a long blank stare before replying, 'Annie, can you fill Barney in with today's investigation at the Farringday Trust and the profiles we need?'

'Of course, inspector,' responded Annie Rock.

Davies nodded his thanks and said, 'I need to make a few 'phone calls. We'll talk later, Barney.' Davies King walked on.

'We'd better talk now, Davies,' advised Barney. 'Our illustrious leader, Keith Jackson, wants Max Fowler and Harry Reynolds arrested for murder, and he wants you in charge of the arrest team. He's been asking for you, Davies.'

'Max is already under lock and key, isn't he?' queried Davies.

'For assault, yes,' replied Barney. 'But that's not enough for Jackson.'

Stopping in his tracks, Davies asked, 'Go on then, Barney. Tell me what we've missed. I presume there's evidence against Max and Harry?'

'Only what's on the Detect computer, Davies, unless Jackson has something up his sleeve,' said Barney.

'Barney, you'd better listen to Annie because our leader, Mister Jackson has his foot in the wrong camp.'

'That's the problem,' said Barney. 'The nick is divided between you and Jackson. There are a lot of youngsters inside that building you're just about to enter. They're having to choose sides between you and Jackson, Davies. For me, it's easy. I'm always going to be on your side. I can retire pretty much whenever I want. The bosses can't hurt me. But Annie here, she could make DI or DCI one day and Webby and the others are all sick of the backbiting and pain that comes with having incompetence, arrogance, and uncertainty as the domineering factors at work; to say nothing of some stupid generic policy that seems to underpin everything and belongs in a shredder. I told you, Davies. I told you not to play politics but you didn't listen, you wouldn't bloody listen as usual; so now people are having to choose which camp to put their foot in, yours or Jacksons.'

'I'm with you, boss,' intervened Annie Rock. 'I'm in no hurry to go anywhere.'

Davies smiled at her and said, 'Thanks, Annie,'

Dealing with an angry friend was never easy but Davies confronted Barney and demanded, 'Surely the evidence is more important than politics, Barney? Surely, the man hasn't lost the plot completely?'

'I don't know any more, Davies. I'm as confused as the next man. What I do know is you'll need to play the game the way Jackson wants it played,' advised Barney. 'At the moment that means playing politics, following the Detect computer, and concentrating on Max Fowler and Harry Reynolds as the main murder suspects.'

Davies King shook his head, spun on his heel and headed towards the door.

There was a sudden cry of pain from Davies King when his knee collided with Bert Allithwaite's briefcase.

'Ah, Davies,' cried Superintendent Allithwaite, 'Just the man, I'm on my way to a meeting at Crillsea golf club. I've left a message with Claudia but the MOD has been on. The Navy has located Conchenta.'

'In the Azores?' queried Davies.

'No, in the English Channel at the mouth of the River Thames off Southend,' replied Allithwaite. 'Has that set the cat amongst the pigeons?'

'No, I think he's going home,' responded Davies.

'Canary Wharf,' declared Annie Rock. 'The family home in Bartholomew Wharf, superintendent.'

'Well, wherever he's going you'd better get down there and get him locked up,' ordered Superintendent Allithwaite.

Davies was stunned for a moment.

'It's what you wanted, Davies. The Navy have responded. It's up to you now.'

'I can't go, sir,' suggested Davies. 'Mister Jackson wants to see me apparently. I understand he wants Harry Reynolds and Max Fowler arrested for these murders. I'll have to do as I'm told.'

194

'Since when did Chief Inspector Jackson run this division?' snapped Bert Allithwaite. 'You wanted an authorised search at sea and I gave you one, Davies. It's time people around here understand who is in charge here. I am. Now get down to London and get your man arrested, Davies. Now!'

'Very good, sir,' replied Davies. 'Barney, you're with me. Annie, find Webby and hit the road. Channel twenty one and not a moment to be lost. Let's go people; no time to lose.'

'The golf club, Davies; I'll be at the golf club, home, or in the office. Keep in touch, man.'

'Daily, sir,' replied Davies. 'On a daily basis even.'

Superintendent Bert Allithwaite threw a twisted glance at Davies, snarled, 'Hourly, Davies, every hour on the hour,' and hurried to his car somewhere in the car park.

Ten minutes later, Davies, Barney, Annie and Webby, were on the open road, out of Crillsea, entering the motorway and heading for London with the accelerator pedal hard down on the floor and Davies King on a telephone to Flying Squad boss, Chief Superintendent Al Jessop.

The journey to London was accomplished in record time.
As the two Crillsea vehicles left the motorway, two silver coloured BMW 1200 GT motor cycles liveried in Metropolitan police Battenberg led a silver coloured BMW series 5 'Touring' armed response unit from the motorway into the heart of the capital. The Crillsea vehicles slipped in behind as Barney fought to keep up with the timely escort provided by one Al Jessop.

They were into the capital with a blare of sirens and blue flashing lights, dodging traffic and running red lights, and Davies King talking on a radio to a sergeant on a police boat following Conchenta down the Thames towards Canary Wharf. They were approaching Millwall and flat out along Pestons Road when the river police sergeant informed Davies King that Conchenta was moving to a berth close to Bartholomew Wharf with her outboards stowed and her sails curled. They were into Bartholomew Wharf with a river police boat nearing the berth but no sign of life aboard Conchenta and no sign of a murder suspect making an escape.

Indeed, the cupboard was bare and the only humans in sight were half a dozen people standing in a bus queue on Pestons Road near a bridge across the waterway into Canary Wharf and the Blackwall Basin.

'Annie, hold at Peston Road, proceed on foot direct to the flat,' radioed Davies. 'Barney and I will take the yacht.'

'I'm closing the area down,' boomed Big Al Jessop intervening on the radio net. 'Secure the arrest. My squad will lock it down.'

As the Crillsea vehicles pulled into Canary Wharf, six unadorned Flying Squad cars swung into Pestons Road and broadsided the road system closing the area down. Jessop worked the radio nets as liveried police cars followed in a colourful display of flashing lights and noisy sirens as London's finest encircled the area and blocked off the roads. Only the London Docks rail system was able to move freely inside Jessop's circle and they were too far from a station for a rushed getaway to be considered.

'Where the hell is he?' asked Barney.

Davies King was out of the car and running towards Conchenta with Barney following and Al Jessop struggling to keep up some distance behind as he rattled orders into his radio.

Meanwhile, Annie Rock and Terry Webster parked their vehicle and cautiously approached Bartholomew Wharf on foot.

'There he is,' shouted Davies pointing from Conchenta along the quayside towards a man walking away from them carrying a large holdall and wearing blue denim jeans and a blue seaman's anorak. 'He's making for the flat,' radioed Davies.

'I have him,' replied Annie.' He's walking straight towards us.'

'The holdall, Annie, the holdall,' shouted Davies.

'Don't mess my operation up,' radioed Jessop. 'Do you have a warrant for the yacht?' screeched Jessop.

'I won't need one, guv,' replied Davies. 'We intend a lawful search of the yacht after arrest to secure immediate evidence... Annie, can you assist?'

'Wait one,' radioed Annie Rock.

The holdall was heavy and long but the walk from the berth to the flat lasted only about two hundred yards. The man was over six foot tall, clean shaven and broad across the shoulders. He walked on unaware of the drama unfolding around him. Clasping the strap of his holdall tighter with his free hand, he became aware of the couple walking towards him.

'Manuel Martinez?' queried the young man.

There was no answer.

'Are you Manuel Martinez, sir?'

'Who wants to know?' he asked.

'Detective Constable Webster,' replied Webby holding up his warrant card for inspection. 'We need to talk to you.'

'Stand still,' boomed a voice.

Webby turned and realised one of the armed response unit had drawn a bead on Martinez and was in the process of taking control of the situation.

'Armed police,' boomed the armed response officer. 'Drop the holdall and stand perfectly still.'

'What do you want?' demanded Manuel.

'To talk to you, sir,' explained Webby. Webby held up his hand and signalled to the armed response officer to lower his weapon.

'About the murder of your wife,' confirmed Annie Rock.

'My.... my wife....' stuttered Manuel. 'I don't understand.'

'I think you do, sir,' declared Annie. 'Put your holdall down and stay exactly where you are. Webby!'

As the armed response officers moved closer Terry Webster withdrew his handcuffs and closed with the Spaniard who responded by saying, 'How do you know who I am?'

Annie replied, 'I've lived with your photograph for a week, Mister Martinez. I'm sorry but we want to have a long talk to you about why you killed your wife and it's not going to be here. We need to go to a police station.'

'You don't understand; I didn't murder my wife. I loved her. There's been a terrible mistake.... I... Oh, no.... Oh, surely not...' waned Manuel.

'Now I don't understand, sir,' explained Webby, somewhat confused at Manuel's diminishing display of fortitude. 'Hold your hands out please, Mister Martinez. I'm arresting you for the murder of Elena Martinez.'

'I didn't do it. I didn't kill her. It wasn't me.'

Manuel Martinez backed off, stepped slowly backwards, and retraced his steps as armed response officers moved closer.

'Not Elena, no, not Elena, I didn't kill Elena,' he said. A stark look of grief, horror and disbelief crossed the Spaniard's face and contorted his features in a mismatch of bizarre incredulity.

Suddenly the penny dropped; it was like a bolt of lightning striking from the sky and opening up a chasm of understanding that penetrated Annie's thinking. Sergeant Annie Rock challenged him with, 'No, of course you didn't; you battered Sophie de Lorenzo to death, didn't you?'

'Yes, I did. I didn't kill Elena.... I killed...'

A look of wide abandoned panic invaded Manuel's' eyes and he turned as if to run back towards the yacht only to see Al Jessop closing with him and the shadow of Canary Wharf Tower stretching out towards him.

Manuel Martinez, discreet corporate banking giant of the city of London, stepped back, threw the holdall at Terry Webster, missed, and ran off haphazardly towards Pestons Road with Al Jessop and Annie Rock in pursuit.

Seconds later, Terry Webster dropped his handcuffs, and joined in the chase with a river police boat sergeant pointing the way and a handful of small boats encircling the Blackwall basin watching proceedings.

The waters churned a black oily image and the reflection of Canada Square's tall buildings shivered in anticipation of events below.

They were along the footpath by the waterside, along the decking path bordering Bartholomew Wharf, and out into Pestons Road with Jessop unable to keep up and Annie Rock reaching out to grab the tail of Manuel's anorak.

Webby closed, rushed into the fray, and saw Annie pull the seaman's anorak from Manuel's back.

All of a sudden, there was a sickening crunch of metal against flesh and bone when Manuel Martinez unexpectedly stepped from the footpath into the front of a big red double-decker London bus.

The bus driver heaved on his brakes but the noise was horrifying when the body of the Spaniard disappeared under the front of the machine and was gobbled up by a clamour of brakes, exhaust fumes and squealing tyres.

'Man down,' screamed Annie into her radio. 'Suspect down.'

Webby ran to the back of the vehicle in what he would later describe as some misplaced ridiculous belief the suspect would reappear at the rear and continue his bid to escape. It wasn't to be but Webby stumbled across the warped and twisted body of Manuel Martinez.

Crashing to the ground beside the Spaniard, Webby tried desperately to find any sign of life. The skull was crushed, a chest caved in, and blood spurted from the lower limbs. It was too late.

Terry Webster took a long look at the body of his first murder arrest and turned to face the garden wall of a house bordering the street. In one swift but nauseous movement, Terry Webster heaved the contents of his stomach onto someone's garden and shook uncontrollably at the thought of the sight behind him.

Annie shouted, 'Davies, the suspect is down. He ran into the front of a double-decker bus and didn't make it.'

The radio net was quiet for a moment before Davies King radioed, 'Is it fatal, Annie?'

'Afraid so, inspector,' responded Annie. 'You don't need a warrant now but we do need a doctor and a recovery team.'

Gradually retracing her steps, Annie bent down, collected the holdall, unzipped it, and rummaged amongst the contents. Annie located a shotgun, broke it like a firearms expert, and radioed, 'I have the weapon and I've made it safe but there's no sign of the laptop, inspector.

Davies King nodded to Barney and quietly said, 'Let's do it.'

Together, they climbed across the decking, boarded Conchenta, broke into a cabin, and searched for a laptop belonging to Elena Martinez.

Al Jessop's office provided the venue for hot coffee, a couple of Chinese takeaways, and a handful of pizzas.

'You don't say,' said Davies King wrestling with a telephone. 'What did the superintendent say to that?'

Annie exchanged looks with Barney and asked, 'What's going on?'

Barney replied, 'The boss is on the phone to Claudia, Annie. Looks like trouble at Crillsea.'

Davies shook his head but, aware he was being listened to, said into the 'phone, 'So have I got this right, Claudia. Bert Allithwaite has fallen out with Keith Jackson but you don't know what it's all about it?'

Listening, Davies answered with, 'Something to do with the four of us being in London, oh dear.'

Munching a sandwich, slurping a coffee, Davies then replied, 'Yes, I know he wants me to arrest and interview Max and Harry for murder but there's no evidence I'm aware of that would make me want to contemplate such a move. I hear you, Claudia, but Chief Inspector Jackson can do what he wishes in respect of discipline proceedings. It's his decision not mine.'

There was another drink taken and another sandwich bitten then Davies responded with, 'Don't you go worrying, Claudia. We'll be home soon.'

Davies ended the call and Ted Barnes asked, 'Well, how bad?'

'Not good, Barney, apparently Jackson is on the warpath, has had a massive argument with Bert Allithwaite and wants me charged with failing to obey a lawful order, bringing the service into disrepute, and a stack of discipline offences a yard long. If he's looking to take me down then you guys are on the wrong team because people like Keith Jackson have long memories.'

'And that's all in addition to the assault file he's prepared for Assistant Chief Constable Patterson,' declared Barney.

'Well, Jackson is hopping mad,' said Davies. 'But I can't do anything about that at the moment. No, let's get on with the job here.'

Annie Rock looked worried but turned her attention to Terry Webster and asked, 'Are you alright, Webby?'

'Yeah, yes, of course,' replied Webby playing with his food. 'Bit of a shock, that's all, the body and everything, I mean.'

'Such deaths are never very nice,' suggested Annie. 'But you need to get used to it, Webby. It comes with the job.'

'I don't think I'll ever get used to it,' replied Webby. 'But maybe you can tell me why Manuel admitted killing Sophie and then ran away like a frightened rabbit caught in the headlights of a car?'

'Good question, Webby,' considered Annie. 'Various reasons, I suppose. Sometimes I think it's just the way you catch someone. You see, there he was totally unaware we were onto him. He'd been at sea for quite a few days; probably lonely, no company, maybe lost in his own thoughts, and then we turn up mob handed.'

'You can never tell how such a person is going to react,' suggested Chief Superintendent Jessop. 'Sometimes they cry their eyes out and can't stop talking about the murder they committed. Some of them admit their crimes because they want to be famous; they want to be remembered in history; even if only for a short time. Then there are those who just don't say a word and it doesn't matter what you say or do, they are never going to talk to you because there's a little mechanism inside their box you just can't switch on. Strange world and it's a strange job trying to second guess your opponent, young man. Don't dwell on it. Move on.'

'And some people even admit to murders they didn't even commit,' stated Davies King. 'And believe me, there's nothing worse than some toxic who wants the apparent glory attributed to a killer when they had nothing to do with it in the first place.'

'Yeah, fine, that's good then,' replied Webby.

'Nothing's ever good until it's finished, Webby,' declared Davies King.

'Inspector,' asked Webby, 'Have I got it wrong. I arrested Manuel Martinez for murdering his wife, Elena, which he denied, but then admitted murdering Sophie de Lorenzo. Where did I go wrong?'

'You didn't,' replied Davies. 'We haven't proved he committed the murder yet. He's admitted it but we have to prove it beyond a shadow of doubt. Personally, I think it's fair to say that we've always thought there were two murders at the same scene and it was never going to be easy sorting out who did what.'

'Agreed,' responded Annie Rock. 'But if Manuel tried to poison Sophie with crocus prior to battering her to death then there's no reason for us to put the Farringday Trust people in the frame. It doesn't add up, inspector.'

'But it will do by the time we've finished, trust me,' replied Davies. 'Look, we need something to place Manuel Martinez on the cliff tops at the time of Sophie's murder. Bearing in mind the time of death given by our learned Professor of Forensic Medicine, we need evidence Manuel was on the cliff tops that Wednesday. We already have his DNA on the murder weapon and Sophie was bundled into his suit cover.'

'And his monogrammed handkerchief was present,' reminded Webby.

'Think of it this way, Annie,' said Barney. 'On the day of the murder, we've always thought the murderer panicked when the poison attempt went wrong. You and Webby have just experienced the same man in action panicking at the time of his arrest. We've got the right man, no doubt. We just need to tidy the evidence up for the inquest, that's all.'

'You're missing the point, guys,' said Webby. 'Chief Inspector Jackson always said it was a straightforward domestic murder and it is in a way. It's just that he killed his wife's girlfriend because he was jealous.'

'Please, don't go there,' said Annie. 'This isn't quite the domestic murder scene Keith Jackson was expecting, Webby.'

'Well, it's my first murder case, my first murder arrest, and I go and nick the suspect for the wrong murder,' revealed Terry Webster.

'It happens sometimes,' intervened Al Jessop.' Just don't make a habit of it, young man.'

'Okay,' said Davies. 'Barney and I found Elena's laptop on the yacht, Conchenta. We've had a good look. The laptop has been most useful. Annie, you and Webby stay overnight and split up in the morning.'

Davies King handed over paperwork and ordered, 'Patents Office, Company House, Advanced Passenger Information, Stock Exchange, and Europol. It's all there and so is the answer to who killed Elena Martinez.'

'And what are you going to do, inspector?' asked Annie Rock.

'Barney and I are going back to Crillsea, Annie. We've people to see and things to do, and, apparently I'm in charge of a surveillance operation tomorrow night.'

'Is that before or after Max Fowler is liberated?' asked Al Jessop.

There was no reply from Davies just a question. 'How did you manage to convince your deputy assistant commissioner to move Benny Abbott from West End Central to Paddington Green nick, sir?'

'I play chess too, Davies. I have a boss who heads up counter terrorism in the United Kingdom and runs some of his operations out of Paddington Green. He didn't take kindly to me using his playground in the manner discussed. What makes you think Benny Abbott was transferred from West End Central to Paddington Green?'

'It was on television,' declared Davies King.

'Was it, indeed, Davies? Did it ever occur to you that the Operational Support Team might just have had an exercise to see how effective a grade one security transfer might take place between London police stations? Do you think we used a real prisoner in such an exercise? Or do you think it was all a ploy? You decide, Davies. You're God's gift to the detective world!'

Davies King smiled, drained the dregs of his coffee, and replied, 'Checkmate, sir, good move.'

'I'm watching your moves, Davies,' announced Al Jessop. 'A murder suspect died on my streets today in the hands of your team. Now I'm not going to fall out with you over this because we were both there and we both know what happened. My problem is that when the top brass hold their 'shudder' meeting at nine tomorrow morning I'm going to be criticised because there was a death during one of my operations to secure a Metropolitan area for you to effect an arrest in. I can hear the voices now; you should have done this, you should have done that. When the same voices learn that Max Fowler is about to be arrested for murder by the same bungling police force that caused a death on my streets today then you can look out. You can look out because the top brass will eat you alive and spit out the remains from the top floor of New Scotland Yard. Do you hear me, Inspector King?'

'Indeed, I do, sir,' replied Davies.

'I'm launching a big raid through the night; it'll keep the top brass occupied most of tomorrow talking to the Press because we've got so much evidence and strong suspicion that we're going to make it into a media spectacular for the Met. But you, you've got twenty four hours to deliver Max Fowler, Davies, otherwise I'll pull the plug on you and Barney's career as night club entertainers.'

'More than enough, sir,' replied Davies King with a nervous glance towards Terry Webster and Annie Rock.

Terry Webster looked directly into the eyes of Ted Barnes and said, 'What night club is he on about? What's going on?'

'Search me, Webby,' replied Barney. 'I just keep the diary; that's all.'

*

Chapter Eleven

~ ~ ~

Dateline: Saturday
London's West End and The Mayor's Ball, Crillsea

Al Jessop briefed his leaders, and his leaders briefed his men and women. It was the best thing to do when there were over one thousand unformed officers taking part in the big raid.

Double doors opened at West End Central police station and the first escort vehicle trundled out into the street with its lights flashing. Within minutes, a constant stream of police personnel vans, dog vans, police cars and scientific support vans had formed a convoy from all over the capital and were slowly merging into the mainstream London traffic.

It was night-time, just gone midnight, and London's nightspots were slowly filling up with people intent on enjoying themselves. And that was the problem for law enforcement officers all over the developed world: someone's idea of enjoyment didn't always match with someone else's idea of pleasure. London was no different to anywhere else in the world; it was a big sprawling capital offering a massive range of diversity to its multi-cultural population, some legal, some illegal. Tonight, Al Jessop had enlisted officers from all over London to take down a criminal empire he'd watched steadily grow over the years.

A sergeant somewhere in the convoy of vehicles heading into the west end radioed, 'Music, Maestro,' and waited for the reply.

A finger reached out and activated a siren, and then another, and then, moments later, it was as if the orchestra had well and truly burst into life. The noise was deafening and the sight of over a hundred police vehicles threading their way through Regent Street, Oxford Street, and the capital was a sight to behold.

Another drugs raid, it was said on the pavement.

Probably a big fight somewhere, it was thought.

Maybe it's a night club raid, ventured a clubber.

But what might have been a bigger than usual overt uniform raid in the capital was much more than that.

Al Jessop and the men and women of the Flying Squad were going to work. They were taking down an empire of pornography, drugs, prostitution, blackmail, racketeering, illegal gambling, illegally held firearms, vice, and criminality that had slowly built up over the years. Of course, they knew they would never destroy crime all together; it's part of human nature, but tonight it was time to claw back some integrity, retrieve some honesty, redress the balance between right and wrong.

They knew who they were going for, knew who their targets were, knew that by the morning the cells of London police stations would be full to capacity. They knew that men and women like Jack Creighton and Lydia Bryant would be in the can by morning. They had no place to hide because Al Jessop was in charge and he was knocking down every door on his list to get the answers he wanted. The doors were pubs, clubs, betting offices, gambling houses, saunas and brothels, council houses and private mansions, top floor apartments and cellar basements. Of course, they knew they wouldn't find the gangland leaders and criminal entrepreneurs in all the clubs and pubs of the capital. Oh, no, they expected to find them in the Home Counties of Essex and Kent, of Sussex and Thames Valley, and the borders of the M25 motorway. That's where the big time criminals lived. A criminal's office might be a dodgy venue in London, but home was in the suburbs amongst the golf clubs and country houses.

The sirens wailed constantly. Al Jessop had explained at the briefing he wanted a 'High Profile'; he wanted a high profile because he wanted everyone in London to know who was boss.

Al Jessop and his squad were going to work; getting stuck in, taking a chance, having a go, following up on information received, acting on proactive intelligence, following on from the Benny Abbott arrest. Al Jessop was gambling, and moving the pieces around a board suggested by Davies King, and with blue lights flashing and sirens wailing Al Jessop was waking up London to do it.

Later that day, in the afternoon, Davies King was back in his office in Crillsea having travelled late at night and slept reasonably well.

In one corner of the office a fax machine was alive and kicking out data requested by Davies and worked on by Barney.

Paper was strewn from one end of the desk to the other. Their murder diary occupied the centre of his desk and was surrounded by statements, documents, photographs, handwritten notes, and the flotsam and jetsam of a detective trying to solve a murder case. Perched on the edge of his desk was a computer, which Davies switched on as he poured himself a mug of liquid caffeine designed to keep him awake and his brain ticking.

Davies knew it was all happening in London; knew of Al Jessop's big raid, and knew Terry Webster and Annie Rock had been out since early doors doing their bit for the enquiry.

Hot coffee raged inside him as he entered his email system and double clicked a mail from Al Jessop updating him on the Flying Squad's activity; who'd been arrested so far, and what evidence had been collated to date. Closing the email, Davies double clicked on an email from PC Mark Tait of Crillsea Meadows. Davies read Tait's email, smiled happily to himself, and drafted a suitable reply of thanks. In addition, Davies revealed to Mark Tait how Manuel Martinez had been arrested in London, how he had met his untimely tragic death, and how important it was to receive an email from him confirming the presence of Manuel Martinez on the cliff tops of Crillsea on the day of Sophie's murder: Wednesday. Davies concluded that he, Mark Tait, had provided an important piece of information that, when added to the rest of the evidence, made a significant contribution to the evidence needed to write off the murder of Sophie de Lorenzo as 'detected'.

But for now, for Davies, it was a hard slog as he studied the evidence gathered from two murder investigations and added his own thoughts and actions from the murder diary to a hotchpotch of notes and papers he'd assembled. Davies King set about his task.

The telephone rang and Davies took time out to talk to Barney. Davies made notes. Then Annie rang and said, 'Go into your emails and find the profiles on the Farringday brothers. That's all I've got so far.'

Davies replied, 'Thanks, Annie. What is it in a nutshell?'

'Usual stuff, dates and place of birth, but it boils down to Rupert: the oldest, he started the business with his father who is now deceased. He's the brains with the technical knowledge on the industry side. He transformed a small family business into a global corporation. He's married; no children, separated from his wife who ran off with his bank manager.'

'Oh dear, bank managers again, and Richard?' asked Davies.

'Single, lives alone in Tevington, majored in law and business studies at Harvard, would you believe. Seems to be well-liked in the area and is the main man when it comes to crime prevention stuff and industrial security. He's quite security conscious apparently and handles all staff and personnel issues. That leaves, Robert. He's the youngest and he's a bit of a lady's man. He dabbles in fast cars and has a Porsche and a Ferrari for weekends and a Bentley for business. He's actually the Financial Director but they seem to wear their badges when it suits them. The reality is they really do run the business together. There's too much money coming out of these three, boss.'

'Thanks, Annie, I'll firm up on your email.'

Davies closed the conversation and then answered a call from Terry Webster. He made more notes and scattered them on the desk in some apparent form of meaning.

Yes, he thought, Barney continued to be the longest serving stalwart backbone of his team whilst Annie Rock was improving day by day as his sergeant. But it was Terry Webster, thought Davies, young Terry Webster who began life in his office probably unsure of his position within it, but now learning fast and not frightened of hard work and long hours.

Blissful ignorance was not a Davies King speciality as he sifted through the papers deciding how he was going to make his final moves. The telephone rang, more emails arrived, and a fax machine chattered constantly in the background.

Rubbing his eyes, Davies hoisted his feet onto the corner of his desk and selected a sheaf of handwritten notes to study again. Gradually, the emails stopped, a fax closed down, and he drifted into an awkward sleep with his papers lying on the desk and his murder diary knocked carelessly to the ground.

Claudia Jones didn't knock when she entered his office. She knew the man, had known him for years. She knew what drove him, what inspired him, and decided long ago he was a unique individual living somewhere between the extremities of brilliance and madness. He existed somewhere between genius and fool as far as she was concerned. Only she was allowed to voice such a view for Claudia Jones was Davies King's most devoted ally, and she preferred to concentrate on the pure intellect of a man she had known all her service.

'Inspector King... Inspector...' Claudia shook his shoulder and gently woke him before retrieving the murder diary from the floor.

'Inspector King. It's time for the surveillance operation.'

207

Rubbing his eyes, stretching, Davies King yawned and said, 'Oh, Claudia, I must have dropped off. I am sorry. Yes, surveillance, yes, that's one of the reasons I had to come back, isn't it. Thanks.'

'No problem, inspector,'

'Look, can you do me a favour, Claudia?'

'If I can; what do you want me to do?'

'Can you type up a report from me to Superintendent Allithwaite recommending PC Mark Tait of Crillsea Meadows for a period of attachment to CID? He's being transferred from Rural Command to Crillsea and I'm always looking for people who understand the importance of intelligence in all its forms. I'd like to give him an opportunity to see if he likes our kind of work.'

'Mark Tait, yes, good choice, if I may say so. I'll use the term 'SCID' so as not to upset anyone. I remember Mister Tait as a pleasant young man.'

'Oh, I don't need him to be pleasant, Claudia,' replied Davies. 'I need him to remember things. You see, Traffic need good drivers; Firearms need good marksmen, Uniform needs the healthy and fit, and I need an odd ball now and again who keeps his notes when others don't, understands the worth of minor intelligence, and has a good memory.'

'Consider it done, inspector,' said Claudia. 'I'm not sure the department can carry another odd ball though.'

'Have there been any more jewellers' burglaries, Claudia?'

'Detectives in the office have carried out a number of different enquiries and spoken to informants but there are no leads, inspector.'

'Yes, I see they've left me a few notes, here and there. Thank you. Has Chief Inspector Jackson been asking for me?' queried Davies.

'No,' replied Claudia. 'He's busy at headquarters and then, of course, it's the Mayor's Ball tonight. Nothing will stop Mister Jackson from attending the Mayor's Ball.'

'Well, that just goes to prove how unnecessary all our work really is, Claudia,' declared Davies. 'The Mayor's Ball takes precedence over everything.'

'Inspector, how inappropriate of you to comment, but as you have brought the subject up…'

'I'm listening, Claudia,' advised Davies.

'You know I seldom speak out of turn but you should know that Chief Inspector Jackson is telling everyone in the office he intends to suspend you as soon as he has got the approval of the assistant chief constable. I think that's why he went to headquarters. I've been here many years, inspector. That's not the way things should be done but it seems you will be suspended soon.'

'That will be this afternoon or tonight, Claudia; whenever Jackson gets hold of Patterson. Look, this might be my last words to you for a while: Thank you for all that you've done. Now take the rest of the day off, go home, and put your feet up.'

Claudia laughed and replied, 'It's gone six o'clock, inspector. I finished over an hour ago. It's time you and Constable Barnes were doing whatever you do on surveillance operations.'

'Oh, no, Claudia, gone six o'clock!' said Davies apologetically. 'What would I do without you?'

'Be happy, Inspector King. If you aren't here tomorrow my resignation will be on Superintendent Allithwaite's desk by lunch time. Goodnight '

With a swish of her cardigan, Claudia Jones was gone from his office, gone from a tired man weighing up the consequences between criminal investigations and internal politics.

Champagne and caviar, and strawberries and cream, vied with gowns and tuxedos, and perfume and aftershave, as the rich and powerful of Crillsea and Tevington on Sea played out their power game at the annual Mayor's Ball. A band played a waltz to which no-one danced and then it played a tango and the floor remained bare. The band moved through their repertoire seeking a balance between what they thought should be played and what their customers thought might be played. The customers were all there: Round Table and Freemasonry, Rotary and Hospice, the Chamber of Commerce, the Federation of this, that and the other, the Association of the Good, the Bad, and the Ugly, and the Society of Do-gooders. And they were all rubbing shoulders and sliding skin with local councillors, a member of parliament, a couple of landowners, a man of the cloth or two, and a Lord and Lady of the Manor.

Mixing, socializing, seeing and being seen, were half a dozen property developers and financiers, bank managers, solicitors, accountants and a host of anonymous would-be, might-be somebody's of the future. Wheelers and dealers in suits and gowns, one might say. Those on the way down meeting those on the way up, one might say, and the ones who were always there.

Collectively, it was called the Establishment and it was more powerful than any criminal mafia could ever be.

During the reception, the Mayor of the Boroughs of Crillsea and Tevington on Sea, Maurice Ashton, welcomed his guests and thanked everyone for twelve wonderful months of memories and experiences. They cheered and applauded and wondered who would wear his chain in the forthcoming year. Then he introduced those going up to those going down. There was much smiling and laughing, and some niceness and sincerity about the evening.

The Chief Constable gave a vote of thanks. The Chief Executive of the County Council, George Samuels, congratulated the Mayor on his term of office, and then secretly winked suggestively at the Mayoress, Abigail 'Abbey' Ashton.

Superintendent Allithwaite and Assistant Chief Constable Patterson discussed tactics and strategy, and kept their voices low in fear of such 'police business' being overheard.

Cyril Leadbetter, the young Chief Librarian, was ever present and spoke repeatedly of his encounter with the Prime Minister. Oh, how exciting that had been, it was said.

Eventually, and without prompting, Chief Inspector Keith Jackson happened to discuss with Assistant Chief Constable Phillip Patterson a dilemma entitled, 'Davies King'.

'You will recall, sir, I stated from the onset these were minor domestic murders and I have been proved correct,' stated Keith Jackson. 'It's just a pity so much money has been wasted on these needless trips to London and elsewhere. It's quite ridiculous and I am angry my attempted intervention has been sidetracked by Inspector King. When they did eventually locate my suspect, King couldn't even organise a proper arrest in secure conditions. What on earth the Commissioner of the Metropolitan Police will have to say to our Chief Constable about a death on London streets due to King's incompetence, I don't know; but it won't be good, I venture to suggest. Indeed, sir, King is a disgrace to the service.'

'Quite,' replied Patterson.

'However, sir, recent developments suggest one of the murders may have been committed by two named persons acting in concert:

namely Fowler and Reynolds. The source for this is impeccable and stems from our latest advanced computerised technology.'

'The Detect computer!' confirmed Patterson.

'Exactly! Moreover, sir, you'll have read my confidential report. King has displayed a complete lack of management skills, poor leadership, and, I believe poor investigative knowledge. In view of the high probability of discipline offences being brought against him, I strongly recommend he be suspended from duty forthwith, sir.'

'Forthwith indeed, you say?' queried Patterson. 'Failing to carry out a lawful order, and bringing the service into disrepute, for example. And then there's the file regarding the assault at the Anchor pub, chief inspector. Not quiet open and shut that one since King did arrest the man he assaulted. I wondered if you had perhaps exaggerated your claims there but when that incident is added to the other matters of which you speak, well, to say the very least, we have a bad apple.'

'Precisely, sir,' declared Jackson.

And so it continued: a tirade of personal attack against Davies King and his actions.

Phillip Patterson listened, agreed, and smiled as he said, 'Personally, I couldn't agree more with you, chief inspector. Moreover, you can suspend him tonight if you wish, Keith. Run a new appointment by me next week, won't you. Someone on side this time, I suggest.'

Keith Jackson nodded and then introduced the assistant chief constable to his brother in law, George Samuels, the Chief Executive of the County Council. Within a few moments Phillip Patterson was able to steer the conversation to an annual budget and an introduction to his Chief Constable.

It was important to be in such a loop, it was said.

It was important to know the person on the 'phone, it was said.

It was important to be on side, in the same team, together, it was said.

Oh how things were contrived, it was thought, and the band played on.

Gradually, the genial scent of divine perfumes took over, and Chief Inspector Jackson's brother in law, George, looked longingly at the Mayoress and her attractive curves. Outside, it was raining hard.

Rainfall splattered Barney's windscreen. He switched on the windscreen wipers and said, 'Why did we abandon the sharp end of a murder enquiry to come and sit on a bloody jewellers shop that might get burgled, Davies? Since when did the value of a burglary surpass the value of human life and a murder investigation?'

'Upset, Barney?'

'I love stake-outs when I know we're onto something, Davies, but this is just a ruse to stop us both going to the Mayor's Ball and upsetting the apple cart.' announced Barney.

'You've made your point, Barney, now switch the wipers off and be quiet. If there's someone on the rooftops looking down at us then you've just signalled to them that we're here.'

'Damn, I should know that, boss.'

'Now I know you're upset when you're calling me boss. Look, Barney, sometimes you need to sit back, lie down, sleep on it, think about it, and all the other things they don't teach you in detective training school. Let it lie for now. But hey, you did me a big favour at Bananos. I don't know what to say.'

'Then don't say anything.'

They watched through the dim light but saw only a stray cat casting furtive shadows in an alleyway.

'You never did tell me how you knew I was there,' said Davies.

Barney considered for a moment and then responded, 'You mentioned to Claudia you were going to war. She thought it an odd comment to make. She rang Annie. Annie rang me. I came into work, took the duty car and sat outside your house until you left and walked to the railway station. I had a hunch you were up to something. I followed you.'

'What?' replied an astonished Davies.

'Well, you instructed my surveillance course,' chuckled Barney.

'I didn't think counter and anti-surveillance methods were required,' replied Davies.

'Well, don't blame me if you didn't teach the two techniques. They're both different you know,' teased Barney.

'Ha Ha Ha!' replied Davies. 'I should have sussed you out within three turns. I could have lost you at the harbour.'

'But you didn't,' laughed Barney. 'Your mind was somewhere else.'

Davies King scratched his nose and rubbed his eyelids before replying, 'Yeah well, it was a stupid irrelevant thing to do but it took us right into the heart of things, otherwise we could have waited for another week or two before we'd unearthed such information.'

'I'm not disputing that,' agreed Barney.

'But Annie and Claudia conspiring together, now there's a turn up for the book,' suggested Davies.

'I told you in confidence,' revealed Barney. 'Don't let me down.'

'Annie and Claudia, well, well, well. Webby?' asked Davies.

'Coming on side slowly,' declared Barney. 'He's going to make a good detective one day, Davies. I can spot them. He's learning the paperwork and the procedures and he's picking up on the practicalities. He'll be all right if you can keep him out of the clutches of people like Keith Jackson.'

'Well, I owe you a big favour, Barney. It was getting a bit hairy and then you turned up.'

'I don't know what you mean, guv. I was never there,' chirped Barney.

'Yeah, I got myself in trouble there and it'll bite back at my arse and give me a nasty bruise one day,' surrendered Davies.

Barney was more serious when he said, 'It could finish you.'

Davies responded, 'It could but there's always a way out. For now, we've got tonight to worry about.'

Barney said, 'The Butterfly Man has deliberately organised a surveillance job to prevent you from attending the Mayor's Ball and taking the opportunity to tell your version of events. He doesn't like the truth, you see. Or is it to prevent you from interfering with the Max Fowler enquiry? I don't know anymore, Davies. Back stabbing is commonplace at work these days.'

Barney crumpled an empty coffee carton, stuffed it into a side pocket of the car, and allowed a huge sigh of boredom to escape his lips.

'Things have changed, that's all,' stated Davies.

'Yes, you can say that again,' said Barney. 'Thing is, Davies, we've been on what, a dozen or more murders together, maybe more? I don't know. I never counted the funerals we went to but it was different then. There was order to what we were doing. Now it's just a bloody farce in the name of progress.'

'It's like this, Barney. We can find seven hundred billion to bail the bankers out and God knows how much to fight wars in Iraq and Afghanistan because of nine eleven but they can't find the money at home to fund public services properly. So we end up with a lot of unqualified people doing some jobs with less than adequate qualifications and at a cheaper price. The knock on effect is poor service all round.'

Barney suggested, 'They'll say we are two dinosaurs the first time we say "it wasn't like that in our day," and we'll stamp our feet and get angry.'

'You think so?' said Davies. 'We'll both be in the convalescence home at Harrogate by then.'

'We'll still be dinosaurs,' offered Barney.

'Opinionated dinosaurs,' suggested Davies. 'We'll be admitted to the Opinionated Dinosaurs Ward where we can be monitored by the State until our time is done.'

There was silence in the car, just a soft hum from the radio net and rain falling on the roof and windscreen.

'Why us, Davies?' asked Barney. 'Why us?'

'Because there's no-one else, Barney; the Butterfly Man could have brought in the Force surveillance team but that would have required paperwork and some positive information that a job was on. Then again, he could have used those community support officers at half the price or he could have hired one of those private surveillance firms. You know what it's like; anyone can do our job when it suits the powers that be.'

'Why didn't he then? I mean why did we get it to do and not them?'

'Because he wants us out of the way, I suspect. But on the other hand there are five jeweller shops in Crillsea and Tevvie and we're just sitting and watching them. It's more observation than surveillance. Hey, who knows! We might get lucky.'

'I doubt it.'

'Me too,' revealed Davies struggling to watch through his side of the windscreen. 'Let's move on to Crillsea. I've arranged to meet Annie and Webby when they return from London.'

'That could be an interesting meeting. Have they completed all those enquiries?' asked Barney.

'I think so, but we'll meet up for a cuppa and go through what they found out at the Patents office and so on,' replied Davies.

Barney pulled away from the kerb and drove towards Crillsea wondering how long it would be before boredom dominated his night.

Meanwhile, the radio worked away quietly in the background telling of road accidents, diverting staff to domestic disputes, and circulating stolen or suspicious cars. As night closed in an odd burglar alarm sounded, the pubs and clubs got out, and the taxi ranks became busier. The hours passed.

Later, turning into a narrow road adjacent to Crillsea harbour Barney pulled his car to a standstill and said, 'Do you see what I see?'

'Well, Well, Well!' remarked Davies, suddenly quite perky. 'I don't believe it. Yes I do. Drive round the block, Barney.'

'What, and miss an opportunity like this?'

'Don't argue, my friend. Just do it. Let's give them both a little time, that's all,' suggested Davies. Then he whispered, 'One door closes and another opens. Nice and slowly does it, Barney, but full headlights on the next pass.'

Without further ado Barney engaged a lower gear and sedately drove round the block again. The rain pitter-pattered gently against his windscreen.

Turning into the junction Barney realised the black Jaguar was still there, still parked in a lane between a jeweller called Hawkman and a cobbler called Littleton. The light in the lane had been extinguished and there were no interior lights visible in the Jaguar; no vestige of a cigarette light burning thinly from within, no hand-held torch being used to read a map, no light whatsoever.

A cat somehow jumped from the roof of the jeweller to a dustbin, and, in so doing, dislodged the dustbin lid. There was a loud bang as the lid made the ground and rolled into a puddle at the kerbside.

'That's finished that then,' noted Barney. 'Bloody alley cats.'

''There's no change, just silence. Wait,' whispered Davies. 'And keep your voice down. Sound carries at night.'

Seconds grew into minutes; the rain lightened, the tide turned.

'Are they at it yet?' asked Barney.

'I can't see for the bloody rain,' answered Davies.

A pair of seagulls took off from the roof into the night skies.

Davies rubbed his window, looked out, and said, 'Here we go.'

'Do you want me to call the troops in?' asked Barney.

Davies King said, 'Well, it's going to go down quite soon, I think.' And then he added, 'Why not, Barney? Why not, indeed?'

Barney radioed, 'All units, all units, from Delta One. Attend Crillsea Harbour Place Back Lane between Hawkman's jewellers and Littleton's shoe shop. Officers require covert assistance. No lights. No sirens. Attend.'

'My God, Barney, you made that sound interesting,' offered Davies.

'Now what?' asked Barney.

'You know what we sing on a Saturday, don't you?'

'You'll never walk alone,' replied Barney confused.

'Precisely! But now and again our friends do have to walk alone, Barney. The Jaguar parked in front of us is the Mayor's car. The Mayoress and the Chief Executive of the County Council are in the back of the car doing what they shouldn't be doing. Agreed?'

'Agreed,' said Barney. 'Politics in action! I can't understand why local dignitaries live in the public eye and do these things so openly.'

'Because they think they're Teflon coated, Barney,' said Davies. 'They reach such a position that they think they are untouchable. It's as simple as that. Anyway, I'm very sure this is where Max responded to that hoax call when the Prime Minister opened the library. Agreed?'

'Agreed,' said Barney. 'I remember, but where's this leading to?'

'A bomb, Barney; can't you see it beneath the Jaguar?'

'What?' Barney activated his headlights again and lit up the Mayor's car.

Davies King stepped from his vehicle into the pouring rain and slowly but deliberately approached the Mayor's black Jaguar. He bent low and carefully and methodically inspected beneath the vehicle. Eventually, he stepped away and radioed, 'Delta One is calling a Red Alpha Foxtrot at this location. I repeat… Delta One is calling a Red Alpha Foxtrot at this location.'

'Was that a Red Alpha Foxtrot, Davies?' requested a voice at headquarters control room on the radio net.

'Confirmed,' replied Davies.

'Confirm you've found an unexploded incendiary device, inspector.'

'Confirmed,' replied Davies.

'Are you sure?' asked the voice.

'Hang on; I'll rattle it and see if it goes bang. Now listen to me, Chief Inspector whoever the bloody hell you are, get your arse off your seat and get me bomb disposal, fire service, ambulance and senior command before half of Crillsea is blown to kingdom come. Now!'

'Roger, Delta One. All received,' came the reply.

Gently, Davies tapped on the roof of the Jaguar and then tried to look in through its steamy windows.

There was a flurry of activity within but Davies leaned close to a window and said, 'Please, don't move. This is Detective Inspector Davies King from Crillsea police and there's an unexploded bomb attached to the underside of your car. Just remain perfectly still. An ambulance, fire rescue vehicle and bomb disposal vehicle will all be here within a few minutes.'

There was a rumbled oath from within and Davies responded with, 'I know it's difficult to take on board but there really is a bomb underneath your car so sit tight and do absolutely nothing.'

He could hear whispers from inside the car and a gentle rustling of clothing. An interior light came on and a face appeared at the window looking directly at Davies. Then the light went off.

Davies remained bent low and explained, 'This is the Mayor's car. It was supposed to be used on the Prime Minister's visit to the library. It wasn't but a bomb disposal officer was called out to a bomb hoax on this street. The bomb was underneath this car all the time. I know this is embarrassing for you but just trust me and I'll have you out of there in a shake. Now please remain calm and don't move at all.'

'I need to get out,' said a male voice from within.

'I'm sure you need to get out of the car,' observed Davies. 'But I can't let you out. It's too dangerous. If the device is triggered by a mercury tilt switch then you'll be blown to kingdom come. So will I come to think of it. Don't move. The device is probably very unstable after all this time'

'It hasn't gone off so far. How many days is it since the Prime Minister's visit?'

'Not long but mercury lives in a thermometer day after day, year after a year. It gets hot and expands and it gets cold and contracts. The problem is you might have triggered it with your...' He paused for a moment looking for appropriate words and then said, 'Your recent movements.'

There was a very long pause as if the occupants of a Mayor's car were working out the pros and the cons.

'If we're lucky the bomb will be on a timer switch,' said Davies. 'The problem there is the device hasn't gone off so it may be faulty. Just be still.'

There was silence from within, just an unheard exchange of whispers before a weak female voice asked, 'What do you want us to do?'

'Nothing,' confirmed Davies. 'Wait there, I'll be back.'

The dance floor was packed and a band was thumping out popular music in wild abundance. The room shook, quivered, and rocked. The Mayor's Ball was a pulsating success until a pager went off. First one, then two, then more. Something was on.

Detective Chief Inspector Jackson's pager was first to sound. And then Superintendent Allithwaite followed by Assistant Chief Constable Patterson.

Pagers were displaced and mobiles rang.

'Bomb!'

It was only spoken once but within a few seconds every guest attending the Mayor's Ball knew something was on. And it was something damn serious because the police, fire and ambulance chiefs were looking worried and the Chief Executive of the County Council was.....

Where was the Chief Executive of the County Council? It was asked.

Where is he? It was asked.

What's going on? It was asked.

The reality was panic had set in because Headquarters had been told by the Metropolitan police that there wasn't a bomb disposal officer to attend. They'd also been told by the military that no-one was available.

'We will, we will rock you,' boomed out from the stage.

'We will, we will rock you,' drowned out pagers and mobiles

'We will, we will rock you,' seemed to be appropriate to the occasion, courtesy of 'Queen' and Freddie Mercury.

And the occasion was two married senior members of the local political fraternity had been caught in a compromising manner in the back of an official car a mile from the venue of the Mayor's Ball and there was a bomb attached to the underneath of their vehicle. The problem was they weren't married to each other and their slightest movement might result in an explosion and the devastation of a goodly part of Crillsea. The situation was compounded by the Metropolitan Police and the military, both of whom were unable to schedule assistance for at least twelve to fourteen hours.

It was time to tell Davies King and Ted Barnes they were on their own.

When Detective Chief Inspector Jackson howled into Harbour Place Back Lane with Superintendent Allithwaite and Assistant Chief Constable Patterson as passengers he was directed by a uniform constable to park behind an ambulance and a fire engine.

When the three alighted from their car a flurry of rainfall dropped from above and reminded them they had arrived.

They stood next to Davies and Barney and looked towards the Jaguar which was now lit up by a circle of lights supplied by the Fire Service and Crillsea Traffic department. The rain was falling; the vehicle occupants were clearly visible, and Davies had lit the scene up as if it were daylight.

'Is it? Is it?' dithered Chief Inspector Jackson. 'Could it be… Could it be a mistake? I mean is it…' he continued.

'Yes, it's your brother in law and he's close up and personal with the Mayoress,' said Davies King.

'Oh dear,' said Superintendent Allithwaite. 'This will finish us. We can't have this. We'll be dragged through the gutter by the press and the Chief…' He was lost for words for a second. 'The Chief Constable? It's a nightmare.'

'My brother in law,' said Jackson. 'This could destroy his career, his marriage. He's finished.' Jackson looked gravely at Allithwaite.

'I dare say his wife won't be too pleased either,' said Davies quietly.

Superintendent Allithwaite decided, 'What can we do? Switch the lights off quickly.'

'No disrespect intended, sir,' said Davies. 'But this is my scene and I'm responsible for the safety of all here. The lights will stay on.'

'Not now,' stated Assistant Chief Constable Patterson. 'I'm in command now and you, King, are suspended from duty forthwith.'

'Very good, sir,' said Davies. 'Come on, Barney.'

Davies King and Ted Barnes turned and walked away from the scene, walked away from the lights and the bomb, and towards the safety of their car.

'Hey!' shouted Patterson. 'Where do you think you two are going?'

'Home,' replied Davies. 'I'm suspended and it's your scene. Goodnight, sir. Mind how you go!' Davies walked away.

'Hey! I give the orders here,' shouted Patterson.

'In that case knock the lights off and work in the dark, Mister Assistant Chief Constable. You've got a couple of hours before the press and cameras turn up so I would establish an outer cordon if I were you.' Davies King looked at his wristwatch and said, 'And by lunchtime when the media are here in their hundreds the Met bomb squad will be here. Good luck!'

Patterson engaged Ted Barnes who was guarding no man's land. Then he looked at a Jaguar with steamed up windows; then he watched Davies King halfway towards his car and striding out.

Patterson looked at the anxious face of Chief Inspector Jackson and then looked at Superintendent Allithwaite who seemed to have aged ten years in as many seconds.

Bending low, Patterson scanned beneath the Jaguar.

Davies King was at his car.

Patterson was searching the underneath of the Mayor's Jaguar. He saw the white plastic sandwich box; he reached out to touch it and then thought better. Fear drilled into his marrow; he backed away from the vehicle in horror, and then stood up and shouted, 'Davies!'

Davies King was holding his car door handle. He stopped and turned.

'Davies, can you dismantle a bomb?'

'No, sir. But I know a man who can,' delivered Davies King.

The heavens were open and rain fell heavily onto the tarmac. An outer cordon had been established. Nearby residents had been evacuated. Emergency services were on red alert. Sandbags had been placed around the vehicle. Senior Command was in attendance, and their tuxedos were wringing wet.

Jackson, Allithwaite and Patterson were at their wits end.

Jackson was worrying, 'He's finished! My brother in law is finished if he's on the telly and this gets out.'

'It'll get out,' said Allithwaite. 'We can't stop this. The Press will have a field day what with the Chief Executive and the Mayoress caught in the back of the Mayor's car at the Mayor's Ball. Can you imagine the headlines?'

'The headlines might be worse if that bomb goes off,' suggested Patterson sternly.

Jackson said, 'Did you have to release Max Fowler?'

'Where's that coffee we ordered?' interrupted Patterson. 'It's bloody raining cats and dogs; I'm soaked to the skin, the evening is spoilt and I haven't a clue how I'm going to explain this one to the Chief Constable. Get on the 'phone and get that coffee moving. And get the library opened up. I need a forward command base. Now!'

A uniformed officer standing nearby heard the order, sensed the tension, and scuttled off to find keys for the library.

'Of course I had to release Max Fowler,' said Allithwaite to Jackson. 'Or do you want me to wait for Crillsea to explode into a thousand pieces? What do you suggest, Chief Inspector?'

'Did we have to do a deal with Max Fowler and drop all the charges?' queried Jackson. He brushed rain from his collar and stepped back beneath the porch of Crillsea library.

'It makes sense if we can stop a bomb going off,' revealed Allithwaite. 'Where's that coffee?' And a raindrop fell errantly from the end of his nose onto his bowtie.

'Yes, but agreeing to drop an investigation into Davies King as well was a step too far,' suggested Patterson.

'You did sanction it, sir,' replied Allithwaite.

Jackson said, 'Did you really have to release Max Fowler? I thought we'd got enough to make a GBH charge stick and enough to rope Davies King in for misconduct and a stack of discipline offences that would sack him?'

'Of course I had to release him. We can't afford to wait fourteen hours for the Met to turn up,' snapped Patterson, tetchily. 'Max Fowler is here in Crillsea. He's the only one who knows what to do. He's a professional, highly skilled, highly trained, the best of the best. Do you know his pedigree? He's a Bomb God and the Met are carrying out a massive raid in London. They've found guns, firearms, explosives, God knows what. Their bomb disposal people are tied up.'

'And the military too, I take it?' asked Keith Jackson.

Do you know how to dismantle a bomb, chief inspector?'

'No, sir!'

'Then shut up, you bloody fool and get me a coffee. Now.'

Wearing his bomb disposal suit, Max Fowler slowly approached the Jaguar and casually threw a slight wave at the terrified occupants. The petrified face of the Mayoress was just visible above the dashboard and the Chief Executive was pressed tight against the back of his seat. Looking into the Jaguar, Max sensed the tension, could only guess the level of fear, and tried a smile that was intended to comfort but probably had no effect whatsoever.

'Control, test my signal,' he radioed.

'Check, check,' from female control.

'Switch the lights off please. The intense beam is spoiling my vision.'

'Check, check.'

The lights went out and Superintendent Max Fowler dropped onto his knees and crawled towards the Jaguar. Almost immediately he saw the device.

'Contact!' he radioed. 'Confirming unexploded incendiary device. It's magnetic and it's live.'

'Check, check,' from Control

'History of this device suggests between two to four pounds of Semtex but it could be linked to more poundage which I have yet to find. The device is similar to a seventy-five minute timeout,' from Max.

The rain had stopped and the reception area of Crillsea library had quickly become a control centre. Wet raincoats and soggy silk scarves were drying out over the back of a chair. Row upon row of paperback and hardback books lined up as if in school assembly. But the assembly was all ears.

'What does all that mean?' asked Jackson.

'It means the timing device will activate at the end of a seventy five minute cycle and it will explode,' advised Patterson.

'Why hasn't it gone off then?' asked Jackson.

'I'm guessing it's faulty. One of the metal pins has ceased moving round and has stopped about a millionth of an inch from the contact. If it touches it will cause a flash from a battery wired to the contact pin. The flash will hardly be seen by the human eye but it will send a charge into the Semtex explosives and it will explode. Do you want to go and check?' said Patterson.

'No, sir,' replied Jackson.

'Then shut up and listen,' ordered Patterson. 'He's going in.'

Underneath the Jaguar Max felt sweat flowing down his neck. His body clock already warned him deep inside that his blood pressure was too high, his pulse was racing, and his respiration had gone haywire. Half a day in a dank police cell with no food, no drink, and no visitors had not helped. And it was really quite amazing how the human mind changed its perspective on things when a cell door remained shut for half a day or more.

Max slid another inch closer to the target.

He couldn't recall how many unexploded incendiary devices he had managed to dismantle in his long career but he did recall that on every occasion it invariably came down to this.

Taking a deep breath Max said, 'Making primary contact. Stand by!'

Inch by inch Max crawled beneath the Jaguar and aimed for a spot directly beneath the driver's seat. A drop of oil fell from the engine housing and spoiled the tarmac beneath. Yet he never lost understanding of how mucky and dirty the underneath of a car could be. Gently and carefully, his hands cleared away dirt that clung to the underbelly. He searched with his eyes for a secondary wire and let out a low breath of satisfaction when his fingers could not find a wire leading away from the main device.

Crucially, Max moved his eyes and his hands all round the box, working away slowly and then carefully inwards and towards the device that was central in his mind. It was as if he were performing a time-honoured ritual as he slowly worked through a manual in his mind and discounted all manner of theories known exclusively to him. He worked slowly. It did not matter to him whether there was a second to go in his life or a minute to go before the device exploded. It was his device now. It was no-one else's. He owned it. He worshipped the bomb, knew it inside out and then some, and the bomb worshipped him. He was a Bomb God.

It was the way he had been taught by a young sergeant many years ago. He remembered the young sergeant: the one who had been taken in Serbia when his hand had prodded and slipped and he was blown into a thousand pieces in a green field far away from home. Ever since, and whenever Max had been up close and personal with a target, he had quietly devoted his bomb, his device, his target, to that young sergeant.

There was a sudden bang from inside the car which resounded downward and deafened Max. He reckoned it might be someone's foot.

'Don't move,' Max shouted. 'Don't move a bloody inch!'

Max slithered further to get purchase and feeling for the target. It was his place of work. He was at home with his fear and oil stains and dirt. An inch more, that's all he needed.

Then he clearly saw a familiar magnet sticking out from the underbelly of the Jaguar by about half an inch: the depth of a magnet securing his device to the underbelly of the Mayor's official car.

There beneath the Jaguar, apparently seconds from life or death, Max chuckled quietly to himself when he read his own writing scrawled in marker pen across the plastic of the device. *Finchley...Case 326/7 For tutorial only...*

Next to his writing someone had written *One nil.... Check...*

Davies King, Max thought to himself quietly. Davies bloody King, Chess Master moving the pieces, thought Max as he gently prised his training device from the Jaguar's underbelly. Yes, that's my device alright, he thought. It was last seen in my van in the yard at Crillsea police station, from which Davies King no doubt snaffled it for his own use.

Max Fowler radioed, 'Clear! All clear,' as he shuffled away from the Jaguar and back into the land of the living.

They greeted him like a hero when he returned to Crillsea library carrying the device. They applauded and clapped when he unlocked his strongbox and secured the device for forensic examination. They thought him so brave, Superintendent Max Fowler: the man of the moment.

'Of course, one can't proceed on the charges now,' declared Patterson.

'It would be wrong to prosecute,' decided Allithwaite.

'Not in the public interest,' acknowledged Patterson. 'And, on reflection, the evidence against him is exaggerated.'

'He's so brave,' suggested Jackson.

'A man of quality,' confirmed Allithwaite.

'It needs to be written up that way,' said Patterson looking out of the library window towards a very shocked and surprised Mayoress and an extremely agitated Chief Executive of the County Council. 'No explosion but we're not out of the woods yet,' he summarised.

A paramedic team treated the Mayoress and Chief Executive for shock.

'Excuse me, sir,' announced Barney approaching with mugs on a tray.

'Yes, what is it?' asked Jackson.

'Coffee, sir,' smiled Barney.

'At long last! Leave it on the table won't you!' suggested Patterson. The assistant chief constable turned to Superintendent Allithwaite and said, 'Yes, we need to raise this Max Fowler chap into the public eye and hope he will deflect the media from the Mayoress and your brother in law, chief inspector.'

'He's on holiday, sir,' interjected Barney still holding a tray.

'Who? What are you talking about, Constable Burns?' barked Patterson.

'Barnes, sir. Superintendent Fowler, sir. He's off duty and on holiday. I believe he volunteered his services, sir.'

'Volunteered his services,' laughed Superintendent Allithwaite.

'Of course,' Barney retorted. 'Off duty bomb disposal man holidaying in Crillsea saves town from loss of life and widespread damage. Isn't that the case? Isn't that what they would write in the newspapers? You guys will know better than me, begging your pardon, sir.'

'Ridiculous!' sounded Chief Inspector Jackson with a scowl.

'Promote the town?' suggested Superintendent Allithwaite with a wry conspiratorially smile.

'Good for tourism?' asked Jackson wavering with the tide.

'Quite!' schemed the assistant chief constable. Patterson selected a coffee and took a sip. 'What's your name? Burns was it? Or was it Barton? I didn't quite catch it.'

'Barnes, sir. Thing is, sir. It's like Inspector King was explaining to me. You see, he was telling me that when we arrived the Chief

Executive, that's Mister Jackson's brother in law, sir; well, he was flashing his headlights. You know the Jaguar headlights.'

'So?' asked Patterson, intrigued. 'What's that got to do with it?'

'Well, Inspector King says, and I agree with him, sir,' offered Barney. 'That the Chief Executive and the Mayoress might have realised their car was booby-trapped and were signalling to us to help. You see, it's how you see things, sir. Perspectives, I think they call it.'

'Have we met before?' asked Patterson.

'Probably, I've got twenty nine and half years service in,' said Barney.

'Quite! I thought I knew you. Allithwaite take this man's name. Now then, Sergeant Barnes. Tell me more.'

'Constable, sir.'

'Surely not,' proposed Patterson. 'You'll be telling me next that you're a dinosaur, sergeant. Now then, what exactly did your Inspector King and yourself say happened?'

The assistant chief constable's hand slid easily onto Barney's shoulder, in time honoured fashion, as he guided him away from the others. Patterson asked, 'Where is Inspector King by the way?'

'He's gone, sir. He said something about a murder we're on but he's gone to the pub first to wet his whistle and get dried off, if that makes sense? His 'phone went. I think he's meeting an informant as well. You know what it's like being a busy detective, sir'

'Quite,' considered the assistant chief constable. 'Quite, indeed.'

'In fact, I think Inspector King might have tracked down Harry Reynolds, sir. I know he's hoping to tie this murder up very soon.'

'Harry Reynolds!' intervened Chief Inspector Jackson. 'Well, there's another one of my suspects going down, sir. You know, it's good to see King reacting to my instructions after all this time.'

'Instructions?' queried Barney. 'Now there's a story, chief inspector.'

'Quite,' growled Assistant Chief Constable Patterson. 'Tell me, Chief Inspector Jackson, does anyone around here know what the hell is going on?'

The Anchor was busy but Davies King found the telephone without much problem.

'Max Fowler is free,' declared Davies King on the telephone to Big Al Jessop. 'And I don't do stalemates.'

'Thanks for the call. Where is he?'

'In the back room, Mister King,' replied Bill. 'On his own, he is.'

'Thanks, Bill.'

'Mister King, Davies!'

'Yes, Bill. What's the problem?'

'I didn't see you here today. I should have said that last week and I didn't and I think you got into trouble because I opened my big mouth and told them everything about you. I'm sorry.'

'Don't worry, Bill. I can get into trouble myself without anyone helping. Trouble is my middle name, I think.'

Bill said, 'But I want you to know, Mister King, that I didn't see you here today.'

'Davies, Bill. Call me Davies. No. Neither of us are here today.' Davies King walked away but then turned and said, 'Bill.'

The licensee looked up.

'Thanks,' said Davies. He turned and pushed open a door into a snug and homely bar affectionately named 'the back room' by all the locals. The bar was decked out with paintings of boats in the harbour, fishing nets, anchors and things mercantile.

Harry Reynolds was on his mobile 'phone. He killed the connection as soon as he saw Davies King approach and ventured, 'Why, Mister King, how nice of you to drop by. Business is it, Mister King? Radios, you said last week. How can I help?'

'I thought I'd find you here, Harry. Just a few questions if you don't mind,' said Davies sitting down beside Harry Reynolds.

'Questions?' queried Harry. 'What kind of questions, Mister King?'

'Legal ones, Harry, with good answers, if you don't mind.'

'Sounds like I need a solicitor,' suggested Harry Reynolds with a wry smile and a shuffle towards the end of his seat.

'Solicitor? No, honest men don't need solicitors, Harry. They just need truth and wisdom. And you do trust me, don't you?' challenged Davies.

'Depends what's on your chess board, as you might say, Mister King.'

'Max Fowler tells me he bumped into you a while back on the cliff paths between Crillsea and Tevvie. Remember that do you?' asked Davies.

'Max Fowler?' replied Harry, thinking. 'Your chess mate. Yes, I do believe we met. Why?

'What were you doing up on the cliff path? That's my question.'

'I live up there, Mister King; near the house where all the trouble has been. Murder, they say.'

'Who says?' asked Davies.

'Voices, Mister King, just voices and what the newspapers say, of course. But I'll tell you now don't go pinning any murder on me, Mister King. It's nothing to do with me that murder or the jewellery.'

'What jewellery?' asked Davies.

Harry Reynolds stood up to go but Davies King grabbed his arm and pulled him down. 'What jewellery, Harry?'

'The jewellery that was stolen from the house; it was in the newspaper, Mister King.'

Davies King tightened his grip. He squeezed slowly and felt a bulge forming in his bicep.

Harry Reynolds was trying to pull away but a vice held him. Nervously, he said, 'The jewellery stolen from the house where that woman was murdered.'

Davies released his hold, smiled, brushed imagined fluff from Harry's blazer and said, 'There was no mention of any jewellery in the newspaper, Harry. We didn't release those details to the media.'

Davies King let the words sink in as he studied Harry Reynolds and then he said, 'You'd best be telling me what you know, Harry. Here or the nick, I don't really care. It's your choice.'

Harry thought for a while and then offered, 'I had nothing to do with the murder but I know about the rings.'

'Never had you down as a violent man, Harry,' offered Davies. 'Bit of a wide boy. Buy one get one free. Oh, yes, bit of a wide boy, you are, but in all the years I've known you I've never seen you violent.'

Davies checked his watch. 'The clock's ticking, what do you know?'

'Mister King! Davies isn't it? Okay to call you Davies, is it?' asked Harry. 'I mean I know you now, don't I? Known you for years, really.'

'You can call me the Queen of Sheba if you like but stop buying time and tell me what you know. You live near the murder scene. You know about the stolen jewellery. You're in the frame whether you like it or not.'

'Problem is, Mister King, I live about a mile from the house in a cottage on the cliff. Me and the wife.'

'Wife? Never had you down as married, Harry, but then I suppose you don't bring your wife down town selling radios, do you?'

'No, I don't but I'm married, alright. And we really do have a cottage industry up there. The wife makes things and I sell them, you see.'

'Make things! What do you make?' asked Davies.

'We put British plugs on foreign made vacuum cleaners, proper batteries into worn out radios, clocks and thermometers onto Lakeland slate. All kinds of things. And we buy bankrupt stock to resell, of course.'

'How do you know the house?' asked Davies.

'A few months ago they moved up here from London. He's a Spaniard and she's a Londoner. He's a real 'un, Mister King. Miguel, Manuel? Something like that, he was called. Tasty for your line of work, I suspect. But the woman, Eleanor, was it?'

'Elena!' said Davies. 'His name is Manuel, as far as I know.'

'Yeah, Elena and Manuel, that's right. She was friendly. She wanted to meet local people, make friends, and settle down. He just wanted peace and quiet. She invited all the neighbours and people from the Trust to come to their house for drinks and a barbecue. Including us! But him? Manuel! He didn't want to know; kept himself to himself, that one. Strange fish, Mister King.'

'And you went to their barbecue?' asked Davies.

'We both went. Me and the wife, neighbourly it was, and in any case my sister, Peggy, kept house for them and it seemed right to look as if we belonged; you know, supporting Peggy and suchlike. Anyway, what a house they have. There's a swimming pool, sauna, and everything, but I expect you know that. Elena showed us round but he kept out of the way and spent the afternoon with his shady friends from the City: financiers and the like. Money men, I think.'

Harry adjusted his tie and released his collar before continuing, 'I saw the jewellery and all the fancy stuff they had. Couldn't help it really, I was just having a look round, you see,'

'On the ratch, you mean,' suggested Davies.

229

Harry Reynolds grew in confidence and looked directly into Davies King's eyes. 'She was trying to impress. Elena was trying to make new friends. You know how it is. Everyone needs to be someone.'

'Are you telling me why your fingerprints and DNA are all over the house?'

Harry betrayed himself by looking away and then lied partially saying, 'Oh, don't try that one, Mister King. Peggy is their cleaner. She cleans twice a week. Peggy told me about the other woman in their life.'

'The other woman?' asked Davies.

'Yeah, Sophie de Lorenzo. Sassy, they called her,' replied Harry.

'Did you ever meet her, this Sophie de Lorenzo?' asked Davies.

'Oh yes. She was there at the barbecue with the sausages, rosé wine and toasted marshmallows.'

'Attractive?' asked Davies.

'I'll say, Mister King, very attractive to both Elena and the Spaniard.'

'Both of them?' queried Davies.

'Like Elena, Sophie was a lesbian,' declared Harry Reynolds.

'A lesbian, you sure of that?'

'Well, I think Elena and Sophie liked female company as much as they liked male company, if you see what I mean. But Sophie! Sassy was a good name for her and she seemed to be hankering after Elena more than the Spaniard. The Spaniard was jealous of his wife and Sophie and what they shared. He even bought Elena a yacht as a gift to try and turn her head back towards him, but it didn't work. Anyway, it was pretty obvious that afternoon.'

'Why do say that?' asked Davies.

'Elena and her husband went inside.' Harry began shuffling in his seat again. 'Words were said because she'd spent time with Sassy.'

'Sophie! Call her Sophie, Harry.'

'Okay! I think the husband was jealous of Elena's relationship with Sophie. I reckon he fancied Sophie. You could tell by the way he looked at her. That's what made me think the Spaniard fancied Sophie. You know me, Mister King. I sell directly to people. I work people out. I know these things. I know when I try and sell something whether I'm going to make a sale within ten seconds of approaching someone and....'

'Yeah, yeah, Harry. I know the score,' interjected Davies.

'Anyway, words were said and when Elena came back she was a bit tearful,' volunteered Harry. 'Crying and everything.'

'And you saw that? You saw Elena crying?' asked Davies.

'Couldn't miss it really.'

'How come?' asked Davies.

'My fingerprints, Mister King, it's my fingerprints and DNA, you see. I know you'll find them but it wasn't me. I was just sizing the job up, looking at stuff, on the ratch, as you said.'

'Planning to come back, weren't you?'

'Not me, Mister King. I was in the house looking at the mortar and pestle. Marble! Antique, very, very expensive, Mister King, that's when it happened.'

'What happened, Harry? Tell me slowly in black and white. No shades of grey or what you thought happened. Tell me exactly what happened.'

'It was in the lounge. I saw the Spaniard hit Elena in the lounge and she got a black eye.'

'Where were you, Harry?'

'In the bedroom searching through the drawers, Mister King.'

'Bad habit you've got there, Harry, and you will know that your sister does keep house for them but she's not the best of cleaners.'

'I reckon, Mister King.... Davies. I didn't steal anything, Mister King. But you've got my fingerprints and my DNA because I was just looking, that's all. I didn't murder anyone. Honest!'

'And the jewellery. What happened to the jewellery?'

Harry Reynolds bent down and rummaged through a holdall. He produced a radio and turned it slowly in his hands.

'Nice one this, Mister King; bankrupt stock cleaned up and repaired by the wife in the cottage. It's yours for a note or two.'

Davies considered the radio with his hands but asked, 'What did you take from their house, Harry. You know, souvenirs?'

'Not a thing, Mister King. Honestly, not a thing.'

'Not even keys, for example?'

'Not even keys, Mister King. Why would I need keys, Mister King?'

'And you mentioned the Trust. You said there were people there from the Trust. Which Trust would that be?'

'Where she worked, the Farringday Trust,' declared Harry.

Davies King nodded and then slowly pushed the radio to one side and said, 'I can bust you now, Harry for this, that and the other, so don't push your luck. The jewellery, Harry, now tell me about the jewellery.'

'It's like this, Mister King. When he went into the nick years ago he owed lots of bad people lots of money. I went to the barbecue with the wife and saw it. I told him there was jewellery in the house: really good jewellery and some real posh fancy stuff. I think he did it, Mister King. He did it for the jewellery, I think.'

'Who?' demanded Davies. 'Who the hell are you talking about?'

'Why, Stan Striker, of course. That's who you want to know about it, isn't it. Stan Striker. You told me last week you were interested. Well, the voices tell me Stan and Reg have a nice little earner going there, so they have. I reckon they murdered her for the jewellery.'

'What makes you say that?' asked Davies.

'They're moving lots of stolen ice around. Didn't you know?'

Davies King looked into space thinking.

'What you going to do about my fingerprints and DNA, Mister King?' asked Harry. Putting his radio away, Harry said, 'I know you got my prints in the house, didn't you, Mister King? Mister King... Mister King.'

Davies King turned slowly to Harry Reynolds and asked, 'Reg?'

Harry Reynolds allowed his eyes to fall for a split second onto his mobile 'phone but quickly replied, 'Reg, that's all I know, Mister King.'

Davies clasped his hand over Harry's mobile, flicked it open and researched the last number called.

'Reginald Arnold Cuttleworth!' pronounced Davies.

'Err, well, oh yes, so it is,' spluttered a worried Harry Reynolds. 'Yeah, Reg, he's only been out about six months or so. That's him, Mister King.'

'Get your things together, Harry. You never were a very good liar. I've got to take you in for conspiracy to commit burglary with Stan and Reg and I have to tell you that we need to talk to you at length about these murders.'

'I'm not going with you, Mister King. It wasn't me. I didn't do any murder, I just told Stan Striker about the fancy ice in the posh house, that's all.'

'Harry, you've got to trust me on this one. You're nicked for conspiracy and I've had one hell of a day. Where are you going to run to? We're both too old for this carry on but you know how these things work. Clear the slate with me on this jewellery affair and things will work out okay, you'll see.'

'And my fingerprints and DNA?' asked Harry Reynolds.

'Are on a cabinet in a bedroom drawer and is the reason you were always going to get nicked, Harry. Now tell me about Stan and Reg before we have a stroll down to the nick for the night.'

'And you want me to trust you, Mister King. You're the top jack in Crillsea despite what Archie and all the others say. You can probably put me away for murder but you want me to trust you on this one?'

'Do you have a choice, Harry?' posed Davies.

'No, Mister bloody Davies King, I haven't, have I?'

Later that night, and from the cell block in Crillsea police station, Davies King telephoned Annie Rock, Ted Barnes, and Terry Webster. He told them he needed them for a job 'first thing' then he telephoned Superintendent Bert Allithwaite and said, 'Superintendent Allithwaite, are you awake?'

Bert Allithwaite hadn't been asleep very long and his restless night bore testament to a bizarre ending to the Mayor's Ball. He pulled himself together and said, 'Davies, what the blazes damn time is this to be calling me?'

'You wanted to know, sir,' replied Davies. 'You wanted to know on an hourly basis, so I'm telling you before I tell anyone else. I'm going to London with my team and we're bringing back the man who murdered Elena Martinez. I thought you'd like to be the first to know, sir.'

'Well, err, thank you, inspector. I'll see you later today then.'

'Indeed you will, sir, Goodnight.' Davies ended the call, winked at the sergeant, and gathered himself for the rush to London.

~

Chapter Twelve
~ ~ ~

Dateline: Sunday
Canary Wharf, London.

As arranged, early doors meant an early start and a drive to London's Canary Wharf, or to be precise London's Dockland Airport.

Canary Wharf Tower presided over affairs again when Barney pulled the vehicle into a space in front of the airport and pulled on the handbrake. Annie and Webby followed suit.

No sooner had they arrived when Al Jessop emerged from the departures lounge, shook hands with each member of the party from Crillsea and said to Davies, 'They're in a private jet on the apron. They think there's a slight delay due to debris on the runway so I suggest you get it over with as quick as you can.'

'We'll do our best,' replied Davies.

'Which one do you want?' asked Al Jessop.

'You should have three,' suggested Davies.

'I'm told all three are on board, but which one do you want?'

'Mmm... I'll let you know, sir,' replied Davies King.

Al Jessop shook his head and said, 'Are you gambling again?'

Davies replied, 'Not at all, come on guys, let's go.'

They were through departures, bypassing security, through the gates and onto the tarmac apron where a beautiful silver private jet sat waiting for permission from the control tower to taxi onto the runway.

Signals were made by ground staff and a handful of airport security vehicles suddenly encircled the aircraft. The pilot shut his engine down and a passenger staircase was transported to the jet.

Davies King was first on board and strode down the aisle towards his target. They were the only passengers and were all called Farringday. At the end of the short aisle the passenger compartment opened up into a wider area where the three brothers sat, strapped in, with seatbelts on, in large plush armchair seats that dominated a carpeted lounge area. The seats were made of deep soft leather and portrayed a certain opulence that was present throughout the aircraft.

'Oh no,' declared Rupert Farringday loudly, 'Not you again, Inspector King. This really is quite ridiculous. What do you want?' He unbuckled his seatbelt and stood to challenge Davies King.

'You, sir,' replied Davies.

'Me?' queried Rupert Farringday. 'Richard, where's our lawyer, this is beyond a joke.'

Davies King was quite assertive when he declared, 'I'm afraid this isn't a joke, Mister Farringday. We are investigating the murder of Elena Martinez. We have reason to believe the man responsible is on this aircraft.'

Rupert Farringday laughed aloud and said, 'Richard, call our steward and get our solicitor here. Remind him we pay him an absolute fortune to represent us. Tell him to bring a writ of 'habeas corpus', if necessary.'

Richard signalled for the steward by pressing a switch in an overhead compartment and moved uneasily in his seat as he unbuckled his seatbelt and began to fidget nervously.

'Inspector,' said Rupert, 'How many times do I have to tell you, none of us were in the United Kingdom when your murders occurred?'

A smartly dressed steward wearing a suit, collar and tie, appeared from behind a curtain, spoke to Richard, and replied, 'I'll make the call, sir.'

Richard Farringday nodded his thanks to the steward, turned to Davies and said, 'I'll tell you something, inspector, why should we listen to you ranting about a murder that happened when we were all abroad?'

'Very well, Mister Farringday, so be it,' replied Davies King. 'I'll start at the beginning with an island codenamed Conchenta and a scientist called Elena Martinez. But I should warn all three of you that you need not say anything unless you wish to do so; anything you say may be used in evidence against you.'

'Oh please do carry on, why don't you? We've done nothing wrong,' replied Rupert with a casual wave of his hand. 'I'm all ears but a little bored already, inspector.'

By now, the three brothers were all free from the shackles of their seats. Richard and Rupert paced the floor but Robert remained seated and alert.

'Let me begin with Elena's husband,' revealed Davies. 'Manuel was a corporate lawyer. He murdered Sophie de Lorenzo, because he discovered she was having a lesbian relationship with his wife.'

'Oh dear,' laughed Richard. 'That would cause some concern in the sedate and demure streets of boring Crillsea, inspector. What next, wife swapping at Tevington on Sea or flower arranging classes in the village hall?'

Davies ignored him and continued, 'Manuel had a fling with Sophie but it didn't work out well. She threatened to tell his wife, Elena, of their affair.'

'Really, inspector,' yawned Rupert Farringday, 'I heard on the radio that he'd been knocked over by a London bus following a botched attempt at arresting him on the streets of the capital.'

'Do you think we're safe, Robert?' added Richard.

There was no response from Robert and Davies continued, 'You're missing the point. Manuel had an affair with Sophie but then Sophie had an affair with Elena and that was just too much for Manuel. He was insanely jealous of his wife's attention to Sophie, so much so that he bought the yacht, Conchenta, for Elena because he needed to try and turn her away from Sophie. There were three in a relationship for which there was only room for two.'

'Inspector, this is all very interesting but you're talking about Sophie de Lorenzo. What on earth has she got to do with Elena's murder?'

'Oh, I can assure you the two murders are connected, sir, certainly from the investigative point of view.'

Rupert nodded with an air of resigned interest and replied, 'Very well, convince me if you can?'

'Standing behind me is Detective Chief Superintendent Alan Jessop of the Metropolitan Police Flying Squad,' said Davies.

Al Jessop confirmed his presence with a nod to the three brothers.

'Chief Superintendent Jessop recently arrested a man by the name of Benny Abbott; indeed, an operation in London has led to the arrest of quite a few people connected to Manuel Martinez and Benny Abbott. You see, Sophie discovered from her relationship with both Manuel and Elena that he, Manuel, represented numerous clients who sought to invest cash overseas with the purpose of hiding it from the taxman. In addition, Benny Abbott and his friends engaged Manuel Martinez to launder money for them, money gained from the criminal enterprises they ran. Isn't that right, Mister Jessop?'

'Correct,' said Al Jessop. 'Benny was a money lender and a money launderer, apart from being one of London's most villainous criminals.

Benny moved money through Manuel. There's a quite complex record of banking movements through offshore accounts that substantiate this but it's fair to say Manuel's job was to turn hard cash into property assets and fund more criminal activities. But Benny wasn't the only one using Manuel's professional corporate services. A Lydia Bryant, protected by a thug called Jack Creighton used some of the same money channels provided by Manuel to move cocaine and heroin.'

Rupert Farringday replied, 'But I can assure you we have never used these channels to move money or drugs. The Farringday Trust is a well ran legitimate business with multi-national concerns, chief superintendent. What would our shareholders think if our company got mixed up in such dealings?'

'If you'd asked me that question last week, I wouldn't have had an answer,' replied Jessop. 'But I can tell you Katrina Kitchener is a well known property developer in the west end. She too has been arrested for money laundering following her friendship with Benny Abbott, but interestingly, she owns shares in the Farringday Trust. Small world, isn't it, Mister Farringday?'

'Well, we can't be held responsible for every share that is bought and sold on the stock exchange, Mister Jessop,' replied Richard Farringday. 'Just what are you suggesting?'

'Yes,' interjected Rupert Farringday. 'What has this to do with us? Just tell me in plain and simple words what the death of Sophie has to do with us? I don't understand at all.'

'Davies?' queried Jessop.

'I'm sure you do to some degree, Mister Farringday,' continued Davies. 'Shareholders, I heard someone say. I think you'll agree that the price of a share in any company goes up and down dependant on market conditions, agreed?'

Rupert Farringday walked away a few steps forcing Richard to respond with, 'That is how the market works, inspector, yes. But our company is a Trust dealing with scientific research and the world of drug discovery and developing drugs for medicinal use. It is not a vehicle to be used in the criminal way you have portrayed.'

'Isn't it,' countered Davies. 'I beg to differ. You see, Mister Farringday, your statement regarding the Trust being involved with drug discovery and drug development captures the connection between the two murders. You will recall I once asked you if crocus are used by yourselves in drug discovery.'

'That's right, you did,' replied Rupert.

'But we don't use crocus in any of our applications,' confirmed Richard.

'No,' responded Davies, 'But Manuel tried to poison Sophie by giving her a mix of crocus in the mistaken belief it would kill her. It didn't, but that's what led us to your laboratory and our interest in the Farringday Trust.'

'Very well,' replied Rupert. 'Is our lawyer here yet? Steward, find out from the control tower.'

The steward scuttled away and was immediately stopped by Annie Rock, who quite clearly said, 'And you're going nowhere. Stand still.'

Unperturbed, Davies King continued, 'Elena was one of your top research scientists at the Trust. She discovered a drug in the plant 'Andorinha': a flowering shrub found all over the Mediterranean islands and the Tropics. We have evidence indicating she believed she had discovered a cure for AIDS. You know she made an application from it and you know she tested it on monkeys before she visited an island off the Azores to test it on the small population there. You knew this because each and every one of you complained to her about exceeding the budget you had allocated to her. She regularly exceeded that budget because she wanted to get the drug development right, didn't she? If she had successfully discovered a drug that could destroy AIDS, your company would have the only proven vaccine in the whole wide world. It would be worth a veritable fortune in the pharmaceutical industry. Barney...'

Ted Barnes stepped forward and said, 'When we located Manuel Martinez, we found Elena's laptop on the yacht, Conchenta. A search through the emails reveals contacts between Elena, you guys, and various scientists in America, Madrid and Lisbon. The emails detail technical questions between Elena and scientists at those locations. Quite clearly, Elena raised crucial matters of concern to her with the foremost brains of the pharmaceutical industry. And, quite remarkably, Elena was questioning the effectiveness of the drug she had discovered. Your problem is one of you knew that whilst the drug had worked in unofficial clinical trials for nearly a year, it failed after six months on younger patients. One of you told her to go ahead anyway and develop the drug.

One of you didn't care enough to stop the procedure. You were all too greedy. It's all here on Elena's laptop.'

Terry Webster stepped forward and said, 'You told us a patent had been applied for and papers had been submitted by Elena. You told us it was all done and dusted and all that was needed was an updated amendment from Elena. The reality is when I went to the Patents Office I discovered that no patent has been lodged and no application is outstanding. There's no trace of any discussion whatsoever between Elena, your Trust, and the Patents office.'

Annie Rock added, 'All those factors didn't stop you allowing the share price to climb to its highest point ever; and you all own shares in your company. So which one of you took exception to Elena Martinez? Or did you all take exception to her? Did you all leak to the market that you'd found a cure for AIDS? Did you all stand idly by and watch the share price grow in the sure and certain knowledge the market was buying up as many shares as possible because you'd quietly told the investment bankers, pension holders, and money market, that you'd made a major discovery? Did you manipulate Manuel Martinez's corporate network and banking friends to invest money into shares in your company? The share price went through the roof; one of you was buying and selling company shares regularly. One of you was making a fortune. And that was the problem, wasn't it? The only people who knew that the Aids vaccine had failed were Elena Martinez and you three guys. But you all allowed the share price to climb up in the knowledge that your buyers thought you were going to make them all a packet.'

Rupert and Richard swopped confused glances.

Robert looked down at his shoes.

Davies said, 'You all knew what was going on. You all allowed the share price to climb and made money because of it. But Elena decided she would spill the beans and threatened to tell the authorities what was going on. Your apparent success was about to be exposed as a sham and a failure. Project VXW 3091 failed on six months, didn't it? The share price was about to dive once the word was out and the company was about to crash, wasn't it?'

Rupert Farringday emerged from his shell and said, 'I think I owe you an apology, Inspector King. I admit we seem to have made a lot of money out of this venture but I, personally, had absolutely no knowledge whatsoever that the clinical trials on Conchenta had failed.'

'Me neither,' added Richard. 'But it all makes sense now, inspector. It's obvious why you have been so dogmatic in your enquiries about us.'

Robert Farringday shouted, 'We were all abroad when this happened.'

Davies turned purposefully to Robert and said, 'My officers carried out numerous enquiries with the Advanced Passenger System Information. You know, before you travel you have to give your details to your flight operator. Your brothers travelled to their destinations. I have video coverage of them arriving at their airports and their hotels, courtesy of international policing co-operation. But you, Robert, you returned to the UK two days earlier, didn't you? I have your flight number and a video of you and Carla arriving at Stansted airport. Oh yes, Carla, and that perfume she wears. What an unforgettable perfume. She wore it one night in a pub called the Anchor in Crillsea whilst you were with her. You interfered with a chess game I was involved in, remember?'

Robert Farringday remained impassive.

Davies challenged, 'All three of you have lied to me. You all told me you had never been to Elena's house but in reality you all went to a barbecue there once before. And you, Robert, you once returned Elena's house keys to her when she left them at work. If you check with your security people at the Trust they'll tell you that you are not allowed to take personal possessions into the laboratory. One day she left her house keys with Security and you told Security you would deliver them to her. You did, and realised how easy it would be to take her keys quite regularly. So the day after you interrupted my chess game, you went up to Crillsea Cliffs, let yourself in with Elena's keys, pleaded with her not to tell the world the AIDS vaccine had failed, and then strangled her to death when she refused to co-operate. Why you? Because we know you have been buying and selling shares for the last eighteen months in the hope of making a few million pounds profit.'

'You can't prove this,' screamed Robert suddenly.

'Let me have a look at your shoes, Mister Farringday,' demanded Davies King.

'What? My shoes... What are you on about?' asked Robert.

Davies declared, 'When Elena was murdered, there was a struggle. I believe I will find traces of pink porcelain on the sole of your shoes. Actually, my top scientists, not yours, will find traces of porcelain on one pair of your shoes, and probably glass, because only the murderer has glass and porcelain on his shoes that match glass and porcelain in the house.'

'You'll never find the jewellery,' screamed Robert Farringday.

'I didn't mention jewellery, Robert, but you did and you're nicked.'

Robert Farringday sunk back down into his chair, held his head in his hands, and began to cry. 'I meant only to frighten her. She wouldn't listen. She was happy to watch us all crash. I did it for us, Rupert. Richard, I did it for us.'

'No, Robert,' said a quiet and saddened Rupert, 'You did it for you.'

Robert Farringday cried aloud, and cried alone.

'And as for all three of you,' said Davies. 'I'm arresting you all for insider dealing, or to be precise, dealing in price-affected securities. You all bought shares on the open market using inside information known only to yourselves regarding the drug discovery that you all thought you had made. And you bought them to sell them for a much higher price intending to fool the market.'

No-one said a word.

There was no run down the aisle, no clamber to an emergency exit, just a resigned understanding of what was about to happen.'

'Take them away,' ordered Davies King.

~

Chapter Thirteen
~ ~ ~

Dateline: Monday Night
The Anchor, Crillsea.

Exhausted, Davies King sat quietly at the bar presiding over a balloon of Magno. A chess set and a chess clock were on a table behind him; a big screen televised a repeat soccer match somewhere, and a darts board was carelessly devoid of players. It was lunchtime and it was Monday.

'Do you think there were only two murders? You know, two deaths?'

'Don't know, Mister King,' said the craggy Archie. 'But I'll buy you a foreign type brandy if you want. You deserve it, so you do, Mister King. You're the governor, Mister King: the governor.'

''You know, I'll just take a Magno with you, Archie. Thank you, that's very kind of you after all these years.'

Archie approached the bar and said, 'Not at all, no problem. I'll get a pint of mild myself, Mister King. I'll put it on your tab, should I? Care for a pinch of snuff?'

Davies chuckled at Archie's response and said, 'No thanks, Archie. Don't mind me, I'm on wind down. Elena and Sophie, do you think they were the only ones hurt in this horrible episode of human endeavour?'

Harry Reynolds moved through the bar, smiled politely and said, 'Mister King, Davies, you need a good night's sleep and some time off, I suggest. Perhaps another time you might unwind. Maybe next week when things are quieter and you're not so tired, Mister King, we'll talk.'

'Yeah, yeah, yeah, Harry, I'll catch you then.'

'Thanks for the word, Mister King,' said Harry Reynolds. 'I'll not forget the words you spoke for me.'

'You will, Harry, but mind how you go,' advised Davies.

Harry Reynolds slunk quietly from the bar, free and on bail and likely to be dealt with sympathetically by a court made aware of a witness statement in a murder case whilst his accomplices Reg Cuttleworth and Stan Striker languished in a cell following their early morning arrest.

Bill said, 'Steady on, Davies, it's getting to you.'

'Who are the bloody victims? I'll tell you who the bloody victims are: The people of Conchenta, that's who. Some poor kid who died in her mother's arms because no-one cared enough to do that one final check, that one final piece of work that would have made all the difference. They just did the basics, and do you know what… The basics aren't always enough.'

There was a rush of air when the front door opened and Annie, Barney and Webby entered and ordered drinks to celebrate a successful conclusion to a job well done. A few minutes later, more detectives turned up from Crillsea police station. Then Bert Allithwaite walked in with Claudia Jones and said to the gang, 'I've an announcement to make. I'm retiring. I've been offered a position as permanent President of Crillsea Golf Club and I'm taking it.'

There was a ripple of applause and hearty cries of 'congratulations' and 'well done, sir' and then Bert Allithwaite approached Davies King and said, 'There's a vacancy you might be interested in, Davies, Privately, the chief constable has informed me that he is somewhat dismayed at the turn of events recently. The generic policy is being reviewed, as they say, and Keith Jackson has been transferred to Ethnicity and Diversity with immediate effect. He's sitting pretty there for promotion to superintendent when Fred Atkins retires in two years time. Phillip Patterson, the assistant chief, on the other hand, has been seconded to the Home Office for an unspecified period to head up a research project looking at computerised crime recording with particular reference to murder investigations.'

Chatter and gossip filtered round the pub.

'By the way, Mark Tait starts with you next week but you will chuckle at this one… I'm told the deputy chief wonders who Patterson will take with him to advise on murder enquiries,' chuckled Bert Allithwaite.

'How times change, sir,' noted Davies. 'And it's only Monday.'

Bert lowered his voice and said, 'The job is yours if you want it, Davies. The chief told me himself. All you need to do is apply when it's advertised and you'll be Detective Chief Inspector King by the end of the month, head of divisional crime. Just say the word."

'Well,' replied Davies. 'Good of you to think of me, sir, but I think I've blotted my copybook as they say. I have no chance of any promotion now.'

'Oh, I nearly forgot, Davies,' declared Bert Allithwaite. 'There's just one thing left to do before I go. It's my final act.'

'I wonder what that is?' asked Ted Barnes with Annie Rock, Webby and Claudia crowding round.

'I've been meaning to give you this for the last few days, Davies. I just didn't get round to it,' said Bert Allithwaite as he handed over an A4 piece of paper. 'Davies, it's my authority for you to carry out undercover operations in Bananos, London. Well, you never know what can happen so it may become useful one day. You never know.'

Davies King read the paper, smiled, and looked up at the friendly faces now surrounding him. 'No, you never know, do you, boss. Thank you, sir.'

There was another brief ripple of applause and Davies asked, 'Who breached security? Who grassed me up? Who typed this? Come on, speak up.'

Webby, Annie and Barney laughed, and raised their glasses but Claudia Jones smiled and led the eulogy to him with, 'Good luck, inspector. Good luck.'

Bert Allithwaite then rested his hand on Davies's arm and said, 'Someone recently advised me that in a career one should promote around you the people you wish to take with you on that journey. That person wasn't quite right. You should promote and take with you people who are good at their job. Davies, it is far more important to take the journey and reach the end knowing you have done a good job rather than taking the journey and reaching the end alone and unsure of where you have been. Success is about making an impact, not about reaching the top of the tree. Good luck in all that you do, my friend. I'm going to miss you, Davies King.'

'Thank you, but by the way, sir,' said Davies.

'What's that, did I forget something, Davies?' asked Bert Allithwaite.

With a huge smile, Davies said, 'You certainly did, Bert. It's your division and you're in the chair.'

'Goodness me,' replied Bert Allithwaite. 'So I am, hey everyone, the drinks are on me!'

There was a clamour to the bar coinciding with the front door opening. In walked Al Jessop and Max Fowler.

Al entered and was quickly introduced to Bert Allithwaite before turning to Davies and saying, 'I had a word with my deputy assistant commissioner today, Davies. I'm looking for a chief inspector on the operational side of things if you're interested.'

'Thanks, Al,' replied Davies. 'Now I just don't know what to do.'

'Well, think on it Mister Chess Master and let me know,' said Al.

Davies nodded and looked for Max Fowler

Max stood framed in the doorway looking towards Davies King.

It was a defining moment for Davies. He viewed life as a game of chess. The first movements in the game were always as a pawn. But as the game grew it was dominated by other pieces. Davies considered he was a pawn because he could only move forward. Other pieces could move to the side, diagonally or backwards. Only the pawn moved forward unable by the constraints of the game to move backwards.

Max Fowler took a seat and a brandy, and then retrieved one half of a chess board from inside his jacket.

Speaking to Davies he said, 'Where were we?'

Davies King sat down opposite Max and withdrew the other half of the chess board from the inside of a jacket which bore leather patches on its elbows. He placed it on the table and joined the two pieces.

The incoming tide crashed against a harbour wall and two men sat in a bar drinking brandy and playing a game of Chess.

Davies King looked into his opponent's eyes, triggered the chess clock with a *thud*, and boldly announced, 'Game on!'

*

Coming Soon....
Moonlight Shadows.... by Paul Anthony

~

Also, by Paul Anthony
The Fragile Peace... by Paul Anthony

~

A thriller of violent prejudices and divided loyalties. This Ulster novel reaches to the very roots of sectarian life and death. Written by a member of the security forces, it penetrates behind the media-screen to reveal a human landscape that is unknown, yet startlingly believable... Everything is here, from the glamour of hi-tech intelligence work to the despairing pub-talk of men locked in the past. Trace the origins of these relentless tit-for-tat killings, often starting in childhood and see how the lives of vastly different people may be mysteriously linked forever against the fatally beautiful backdrop of Northern Ireland...... 'A bomb will explode in Downing Street in half an hour'... The chilling Ulster accent, echoing a world of grey streets and grim death... The correct password, confirming a deadly threat to the UK government.... As more Irish republicans come to the negotiating table, one fanatical group sets out to smash the peace talks beyond hope. Highly trained and well-armed, they have the power to strike a devastating blow at the very heart of the establishment, but the police keep intercepting their plans – until they gradually realize that one of their own number must be a double agent. When you read this topical thriller, you'll see why this crime-fighting author had to use a pseudonym.

The Keswick Reminder: A powerful novel... A hard hitting tale of intrigue and suspicion, treachery and tension...

The News and Star: A remarkably balanced piece of fiction... Gripping

Published by Janus Publishing Company, London

Bushfire... by Paul Anthony

~

'Bushfire' is a terrifying thriller of greed and deceit. The action spans the oceans, from Colombia to the British Isles and is set against the inferno of a raging drugs' culture...

Cumbrian undercover detective, Boyd, and the covert power of the State, battle against globally organised crime syndicates unaware that some amongst them have different plans: Private and personal revenge.

The Cumberland News: A gripping story.... Take a bow...

*

The Legacy of the Ninth... by Paul Anthony

~

'The Legacy of the Ninth' is a whirlwind thriller of bitter conflict and religious mystique, echoing through the centuries of time from the Roman Empire to the luscious green valley of the Eden River and the land of the Lakes. Behold, the noble Domitian: A valiant Roman centurion who witnesses an appalling act of mass suicide in the Negev desert, and Hussein who plunders a Jewish artefact from its rightful owner. Centuries later Boyd tries to find out why events in Masada are now so closely linked with nearby Hadrian's Wall. Indeed, Boyd realizes that the links are so strong that prospects of peace in the Middle East are in danger of collapsing. Things can't get any worse, can they?

Keswick Reminder: Full of intrigue, espionage and cold-blooded murder...the action is on-going, the descriptions vivid.
Cumberland News: A thriller mixing fact and fiction, stacked with intrigue.

Published by Paul Anthony Associates
www.wix.com/tscougal/paulanthony

Printed in Great Britain
by Amazon